THE GHOST OF

AKHENATEN

FICTION

The Egyptian Sequence:
Hatshepsut: Daughter of Amun
Akhenaten: Son of the Sun
Tutankhamun and the Daughter of Ra
The Ghost of Akhenaten

Guardians of the Tall Stones:
The Tall Stones
The Temple of the Sun
Shadow on the Stones
The Silver Vortex

Weapons of the Wolfhound
The Eye of Callanish
The Lily and the Bull
The Tower and the Emerald
Etheldreda
The Waters of Sul
The Winged Man
Child of the Dark Star
The Green Lady and the King of Shadows

MYTHS AND LEGENDS
Crystal Legends
Three Celtic Tales
Women in Celtic Myth
Myths of the Sacred Tree
Mythical Journeys: Legendary Quests

More information is available from
www.moyracaldecott.co.uk

THE GHOST OF AKHENATEN

by

Moyra Caldecott

Published by
Bladud Books

Moyra Caldecott has asserted her right under the Copyright, Designs and Patents Act, 1988, to be identified as the Author of this work

First published in Great Britain
by Mushroom eBooks 2001

This edition published in 2003 by Bladud Books,
an imprint of
Mushroom Publishing, Bath, UK
mail@mushroompublishing.com
www.mushroompublishing.com

ISBN: 1-84319-024-9

CONTENTS

Introduction

The Pharaoh Akhenaten reigned in Egypt from *c*.1353-1335 BC.

He was the son of the powerful Pharaoh Amenhotep III, and succeeded his father as Amenhotep IV. However, early in his reign he changed his name to Akhenaten, indicating that he revered the god Aten instead of Amun. Within a few years he had virtually dismantled the elaborate religious system of ancient Egypt, abolishing the worship of its many gods, demolishing their temples, and dispossessing their priesthoods. He declared the Aten, represented by the Sun's Disk, the only true god, and himself and his wife, Nefertiti, the sole channels for its influence on earth.

No one knows how he died, but after his sudden death his successors declared his name anathema and everything he had put in place was destroyed. The temples of the other gods were rebuilt and the power of their priesthoods reinstated. His name was removed from the King Lists and it was as though he had never been. It is only in recent years that the persistent curiosity of archaeologists has uncovered his story. The city he built to the glory of his One God was excavated and an archive found that tells us much about his life.

There has been much speculation as to whether he was assassinated by the powerful priests of Amun who had suffered so much during his reign, and more than one source mentions a curse that doomed him to wander as a ghost for the rest of Time as punishment for his heretical deeds.

While I was writing the novel *Akhenaten: The Son of the Sun* many strange and extraordinary experiences in dreams and through mediums led me to believe in this curse, and after the book was published I came upon someone who claimed to have personally encountered the ghost of Akhenaten in the Egyptian desert. A friend lent me *Tombs, Temples and Ancient Art* by Joseph and Corrina Lindon Smith, who describe a mysterious encounter they themselves had with the priests of Amun when they tried to set Akhenaten's soul free from the curse in 1909. The archaeologist Arthur Weidgal who witnessed it also reported the incident.

In response to my novel about Akhenaten I received many letters from around the world claiming to be from reincarnations of Akhenaten or of members of his family. I also received reports of channelled messages from Akhenaten. It seems that whatever happened at his death, and in spite of all the efforts to wipe his name from history, Akhenaten is very much an active force in the world today. The books about him run into many hundreds – from cautious archaeology to wild speculation.

1

The Dreams Begin

The man lay on the desert sand, his body twisted and broken.
Dark shapes circled around him like jackals around a lion's kill.
Deep voices intoned the malevolent words of a curse.

'This man will not rise again.
This man will not go to the stars.
This man will lie forever in the desert cut off from those who
loved him and those whom he loved.
His god will have no access to him.
HIS GOD IS DEAD.'

The sky deepened from the colour of fire to the colour of blood.
One broke off from the circle, crouched and wrote hieroglyphs in
the sand – each one reversed.
The chanting continued.

'May you never enter the barque that glides among the
unwearying stars.
May you forget the names of those who guard the seven
doors, the fourteen gates, the twenty-one mounds of the
Otherworld, and may you never be vindicated in the presence
of the forty-two assessors. May your heart weigh heavy
against the feather of Maat in the Hall of Osiris, and Ammut,
the Devourer of the Dead, feed on it. You have denied the
gods of your ancestors, may they in the Everlasting deny
you.'

Darkness fell and absorbed the figures of the priests who chanted
these fearsome words, as though they were part of the darkness itself.
When the dawn came and the sun rose in a splendour of blue and
gold, the man who lay, twisted and broken, alone at the centre of a
vast and featureless desert, did not witness it.

* * * *

Eliot rang the bell in shabby Swallow Street and Emma looked around curiously. She had never visited Eliot's friend Jack before. The place did not look promising. The door paint was peeling and scuffed, the wall grimy, and the beautiful honey-coloured stone almost unrecognisable. The whole street resembled the back of a stage set that no one had time to tidy up before the play started, while just around the corner – the front of the stage – was resplendent with reproduction Roman buildings housing a genuine ancient Roman bathing and temple complex.

At last, a disembodied voice greeted them and a buzz indicated that the door was unlocked. A steep, dark staircase confronted them, and they started to climb. The first indication Emma had that she had not entered the den of some impoverished troglodyte was the shine of leaves caught in sunlight from a skylight high above the landing. From then on the place was a delight.

A life sized Egyptian statue of worm-eaten wood that had once guarded the secret entrance to a tomb in ancient Egypt, stood beside the door to the living room. The statue held a staff that was irreverently draped with Jack's red winter scarf, and a ski hat graced the forbidding head.

The front room, the living room, was large and light, with a view of chimneys and rooftops.

Emma knew that Jack had inherited money from his father, and many of the precious artefacts in his apartment from his great-grandfather, Ben Wilson, an archaeologist. He was in the enviable position of not having to work too hard at making a living. He fancied himself as a writer, but had never written a book, though he had a drawer full of titles and discarded first chapters. However, he had had some travel articles published and, if anyone asked, he claimed to be a freelance travel writer.

The tomb guardian had been inherited from his great-grandfather, taken out of Egypt, no doubt, before the authorities fully worked out their strategy for preventing heritage artefacts leaving the country. He also had from his great-grandfather an old leather suitcase stuffed full of ancient manuscript fragments on papyrus. He only looked at them when he was showing off to a visitor and had no idea what they were. Since they had come into his possession he had intended to have them deciphered by an expert, but never got around to it. He and his friends enjoyed speculating on their origins and meaning.

Emma stared at his mantelpiece, which was full of ancient Egyptian artefacts – a couple of ushabtis, faience slaves waiting to

4

labour for the deceased in the afterlife, a blue pottery hippopotamus painted with flowering lotus on its sides, and several exquisite stone bowls filled with paper clips and boxes of matches. Most impressive of all were a pair of tiny ancient Egyptian silver statues of gods: Anubis, the jackal headed protector of the necropolis, and Isis, the Queen of Heaven.

On the wall above the mantelpiece was a flat piece of white chalk-like stone with the symbol of the sun painted in thin black lines, each ray ending in the stylised drawing of a hand holding an *ankh*, the Egyptian sign for eternal life. Something was scrawled under it in hieroglyphs, but the end sign was broken off and so the inscription, whatever it was, was incomplete. Beside it a similar shard of stone was carved in relief. It was of a hand with long, sensitive fingers reaching out to touch something that had been broken off and lost.

The hand had pride of place, mounted so that the best light in the room fell on it.

Eliot and Emma were visiting Jack because they were worried about him. Jack and Eliot had been close friends since Jack visited the United States as a teenager, and had stayed at Eliot's home as part of an educational exchange programme. They kept up their friendship at long distance until Eliot decided to come to England, to Jack's home town, to work.

Jack had recently been having disturbing dreams.

The first dream that he told Eliot about had occurred about a month before. In the dream the ancient Egyptian hand seemed to be beckoning, instead of reaching out. He was in a desert among the columns of ruined Egyptian temples. Whenever he looked directly at the figures painted and carved on the columns and walls they were still and lifeless, but as soon as he turned his head away, out of the corner of his eye, he could see them move.

He had lain awake for some time after this dream feeling uneasy, as though he had woken too soon and missed something very important. When he went into the living room his eye went straight to the hand. It appeared as it had always done – inanimate. And yet he sensed a subtle difference.

Eliot had laughed.

'You really ought to write that novel you're always talking about,' he said. 'Your imagination is getting out of hand!'

'I didn't imagine it,' he had protested. 'I really felt...'

But already he was not certain how he had felt – and the dreams kept coming.

Some were only made up of the flotsam and jetsam of his ordinary day-to-day life, but others were more disturbing and powerful. He seemed to be recalling, in great detail, people and places in what seemed to be ancient Egypt.

Emma, an ardent New Ager, had pricked up her ears at once when Eliot told her that Jack was having disturbing dreams about ancient Egypt.

Eliot himself had no time for the New Age and had often indulged in jeering at it before he met Emma. She had not converted him or even lessened his scepticism and distaste, but he was prepared to humour her.

Emma paused a long time beside the battered old leather case containing the papyrus manuscripts. Eliot was talking, but Jack was watching Emma. Tentatively she put out her hand and touched the case. She withdrew it at once, but then put it back again and left it there for a long time, frowning in concentration.

'What is this?' she asked at last.

'Oh, that's a lot of old useless stuff from Egypt – bits and pieces of papyrus no one can read,' Eliot answered for Jack. 'I don't know why he doesn't just chuck it away or give it to some old museum.'

Emma looked at Jack. 'It must have come into your possession for a purpose,' she said. 'You should have it translated.'

'The case has been in my family for ages,' he replied. 'It contains mostly fragments. I can't see that any sense could be made of them.'

'Perhaps one of them would explain your dreams.'

Jack glanced at Eliot crossly. So he had been spreading it around about the dreams!

There was an awkward pause, and Emma moved away from the case. To break the tension she lifted up a small earthenware lamp.

'This is Roman. Was it found in Bath?'

'I don't know. I bought it at the flea market in the old tram sheds in Walcot Street.'

She held it up and turned it over, examining it closely.

'Perhaps you should rub it,' Eliot mocked, 'and a genii will come out and grant your every wish!'

'What would be your wish?' Emma asked seriously, holding the lamp up, her hand poised ready to rub it.

Even Jack laughed, and then, because she seemed so earnest and was so beautiful, he said: 'I'd wish to understand what is going on in my dreams.'

Emma rubbed the lamp.

Nothing happened. Of course!

She put it down and returned thoughtfully to the leather case.

'I sense very strongly that this is a key to something,' she said. 'You really should have the fragments translated.'

Jack crossed the room and opened the case. Inside lay the yellowing scrolls, half worm-eaten, covered in strange markings – writing, but to him indecipherable.

'They are powerful,' she said. 'I'm not surprised you have strange dreams!'

He frowned, shutting the case. He had been finding his attention drawn to it more and more recently. In several of the dreams he had about Egypt it seemed as though someone was calling him, urgently, as though there was some danger. He had the feeling he was expected to do something he did not want to do.

If he had a second chance to wish on the Roman lamp he would wish for the dreams to go away, not for him to understand them.

'Aren't you going to offer us a drink?' Eliot asked, impatient with what he would term a 'spooky' turn to the conversation.

Jack left the room at once.

'You were supposed to be trying to help him,' Eliot said accusingly. 'Not freak him out even more.'

Emma moved reluctantly away from the case.

When Jack returned with three glasses and a bottle of wine, she told him she knew someone in Glastonbury who might be able to interpret his dreams for him.

'She might even be able to give you a past life reading,' she added.

Jack shrugged. He was uneasy that they were having this conversation about something so personal, and was not about to expose himself further to a total stranger. He knew enough about Freud to be very wary of letting anyone loose on his inner motivations. Who knew what an 'expert' would make of what happened to him at night in the privacy of his subconscious!

No. Emma was well meaning, but he needed no witch at Glastonbury to analyse him. He was irritated with Eliot for dragging her into it, and wished he had told his friend nothing about the strange events he was experiencing in the 'twilight zone'.

Luckily Emma did not press the point, and the conversation turned to what Eliot had been doing since he last saw him. It seemed he might go to Chile soon to attend the wedding of his sister to a rich rancher.

Emma sat quietly, cross-legged on a cushion on the floor, and seemed removed from the conversation. Jack glanced at her frequently and saw that she was gazing at his Egyptian treasures intently. Eliot was lucky, he thought. Her hair was brown and long but shining like fire in the sunlight that had now suddenly broken through the rain clouds. Her eyes were deeply grey, her lashes long. She wore a tight jumper that did not meet her jeans, and had kicked off her sodden shoes to reveal beautifully shaped feet. The wine glass was on the floor in front of her and she was meditatively drawing her finger around the rim, listening for the high, fine sound she hoped it would make.

Eliot's voice seemed further and further away. Jack felt he and Emma were alone in the room. The sound started on the glass and it seemed to him it was a thread drawing him away, like the voice calling in his dreams.

He struggled to free himself from the web he felt tightening around him, and turned his eyes to Eliot – good, solid, down-to-earth Eliot.

That night he dreamed again.

'Will this exile never end ...will there be no pity ... Other men have failed, but their punishment has had a season and then it has passed and gone, and they have sailed the golden barque among the stars...

I reach up ... I cry ... but even the God I have served so faithfully has deserted me ... Ai-i ... Ai-i...'

The voice was in the wind that wailed over the desert dunes, lifting the sand like fog around the bleak and lonely figure.

Jack in his bed reached out his arms, but he could not touch him.

When he woke he found that tears were streaming down his cheeks.

He dressed and went out. He walked by the river and stared at it long and hard. The water rushing over the curved weir almost mesmerized him, but not quite. He could hear the early rush hour traffic building up behind him, the coaches with their air brakes breathing heavily as they stopped for the lights. The covered market was already busy and bustling. A lone canoe came into sight, but turned and left before the rough white water of the weir. Along the far bank, downstream, the houseboats sent up little signals of smoke as their inhabitants boiled water for their morning coffee. The rugby field on the other side lay silent, wet with dew, and beyond it the wooded hills rose, holding the town, nesting, between them.

At last he walked away, hands in pockets, head down. He could not go on living like this. He had to know the meaning of those dreams.

He found a phone box and dialled Eliot's number. Emma

answered. He invited himself to breakfast and put the phone down before she could demur.

When he arrived Eliot was about to leave for work in smart suit and impeccable tie. Emma was still in her dressing gown with her hair tangled and unbrushed. He scarcely noticed how lovely she looked.

'You know that interpreter of dreams in Glastonbury you mentioned?' he said. 'I've decided. There's nothing for it. I have to see her.'

'She's away for a few days,' Emma said. 'Have some camomile tea.'

He was disappointed. Having made the decision, he was impatient to get started.

'You look terrible,' Eliot said cheerfully, slapping him on the shoulder. 'Give him some strong coffee Emma. He needs it.'

Emma looked as though she might argue, but gave in and poured him a strong black coffee. He sipped it distractedly.

'I've got to go,' Eliot said. 'Emma will set you right.' And he leaned down and kissed her as he left.

'Ciao!' he called at the door and was gone.

Emma looked at Jack thoughtfully.

'Sit down,' she said. 'Have some fruit. You look unhealthy.'

'I feel unhealthy,' he said. 'I think I'm going mad. Half the time I don't know whether I am dreaming when I'm asleep or dreaming when I'm awake. Which is the reality?'

She laughed. 'Probably both,' she said.

'I dread going to sleep. Or rather...' He hesitated. 'I both dread and long for it.' He began to pace, frowning.

'Sit down, for heaven's sake; you're making me dizzy! Have an apple while I go and get dressed. Calm yourself.'

Jack sat down and poured himself another strong coffee.

He tapped his fingers on the table while she was gone, thinking of Egypt. He had been there only once, briefly, and only to Cairo – busy, noisy Cairo which gave no hint of its ancient past. He had not even been to the Museum there. He was writing an article on its restaurants and hotels and he had felt no urge to sample anything else. Islamic Cairo had been visible with its mosques and the way the men washed and prayed so often in the day, but the Egypt of the Pharaohs was another country. He had promised himself he would visit it one day, but that day had not yet come.

When Emma returned they talked about his sudden impatience to have the dreams interpreted, and the fact that the woman she knew in Glastonbury was not yet available.

'I have a friend here who might be able to help you,' she said. 'She isn't a professional past-life reader and she won't even admit to being a psychic, but she has visited Egypt many times and some pretty strange things have happened to her!'

'I'm not sure that I want to spread it around that I'm going crazy,' Jack said cautiously. 'A professional is one thing...'

'Believe me, she won't spread it around.'

He looked doubtful.

'It's worth a shot,' she urged. 'If you don't feel comfortable with her you don't need to tell her anything. We'll just visit. I often do. I enjoy her company. And her house is even more cluttered than yours with beautiful and interesting things to look at.'

Eventually he agreed, and she rang Mary Brown. She could see them that very day.

They drove almost to the southern limits of the city before they stopped at a house half hidden behind a high shaggy privet hedge in urgent need of cutting. The gate was tall and solidly panelled with grey and splintering wood, so they could see nothing of the garden until they opened it and stepped inside. Jack almost gasped. It was a tangle of wonderful plants and colours. Oriental poppies gleamed and shone in the sunlight. Peonies leant untidily against the hedge in brilliant crimson. There did not seem an inch that was not burgeoning and blooming. When the gate shut behind them, they were in a magical and private place – a miniature nature reserve in the city.

Emma rang the bell and while they waited Jack gazed into the conservatory, which was a jungle of exotic plants that he recognised from his travels abroad – bougainvillea and plumbago, hibiscus and lemon, a ten-foot tall Egyptian papyrus plant and several African aloes.

Through the glass door he saw Mary approaching. She was an old lady leaning heavily on two sticks.

She greeted Emma warmly and ushered them into her home. In the small front room two of the walls were lined with books up to the ceiling. The other walls were covered with real pictures – not prints. The windows glowed and gleamed with the vibrant colours of stained glass.

If his own home was deceptive from the outside, hers was even more so. He had passed down this road many times and never thought that the people who lived there might be like this.

She offered tea and while she was away in the kitchen Emma showed him round, pointing out that the pictures were all painted by members of her family; the blown glass was made by her son-in-law, and the stained glass in the windows was by Mary herself. She showed him the books Mary had written and the extensive library she kept for research.

'Everything in this room has personal significance,' Emma said enthusiastically. 'That is why it feels so good. I knew you would like it!' she added triumphantly, reading his face.

'You wouldn't think such an old woman would...' Jack began, but stopped at once when she came back into the room.

Mary laughed.

'It's my disguise,' she said. 'We all use disguises to hide the fact that we are eternal beings on a journey through the universe! Yours is of a rather feckless young man intent on nothing but a good time.'

'I may have used that disguise once, but not any more,' Jack said. 'Things have changed a lot lately.'

'Which is why Emma has brought you to me. Do you have milk and sugar?'

He nodded and there was a pause while milk and sugar were dispensed and biscuits offered. He was impatient to get to the crux of his visit and would gladly have forgone the tea and biscuits. But Mary seemed intent on playing out the little ritual, as though it had some importance.

'Perhaps she holds to these little ordinary things to keep her sane,' he thought, feeling that in her presence he could very easily leave this reality behind and swing off into unknown realms.

Emma smiled at him, amused, as though she sensed his impatience.

He tried to be patient.

At last the cups were put away, Emma carrying them through to the kitchen.

He met Mary's eyes expectantly.

She smiled.

'Tell me about your dreams,' she said.

The floodgates burst open and out came the torrent.

She heard how he had never been particularly interested in Egyptian history, but now almost every night he seemed to be in ancient Egypt. She sat with her hands folded in her lap, listening and waiting. Emma held her breath. She began to feel a strangeness growing in the room as though the world outside had ceased to exist.

'I can never make the dreams come,' he said, 'and they rarely come in sequence. They seem to be scattered fragments of another life I am beginning to think I once had, and yet I don't believe in reincarnation.'

Emma spoke for the first time.

'His apartment is full of things from Egypt left to him by his great-grandfather.'

Mary's eyes flicked over to Emma when she spoke, and then back to Jack.

And then she stood up and limped across the room. She pulled out a book of astronomy and handed it to him without a word. Puzzled, he turned the pages. The most wonderful photographs of the universe he had ever seen were there, taken through the most advanced telescopes, some based on satellites above the earth's pollution. The whole magnificent panoply of what surrounded us in outer space, but which could not be seen with the naked eye, filled him with awe.

'Take this picture,' she said, pointing. 'All these stars look as though they are clustered together, yet what we are seeing is actually an illusion. Our experience of them is simultaneous, yet they are separated from each other by millions of light years.'

He studied the picture carefully. He could see no difference between them.

She watched his reaction.

'Do you understand what I am trying to say?'

He hesitated. He was not sure. Something was glimmering at the back of his mind, but he could not bring it into focus.

'There is a sense in which we experience events as simultaneous, although they are in fact separated in time by millennia,' she said. 'Our minds are skilled beyond belief at surfing the ocean of consciousness in which we have our being.' She paused. 'Everything that has ever been is still present, though we may not be aware of it because it is in a form usually inaccessible to us. Some call it the Akashic records, but perhaps we should not use the word "records" because it suggests something inanimate, stored on shelves, gathering dust. The Akashic is rather an imprint from life in dynamic motion, interacting, interrelating, influencing. Eternal and yet ever present...'

Jack struggled to come to terms with what she had just said.

'We are just part of the choreography of that universe,' she continued, indicating the pictures once more. 'We are, it is true, hurtling through space on the surface of a very small planet, but our consciousness is free of time and space. You can experience ancient Egypt as though it is present in your life now because you can see the bigger picture where everything that has ever happened still exists in some form. You are in a sense seeing two stars separated by millions of light years, simultaneously...'

'Whew!' Jack laughed nervously. He needed to think about this. The unfamiliar ideas were crowding in too fast.

After a long pause when each sat wrapped in their own thoughts, Jack spoke again.

'You mean you don't think I actually *lived* in ancient Egypt, but am just picking up impressions floating around?'

'But why does he just pick up *those* impressions?' Emma asked. 'Why are we not continually bombarded by all sorts of things so that we don't know what is now and what is not?'

'Because we could not live like that,' Mary said. 'We have filters. We have screens to protect us. When you walk down a street you don't notice everything that is there. A baby in a pram might notice only the dogs and the other babies. A gardener might notice only the gardens. A young girl the clothes in the shops ... a young man the cars ... Not one of us sees everything. Only occasionally we focus on one or two of the host of impressions that are with us all the time. When we are in a relaxed state, sleeping for instance, we may lower our screens, and extend our range.'

'But why do I feel that I am personally in ancient Egypt experiencing those things?'

Mary shook her head. 'You must not think I am claiming to know for sure everything about the nature of reality. No one does. But I see no reason why we can't access the past, because it is part of the universal consciousness, and we are part of that. Even in the physical universe nothing is ever destroyed, but only changes form.'

Jack had heard that every cell in the body changes every seven years. If this was so, he could not be the person born to his mother – yet he knew that he was. Something continued through all the physical changes, something that was not physical. This non-physical element could be in touch with a non-physical universe.

'The ancient Egyptians believed that the human being is made up of nine parts, or aspects,' Mary continued. 'I understand the *Khu*, or *Akh*, as the Spirit, the original and eternal Being of a person. The pharaoh Akhenaten incorporated that word into his name to indicate that he, as eternal spirit, was in touch with his god, the Aten. In ancient Egyptian iconography it is represented by the sacred crested ibis, a bird whose feathers are iridescent. Through it we are in touch with Eternity, for Eternity is where it actually dwells. It only temporarily overlaps, as it were, with this world, while we are in the body. By becoming conscious of the *Akh* we can communicate mystically with what is normally beyond our comprehension.

'The *Ba*, or soul, is more local to oneself as a personality formed in time. It is represented aptly by a migrating bird, a stork, standing beside a pot with a flame burning brightly, or, perhaps more frequently, by a human headed bird. This *Ba* is judged after the death of the body. If its thoughts and actions in life can balance against Maat, the ultimate arbiter of truth and justice, it could pass on to rejoin the *Akh*, or eternal spirit. If it is judged not to be ready and has failed in some way to satisfy Maat, the ancient Egyptians believed it had to return to earth and try again as a reincarnated being, or, in some extreme cases, be flung back into the void where it ceased to have any individuality at all.

'The third aspect of the non-material part of us was named the *Ka*, this was represented by two upraised arms. It seems it was thought of as being much more earthbound than the spirit or the soul. It may be what sometimes appears to us as a ghost, or helps us in invisible form as our guiding spirit. In the tomb, a false door was placed for its convenience so that it could pass in and out of this world after the death of the physical body. Food and drink were left for it, sometimes in a literal sense, but mostly in picture form. The ancient Egyptians had much more of a sense of the vital essence, the life, of a thing, not only residing in its material form, but in the idea of it. We might call the *Ka* the astral body – but that would not be totally accurate.'

'What on earth is the astral body?' Jack asked, groaning inwardly at all this mumbo-jumbo.

Mary laughed and threw up her hands. Where to begin!

Emma helped her out.

'We also believe our physical bodies are not all there is of us. The astral body is a sort of invisible envelope around us while we are in this world, operating on a different vibrational wavelength to the physical or the spiritual, but nevertheless connecting the two. Healers can sense it and use it for diagnosing and healing what is wrong with us. When people have out-of-body experiences it is usually believed that it is this astral or etheric body that detaches itself from the physical, floats away and observes the physical from a distance. This could happen during the shock of a near death experience, or under the influence of drugs. A friend of mine experienced astral travel under morphine during the long labour to deliver her first child. I have experienced it, without drugs, unexpectedly. There are stories of saints experiencing it in states of high mystical ecstasy, and Eastern holy men inducing it deliberately by practising certain esoteric disciplines.'

'The other six aspects the ancient Egyptians believed in are easier to comprehend,' Mary said, laughing.

'I'm glad to hear it!' Jack said thankfully.

'The Name had special significance because it was the one thing that held all these disparate elements together in the minds of others, identifying an individual. The Heart represents the motives, the will of the individual. The Shadow we might call the sub-conscious; the Double, the template given at birth to guide the individual into what it *should* become.'

'You mean like that story, "The Portrait of Dorian Gray",' Jack asked, 'where the portrait kept in the attic changes throughout the man's life into a hideous monster to reveal at last what he is really like, as opposed to what he pretends to be?'

Mary smiled.

'Well, that would be the principle working the opposite way! But it just shows how these ancient beliefs are still part of our culture, though we may distort them or deny them.'

'I have seen Egyptian images of a potter god fashioning newborn twins on a potters wheel,' Jack said.

'Not twins,' Mary corrected him, 'but the newborn and its Double. Some Christians believe one's guardian angel is assigned to one at birth. Perhaps this is what the Double is – not just a template which holds the image of us as we ought to be, but someone who helps us to fulfil that potential.'

But Jack had had enough. He was becoming confused and uneasy. He felt that the ground that had always seemed so firm and solid under his feet was shifting and dissolving. He needed to get away.

He stood up.

Emma seemed surprised.

'Are we going?'

'Yes, I have another appointment,' he lied.

Mary smiled and stood up at once, leaning on her stick. She knew he was running away, but she knew also that he would be back.

'But we haven't told Mary about the papyrus fragments you have,' Emma cried. They had been uppermost in her mind when she had arranged the meeting. She knew that Mary had studied hieroglyphics at evening classes, and, although she was no expert, she might have been able to decipher enough to tell them if they were worth getting properly translated.

Mary shook her head.

'Another time,' she said. 'We must not make Jack late for his appointment.'

He could see that she did not believe that he had an appointment, but she spoke in a way that suggested she might know of an appointment that *he* did not yet know he had.

They left, Jack not looking back. Emma turned at the gate to wave at the old lady still smiling in the doorway.

* * * *

15

That night he dreamed again. Was this the appointment he had to keep?

He found himself walking in a beautiful garden, but one unlike any he had seen in England. The trees were tamarisk and sycamore fig, with tall palms against the perimeter walls, bushes scarlet with pomegranate flowers, and lilies everywhere. The sun was low in the sky but still blazing hot.

He turned a corner and found himself looking at a rectangular pool lined with flowering shrubs. On the water a variety of water lilies rested – an exquisite waxy blue the most common. At the far side, a lotus raised its long stalk and held up a luminous white flower in the fragrant air. He glanced down at his feet and was surprised to see his legs were bare and he was wearing a pair of flimsy sandals. A white linen kilt was fastened around his waist.

A slight sound made him lift his head.

On the far side, just emerging from a leafy avenue, was a woman. He caught his breath. He had no doubt now where he was. He had seen paintings of ancient Egyptian gardens and women dressed in that way, finely pleated, almost transparent fabric revealing every curve. As she paused beside the pool, the sunlight, shining through the leaves, flickered over her, turning her skin to gold and black like a leopard's...

'Ah, but she is beautiful,' he thought.

'Will she turn? Will she see me standing here ... waiting?'

'Will her eyes – deep as the Great Green Ocean – look into mine and smile?'

There have not been many smiles lately.

She will turn to me, but her eyes will be cold and sad... Will I ever bring back the light to them?

2

Glastonbury

Soon after the visit to Mary Brown, Emma set up an appointment with Denise, the dream-interpreter and past-life reader she knew in Glastonbury.

As they sped along the road in his red sports car they hardly spoke a word to each other. They had not met since the visit to Mary, but Emma knew that Jack had been dissatisfied with what she had said. He did not want to find that he was only in touch with a vague 'sea of events' preserved in some unspecified way outside time. He, who would never have given mind-space to the possibility of reincarnation before, now wanted it to be true. The dreams were so vivid he had begun to believe they were memories, and wanted more than anything else to have a clear storyline from ancient Egypt with himself as protagonist. He pressed Emma to make the appointment with Denise in spite of his former resistance to the meeting.

Emma glanced at him sideways and a strand of hair blew across her face. He was staring straight ahead, driving too fast. When she looked back at the road she found that they were approaching her favourite stretch of the route.

They were on the crest of a hill and were looking down on a wide vista of what had once been low-lying marshland punctuated by islands. Glastonbury Tor, an extraordinary hill, rose high above the flat farmland, crowned by an abandoned church tower.

Emma could see that Jack was impressed with the distant view of the Tor, but was anxious to keep his appointment, and did not slow down.

'I don't wonder there are so many legends about Glastonbury,' Emma said. 'From this distance it looks such a magical place – and when it was an island rising above the marshes with the mist swirling among the reeds below it, it would have been easy to imagine it as the gateway to the Otherworld. I can almost see the mighty figure of Gwynn ab Nudd greeting the souls of the Celtic Dead as they are ferried across the waters and through the mist...'

She stopped speaking, dreaming of a later time when Glastonbury was thought to be King Arthur's Avalon. She imagined Arthur and his knights riding out in search of the Holy Grail, when, according to another legend, the sacred chalice was lying hidden nearby all the time, placed in the well at the foot of the Tor by Joseph of Arimathea after the crucifixion. She dreamed of Merlin weaving his spells and teaching his Druidic wisdom ... of Guinevere meeting her lover... She wondered if the monks had indeed found the grave of Arthur and Guinevere in 1190 as they claimed, re-interring their bodies before the High Altar in the Abbey.

The road dipped and the Tor disappeared. They were coming down the long slope of the hill towards the town of Wells. They passed through a green tunnel where the trees on either side knit their canopies together, to emerge where houses lined the road, and Jack had to slow down for buses and cars. The great Cathedral of Wells rose impressively before them.

'This must have been how Glastonbury Abbey once looked,' Emma thought, and decided she preferred the romantic ruin to the busy building with coach loads of tourists crawling all around it like ants. The architecture of Wells Cathedral was certainly grand, but her favourite thing was a tiny panel on one of the walls inside that Mary Brown had once pointed out to her. It was a relief carving of the Ascension of Christ to Heaven – a group of astonished people were gathered on the ground staring upwards to where a pair of feet comically disappeared into a cloud!

She would have liked to show it to Jack, but she was not sure he would be willing to stop. There was something of awkwardness in their friendship. She was, after all, his best friend's lover, and although Eliot seemed happy enough for her to help him with the mysterious dreams, she did not know how he would react if they seemed to be getting too friendly. Jack himself seemed obsessed with solving the puzzle of his dreams and, although she caught him looking at her occasionally in a way that might have worried Eliot, he glanced away at once when her eyes met his, and kept the conversation strictly to the matter in hand.

Emma always felt she was entering a special realm when she entered Glastonbury. Not only did it resonate with its extraordinary history, but also the contemporary scene itself was like nowhere else she had ever encountered.

Eliot was cynical about Glastonbury. He claimed that it was all sham and fake. He hated the vegetarian cafes, the shops that sold crystals at exorbitant prices just because they were supposed to be impregnated with healing energies. He hated the women who had substituted one gender of an impossible god for another, and the statues of gross fat women purporting to be images of the Earth Goddess. But most of all he hated the ragged unemployed who hung about the streets like hippies left over from the sixties, with matted hair, ear-rings and dogs on leads of frayed string.

Emma saw it as an exciting mix of many different cultures. The farmers used it as a market town. The Christians earnestly paraded through the streets with crosses and candles on certain days of the church calendar. Then there were the New Agers who built invisible temples and walked an invisible maze on the Tor, who had rituals they believed dated back to ancient times. Shops sold Christian icons beside images of pagan gods and goddesses, magnificent reproductions of Medieval and Renaissance archangels beside impossibly fey paintings of tree devas and angels looking like winged Barbie dolls. And on every notice board were advertisements promising alternative and complementary healing.

Emma believed that there were genuine seekers after enlightenment there, and inexplicable miracles of healing. She claimed that for every charlatan overcharging for bogus alternative healing there was one who was truly in touch with the spiritual dimension that brings wholeness to the fractured psyche. She believed that tucked away among the bookshelves in shops and libraries housing so many superficial panaceas for the ills of the world, there were genuine gems of wisdom that could change your life for the better and divert the world from destruction.

The trees surrounding the house of Denise, the Psychic, were hung with wind chimes. Jack and Emma approached the front door setting off a discreet and delicate cacophony of fairy sound. Huge white roses brushed against them, and white doves circled above their heads.

Jack took hold of Emma's elbow.

'Let's go,' he whispered urgently. 'I don't want to do this.'

'We can't go back now,' she replied, shaking her arm free of his clutch. 'She probably knows we're here.'

'I don't care.'

He turned to go, but the door opened and a woman in a flowing robe stood squarely in the doorway.

'Welcome!' she cried in a voice that could not be disobeyed.

Like a child caught in a naughty act, he turned and stood before her. He scarcely heard Emma introducing them.

She had pitch-black hair flowing almost to her waist, and a huge Egyptian ankh studded with semi-precious stones rising and falling on her ample bosom.

'Come!' she said, and reached out her bejewelled hands to him.

He stepped meekly forward and entered the house.

Surrounded by portraits of her spirit guides – wispy Tibetans, stern ancient Egyptians and one magnificent Amerindian in full feathered head-dress – he was offered herbal tea, and sat, sipping it out of a bone china cup, as Emma and Denise talked.

Emma had promised she would not tell Denise any details about his dreams, but just that he needed a past life reading to see if they had any relevance to his present life. He wanted to see what she could pick up psychically.

He soon felt uneasy under the stare of the disembodied beings she believed communicated with her. Emma and Mary seemed to be unperturbed by the belief that they were surrounded by invisible beings of various species and orders – some the dead who chose to return to try to help the living, others who had never lived on earth yet interacted with it in a dynamic way... Had not Abraham been visited by angels, and Paul heard voices on the road to Damascus? But what if Denise's voices were mischievous or ignorant? Enlightenment might not come as an automatic result of dying, but have to be won by passing further trials and tests in the Afterlife.

After tea Denise told Emma to stay where she was and took Jack alone into her inner sanctuary, a small room resplendent with crystals. A candle burned inside a giant half geode of amethyst. There was no furniture, only a rich Indian rug on the floor.

She indicated that he should sit, and he sat, cross-legged, in front of her. A narrow arched window was the only daylight source. The sun was shining directly through it, illuminating with unearthly beauty one huge quartz crystal ball on a silver stand close in front her.

He was feeling extremely nervous and not a little resentful. Emma had not prepared him for the weirdness of everything in this house.

'I don't want to be here!' he thought.

He was just about to rise and leave when she started to speak, and the power of her voice gave him pause. Like a wild animal held transfixed by the headlights of a car, he stayed where he was.

'Don't be afraid,' she said. 'You are held in the heart of Spirit. No harm will come to you.'

Out of nowhere soft music started to pervade the room.

'Listen to the music. Relax. Stop fighting.'

He shut his eyes and tried to accept what was happening. Emma had been so sure that Denise would be able to help him.

'I have come all this way, I might as well give it a try,' he decided. 'But as soon as I feel her taking over my mind, I'll leave!'

She had started intoning strange sounding words, and at first he let the sound wash over him, but then, when the power of her voice became almost unbearable, he opened his eyes, alarmed.

Her appearance seemed to have changed. Her pale blue eyes were dark and unfathomable. There was a kind of beauty about her he had not noticed before. The voice that he heard seemed not to be her own.

'Oh God!' he thought. 'She has gone into trance!'

But he was now too curious to leave.

She claimed to be Isis, the Great Goddess of the Two Lands.

'Egypt!' he thought. Had Emma disobeyed him and told her more than he had wanted to tell her?

'You have come to ask a question. Ask it, my child.'

He hesitated. If she was indeed the Goddess Isis surely she should know without being told what his question was. Those dark eyes certainly seemed to be gazing into his very soul! He must be careful what he said out loud if he wanted to test if she was really who she said she was.

'I am having strange dreams. I wanted to know the meaning...'

'Let your mind form images,' she commanded.

'Of the dreams?' he asked.

'You are resisting – fighting against yourself. You don't want to know what they are trying to tell you. Stop fighting ... let your mind drift... It will take you where you need to go.'

'I would rather be guided by you.'

'If the answer comes from me, you will not believe it. You have to find the answer yourself. Drift ... let images come ... first the water will be muddy from the tap ... then it will run pure...'

It crossed his mind that an ancient Egyptian would not know about taps.

'I am not in ancient Egypt now,' she said in answer to his thought.

He sat up straight. He would try to do what she said but the images that floated like smoke through his mind were at first of the landscape he and Emma had just driven through ... then Mary Brown's room with all the glass gleaming in the sunlight... He even saw an image of his old school playground. But gradually other images came ... ships tossed on a stormy sea ... a Roman villa in a Roman town ... the columns of an Egyptian temple ... the carving of the Egyptian hand in his room in Bath ... the graffiti of the sun with all the rays ending in little hands ... a man and women raising their arms in adoration to it...

She listened impassively as he talked on, warming to his theme, having no idea if he was remembering things or just imagining them...

21

At last she raised her hand and stopped the flow.

'You have had many lives,' she said in that strange voice. 'But the one you are describing now is the one that troubles you most.'

He was puzzled. It did not seem to him that he was describing a life, but the objects in his room and drifting images they evoked.

'I sense you are holding back because you are afraid of the truth. The sun's rays ending in hands is the symbol of Akhenaten, the symbol of his God. The hand you describe is the hand of Akhenaten reaching out to his God. You have something in your possession that proves to you who you are.'

'But...' Jack started, and then lapsed into silence.

He felt very strange as though he was standing at the edge of a precipice about to be pushed over.

Was she implying that he had been Akhenaten in a past life?

'You cannot avoid your destiny,' she said. 'The more you try to do so, the more it will pursue you.'

'What is my destiny? I'm not trying to avoid it. I just don't know what it is.'

'You will.'

He began to feel angry. He was to pay a hundred pounds for this 'reading' and so far he had done all the work and was nowhere nearer enlightenment.

'Will you tell me who I am, and why I am having these dreams about Egypt?' She must have heard the impatience in his voice, but she took no notice.

'Does the hand on your wall feel like your own hand?' she asked.

'Yes,' he said at once without thinking. 'No. I don't know. It is an old fragment of sculpture, of course it can't be my hand! In the dreams it beckons me as though it belongs to someone else. But sometimes I have felt it is mine...'

She smiled pointedly.

'Are you implying that I was Akhenaten in a past life?' he demanded angrily.

If she did not give him a straight answer now he would get up and leave, strange feelings or no strange feelings!

'Do you think you were Akhenaten?' She asked.

He had been to a psychiatrist once who had persisted in asking questions and giving him no answers. He was annoyed then, and he was annoyed now. With an exclamation of disgust he rose to his feet and strode out of the room, slamming the door behind him. A hundred tinkling mobiles moved and spun.

Emma looked up, startled, from the book she had been reading.

'Let's go!' he snapped. He put his hand into his wallet and pulled

22

out two fifty-pound notes and flung them on the coffee table. One missed and fluttered to the floor. He did not wait to pick it up but made for the outer door without a backward glance.

Emma looked anxiously back at the door he had just slammed, but hesitated only a moment before she followed him out of the house.

'What's the matter?' she asked as he furiously started up the engine.

'Nothing!' he snapped. 'A waste of time. I don't know why I let you talk me into it!'

Emma gritted her teeth and prayed to her Guardian Angels for protection as they hit the road much too fast.

3

The Tomb Guardian

Several weeks passed in which Jack resisted any discussion on the matter with Emma. He tried to get his life back as it had been before the dreams started. He went drinking with Eliot and his other friends and treated Emma, when she was in their company, like a stranger, except when he made barbed jokes about the New Age, which she interpreted as criticisms of herself.

At first she was hurt and upset by his treatment of her, and then began to resent it. By the time he was ready to ask her help again she did not want anything to do with him, and told Eliot that if he wanted to see Jack he would have to see him alone.

Jack made sure he drank so much he fell into bed in a stupor most nights, and if he had any nocturnal adventures, he certainly could not remember them in the morning. He was just beginning to believe he had imagined the whole thing, when, one night, he inadvertently went to bed without drinking, and he dreamed one of 'those' dreams again.

He found himself in a vast desert, featureless to every horizon. The feeling of loneliness and aloneness was overwhelming. The sun was directly overhead, casting no shadow. He had no idea whether he was facing north, south, east or west.

He was near to despair when he spotted a tiny smudge on one horizon, which steadily manifested itself as a figure walking towards him. He was greatly relieved. Rescue was at hand.

But when the figure was near enough to distinguish, he was startled to see that it was the figure of the tomb guardian he had in his apartment – worm-eaten, black painted wood with gold belt, gold painted staff and eyes of black onyx. There was a bitter taste of disappointment and fear in his throat. He turned to run, but his feet sank into the sand.

He braced himself and waited.

The striding figure reached him and passed him. Its eyes, staring straight ahead, showed no recognition. It moved like an automaton.

Jack stared, astonished, as the statue strode past him, making no indentation on the soft sand into which his own feet were sinking, each step precisely the same length as the last.

'Wait!' he cried, suddenly realising that he would be alone and lost again when the figure had reached the other horizon. Anything was better than that!

He stumbled after him and was still stumbling and sweating, struggling and calling, when he awoke...

It took another week of heavy drinking to ward off further disturbing encounters.

Meanwhile the statue of the tomb guardian was becoming a problem.

Occasional visitors had complained that it was frightening, but Jack had never found it so. Now he was aware of it all the time he was not drunk. Its eyes seemed to follow him whenever he passed it, and on more than one occasion he swung round in the bedroom or the living room convinced it had followed him and was standing behind him.

He threw a patchwork quilt over it, one his grandmother had made for him when he was a child, but this only made things worse. He *knew* its eyes could still see him through the fabric.

At one time he almost threw it down the stairs, wanting to break it into a thousand pieces, but he could not bring himself to touch it.

'I'll sell it to a museum,' he thought, and phoned an archaeological friend of his fathers, saying the matter was urgent, as he needed money desperately. The man, Colin Meredith, was excited at the prospect of getting his hands on a genuine ancient Egyptian tomb guardian and made an appointment to come to see him the following Friday.

Jack decided to stay with Eliot until his visit. He could not face sharing his apartment another night with the ghostly figure. He was determined to tell no one of this latest turn of events. Not even Emma, picking up that something dramatic had happened, could wheedle a word out of him.

Every evening he and Eliot drank a lot and she went to bed early to escape the maudlin songs and the exaggerated memories of the time they had spent travelling the States on a Greyhound bus before she had met either of them.

When Colin Meredith arrived to view the statue he was tremendously excited and said at once he would take it to Sotheby's for valuation and possible auction.

'But I'm afraid I can't get you a buyer quickly and easily. We will have to have documentation of provenance, and I'm sure there will be questions about the legality of your great-grandfather taking it out of Egypt.'

'I thought there were no such laws in his day.'

'Certainly not as strict. But this is a very valuable piece and I very much fear your right to hold it privately may be questioned. Are you sure you want to start all this? Would you not rather just keep it away from the limelight as your great-grandfather did?'

'I need the money,' Jack lied stubbornly.

'You have a lot of treasures I see,' Meredith said, glancing appreciatively around the room. 'Perhaps something else, less controversial, will bring you in the required amount.'

Jack frowned. He did not want to admit to his fear of the statue. He imagined an ironic glint in its eyes as though it were listening to the conversation and knew that he would not be able to get rid of it as easily as he wished.

He tried to pull himself together. He had lived with the statue most of his life and had never felt this way about it before.

Meredith was meanwhile exploring and had come across the leather-covered case left by Jack's great-grandfather. His initials were embossed in faded gold on the top and were recognized at once by the young archaeologist.

'Some old papyrus manuscripts. Mostly fragments,' Jack said abstractedly.

Meredith opened it and started to riffle through it carefully, but with growing excitement.

In the dust at the bottom he found an insignificant looking dull silver ring with a flattened turquoise bezel, and put it aside on the coffee table while he examined the documents.

'Not much in hieroglyphs,' Jack said apologetically, 'so they can't be very old.'

'Hieroglyphs were mostly used for formal or magical texts. They themselves were believed to carry a direct magical charge. A much easier writing developed for everyday use called hieratic, and, in the seventh century BC, it became what we call demotic. These are mostly demotic, but still very interesting.'

He held up one of the larger fragments covered with hieroglyphs.

'This looks pretty old,' he said. 'It looks like ... it looks like a list of names... a genealogy perhaps.'

He held it up to the light by the window. Many of the characters were faded and some eaten away by insects.

'I see the name Wa-en-ra,' he said thoughtfully, and then looked round at Jack, his face astonished. 'One of the names of Akhenaten,' he cried.

'Oh, no!' Jack thought. 'Not that again!'

'I really think you should have these properly translated and evaluated,' Meredith continued, his eyes alight. 'I don't know enough to do them justice. But there are plenty of scholars I know who would appreciate a chance to study them.'

'Take them if you want,' Jack said impatiently. 'They are no use to me as they are now.'

The archaeologist could not believe his good luck. He started immediately to pick up the papyri, before Jack could change his mind. It was clear they would deteriorate further without proper care, and who knew what information they would reveal about the 'heretic' king!

'It's the statue I really want to get rid of,' Jack said suddenly. 'It's too big for this apartment and it frightens my guests.'

'I don't wonder,' Meredith laughed. 'Those tomb guardians were fortified with all sorts of magical spells.'

He did not notice Jack's expression, because he was still poring over the papyrus fragments.

'If this is a genealogy,' he mused aloud. 'We might finally be able to solve the mystery of Tutankhamun's antecedents, and whether Smenkhkare was a separate male king or just the throne name of Nefertiti... There might even be something about what happened to his daughters after his death...'

But Jack was not listening.

'The statue has to go today,' he announced.

'What?' Meredith exclaimed, looking at Jack in surprise.

'I really want to get started on selling it at once,' Jack insisted.

'But...'

'You can take the papyri to translate,' Jack said stubbornly, 'only if you take the statue away today.'

Meredith looked at him as though he had gone mad.

'You must know that is impossible.'

'We could wrap it up and put it in your car. No one will know what it is. We could phone Sotheby's to tell them it is coming...'

'I'm sorry. It is priceless. It must be properly crated and transported. There are procedures...'

'I tell you. I'm fed up with it. I want it out of the house. If you don't take it today, I'll crate it up myself and put it in storage somewhere where it will not be seen again until I die.'

* * * *

And so it was that Colin Meredith found himself driving down the motorway towards London in his Vauxhall station wagon with an ancient Egyptian tomb guardian wrapped in a blanket in the back, and a box of precious papyrus fragments on the seat beside him.

That night Jack went to sleep in his own bed, sober, and had no dreams. He had not noticed that Meredith had left the ancient ring on the coffee table. It was Emma who found it on her next visit with Eliot.

Since the departure of the statue Jack had almost returned to his former self. He was not drinking so much and was good company again. She did not ask if he was still having the dreams, although she longed to.

As she put her coffee cup down on the low glass tabletop the ring was knocked off onto the floor. She picked it up and examined it curiously.

'What's this?' she asked.

Jack peered at it without interest.

'Oh, just some old ring that came with the papyri,' he said. 'Meredith must have left it behind. He could probably see it was of no value.'

'But it looks old,' Emma mused, turning it over and over.

'Oh, I'm sure it is old!' Jack laughed.

'There is a cartouche. It must be the name of a pharaoh!'

Jack shrugged. 'I have no idea who it belonged to.'

'Mary Brown has lots of books on Egypt,' she said. 'She will probably be able to find out.'

She put the ring on her finger and held her hand up to admire it. The ring fitted well, but her finger began to tingle uncomfortably. She removed it and returned it to the table.

Jack's coffee table was one of those display units, consisting of a heavy piece of thick glass over a wooden base. In the tray under the glass he had a good many fossils displayed – whorled ammonites, bi-valves changed to shining pyrites, ancient shark's teeth, and skeletal fish caught in a moment of graceful movement and locked in stone forever. Emma stared down at it, and, in the glass, she could see her own reflection and, behind her, that of Jack.

A strange shift in focus occurred and suddenly she was aware of the fossils that had been living creatures millions of years ago, the ring worn on the hand of a living being several thousands of years ago, and she and Jack living and breathing at this time, yet all part now of the same moment. She remembered Mary Brown's image of the starry heavens to illustrate the interconnectedness and simultaneity of everything.

She glanced up, eager to pass on her insight to Jack, but he and Eliot were laughing at some joke and she knew it would not be appropriate.

When they were ready to leave, Emma managed to extract a reluctant agreement from Jack that together they would take the ring to Mary for an interpretation of the cartouche.

Over the next few days Jack heard from Meredith, who was handling the sale of the statue at Sotheby's, that most of the difficulties had been ironed out and that it would not be long before it was put up for auction. He also reported that the papyrus fragments were well on the way to being translated. He had found just the scholar for the case. Jack listened with only half his attention. The only news he wanted from Meredith was that the statue had been sold and was out of his life forever.

And then he had another of 'those' dreams. This time it concerned the ring. He dreamed he put it on and could not get it off. Someone was demanding it of him and he tried to pass it over, but tug as he might it would not budge. Suddenly he saw the flash of a blade, and the shadowy figure before him cut his ring finger off. For a moment he stood there, in agony, watching the blood spurt out, and then he awoke.

Shuddering, he climbed out of bed, and, in the light, examined his hands. All his fingers were intact. He went to the living room and looked for the ring. Emma had put it on the mantel shelf, saying it would be safer there than on the coffee table.

He stared at it where it lay, but did not pick it up.

Next morning he phoned Emma and they made an appointment to visit Mary Brown.

Mary examined the ring with great interest, and Emma noticed, if Jack did not, that there was a growing excitement expressed in her face as she began to translate the glyphs. But before she would tell them what she had discovered she drew out several books from her shelves and consulted them.

At last she held it up and declared with conviction that it was the seal ring of the pharaoh Akhenaten.

Emma gasped, for Jack had told her that Meredith had isolated one of the names of Akhenaten on the papyrus fragments.

There was silence in the room. Both Emma and Jack felt a chill down their spines, Emma remembering the tingling she had felt in her finger when she had worn the ring, and Jack remembering Denise's suggestion that he himself was a reincarnation of Akhenaten. Mary seemed deep in thought.

'It is strange that Akhenaten's ring should come our way,' she murmured. 'It seems as though something connected with him is stirring again and we are being drawn into it.'

'An archaeologist friend of Jack's said the name of Akhenaten was on one of those papyrus fragments of his,' Emma said eagerly.

Mary looked up at Jack sharply.

'Are you having them translated?'

'Yes.'

'I would very much like to see the translation.'

'Of course I'll let you see it,' Jack said. 'But...' He paused.

Mary looked at him steadily, enquiringly.

'But ... I don't really want to get involved in anything spooky...'

'You are involved!' Emma cried. 'Tell Mary what Denise said!'

As he hesitated to speak, Emma took the initiative.

'A famous psychic and past-life reader in Glastonbury said he was a reincarnation of Akhenaten!' she cried.

'She didn't say it, she implied it,' Jack said testily, wishing he had not given in and told Emma what had occurred between Denise and himself. 'She was pushing me towards admitting it, but I knew it was nonsense. She was absolutely off the mark.'

Mary was listening intently, her hands resting in her lap, still holding the ring.

'We will know more perhaps when those manuscripts are decoded,' she said quietly.

Jack frowned, convinced he did not want anything more to do with Akhenaten and his mysteries.

As though she had heard his thoughts she said sympathetically: 'I know how you feel, but once something like this has "chosen" us, we cannot escape. It's better to see it through to its end. I know from my own experience how mercilessly one is hunted until one capitulates.'

He did not like the sound of this, and rose to go.

'Do you believe Jack is Akhenaten?' Emma asked eagerly, not at all keen to end the conversation.

Mary smiled.

'I have met at least five people who claim to have been Akhenaten in a past life, some of them with very good credentials.'

'There you see!' cried Jack. 'The whole thing is absurd.'

'I would not say that it is absurd,' Mary said, 'but that something is going on that needs investigation.'

'It might just be a matter of people trying to give their own pathetic lives some kind of significance,' he said scornfully.

'Is that what you are trying to do?' she asked.

He flushed angrily.

'I didn't *ask* for these dreams! I didn't *ask* for all these things to be happening! And I absolutely deny that I was Akhenaten in a past life. Denise is a manipulative, misguided woman with no more psychic ability than a horse!'

Mary laughed. 'They say horses have very strong psychic abilities,' she said with a mischievous twinkle in her eyes.

Jack glared at Emma and jerked his head towards the door.

'Whatever!' he snapped.

Mary rose to her feet and led the way to the door. Emma followed reluctantly.

As they parted Mary reached out the ring to him.

'Keep it,' he said brusquely. 'It probably means more to you than to me.'

'I don't think so,' she said softly, and pressed it into his hand.

4

The Window of Appearances

He was in a city – in a street where a throng of people pushed and crowded around him. All were facing one way, steadily making their way towards the east where a bridge spanned the street from one building to another. It was a city he knew well although he had never seen anything like it in his life as Jack Wilson. The buildings were low and angular. Flags fluttered from tall flag poles in front of angular stone pylons, while gigantic statues guarded the gates of the temples – each one the divine pharaoh himself.

Over all the sun was blazing down, the one round object in all these straight lines.

As the crowd pushed him near the bridge, the small figures that were standing on it became clearer. The royal family ... Akhenaten, the Son of the Sun, Nefe-Kheperu-Re, sole one of Ra, and the beautiful wife of the God, Nefertiti ... both naked but their skin gleaming with gold dust. Ranged beside them were their six daughters, the three youngest chattering and pointing at the crowds like excited children anywhere, the three eldest standing quietly, somewhat bored. High officials were dispensing gifts from the King – gold collars – jewels – fine transparent alabaster goblets and jars of precious ointment...

People were falling into the dust in obeisance.

Jack was awed. He was witnessing the love and generosity of a god towards his people.

With tears in his eyes he fell to the ground and put his forehead in the dust. If he died now there would have been no better moment in his life.

He felt a hand under his shoulder, raising him. He looked up and it seemed to him Akhenaten himself was gazing straight into his eyes with a knowing tenderness that melted his heart.

Ah, Wa-en-ra Akhenaten, Saviour of the World, Lord from Everlasting to Everlasting...

He scarcely noticed the official putting a jewelled menat around his neck.

Weeping he knew that he would serve his lord until the end of time.

* * * *

'No!' he shouted, leaping up and pacing about the room. The dreams had started up again.

The noise of drunken revellers in the street gave him pause for a moment. Had the sound of crowds rejoicing in the street below his apartment influenced his dream? He banged his knee against a chair in the darkened room and swore. Now he had no doubt where he was and who he was, yet the experience in Egypt had been so vivid he could not believe that it was only a dream. Were Mary Brown and Emma right about there being more than one type of reality?

He calmed down after a while and pulled a beer out of the fridge, sitting in the kitchen, drinking and thinking.

Then he went to the living room and picked up the ring Mary Brown had said was the seal ring of Akhenaten, and stared at it long and hard.

Jack knew very little about the history of Egypt and he decided, for the first time, to open a book that Emma had lent him. He found a list of pharaohs. Akhenaten was given the dates 1353-1335 BC.

It seemed Akhenaten had turned his back on the ancient Gods of Egypt, and instituted what amounted to monotheism. He moved his court from the traditional royal cities of Memphis and Thebes, and built a brand new one in the desert uncontaminated by the old religious cults of Egypt. Akhetaten, City of the Sun. From the line drawings based on ancient tomb reliefs he could see how it once was, and it was remarkably like the city he had seen in his dream. There had been 'a window of appearances' on a bridge across the main street where Akhenaten and his family appeared from time to time to greet their people and dispense rewards.

Jack shivered. He felt he was being drawn inexorably closer and closer into a web. He felt someone was setting him puzzles and watching to see how he solved them. He felt that every move he made, awake or asleep, was somehow being observed.

'What do you want with me?' he shouted aloud in the oppressive stillness of the night now that the revellers had gone. 'What do you want me to do?'

Someone was playing games with him – but they were not children's games.

He paced the rest of the night away alternately angry and afraid. When first light came he fell on his bed into a dreamless stupor and was still sleeping when Emma rang the bell at noon.

Bleary eyed and dazed he pressed the intercom button. Emma's voice, bright and cheerful, seared a path through his head. Groaning, he pressed the button to activate the door opening and leaned against the wall with his eyes shut.

Where was he? Part of him was aware of his room, curtains still drawn shut, a dim light diffusing over familiar objects – but somewhere else in his consciousness he heard a voice calling – a voice he had heard before but did not recognize.

'What's happened? You look like hell!' were Emma's first words.

She stared at him for a moment, and then went straight to the kitchen and put on the kettle.

When she came back he was gone, and there was the sound of water splashing in the bathroom. Emma decided he must have had another of those dreams, and was impatient to hear about it. But she knew she would have to wait.

When the water stopped running, she called out the question she had come to ask.

'Have you heard from Meredith yet?'

'What?'

'The papyri? Have they been translated?'

He grunted his reply, which she could not catch.

'Sotheby's? When is the auction of the statue?'

This time she got an audible reply.

'Next month. The 20th.'

'And the papyri?' She tried again.

'Haven't heard. I think he has found someone, but nothing has come my way yet.'

Later, after three cups of strong black coffee, he volunteered a description of his latest dream.

'At least it proves I was not Akhenaten himself,' he said with relief.

'But you *did* live in Akhenaten's time!'

He frowned.

'I don't understand why it is all happening to *me*. You would be a much better candidate for these things!'

'All the more reason to believe it is all really happening. It cannot be a case of manifestation caused by wishful thinking. I would love it to happen to me. Yet it does not.'

'Perhaps if we slept together I could pass the dreams on to you!' He looked at her in such a way that she could not be sure if he was just joking or not. She decided the only way to react was to pretend she thought he was.

She laughed, but a bit nervously. His hair was still damp and ruffled from the shower, his shirt open. She noticed a trickle of water tracing its way slowly from his neck to his waist. She stood up quickly and drew the curtains aside vigorously, letting in the bright sunlight.

He was still looking at her, quizzically, when she turned around. She could not meet his eyes.

'We should see Mary Brown again,' she said briskly. 'Or perhaps Denise. One of them might be able to make sense of what is now emerging.'

'I don't want to go back to Denise,' he said firmly. 'And I don't think we should see Mary again until I have the translations of the papyri. There would be something definite to report then.'

'You have something definite to report now,' Emma insisted, not wanting to wait before another piece of the puzzle was fitted into place.

He shrugged. 'Who knows,' he said, 'it is all probably just imagination!'

'I hate that phrase "just imagination"! Imagination helps us to extend our understanding beyond our own limited experience. Mary says it is the greatest learning tool we have.'

'Okay!' Jack laughed. 'Okay. I admit imagination may have its uses.'

'Mary says there are three main types of consciousness. The super, or higher consciousness, in which we are in touch with what she was trying to describe the other day, the Inter-Related. Everything. Then there is the ordinary practical consciousness with which we operate day by day in our immediate lives on this earth – which has shields up against too much input. The subconscious is the third type. It draws on both of these and is the hidden agenda we all have whether we are aware of it or not, the half forgotten memories, needs and desires that influence our decisions and our actions.'

'So, you are saying...?'

'I am saying that even if the dreams you are having spring from your subconscious and are given form by your imagination, that does not mean they are not expressing or revealing a significant truth. They may be coming from the Higher Consciousness via the Subconscious, because your Ordinary Consciousness will not listen.'

Jack rose and crossed the room. He moved an object on the mantelpiece to a different position, and then back again.

Emma watched him, waiting. Would he turn the matter aside with a joke, or make some excuse to be somewhere else?

He looked at his watch, but before he could dismiss her with a lie, she herself said she must go.

'Let me know when you hear from Meredith,' she said at the door. 'Especially about the papyrus with Akhenaten's name.'

'That will probably turn out to be someone's laundry list,' he said. And they parted with a laugh.

Jack did in fact speak to Mary Brown again before he received the translation from Meredith. He was crossing the Abbey courtyard and saw her sitting on one of the benches, staring up at the 'Jacob's ladders' that were carved on the twin towers of the Medieval church. He could have passed without her noticing him, and at first he quickened his pace hoping to avoid recognition. But then he stopped and glanced back at her, remembering her remark that it was only her disguise that made her look like an old lady.

He followed her gaze up at the ladders on the towers. Angels were going up and down as in Jacob's dream. He had seen, or rather half-seen, these ladders and these angels hundreds of times without paying them much attention. But now, experiencing, as he was, the power and significance of dreams, he paused and stared at them with new eyes.

He walked back to Mary and sat down beside her. She lowered her eyes to his and smiled without surprise.

'It seems Jacob had interesting dreams too,' she said.

He grinned. 'Do you think he really saw angels?'

'Of course,' she said. 'Why not?'

'Well...'

'You don't believe in angels?'

'Not ones that have to climb ladders!'

She laughed. 'Metaphors and analogies are always crude compared to the real thing,' she said. 'How else can we express what we feel to be spiritually higher or lower? Of course we know heaven is not *up there*. The other realms of being are simultaneously with us. They are around us in this courtyard even as we speak.' She waved her hand to indicate the passing throng of tourists, the stone buildings, the busker dressed in eighteenth century costume playing his flute at the abbey door. 'We may not see them but they are here as surely as those people there...'

As she spoke Jack could almost see the invisible worlds around him passing through him like smoke. How many tourists were aware that what they could see was only a very small part of what was actually there? How many would go home thinking thoughts that changed their lives, never knowing how they had come by them? How many others would go home carrying no more than dull photographs of themselves posed before buildings.

'Dreams and interpretations of dreams come a lot into the Bible,'

Jack said thoughtfully after a long pause. 'People in ancient times were always altering their lives because of a dream. I grew up believing that we knew better.'

'We know nothing. We are still in kindergarten.'

There was a long silence between them, Jack pondering Jacob seeing beings from another reality.

Mary spoke first.

'Emma tells me you have had another dream about Akhenaten,' she said.

He experienced a moment's irritation. He was not sure he wanted his private dreams discussed behind his back.

'Its funny,' she continued musingly,' that Jacob, whose dream we see in stone before us here, had a connection with Egypt too, and possibly with Akhenaten.'

Jack looked surprised.

'Jacob was the father of Joseph of the many coloured coat. He was sold to slavers by his jealous brothers, sojourned in Egypt, and was thrown into prison when he was falsely accused of seducing Potiphor's wife. Then he interpreted Pharaoh's dreams and became a power behind the throne in Egypt. Jacob himself visited him there. Genesis chapter 46.'

Jack tried to recall the story from his Sunday school days. He could only remember the musical by Andrew Lloyd Webber, 'Joseph and the Amazing Technicolour Dream Coat'. One of the songs started to run through his mind, blotting out everything else.

'I would give anything to know who the pharaoh was,' Mary said. 'Some say it could have been Akhenaten, in which case the idea of the one God could have come from Joseph. People have noticed the similarities between Psalm 104 in the Bible and Akhenaten's hymn to the Sun. But it is impossible to tell from the Biblical story, and the Egyptians themselves left no record of the event.'

'Can't we tell by the dates?'

Mary shrugged. 'The dating of ancient events is mostly inaccurate. Each pharaoh's reign began at year one, and the next one that followed also began at year one. Egyptologists make neat lists, but they are mostly approximate, based on incomplete data. They frequently find evidence of pharaohs they hadn't known existed! Even comparison with other events in other ancient civilisations is suspect. And as for the Old Testament! We don't know how lucky we are to have a fixed date in the Birth of Christ on which to base our historical records.'

'I believe even the date of the birth of Christ is controversial.'

'It is based on the known dates of Herod the Great and the

massacre of infants that was supposed to have taken place near the end of his reign. We have no independent confirmation of the massacre, but Herod from all reports was quite capable of such a monstrous act.'

'If I've learned anything over the past few months,' Jack said, 'it is not to take anything at face value.'

She smiled, and Jack suspected she was thinking: 'I hope you have learned more than that!' But she said nothing.

He stood up.

'Will you be staying?' he asked.

'No. I'm going now too. But you go ahead. I'm so slow.'

He hesitated, but she waved him on, and he turned to go.

A busker at the other end of the forecourt was playing the theme tune from Lloyd Webber's 'Joseph' that had been running through Jack's mind a few minutes before!

5

The Shemsu Benu

Meredith returned in early September with some of the papyrus pieces translated. They were, he said, fragments from many different times and places, written sometimes in old Egyptian demotic, some Greek or Latin, with a smattering of hieroglyphs from earlier times.

'Do any of them make sense?' Jack asked.

'My friend concentrated most on the largest fragment. Some of it had been eaten away by insects, and it seemed to have been added to from time to time. Mostly it was a list of names, starting with reference to Akhenaten. At first we thought it might be a genealogy, but the names don't seem to have any royal family significance except, possibly, Setepenra, which was the name of one of his younger daughters. But that may be coincidence. However there does seem to be a hereditary element in the list, for many of the names are apparently sons or daughters, or even grandsons and granddaughters, of the people named earlier on the list.

'As far as we could make out they all seemed to be "Companions of the Benu". The words Shemsu Benu appeared frequently and there seems to have been a strong connection with Akhenaten because many of the phrases used are typically Atenist.

'Other fragments were just bits and pieces we know from other texts, spells from the Book of the Dead, and something that seemed to be part of a judgement in Roman times against one Ra-hotep who had been plotting against the Prefect.'

Jack picked up the transcript of the fragment that mentioned Akhenaten and read it carefully. He found it maddening that so much of it was missing. Who were these Companions of the Benu? Why was there a prickle down his spine as he whispered the words 'Shemsu Benu'?

'Time we went for a spot of lunch,' Meredith said briskly. 'Any good places around here?'

'We'll go to the Crystal Palace pub around the corner,' Jack said. 'Its not bad.' He would be glad to get away from the list that was inexplicably bothering him, as though a memory was just hovering out of reach.

They walked around the corner to Abbey Green dominated by a huge old plane tree, the girth of its trunk formidable, its uppermost branches almost touching the buildings on every side of the tiny square, its roots stitching the buildings together underground.

It was a fine day and they chose to sit in the open area at the rear of the pub in the dappled light that penetrated through vine leaves. Jack recovered his equilibrium and ate a hearty meal.

Meredith told him one of the smaller fragments had been part of a Gnostic Gospel missing from those found at Nag Hammadi.

'You'll get a good price for that,' he said. 'Scholars will jump at a chance to fit it into the jigsaw.'

'What is a Gnostic Gospel?' Jack asked.

'You've heard of the Dead Sea Scrolls?' Meredith asked.

'Of course – early Essene writings from about the time of Jesus found in Israel.'

'Well, it is less well known that very early Christian writings were found in Egypt in 1945, in caves in the mountains near the town of Nag Hammadi, dating from the first and second centuries AD. They must have been hidden when the Gnostics were declared heretics by the emerging Christian Church, probably at the time of Constantine in the fourth century when the penalties for being a heretic were severe. One of their more controversial beliefs was that there was an ultimate unknown god who started off everything, and that the god described in the Old Testament, the jealous, punishing god, was actually only a demiurge, a lesser being. The Gnostics believed our lives should be devoted to discovering the Real God, and we could do this through our own efforts, through the pursuit of knowledge and wisdom inspired by the spark of Divine Fire from the Real God, which is in all of us, waiting to return ultimately to its Source. To the Gnostics, Christ Jesus came to earth to teach us about the Real God and we are saved by the knowledge, the Gnosis, we gain by following him, and not, as the Church would have us believe, because God accepted his blood sacrifice on our behalf.

'Many of their gospels give a different slant to the Biblical stories. For instance, in their version of the Garden of Eden, Eve does not bring about the downfall of man but, realising the god who had forbidden them to eat of the Tree of Knowledge was a false demiurge, she led Adam to rebel against him and thus gave him the chance of salvation through Gnosis.'

'Wow!' said Jack, and laughed.

'Sometimes I wonder if modern psychiatrists and therapists have learned anything since the ancient days,' Meredith mused. 'There is a passage I remember from the Secret Gospel of Thomas which is supposed to be a direct quote from the living Jesus. Jesus said: "If you bring forth what is within you, what you bring forth will save you. If you do not bring forth what is within you, what you do not bring forth will destroy you".'

Jack sipped the very good wine Meredith had chosen. Would what was coming forth from him save him? And if he did not follow what was coming forth, would he be destroyed?

As soon as Emma knew that he had the translations she pestered him until he agreed to take them to show Mary Brown.

'You haven't heard half of the story about her own links with Akhenaten,' she said. 'She might even have heard of the Shemsu Benu.'

'The connection with Akhenaten is very tenuous,' Jack protested. 'Just because his name appears once...'

'And his seal ring was found, remember, with the papyrus that mentions his name.'

'We don't know if my great-grandfather found it with the papyrus that mentions his name. Most of the fragments in the case were totally unconnected. Some were from as late as Roman times. Old Wilson must have picked them up all over the place. When the family packed up his things after he died, the ring may have got in there purely by accident.'

'Did he not keep a diary or a journal about his discoveries?'

'Not that I know of.'

'I bet he did! It would tell you if the ring was found with that particular papyrus or not. I believe it was.'

'You would believe anything!'

'Mary would believe it too!'

'Believing something doesn't necessarily make it true.'

'No, but neither does doubting it make it untrue.'

He grinned. 'Okay. It is an open question. We'll leave it at that.'

'No we won't!' she said. 'He must have kept a journal. All those old archaeologists did. You must try to find it. You seem to be on some kind of trail, following clues and signs laid down for you.'

'That is what I'm afraid of!'

'The journal might help.'

'If there was one – it was probably destroyed.'

'Don't be so negative! The whole thing is tremendously exciting. You must admit it beats spending your life at the pub talking about cricket all the time!'

'Are you saying that is all I did with my life before these things started happening?'

'No, of course not. But you must admit you did not do much.'

Jack surveyed his past life and had to admit there was not much there that he was proud of. Even when he went abroad to write a travel article he tended to travel well and comfortably and write about the wine and food and water-skiing.

He agreed reluctantly that he would make enquiries about a possible journal.

Mary, as Emma anticipated, was very interested in the translations, particularly in the list of names.

'It is so frustrating that it is so damaged,' she said. 'A lot of the links are lost.'

'Do you think they all have something to do with Akhenaten?' Emma asked. 'Maybe its a genealogy.'

'I don't think so,' Mary said thoughtfully. 'They seem rather to be members of a society: the Companions of the Benu.'

'What's the Benu?' Jack asked.

'The Benu was a mythical bird, resembling the blue heron, supposed to have landed on the first mound of earth that emerged from the primeval waters, and laid the egg out of which all that we know emerged. Later it was believed it was a kind of phoenix, burning itself up on the altar of the Sun God Ra, encased in an egg of myrrh, and emerging, reborn, from the flames. It became a symbol of resurrection.'

Mary's thoughtfulness was giving way to a growing excitement.

'I am beginning to see where this is leading us,' she said.

'Where?' Jack's face was blank.

'I think the time has come for me to tell you the story of my encounter with Akhenaten. Perhaps when you hear it you too will see the significance of the Shemsu Benu.'

Jack was prepared to listen now to anything that made sense of the story that was unfolding in his own life. He listened with growing interest as Mary spoke.

'I don't know how or when my fascination with ancient Egypt started,' she said, 'but from an early age, certainly. I remember my project on Egypt at Junior School was read out to the class. My mother took me to the British Museum in London and I could not be drawn away from the Egyptian exhibits. But the first time I noticed Akhenaten was when I was a young woman visiting the Louvre Museum in Paris. I was heading for the Egyptian galleries, climbing a staircase. At the head of it, looking over me and, I swear, meeting my eyes, was this huge stone bust of the pharaoh Akhenaten. He had such a strange face, elongated, with slightly slanting eyes and very full lips. I have since read in books that he was ugly and deformed, but to me that day, and ever since, he was beautiful! I stopped and stared for a long time, and came back many times to gaze at him. In the galleries I sought out any artefacts that might have been from his time, and after I left the Louvre I began to read books about him. I was totally intrigued by the mystery that surrounded him. It seems that when he succeeded his father he took the name Amenhotep IV, but soon changed his name to Akhenaten as he became more and more convinced that there was only one true God, and that God was Aten, represented by the burning disk of the sun.

'For thousands of years the complex pantheon of Egyptian gods had been stable. Each of the forty-two nomes (or districts) in the country had developed their own particular religious myth, with its group of divine protagonists, in an attempt to understand and explain the mysteries of existence. Some became so popular and were so appropriate to the human condition that they became accepted more widely than the district in which they originated.

'One of the most important and widespread myths was that of Isis and Osiris. This was part of the Ennead of Heliopolis. Here it was believed the creator sun god was Atum, or Ra-Atum, the Totality, 'an ultimate and unalterable state of perfection'. From him descended two divinities, Shu and Tefnut (air and water), and from them two more, Geb and Nut (earth and sky). From these, four offspring followed: Osiris, Isis, Set and Nepthys. Rich mythic material was woven around these four. Osiris and Isis, brother and sister, were also lovers. Set killed his brother Osiris and scattered his chopped up body far and wide. Isis, grief stricken, searched and found the pieces, bound them together, and, fanning them with her wings, restored enough vitality to him that he fathered their son Horus on her. From this event grew his role as Lord of the Otherworld, representing resurrection, rebirth, life after death. Horus, their son, tried to avenge his father's murder, and represented the fight of Good against Evil in many of the sacred stories.

'The Aten, as represented by the shining disk of the sun, was another of the many gods of Egypt, scarcely a major protagonist in the Great Drama before Amenhotep IV chose him as his favourite, changing his own name to Akhenaten, 'Beneficial to Aten'. He looked on the Aten as King of the gods, thereby displacing Amun of Thebes who had borne that title before. To the Aten he attributed the creation and ordering of the world, and the ultimate power to preserve or destroy. Afraid that the purity of his vision would be corrupted by others, he declared that he and his great Royal Wife, Nefertiti, would be the sole channels through which the Aten communicated with earth and bestowed its blessings.

'The most powerful priesthood at that time was attached to the worship of Amun with his great temple complex at Karnak. No doubt because the female pharaoh Hatshepsut, a century before, had brought her favourite god Amun to prominence, and given his priesthood unprecedented riches and power, they were not at all pleased to find their temple and themselves starved of power and funds, and later even physically attacked and destroyed. It was a very important tenet of belief that the gods performing their traditional roles kept the universe, not only in order and balance, but in existence. It was thus dangerous to alter anything, for in doing so one might bring about the end of all things. Statues of gods in Egypt were sacred objects which, it was believed, the gods themselves might inhabit from time to time. When statues of Amun were smashed and his temples desecrated, Akhenaten was putting the whole universe in jeopardy.

'Akhenaten reigned for about twenty years and in that time he left behind the great cities which had for millennia been the seats of power, and built his own totally new city, Akhetaten, now called Tell el-Amarna in Middle Egypt. No one knows how he died, but there has been much speculation that he was assassinated by the disaffected Priests of Amun, possibly with the support of General Horemheb, who, although a commoner, became pharaoh himself a few years after Akhenaten's mysterious disappearance.'

'After his death,' Emma interrupted enthusiastically, 'Akhenaten was reviled as a criminal and a heretic and they tried to remove every trace of him from history. The king lists at Abydos do not mention him. It is as though he never was.'

'How do we know about him then?' Jack asked.

Mary smiled. 'The persistent curiosity of archaeologists,' she replied. 'Just as we found the far outer planets because we noticed certain anomalies in the orbits of other bodies in space, archaeologists began to notice gaps in records and artefacts that did not fit known facts. Then the ruins of Akhetaten were found at Amarna, and the archives with hundreds of clay tablets recording the daily business of the city were unearthed. Akhenaten is now almost the best-known pharaoh from ancient Egypt. Hundreds of books have been written about him.'

'Tell Jack about your dreams,' Emma prompted eagerly.

'Dreams?' Jack exclaimed with interest.

'I never entirely forgot the impact the face of Akhenaten in the Louvre had on me, but I was busy bringing up my children and living my life, and it faded into the background. And then, about twenty years ago, I began to dream about it. More often than not the statue of Akhenaten would come alive, climb down from its plinth and walk towards me. In the museum it was only the top half of a statue, but in my dreams it was always complete. I always woke up before it reached me, but I could see its mouth moving as though it was trying to tell me something. It seemed to me it was pleading with me to do something, but I couldn't understand what. I was frightened and retreated down the stairs. When I woke I always regretted my cowardice in running away, and told myself that the next time I would stay to find out what he was trying to communicate.

'Then I read a book that seemed to explain what was happening: 'Tombs, Temples and Ancient Art' by Joseph Lindon Smith. Lindon Smith was an artist who accompanied archaeologists in Egypt to record their findings. In 1909 he and Arthur Weigall decided to put on a play about Akhenaten in the Valley of the Queens. The idea behind it was that the Priests of Amun had cursed Akhenaten so that in death he would not be able to travel to the Otherworld, but would be doomed to walk the earth forever as a powerless ghost. The play intended to lift the curse and free the soul to travel on.

'In January 1909 several archaeologists and their families and friends gathered in the Valley at Luxor to watch the dress rehearsal. Arthur Weigall and Joseph Lindon Smith had written the text between them and they and their wives were taking the major roles.

'The rehearsal was performed in a natural amphitheatre in the valley of tombs with the actors appearing and disappearing from above and behind rock formations, the perfect setting for a drama about ghosts and ancient curses.

'Lindon Smith had planned the whole performance well. The costumes were excellent. His wife Corinna was dressed in a swathe of red silk as Queen Tiye, Akhenaten's mother, to be called upon to intercede in the Otherworld for the release of her son. Hortense Weigall as Akhenaten himself was costumed according to ancient wall paintings. Head dresses of papier mache for the gods were extraordinarily effective. Haunting music had been specially composed. Lindon Smith as Horus appeared from the Underworld with his magnificent mask glowing in red light that was shone up from below, and intoned words that were echoed back from the rock cliffs and seemed to reverberate deeply inside the tombs.

'After the invocation Hortense as "Akhenaten" appeared on a crag above the stage. As the actress raised her arms in supplication to the god, a devastating peal of thunder and a blinding flash of lightening struck. A wind sprang up as if from nowhere and rushed screaming through the narrow valley. Lindon Smith described how they clutched their possessions at once and bent double against the blast. The donkeys, which had brought them to the valley, set up a terrified braying.

But almost as suddenly as it had started the storm was over, and they decided to continue the rehearsal, laughing at the dramatic interruption, and joking about the Priests of Amun trying to intimidate them.

'The rehearsal continued, but again, later, when Queen Tiye was declaiming Akhenaten's Hymn to the Aten and making an impassioned plea for his release, another violent storm swept through the valley, this time with squalls of rain and hail stones as big as tennis balls. Most of them fled at this point to the shelter of a tomb, but Corinna in her persona as Queen Tiye stood dramatically and firmly on her rock and continued her recital of the long hymn to its very end. When her husband drew her away she was soaked to the skin, but wild with excitement that she had defied the elements and the ancient Priests of Amun.

'It was impossible to continue this time, and they retreated to the tombs for shelter. That night they slept uneasily.

'In the morning it emerged that both Corinna and Hortense had had an identical dream in which one of the statues in the Ramesseum had come alive and whipped her with his flail, Corinna in the eyes, and Hortense in the stomach. Both women were in great pain in the part of the body where they had been hit in the dream. Later Corinna had to be rushed to a Cairo hospital with a dangerous case of trachoma. Most of those who had been at the rehearsal were ill. The play was abandoned.'

When Mary finished speaking there was silence for a while in the room.

Emma shuddered. 'The dark forces are very real and we challenge them at our peril!' she said.

'Do you believe there really is a ghost and a curse?' Jack asked Mary.

She shrugged. 'My persistent dreams make sense if there is,' she replied. 'And then, just at the time I was really pondering the truth about all this, I met a man who claimed to have seen Akhenaten's ghost in the desert in Egypt. He claimed that Akhenaten himself told him he had been cursed, and pleaded with him to try and release him. I felt I could no longer ignore the possibility that it might be true, and began to wonder what I could do about it. Archaeologists and

46

Egyptologists don't know what happened to Akhenaten in the end. His successors did everything in their power to eliminate all record of him from history. Something sinister must have gone on!'

'Tell Jack about your experience at Abydos!' Emma prompted.

Mary smiled indulgently at Emma and then continued her story.

'Some time later I was in Egypt with a group. We were all seeking some kind of explanation for our fascination with ancient Egypt. I was particularly interested in Akhenaten after my dreams about the statue in the Louvre, but we didn't go to Amarna where the ruins of his city lie. It was at Abydos that I unexpectedly had an experience connected with him. The temple itself is still in a remarkable state of preservation. It was built some years after his death by Sety I who might well have been alive at the end of Akhenaten's reign. Sety was the son of the aged Rameses I who succeeded Horemheb – and Horemheb was the man who is believed to be responsible for the overthrow of Akhenaten and the restoration of the ancient religious cults.

'The temple itself is impressive enough, built in a region that was extraordinarily sacred. In the myth of Isis, Osiris and Set, the head of Osiris, severed by his brother Set, was believed to be buried there. In the desert nearby archaeologists have found thousands of pieces of broken pottery. Those who could not be buried in this special ground had pots broken in their name as a way of connecting them with the place.

'The group took a long time exploring the temple itself, but I felt drawn to the desert beyond and wandered off by myself. I will never forget that day. As I left behind the temple and the village I left behind all noise... all comfortable sound of voices, of chickens clucking, cocks crowing, dogs barking ... One moment I was on fertile soil, the next on barren desert. Soon I was stepping over pebbles and then wading through sand, aiming towards the range of mountains that bordered the sacred land. From a high mound I looked back and saw the broken mud brick walls that had once cut off the temple complex from the rest of the community. What had seemed so mighty when I was there gazing up at the gigantic columns, seemed small and insignificant now against the vastness of the desert surrounding it and the towering rock of the mountains that lay beyond.

'A million earthenware or stoneware pots must have been lying broken in the sand, some weathering on the surface, others lying deeply buried, the restless sands of the desert continually covering and uncovering them, each one a story in itself. What lives were represented there! What joys and sorrows! I began to feel really strange. I think it was at that moment I became aware for the first time of the invisible worlds that inhabit the same space as our own. I looked around and I was alone in a vast and empty desert, but I felt as though I was standing in the middle of a crowd. When I shut my eyes I could almost see them.'

Jack remembered how he had felt in the forecourt of the Abbey when Mary had first pointed out to him the existence of the invisible worlds. He still did not want to believe in them.

'I walked a long time among the shards of others people's lives,' Mary continued, 'wondering about those who had put them there; wondering about all the stories of an afterlife I had ever heard...'

Mary stopped speaking and they sat quietly for a time, each absorbed in their own thoughts.

'It was hot,' Mary resumed,' and I could see rocks and mountains ahead. I made for them, hoping to come upon a particular wadi I had been told about which was supposed to be a kind of gateway between the worlds. I don't know what I expected of it, but I was curious. My mind was very much on the mystery of death at that time because my mother had recently died and I was missing her desperately. Its funny, all your life you know about death, it is the one certainty in life, but until someone close to you dies, you don't really believe in it!'

Another pause. Jack was beginning to feel uncomfortable. He did not want to think about death.

'I was nearly collapsing with heat exhaustion when I finally found shade. Ahead of me was what had been described to me as the gateway between the worlds – two dark cliffs between which a river of golden sand seemed to flow. The air was very still. Very heavy. Very hot. I felt as though I was waiting for something to happen.

'I waited. The desert waited. The sky waited.

'And then suddenly a light breeze sprang up and the loose sand around me began to stir.

'Then it was still again. The silence seemed even more oppressive than it had been before.

'After a long while I heard a strange and distant sound. A kind of howling and roaring, faint at first, but growing stronger and more fearsome every second. I stood up, alert, startled, staring at the gap in the mountains from behind which the sound seemed to be emanating.

'And then a cloud of sand began to pour out from between the gap, propelled by a mighty wind, and in that wind I swear I heard voices crying! The Dead were rushing into the sacred space around me!

'I suddenly panicked and turned to run, but the sand was already whipping up around me and cutting into my skin. I was terrified – and not only of the Dead. I thought I would be buried alive and would never be found.

'I remember thinking that I was falling into a dark void.

'But gradually the darkness lifted and it seemed to me I was surrounded by a golden mist. And then I saw the figure of the Pharaoh Akhenaten walking towards me through the mist, his flesh shining like gold. He reached out his hands to me, and rays of light shone from every finger, enclosing me in a web of light. He spoke, but I could not understand what he was saying. I remember wondering why he did not speak in my language as channellers and mediums do when purporting to be transmitting messages from the Dead.

'But then he suddenly vanished. The golden light vanished, and I found myself lying in the hot sand of the desert.'

There was a long silence in the room when Mary finished speaking. Jack was stunned. He was thinking about the dreams in which he had felt so lost and alone in the desert. He was remembering how he had heard his name called desperately as though someone was pleading for help. He had a vision of the tomb guardian walking like an automaton to the horizon. Could he have been trying to lead him to the ghost of Akhenaten? At one moment he felt that he himself was the ghost of Akhenaten in his dreams... Why else would he feel so alone? At the next he believed Akhenaten was calling him... What *was* going on?

'It seems to me...' Mary was saying thoughtfully, hesitatingly, 'that what has been happening to you recently, Jack, is a continuation of what was happening to me. We were not brought together by chance.'

He knew she was right, but he wished she was not.

'When you started speaking Mary, you said you might have some idea how the Shemsu Benu fitted in?' Emma asked suddenly.

Mary nodded, but was slow to reply.

'It could be,' she said at last, 'that if it is true about the curse on Akhenaten and if his loyal friends knew about it at the time, the Shemsu Benu might have been a secret society founded by them to bring about his rebirth by removing the curse. You can imagine the chaos and confusion that must have followed the king's murder. Many of his followers would have been killed too. Some might have got away, and met again later.

'His enemies had left him no power in this life or the next. His loyal companions were determined to restore it to him.'

'One of his daughters, Setepenra, was one of them!' cried Emma excitedly. 'She was a child when he died, and probably also went into hiding. She may have emerged as a powerful lady when she joined the Shemsu Benu and gave it her blessing.'

Emma's eyes were shining. She had always been particularly interested in Akhenaten's youngest daughters, about which so little is known.

'It would seem they did not succeed in their aim if three thousand years later he is still a ghost wandering the earth,' Jack said.

'Perhaps the society went the way of most secret societies,' Mary said sadly. 'It started with enthusiasm and courageous dedication, but as the difficulties they encountered appeared more and more insurmountable it may have gradually lost impetus until the secrets passed down by father or mother to son or daughter became so diluted they became meaningless. Perhaps centuries after Akhenaten there was still a Shemsu Benu, but they had long since lost the knowledge of their founders, and the rituals they performed had become more and more elaborate, and more and more obscure.'

'Like the Masons today,' Jack mused.

'Perhaps there is still a Shemsu Benu today!' cried Emma. 'And we are members of it!'

Both Jack and Mary looked at her, Jack in shock, Mary with interest.

'Perhaps,' Emma continued, her eyes shining with the excitement of genuine inspiration, 'all those people who believe they are reincarnations of Akhenaten today are actually reincarnations of members of the original Shemsu Benu. Perhaps,' and here she almost shrieked, 'perhaps we are reincarnations of the original members of the Shemsu Benu!'

'For heaven's sake!' Jack said irritably.

But Mary was thinking seriously about what Emma had said.

'It makes sense, Jack,' she said quietly. 'Both of us have had the overwhelming sense that something was expected of us in connection with Akhenaten. Why else have all these things been happening?'

'There could be many explanations other than this one,' he replied stubbornly.

'Don't you see Jack?' Emma cried. 'You and Mary have been chosen to go to Egypt and rescue Akhenaten!'

'Hang on! Don't get carried away!'

Mary laughed and raised a calming hand to her friend.

'It is a tempting solution to many of the puzzling things that have occurred to us Emma, but we must not be too hasty. The matter needs more thought.'

'I know you'll find I'm right!' Emma, though disappointed at their reaction, was determined not to give up her idea.

'We may very well find you are,' said Mary soothingly. 'But if the

Priests of Amun have kept such a curse going for more than three thousand years, it may not be so easy for us to lift it. Magic was very real and very powerful in ancient Egypt. What makes you think we would have any hope of success in challenging it?'

'Why else would we be called to the task? Someone "up there" must think we have a chance of success. Perhaps we failed before because we were not ready.'

'I don't feel very ready now,' Jack said firmly.

'You don't know. No one knows whether they are ready or not until they are tested. We'll only know if we try. Its worth a try – surely?' she pleaded.

'I don't think I am physically capable of going to Egypt again,' Mary said regretfully. 'It is not an easy country to visit even if you are fit, and I can't walk more than a few yards these days.'

'Perhaps that is why Jack is having the dreams. "They" know you can't go, but you can guide and advise us.'

Jack glanced at Emma. Us? Were they a couple now?

Mary was looking deeply thoughtful.

'Do you propose we just waltz into Egypt, accost the ghosts of the Priests of Amun, demand that they release Akhenaten, and waltz out again?' Jack jeered.

'No, of course not!' Emma flushed with annoyance. It seemed so clear to her that something had to be done and they were the ones to do it, that she could not believe he was being so negative.

'How do you propose we do it then?' he demanded

'I don't know,' she said impatiently. 'I feel we should just open ourselves to possibilities. I'm sure once we get there we will be guided. All those invisible presences Mary talks about will surely be there to help us.'

'What of the ones who will be there to stop us?' he asked.

'I can't understand why you are the one who is having all those dreams,' she cried in exasperation. 'They are wasted on you!'

Mary, sensing the mood turning ugly, intervened.

'None of us can know the reason why things happen to us rather than to another,' she said mildly. 'But I'm sure there is a reason why Jack is having those dreams.'

Emma's eyes were filling with tears.

'Its so unfair,' she said bitterly. 'I would love to have them.'

'You're welcome to them! I don't want them.'

'Perhaps we have worried enough about the matter for now,' said Mary hastily. 'We should let some time pass and see what else occurs.' She put her arms around Emma and gave her a hug. 'Come, Emma, don't be so upset. All will become clear.'

'Jack is such a...'

'Such a beginner,' Mary cut in tactfully. 'Remember Emma, you and I have been thinking about these matters for a long time. They are strange and new to Jack.'

Emma blew her nose noisily.

Mary met Jack's eye.

He cancelled what he was about to say, and stood up.

'Come Emma, Mary looks tired. We ought to go.'

Reluctantly Emma stood up.

'Don't worry,' Mary said soothingly. 'If what you believe is meant to be – it will be.'

'Not if I can help it,' Jack thought. He wanted nothing more to do with this craziness.

6

Akhenaten Speaks

Sotheby's sold Jack's tomb guardian to a country museum for a considerable sum.

The night he heard about the sale, the guardian returned to his apartment. He saw its shadow out of the corner of his eye as he passed from the living room to the kitchen. He spun round to face it, but there was nothing there. He switched on the light. The shadow was gone. He peered at the plants hanging below the skylight to see if they could have cast the shadow. But it was not likely.

He glanced angrily at the place where the statue had stood for so many years, and then went back into the living room. He dragged a great sea chest filled with linen and other things out and placed it exactly where the statue had been.

And then he went to bed.

This time in his dream he saw the guardian as one of a pair guarding a tomb in ancient Egypt. He peered at the wall carvings and paintings and noted that the characteristic sign of Aten worship was there – the sun disk with rays spreading out, each ray ending in a hand blessing the earth.

He knew that Akhenaten's tomb had been robbed in ancient times. There were no grave goods or guardians there when his great-grandfather visited it. Or were there? In his dream he remembered the seal ring and the statue he had inherited. Had his great-grandfather taken them from here and not declared them in his records of the dig?

As he watched, one of the guardians moved, and with the stiff, wooden steps of an automaton started to walk away up the long corridor to the surface. It passed right by him, but did not acknowledge his presence.

In his dream Jack followed him, now convinced that he would lead him to Akhenaten. Since Mary's revelations he had thought a great deal about Akhenaten's fate and his own vocation as a member of the secret society. He was almost convinced he was meant to find the king's ghost and release him from the curse.

They seemed to pass right through the great slab of stone that blocked the entrance and walk down the dry and dusty wadi beyond. Rocks towered on either side casting deep shadows. Where the sun penetrated, Jack could feel the heat as though he had entered an oven.

Within the dream he knew he was dreaming, though every part of it was so vivid it could have passed for reality.

Before long they were in the open desert and Jack experienced again the lonely desolation he had experienced before. But this time he knew he had to follow the guardian, and was determined to do so.

He tried to quicken his pace as the figure began to draw too far ahead. He felt his feet sinking into the sand and struggled to extricate them. Every step was more difficult than the last and he knew he would never catch up.

'Stop!' he called out. 'Wait for me!'

But the automaton continued, his stride unbroken.

Jack found tears running down his cheeks when he woke.

'If you want me to do something, why don't you make it easier?' he shouted aloud into the night. 'I want to help, but you won't help *me*!'

He sat up in bed, his arms around his knees, and his chin resting on them. He told himself it was natural that he should have dreamed about the guardian that night, having just heard about the sale. He told himself that everything that Mary had told him was a load of rubbish.

'I'll tell Emma as soon as it is decent to phone her that I want to be shot of this whole Akhenaten business. Mary and Emma will believe anything! But I,' he thought, 'am a rational human being. One dreams all sorts of things. If I followed the half of them I would have to be locked up in a mad house!'

He lay down again and pulled the duvet over his head.

'I am not going to dream this time!' He declared fiercely, and then added in a small voice: 'Please don't let me dream any more.'

He must have got his wish because when he woke it was morning and he was unaware that he had been asleep.

When he finally got through to Emma that afternoon he told her gruffly that he wanted out. She, at once said she was coming round to talk it through.

'No. I don't want to talk it through. As far as I am concerned I want nothing more to do with this mumbo jumbo. And I advise you to steer clear as well.'

'We must talk. I'll see you in ten minutes!' And she cut him off.

He could imagine her face and the room she was in, the door slamming, her running down the stairs.

He put his own phone down and left the apartment, determined not to be there when she arrived.

He managed to avoid Emma for a couple of days by not answering his phone or his doorbell, but she caught up with him at last with Eliot in a pub on the London Road. It was not their usual venue, but they had all come to hear the Irish music that was such a feature of the place on a Friday night.

Eliot spotted him at once and called out to buy him a drink, otherwise he might have slipped away as soon as he saw them. He pushed his way through the tight crowd and mouthed what he wanted. The fiddle, the Northumbrian pipes and the bodhran, the peculiarly Irish drum, were in full storm. No words, however loud, would have been able to penetrate.

'It will be all right,' Jack thought. 'We won't be able to talk here.'

He settled down to a noisy but enjoyable evening. Emma grinned and nodded to him and there was no hint that she was aware of any bad feeling between them. He tapped his foot to the music and began to relax.

During the evening a man attached himself to them. Emma seemed to know him, but Eliot ignored him. He was lean and haggard, with a thin black beard and long black hair hanging in strings over his shoulders and down his back. He had earrings, of course, one side an Egyptian ankh and the other a Celtic bird. Around his neck and resting on his bare chest was a magnificent piece of jewellery – the sign of the Aten – worthy to have been in Akhenaten's tomb.

Once again Jack was glad there would be no conversation, and determined to leave before the music stopped in case the man should bring up the subject of Egypt. He would not have put it past Emma, he thought, to spread the word around about his involvement in the Akhenaten mystery.

After a while the man produced a flute from somewhere in his voluminous but ragged coat, and began to play like an angel. Jack listened amazed. He looked like a typical homeless beggar and yet played like a concert professional. Emma was watching him with shining eyes as though only he and she were in the room. Jack was shocked at his own reaction. He felt a twinge of proprietorial anger as though Emma were his girlfriend and had no right to be looking at anyone else like that. He glanced at Eliot to see if he also had noticed the bond between the two, but Eliot was ordering another drink. When he returned he shouted at Jack that the place was too noisy and they would be leaving soon. Jack suspected he had not wanted to come. It had been Emma's idea. Not for the first time Jack wondered how they had ever become lovers. He looked at Eliot's handsome, amiable face, and felt for the first time in their long friendship that he and Eliot themselves were not really compatible. Without realising it, in the past few months, he felt as though he had woken from a long sleep, whereas Eliot was still unconscious.

Jack turned his gaze to Emma and saw her moving to the music within her own space; following the fine hypnotic line of the flute sound as though she were a nymph alone in an enchanted forest.

She was at this moment beautiful beyond belief.

When the set stopped for a moment for the musicians to replenish their glasses, Eliot took Emma by the elbow and told her they were leaving.

'No,' she said. 'Not yet.'

'It's too crowded,' Eliot said.

Jack saw the flautist moving back towards Emma.

'We could go for a drink somewhere else,' he suggested.

They could hardly raise their arms to their mouths for the crush, and every moment more and more people seemed to be pushing in, many of them with musical instruments. This pub on a Friday evening was a 'free for all' and anyone who could play Irish music was welcome. There was quite clearly a hard core of regulars, but Jack had noticed several youngsters hanging around the outside trying to pluck up the courage to join in.

'Let me introduce you to Finn, Jack,' Emma said, pulling the man towards her and almost thrusting him at Jack. Eliot apparently had met him before and nodded a rather unenthusiastic greeting.

Jack looked into eyes that were almost totally black and were looking into his as though he could see right down to his boots. He felt uncomfortable.

'You play a mean flute,' he said – anything to break the power of that stare.

'Doesn't he just!' Emma laughed. 'I've been wanting you two to meet for ages.'

'Why?' Jack asked, and wished he hadn't.

'You have so much in common. Finn is...'

But before she could complete the sentence Jack put his glass down on the counter and turned away.

'Sorry. I have to go before they start playing again. I was just leaving.'

'So are we,' Eliot said at once. 'We'll make a bit of space in here for others.'

Finn had not said a word, but Emma was leaning on his arm as though they were old friends.

'You two go then,' she said. 'I want to stay. I might even sing.'

Jack hesitated. He did not know she sang. He was torn between wanting to hear her and wanting desperately to leave. He could feel the atmosphere charged by the presence of Finn, and he did not like it. But to leave Emma with him...! He glanced at Eliot hoping he would make a stand. But Eliot did not seem to see the danger.

'Okay,' he said. 'We'll be at the Hart if you change your mind.'

And he walked out without a backward glance.

Jack followed him in some agitation.

'Will she be all right?'

Eliot grinned. 'Sure. She loves that sort of thing. Its not my scene though.'

'But it is a pretty rough neighbourhood.'

'Oh, she'll be fine. She tells me she has good guardian angels!' And Eliot laughed as though he saw this as a joke.

Jack wanted to go back. But if he did so he knew he would be dragged into a conversation about Egypt. Finn, in spite of his Irish name and Irish music, was obviously connected with ancient Egypt in some way. No one wore such jewels so ostentatiously if they did not want to make a statement.

He followed Eliot out into the street without another word.

Jack found himself thinking about Emma the next day. He was no longer wanting to avoid her, no longer categorizing her as an interfering busybody, a New Age gullible nut, but as a desirable woman about to be taken away from his friend Eliot by another man. He waxed so indignant on Eliot's behalf that anyone listening in to his thoughts might have suspected it was not Eliot he was worrying about, but himself.

At noon he could bear it no longer and phoned her. She sounded surprised when he invited her to lunch, but accepted.

They drove out of town to a quiet restaurant with extensive gardens and terraces overlooking the river.

When they had ordered and were seated in the dappled sunlight on the terrace, Emma asked why he had been avoiding her.

'You know why,' he replied.

She grinned. 'And you know it cannot be avoided!'

'Look,' he said, 'I didn't bring you here to argue about Egypt.'

'Why did you bring me here?'

'I don't know. I suppose I felt bad about running out on you that day and not returning any of your calls.'

'I've seen Mary again,' she said, 'and she is almost convinced I am right about us and the Shemsu Benu. She thinks the possession of Akhenaten's seal ring is a clincher.'

'Ben Wilson found a lot of things in Egypt. He was like a magpie collecting things at random. You can't read any specific significance into the collection.'

'How do you know? Have you found his journal yet?'

'No.'

'Have you even tried to find it?'

'No. But...'

'You don't want to solve the mystery of your dreams. But they won't leave you alone until you do. Mary found that when it started happening to her.'

'Mary and I are two very different people. I'm really regretting mentioning the dreams. You can make something out of anything if you try hard enough.'

'But you have his ring and you have the list of Shemsu Benu members and you have the dreams! Surely...?'

'I admit there are a lot of coincidences...'

'Coincidences? Pooh!' she sneered.

Jack took advantage of the arrival of the waitress to change the subject.

'Do you often go to that pub?'

'Sometimes I go on a Friday when they have Irish music – but most times Eliot won't come with me.'

'That flautist was good,' Jack said with deliberate casualness.

Her face lit up. 'He is also one of the Companions of the Benu.'

'What do you mean?'

'He believes he is a reincarnation of Akhenaten.'

Jack raised a quizzical eyebrow.

'You may mock as much as you like, but mocking doesn't change the truth if it is there.'

'If it is there!' Jack muttered bitterly. He felt the web closing in around him again, the web that existed in so many different realms of reality at the same time. The multi-dimensional web.

'We had a long talk after the music last night, and I told him what has been happening and about the Companions...'

'And...?'

'He was fascinated, but...'

'But...'

'He wasn't too keen to give up the idea that he actually *is* Akhenaten... but he is quite prepared to consider it if we can produce some proof that Akhenaten is still wandering about as a ghost. Even then, with the Egyptian idea of the nine parts of being, it might be possible for him to be linked directly with Akhenaten and yet there still be a *Ka* wandering in the desert.'

'I suppose you told him all about my private dreams?'

'I don't look on them as your private dreams. We are all involved. Finn wants to meet you again.'

'Well, I don't want to meet him,' thought Jack sulkily.

'I'll arrange a meeting tomorrow.' Emma ignored his expression. 'We'll take him to see Mary.'

'I'm sure Mary...'

'She'll love him!' Emma cried. 'She will see at once how he fits in. And you must find Ben Wilson's journal. Don't you have any other relatives who may have inherited things from him?'

'He left some things to museums.'

'He wouldn't have left his private journal – or not if it documented the things he stole from Egypt.'

'My great-grandfather did not steal them! It's just that the laws were not so strict in his time.'

'But there were laws. I heard that the only way the Berlin Museum obtained that magnificent head of Nefertiti was because it was smuggled out in a box of broken shards.'

'My father's aunt is still alive. Great Aunt Bella. She was Ben Wilson's youngest daughter. I suppose it is just possible she might have some things of his.'

'There you go. That is somewhere to start. Let's go back to your place after lunch and phone her.'

'She's very old. She probably has a nap after lunch.'

'Quit making excuses! You know it would be really helpful to have that journal.'

Once again Jack was irritated by Emma and wondered why he had been so jealous of Finn. Yes, it was jealousy, he finally had to admit.

The lunch date in its beautiful setting proceeded uncomfortably. Leaves like stained glass with the light shining through them ... flowers glowing in vivid red and virgin white ... slender canoes passing the jetty where the punts were tethered waiting for the Sunday crowd ... None of these could lift Jack's spirits. He had to accept he was back in the Egyptian labyrinth, a signed and sealed member of the Shemsu Benu.

* * * *

When Jack, Emma and Finn visited Mary, they found she already had a guest – a dapper, middle-aged man as smartly dressed as Finn was ragged. Jack, surveying the room as they took tea and biscuits, found them an incongruous group and wondered, yet again, why he was going along with all this nonsense.

'Bernard is a medium and has been channelling Akhenaten for some time,' Mary said mildly.

'Oh, no!' thought Jack. 'We're not going to have messages direct from a fake Akhenaten now!' Apart from his irritation with Denise in Glastonbury, he had once been to a spiritualist meeting and had listened with derision to a message about dog-food and one from an aunt who wanted her niece to locate a necklace of hers. But derision had turned to alarm when a friend of his had been told by a medium to leave her husband because he was no good for her, and had done so, ruining several lives. But here was Bernard, a medium, and he was shaking his hand.

Mary looked at him and smiled as though she had read his mind.

'I believe you have had some bad experiences with mediums,' she said. 'But like everything else, there are good and bad mediums. We have to beware of power hungry channellers and power hungry discarnate beings, and I cannot emphasize enough the dangers of the uncritical acceptance of the advice of others, alive or dead. As you can imagine, advice with the apparent authority of the spirit world behind it is formidably persuasive. But channelling is easy to fake. Even if the channeller genuinely believes he or she is honourably and honestly channelling a message from a discarnate entity, they may be deceived for any number of reasons.'

Jack looked at Bernard.

'Bernard, I believe, is one of the good ones,' Mary said confidently. 'But I would still treat his transmissions with caution.'

Jack turned his attention to Finn. If Finn believed he was himself Akhenaten – how would he react to the implication that Akhenaten was still in the spirit world channelling through Bernard. What was the truth? It was clear, hearing Finn and Mary talk, that they were both convinced their experiences were real, as he was, after having just woken up from one of those dreams.

For a while he lost track of the conversation, but when he returned to it, he heard Emma suggesting that Jack let Finn try on Akhenaten's seal ring. She had persuaded him to bring it, and he now took it out of his pocket. The room fell silent and everyone stared. He was reluctant to allow Finn to touch it, but the pressure from the others was strong. At last he decided that it would settle things one way or another if he gave in, and handed it gingerly to Finn.

The Irishman held the ring a long time between his thumb and forefinger, staring at it, while the rest of them waited breathlessly for a reaction. Slowly he put it on. His hands were thinner than Jack's and it had to go on his thicker middle finger. He held his hand up.

Jack was convinced that this was not Finn's ring. But what line of bullshit would Finn spin to make it appear that it was?

'I feel nothing,' Finn said at last.

Jack was surprised. It would have been so easy to put on a performance. Perhaps Finn was not such a fake after all. At least about this he was being honest, unless it was something like a double bluff?

Bernard reached across eagerly.

'Let me hold it,' he said. 'If it is Akhenaten's ring surely it will strengthen the link of communication between us.'

Finn removed it from his finger, held it a long moment, gazing at it in disappointment, and then handed it over.

Bernard's hand was trembling when he took it in his own. He did not put it on, but held it in front of him staring at it intently. They were all silent, waiting, hardly daring to draw breath.

Subtly Bernard's face began to change. From being a slightly pudgy-cheeked Englishman, his features seemed to lengthen until he slightly resembled the lean image of Akhenaten that Jack had seen in Mary's book about ancient Egypt.

Bernard exhaled a rasping breath that certainly sounded as though it had come from beyond the grave! And then began to speak – in English but with an odd accent.

'How do they all know English so well?' Jack caught himself thinking. His irreverent thought must have shown on his face, because he was given a sharp, accusing glance by Emma. Jack looked across the room at Mary. How would she react to this? She was sitting back in her chair comfortably, as though the addition of a dead pharaoh to her tea party was the most natural thing in the world.

'My friends,' the sepulchral voice coming out of Bernard was saying. 'Welcome.' A long pause. Jack looked at Finn. He was sitting forward on his seat, scowling at the man. 'You are all gathered here today because you are all very special people ... (another rasping breath) ... My children, chosen by me, to perform a very special task...' Long pause.

'What task?' Jack asked impatiently. Partly he asked the question because he seriously wanted the answer from Akhenaten's 'own lips', but partly he was still sceptical that there was anyone there but themselves, flesh and blood, and one of them putting on a pretty convincing imitation of a dead pharaoh for purposes of attracting attention to himself.

61

'Why do you resist me? I have called you and yet you refuse to come. Why?'

'I need proof that it is indeed Akhenaten, pharaoh of Egypt, speaking.'

Bernard's lips twisted in the semblance of a sardonic smile.

'I am no longer pharaoh,' he said. 'In the spirit world there is no distinction of rank or privilege as there is in your world. I am one who needs your help – a spirit such as you are, in trouble.'

'I am not sure I believe in curses that can hold a man's soul to the earth for three thousand years.'

'There are many things you do not believe that are true. And there are many things that you do believe, that are untrue. You have been called. Come.'

'Wa-en-ra,' Emma interrupted gently. 'We are not resisting you, but we need to know more. What precisely do you want us to do?'

The expression on Bernard's face softened, and his voice was softer when he spoke to Emma.

'You, my daughter, will know what is to be done. You will lead them and they will follow.'

'But...'

A great rasping sigh ended the transmission and Bernard's round and amiable face reappeared.

'What happened?' he asked eagerly. 'Did I say anything?'

The rest were silent, staring at him.

Emma was thinking: 'Did he say "my daughter" because I *am* his daughter, once the child of his wife Nefertiti – Setepenra? Or did he say it only in the way all channelling spirits refer to the living as "children" or "dear ones"?'

Finn challenged Bernard to prove that it was indeed Akhenaten speaking through him. 'Nothing you said could not have been said by someone else!'

'There were certainly no distinguishing features in the transmission,' Mary said mildly, sensing the antagonism growing in the room between the two men. Finn's face was pinched and accusing; Bernard's flushed and defensive.

'I just know who it was!' he was saying. 'He might not have identified himself this time, but he has to me, many times.'

'How?' persisted Finn.

'He has quoted Akhenaten's Hymn to the Sun. He has spoken of his life as Akhenaten.'

'His Hymn to the Sun has been translated. I, one of many, know it by heart. Has he told you anything you could not have learned from books? Anything that the archaeologists don't know?'

'I hadn't read his hymn before he quoted it through me. I only read about it afterwards. I haven't studied ancient Egypt like you have! I hadn't even seen a map or a plan of his city before he started to tell me about things there. And when I looked up the printed information there were some things about which he told me that were not marked.'

'Have you had them checked?'

'I didn't need to. I never doubted his words.'

Finn snorted triumphantly.

'What proofs have you that *you* are Akhenaten?' Jack suddenly turned the tables on the Irishman.

All eyes turned to Finn. He tried to shrug it off, but when even Mary suggested he should tell them on what grounds he believed he was a reincarnation of Akhenaten, and Emma gazed at him with eyes brimming with affection and trust, he could not very well refuse.

'Since a child I have known it.'

'How?' demanded Bernard, almost spitefully.

Finn paused. His eyes seemed to go darker as he gazed into the distance beyond them. He was already retracing his steps in memory to when he first knew for sure who he was.

'I grew up in the Burren in Galway,' he said. 'Sure, my greatest joy was to run wild, until one day, I must have been eight or nine, ten at the most, I opened one of my father's books and saw in there a picture that changed my life.'

'Finn's father was the village school master,' Emma told the others, 'so he had books in his house unusual at the time in such a small village.'

Finn glared at her.

Emma flushed. 'I'm sorry. I didn't mean to imply... but one wouldn't have expected books on ancient Egypt to be common in those villages.'

'In ancient times,' he said haughtily, 'the Irish race were in contact with civilisations as far away as Ethiopia. Egyptian faience beads were found in an Irish Bronze Age tomb. We have a legend about the daughter of a pharaoh coming to Ireland, and the invasion of a race of people, the Milesians, who may well have been ancient Egyptians.'

Mary stepped in. 'That is not in dispute, Finn,' she said quietly. 'The earth's people are restless – constantly on the move – constantly cross-pollinating other cultures. The Irish story is a rich and complex one, and links with ancient Egypt may well be part of their history. I believe I read somewhere the Berber language of North Africa has much in common with ancient Irish.'

Jack was surprised and would like to have pursued this line of thought, but Finn had simmered down and returned to his story.

'As Emma says, the book was about ancient Egypt – about Akhenaten in particular. I stared at a full-page photograph of a statue of him and knew that it was a statue of me. I hadn't heard anything about reincarnation at that stage, but my skin just prickled looking at the statue, and as I turned the pages I saw the bits and pieces that had been dug up in his city as though they were not broken shards, but complete. Broken floor tiles gave me an image of the whole floor of reeds and flowers and duck ... slivers of pottery gave me images of complete drinking vessels and oil jars.

'After that there was no going back. I pestered my father for information about the man and his life in ancient Egypt. I stopped playing with the other kids in the village and went off in every spare moment into the Burren by myself. I became Akhenaten! I dressed up in clothes I raided from the attic to look as close to an ancient Egyptian as I could. I remember the cloak I borrowed from my grandmother. When I put it on and raised my arms I *was* the Pharaoh himself. My mother fed me books by Joan Grant – novels about ancient Egypt supposed to be the author's own far memories of the times when she had lived there in a past life. I became obsessed. I preached to the flowers hidden from the wind between the cracks in the rock about the One God, The Sun, The Aten, who gave life to all things. Luckily I had the sense to keep my activities and my beliefs secret from the other villagers or I would have had the priest down on me believing I was possessed by demons. Even at that age I knew to keep what was desperately important to me secret. Not, I think, because I feared ridicule and punishment, but because my secret life was so precious to me that I couldn't bear to let anyone else into it. I built models of what I believed Akhenaten's town to be like. I acted out all the little tableaux depicted in wall reliefs and paintings of the time. I learned Akhenaten's Hymn to the Sun and chanted it at every dawn – sometimes in a strange language that came to me and which I believed was ancient Egyptian itself.

> *"Beautiful is your appearing in the horizon of heaven, you living sun, the first who lived! You rise in the eastern horizon and fill every land with your beauty. You shine and are high above every land. You are Ra. You are far off, yet your rays are upon earth.*

> *"When you go down in the western horizon, the earth is in darkness as if it were dead. They sleep in the chamber, their*

heads wrapped up, and no eye perceives the other. Though all their things were taken, while they were under their heads, yet they would not know it. Every lion comes forth from his den and all worms that bite. Darkness... the earth is silent, for he who created it rests in his horizon.

"When it is dawn, and you rise in the horizon and shine as the sun in the day, you dispel the darkness and shed your beams. The Two Lands are in festival, awake, and standing on their feet, for you have raised them up. They wash their bodies, they take their garments, and their hands praise your arising. The whole land, it goes about its work.

"All creatures are content with their pasture, the trees and the herbs are verdant. The birds fly out of their nests and their wings praise your Ka. All wild beasts dance on their feet, all that fly and flutter – they live when you arise for them...

"Ah, beautiful is the rhythm of your setting and your rising. Each day a renewal and re-affirmation."

'Then, when I was sixteen, some friends and I played the ouija board.'

'What's that?' asked Jack, frowning.

'Another dangerous activity,' Mary said. 'In this case communication from the "dead" is sought not through the voice of a medium or channeller, but through a board set up with the letters of the alphabet arranged in a circle. At the centre is an indicator, or in the case of home made ouija boards, an upturned glass that can easily slide across the surface. Everyone present, seated around the board, puts a finger on the glass. Questions are asked of the "dead" and the glass or indicator may start to move, apparently of it own volition, spelling out the answer to the question.'

'I was told outright by the spirit who was communicating with us that I was the reincarnation of Akhenaten,' Finn said. 'It confirmed what I had always believed. I was also told that I would die at the age of thirty-five,' he added in a lower voice, almost as an after thought.

'How old are you now?' Jack asked curiously.

'Thirty-five,' Finn replied.

The room was silent.

'Tell about your friend dying,' Emma prompted.

Finn shook his head.

'One of his friends was told by the same spirit that he would die at twenty-seven. And he did!'

65

Jack was startled. Hovering as he did on the edge of believing in all these things, this was an alarming piece of information.

'What did he die of?' Bernard asked.

'He was killed by a bomb in Belfast.'

'That's why I think we should hurry to fulfil our duties as Companions of the Benu,' Emma cried. 'I believe we have all been brought together for a purpose at this time. Whether Finn is Akhenaten or not, whether Akhenaten is still a ghost haunting the desert near his city, channelling through Bernard here, or whether Jack or Mary or I are who knows who in the ancient drama – I feel an urgency ... a demand that we act immediately.'

'How? Act how?' Jack asked, a slight sneer curling the edges of his mouth as she paused.

How indeed?

'I don't *know*!' Emma burst out irritably. 'But I believe we'll know when we get there!'

'Have any of you ever been to Egypt?' Mary asked quietly, trying to restore the peace. 'In this life I mean,' she added with a smile.

'I've been to Cairo,' Jack said grudgingly. The others shook their heads.

'I've been twice, but never to Amarna. I always wanted to go there, but never managed it. And now I am too old and decrepit.' She sighed. 'Egypt was never an easy place to visit, and it must be more difficult now with the Islamic Jihad shooting tourists in an attempt to bring down the government.'

'I always intended to go back,' Jack said thoughtfully. 'It's a pretty amazing place.'

'Well, now's the time!' Emma said at once.

'I couldn't afford it,' Finn said.

'Oh, Jack will lend you the money. He's got plenty.'

'Thank you!' Jack said angrily.

'I mean you've just sold that tomb guardian for a fortune. How better to spend it than on finding out the truth about Akhenaten, whose tomb it used to guard.'

'We don't know that!'

'Your dream...'

'Blast my dreams!' Jack shouted, suddenly standing up. 'I'm sick of the whole thing. It is all bullshit! The whole thing! Get off my back Emma! What are you trying to do? You are the most manipulative bitch I have ever encountered!'

'Don't speak to her like that!' Finn rose to his feet, fists at the ready.

Bernard retreated out of reach hastily. Mary rose too and stepped between them.

'This is not the way to go,' she said, 'fighting among ourselves. I believe Emma has a point. It is no coincidence that we have been brought together, and I feel very strongly that there is something very important here for us to resolve.'

'Well, resolve it yourselves,' Jack snapped. 'Count me out. *You* lot go to Egypt and get shot by terrorists! Send me a postcard.'

'Jack...'

'And with your own money!' he snarled, turning his back and storming into the bathroom. The door slammed behind him.

They looked at each other in shock for a moment, and then Mary broke the tension by laughing out loud.

'Well, isn't it fascinating how an event that occurred three thousand years ago still has the power to raise such emotions among us?'

Bernard and Emma laughed nervously.

When Jack came out of the bathroom Mary suggested they should part company and re-convene another time.

Still protesting that he would not be present at the next meeting, Jack left.

7

The Journal

The next time Jack dreamed, he found himself in a bare stone chamber. The floor was covered with sand, much whiter and finer than he had seen in the desert. He and four others were squatting in a circle, while one, a woman with grey in her hair, was drawing with a rod in the sand. The rod was no ordinary stick, but a pharaonic crook of black ebony bound with strips of silver and gold alternately. He leant closer to see what she was inscribing. It was the Atenist sign of the Sun with its rays ending in hands.

As the sigil was completed all present bent his or her head and murmured:

'Arise, Son of the Sun, dispel the darkness that surrounds us. Lift our hearts to the light of your Being.'

There was a profound silence as the whispering ceased.

He experienced a great sadness. The lamp flickering in the corner cast elongated and distorted shadows around them.

Then, one by one they spoke, each following each to complete a passage of the sacred texts they all knew by heart.

'He is not the sun of this or that moment, but of yesterday, today and all eternity, the One proceeding from the One. We call him Ra-Harakhi, Kepher, Aten and Atum in his different aspects, and in all the naming we do not forget he is none of these...
But mysteriously, powerfully, ultimately the One proceeding from the One.
Lord of Eternity and Everlasting – hear our prayer.
Lord of Eternity and Everlasting – free us and our beloved from the shadow that shuts off Thy Light from us.'

They all then bowed their heads to the ground. He felt the cool sand on his forehead. He felt hopeless, despairing, and suicidal. What was the point of this secret ritual? They had been doing it for years as their hair turned white and their limbs became less flexible. His body ached as he held his position of obeisance to the sign that lay in the sand. They were no nearer finding their king than they had been at the beginning. No nearer lifting the curse on him.

Year after year they pretended worship of Amun and the other gods – all the time feeling guilty that they were betraying him. But what were they to do? Others had died for him. Where were they now? In Amenti? Or were they too wandering the desert never to be reborn?

The woman, Akhenaten's daughter, Setepenra, erased the sigil from the sand and stood up. She held them together. She kept them strong in faith.

As though she sensed his doubt now, she met his eyes. He was held in the depth of her gaze and felt ashamed of his wavering.

'We will go our separate ways once more,' she said. 'But we will be together forever in his love. And we will gather here again to pledge ourselves to him.'

As each one left he bowed his knee before her and she touched his head.

As he felt her hand on his, Jack trembled. He had watched her as a child sitting on her father's knee. He had been with her through the darkest times of exile. They had been parted. Only recently they had been reunited with the founding of the Shemsu Benu.

She had her mother's delicate features matured by hardship into an extraordinary and powerful beauty. He could not be in her presence but he feared and desired her.

Her hand rested on his head a moment longer than the others.

His heart beat fast. Did she remember what they had shared?

But she lifted her hand and turned away from him to lift the lamp.

'We must hurry,' she said. 'The night is almost gone.'

He found himself stooping to enter the long narrow corridor to the surface. They had been in an unfinished tomb, abandoned by workmen when the owner chose another site for the final resting place of his body.

They met there at night, and left one by one, slipping out into the dark like shadows.

As he reached the surface he could see the first grey light touching the land, and felt the relief he always felt at the coming of the dawn.

When Jack woke he lay a long time thinking back over what he had just witnessed.

The fineness and the whiteness of the sand had struck him as significant, and he remembered that recently a small door had been found in one of the so-called air vents in the Great Pyramid at Giza.

Archaeologists had not been able to open the door, but a robotic probe had been sent through a small aperture and had discovered fine white sand, unlike that of the desert around the pyramid. Jack wondered if this had a special significance because it had been taken from a particularly sacred place, and this was also why the Shemsu Benu had used it for their secret meeting place.

Pondering the matter Jack was led back to Mary's fascination with the stars and how it echoed that of the ancient Egyptians. Some scholars believed now the air ducts in the Pyramid were not air ducts at all – or not primarily. Bauval and Gilbert in *The Orion Mystery* claimed that they were channels so precisely aligned to the major stars in the constellation of Orion, and to Sirius, that they had to be taken seriously as launching channels for the spirit of the deceased on the way to the stars. Mary had quoted very ancient pyramid texts in this connection: 'He climbs to the sky among the imperishable stars.' But what did it mean – 'climbing to the imperishable stars'? Was it purely symbolic, or did it literally mean that the soul journeyed to another planet orbiting another star and was there reincarnated?

Jack wondered if the fine white sand of his dream was linked in some way to the fate of Akhenaten. They, the Shemsu Benu, were trying to release his soul from the earth and send him to the stars, and this fine white sand, similar to that in the Pyramid, may somehow be an integral part of the ritual process.

And then he pondered the use of the words Eternity and Everlasting used so often in the ritual of the dream. Before the dreams started and he began to learn so many things from Mary Brown and Emma, he would have thought the two words were referring to the same concept. But now he could see that they were different. Eternity cannot be comprehended by us. It is a state of Being utterly other than any we know on this earth. It is the quick of a moment, with no beginning, no extension, and no end. We as 'Spirit' are in Eternity even now. But we as 'soul' and body are subject to linear Time – one thing following another in succession. 'Everlasting' is a succession of days with no end in sight – but with an end always as a possibility. Eternity has no possibility of ending, because it never began. It just Is. What had the priests of Amun done to Akhenaten in that fearsome curse? Was it his Spirit, his *Akh*, they had chained to the earth? Or his Soul, the *Ba*? Surely no one could have power over the Eternal Spirit? But could the Spirit know itself complete and rest in contentment in Eternity if some part of it was missing? There must be some link between the two that is only severed when the Soul is ready – like a child leaving its parents when it is mature enough to do so.

Jack climbed out of bed impatiently and drew the curtains. Light poured in.

Akhenaten, channelled by Bernard, had said they must follow his daughter. Emma believed she was Akhenaten's daughter Setepenra. He, in the dreams, seemed to be in love with Setepenra. He would follow her – come what may.

Jack went to Oxford to see his Great Aunt Bella.

Her middle-aged companion-housekeeper opened the door to him with a barely disguised suspicious look in her eyes.

Bella had never married, and had no children of her own. Mrs Martin had been caring for her for years and resented the fact that her relatives made only occasional duty visits. The last time one of her great nephews and his wife had visited it was quite clear they were evaluating her possessions. They made a particular fuss of a clock of obvious antique value, suggesting that they should take it to be valued at Sotheby's for her.

Great Aunt Bella had smiled and nodded, but Mrs Martin had seen to it that the clock had not left the premises that day.

Now here was another great nephew. What did he want?

She ushered him in with a bad grace, and left him standing before the frail old lady in the Morris chair while she went to make a pot of tea.

Jack had to remind his great aunt who he was, spelling out his branch of the family tree several times before she grasped the relationship. She was clearly delighted to have a visitor and was as welcoming as Mrs Martin was resentful. He settled on a stool beside her and began to listen as sympathetically as he could to her saga of ailments.

Mrs Martin brought in tea and biscuits and joined them by taking up her position on a straight-backed chair the other side of the cold unlit fire.

Jack tried to answer all his great aunt's questions about family, but had long since lost touch with his numerous cousins. Christmas usually brought a slew of Christmas cards from strangers claiming to be relatives, but apart from glancing at them he never thought to follow up the news in them. 'Johnny has a scholarship...' 'Edward has a new son...' 'Martha has passed her finals...' etc.

He wondered how soon he could bring up the subject of his great-grandfather's journal. Mrs Martin was keeping a sharp eye on him, daring him to ask a favour of the old lady.

At last he took the plunge.

'I have recently become very interested in your father's work as an archaeologist in Egypt, Aunt Bella,' he said. 'And I wondered if you had any papers of his ... journals perhaps ... letters ... that might help me in my research.'

Mrs Martin's face immediately registered triumph. So he had come a-begging like all the rest!

'I don't know my dear. Mabel ... do we have any of my father's papers?'

'No, we don't,' said Mrs Martin without even considering the matter. It was clear that even if they did, she was not about to hand them over to Jack.

'I was almost certain you would have, Aunt Bella,' Jack said smoothly to his Great Aunt, avoiding meeting Mrs Martin's eyes. 'I was given some of his papers, but the rest, I'm sure, came to you. Don't you remember? I had the ones written in foreign languages, but you had the ones in English.'

'I'm sure I did not...' Great Aunt Bella tried to focus her mind.

'I remember my father telling me about them,' Jack persisted.

'Who is your father, dear?'

Jack took a deep breath and repeated for the fourth time that day: 'My father was your nephew, Reginald. Don't you remember?'

'Ah, yes.' Bella smiled benignly. 'And how is he, my dear?'

'I'm afraid he is no longer with us, Great Aunt. He died in '93.'

'Poor boy. I remember him well. He was very good at cricket.'

'Yes. He played for his county. I inherited a lot of your father's stuff from him, but there were letters and journals I didn't get.'

'And now you want them,' Mrs Martin put in sharply.

'They are of no great monetary value,' Jack said, trying to keep his temper. 'But they may help to solve a puzzle I have come across in the papers I have. Could I at least see them, Great Aunt?'

'I don't see why not, my dear. Mabel, do we know where they are?'

'I'm sure I don't!'

'Do you mind if I look for them, Aunt Bella? They're probably in a box in the attic.'

'I'm sure your aunt does not want you rummaging about in her house,' Mrs Martin said. 'You – a virtual stranger!'

'He is not a stranger, Mabel. He is dear Reginald's boy. I remember holding him in my arms as a baby. Fetch me the albums, Mabel. I'll show you.'

For the next hour they looked through old photograph albums.

Jack stared at all those people staring back. How strange to be caught thus in a moment of time and frozen there in image while every cell in your body changed, wars came and went, marriages came and went, life came and went.

There was a picture of Great Aunt Bella as a much younger woman, standing straight and tall holding a baby in her arms. Under it was written, 'Reginald's boy'. That was him! To her he would always be 'Reginald's boy'.

He remembered Mary Brown's insistence that we are all eternal beings journeying through a magnificent multi-dimensional universe. It was hard to think of Great Aunt Bella with her wandering mind, and Mrs Martin with her small and pinched one, fitting that description. But, improbable as it seemed, he believed Mary had a profound insight into the nature of things. Perhaps, he thought, what is wrong is that we look at others always as though they are photographs, static, two-dimensional, without depth or possibility of change. We judge them as they appear, and not as they really are. And yet we expect them to see *us* as we really are, with all our complexity and our multi-layered motivations, continually changing and learning and growing.

When Mrs Martin left the room to attend to something in the kitchen, Jack again brought up the subject of his great-grandfather's papers. This time, perhaps stimulated and refreshed by sharing the photographs and their accompanying memories with him, she told him she could remember that there had been a bound volume of papers from her father and it would probably be on the shelf above the wardrobe in her bedroom.

He went there at once, and located it among an extraordinary collection of shoeboxes containing yellowing theatre programmes and letters dating back fifty years or more. Great Aunt Bella, not having a family of her own, kept everything that came to her from any member of the wider family, even to inept pictures of dinosaurs sent on birthday cards from small nephews and nieces.

He found what he was seeking at last – a black journal with dog-eared pages, yellowed with age, covered with fading, spindly writing that would be difficult to decipher. Between some of the pages leaves had been pressed – leaves of exotic plants not grown in England.

He carefully placed everything back as he had found it, except the journal. That he took to Great Aunt Bella and humbly asked if he could borrow it.

Smiling benignly, she agreed at once, ignoring Mrs Martin's protestations.

Jack showed the book to the companion.

'You can see it is of no value as it is,' he said. 'I will make a legible copy and return it to her, if you really think she wants to keep it.'

Suspicious as she was, even Mrs Martin could see that the book was of no use to Bella Wilson. She decided to stop objecting and let it go.

'We arrived at the Royal tombs of Akhenaten and immediately our hopes were dashed. They had been more thoroughly looted and vandalised than we had feared. Almost nothing was left. One of the tomb guardians had vanished altogether, while the other was lying on its side, in a good state of preservation, in spite of having most of its gold stripped from it. I staked my claim to it, and Stuart agreed, but only if he could have the sarcophagus lid, which lay smashed to pieces in the dust. A few flowers lay in the corner. I believed they might be from Akhenaten's funeral wreath, and lifted them with great care. But they instantly disintegrated.

We made our measurements and notes, and Stuart did the drawings. We found some few objects – ushabti, diorite bowls, broken flasks of wine. One was still complete with seal unbroken. We wondered what it would taste like after all this time and put it in our packs to try later.

There was a gloomy chill about the place, and I, for one, was pleased to leave.'

Ben Wilson's journal continued with page after page of spidery writing. Jack sat up late into the night until his eyes ached with the strain of trying to read it.

There was no more mention of Ben Wilson taking the tomb guardian out of the tomb, but he had said enough for Jack to be convinced the one he had inherited was indeed the one from Akhenaten's tomb.

Many pages later it was mentioned again.

'Elizabeth hates the tomb guardian. She says its eyes follow her, and she won't have it in the house. It has had to be stored in the shed.'

Jack was curious as to whether Stuart and his great-grandfather had drunk the wine they found in the tomb. But there was no record of it. There was also no record of his having found Akhenaten's ring in the tomb. But Emma, who had been invited to read the journal, found mention of it on a date almost a year later. It seems he had found it in the eastern desert beyond Akhetaten. She was tremendously excited by this, and said at once that when they went to Egypt this would give them a clue as to where to start looking for Akhenaten's body and presumably his ghost.

'But surely Ben would have mentioned if he had found the body?'

'He would have – if he had. But after thousands of years of wind and shifting sands no doubt the dry bones would have been scattered. The ring would have worked loose from a skeletal finger and parted company from it.'

'The eastern desert is vast. Where would we start looking?'

Emma, with puckered forehead, considered the matter.

'There are sketch maps in your great-grandfather's journal,' she said. 'They would give us some idea of where he went and thus some idea of where he might have found the ring.'

Since Jack had been reading the journal he had found that his resolve not to be part of this mad scheme to go to Egypt was weakening. He was becoming more and more fascinated and intrigued. Perhaps after all it was not such a crazy scheme if they followed in Ben Wilson's footsteps. He could claim to be investigating history for biographical purposes, rather than going off on some wild and improbable ghost hunt.

8

Cairo

On 2nd November the four of them set off for Egypt.

Eliot was attending his sister's wedding in South America and had agreed reluctantly that Emma should go to Egypt without him.

'You'll keep an eye on her,' he said confidently to Jack. 'Don't let any harm come to her.'

It crossed Jack's mind that his request was rather like someone asking the fox to look after a chicken, but he dismissed the thought as unworthy at once, and assured Eliot, and himself, that he would be responsible for Emma's well being.

Mary felt she would hold them up if she joined them. She found it very difficult to walk and was in continual pain from arthritis. She primed them with books and information and sent them off with her blessing. She made an arrangement with Emma that they would try to be in telepathic contact at certain times and in certain places.

Jack had been persuaded to lend Finn the money for the fare. Eliot paid for Emma, and Bernard paid for himself.

They seemed an ill-assorted group at Heathrow waiting for their flight number to be called. Jack, a handsome but fairly ordinary looking young man, Emma and Finn shamelessly 'New Age', and Bernard looking as though he had just stepped out of a conference of accountants. Both Emma and Finn were travelling light. A rucksack that had seen better days was attached to Finn's back with the box containing his flute tucked in under the flap at the top. Emma had several bulging string bags hanging from her person. Bernard carried two neat and expensive suitcases with shining locks and brand new labels. Jack himself brought only one case but it was covered with badges from the countries he had visited in the past. All of Emma's string bags came with them into the cabin, and Finn's flute, but the rest of the luggage went into the hold.

They did not speak much as they waited. Jack in particular was morose. Having made up his mind he would go to Egypt he would rather have gone alone, or just with Emma. He did not like or trust the other two men, and had reservations even about Emma. He felt he had been bulldozed into the expedition by her, and given no chance to state his own preferences for how the journey was to be organized. But it was too late to back out now – their flight was being called.

When they reached their Egypt Air plane, Emma was shocked to see that it was named 'Amun-Ra'.

'That is a bad sign,' she cried, tugging on Jack's arm and pulling him back. 'We shouldn't go on that plane.'

'Don't be silly,' he said impatiently. 'Its just a name given by a commercial airline. It has no religious significance whatever!'

'Finn, what do you think?' Emma appealed to the Irishman.

He shook his head. 'We're committed to going. We know there will be opposition from the forces of Amun-Ra. We should take this only as a warning for us to be on our guard.'

'Well, I'm going,' Jack said firmly, shaking his arm free from Emma. 'You can turn back if you like.'

Emma fell back and other passengers crowded past her, giving her curious glances. But when Jack was settled in his seat, almost at the point the doors were being closed, Emma joined him.

'Finn's right,' she whispered. 'We have to defeat them – not run from them.'

Jack frowned, but said nothing.

Cairo assaulted every sense. Their taxi from the airport was soon immobilised within a huge traffic jam, with drivers pounding their hooters. The cacophony was deafening. All the stationary cars kept their engines running and belched out toxic fumes. The polluted air was suffocating. Sometimes the blare of pop music and the shouts of one driver to another added to the noise.

Emma stared through the dusty windscreen, past the tassels and amulets that hung in their dozens from above, and her heart sank. She had a romantic idea that they were going to ancient Egypt – magical, fascinating, ancient Egypt. She had forgotten they would have to negotiate modern Egypt as well.

It took them several hours to travel less than two miles, but at last they were at their hotel. She had insisted that they were not to stay at any of the five star hotels, but the cheaper one they were booked into on Ghezira Island seemed to be only half finished. The entrance hall was grand, but as they travelled up in the lift they passed many floors that were still open building sites, and in her room she found the electric fittings only partly installed, with live wires sticking out of the wall. She flung herself down on the hard bed and burst into tears.

They had planned to see two things while they were in Cairo before they set off for Amarna. One would be the Museum, the other the Giza plateau with the pyramids and the sphinx. Although the latter had no connection with Akhenaten, they could not resist the pull of monuments so ancient and so famous.

The Museum was dusty and ill organized, the numbers in the guidebook not always coinciding with the objects they described. But it contained even greater treasures from ancient Egypt than the British Museum. There was a section devoted to the era of Akhenaten where they stood before carvings of the divine family. Although all they had seen before had been magnificent, there was a different atmosphere in that particular room... The figures were more life-like, more approachable, more human. Emma gazed at a little statue of Akhenaten holding a child on his lap. Father and daughter were kissing with such love and affection that it was difficult to remember they were just images in stone. The full emotion of the relationship was palpably there three thousand years after the event. Jack stood beside Emma in silence, remembering the Setepenra of his dream ... wondering if Emma had been that princess, as she believed she was.

Finding the sadness he felt while standing before the statue disturbing, Jack moved away and searched for a portrait carving of Nefertiti. There were two that drew his attention. One young and beautiful, the other tired and drawn. He wondered about her life. In the early years they must have been full of the energy of idealism, sustained by their love for each other. In her portrait he saw the weariness of a woman who had spent years supporting a difficult man ... with dangers threatening her children and shadows gathering around her.

Jack shivered. Everything in the room appeared familiar, and an overwhelming sadness almost brought tears to his eyes.

Then Bernard spoke and broke the spell. He announced he was going upstairs to see the treasures from Tutankhamun's tomb. Finn and Emma agreed and started to move away. Jack looked back at Nefertiti, but now he saw nothing but cold stone.

He knew he would not be able to recapture the mood however hard he tried, and followed the others resentfully along the corridor and up the stairs. Tutankhamun might have been Akhenaten's son by a secondary wife, and Jack knew at least he had been married to Akhenaten's daughter, Ankhesenamun. There would still be connections for him in that room of the Museum.

Mary Brown believed Akhenaten had been assassinated by the

corrupt priests of Amun whose power he had tried to break. Whether this had really been the case it was impossible to tell. He had disappeared suddenly from history, his body lost, and the few years that followed his disappearance were confusing for the Egyptologists who tried to make sense of them. Smenkhkare, whoever he or she was, reigned briefly and was succeeded by the boy Tutankhaten. Under the guidance of General Horemheb he had changed his name to Tutankhamun and reinstated the worship of Egypt's pantheon of many gods, led by Amun-Ra. He too had mysteriously died a few years after his accession from a blow to the head, and was succeeded by Ay – an old man, master of Chariots and possibly the father of Nefertiti. There was some evidence that he had married Ankhesenamun, Akhenaten's daughter and widow of Tutankhamun, to give his claim to the throne legitimacy. After his death, the commoner, Horemheb, had taken the throne and become a powerful and long-lived pharaoh, bringing the magnificent Eighteenth Dynasty finally to its end. Ankhesenamun also disappeared mysteriously after writing a letter, which is still preserved, to the King of the Hittites asking for one of his sons to be pharaoh of Egypt on the throne beside her.

Because Tutankhamun's hastily prepared tomb had been found relatively undisturbed by Howard Carter in 1922, most people today knew about him.

Jack had seen the treasures from his tomb illustrated in expensive and glossy books. As a child he had been shown the pictures of one of the golden shrines inscribed with amazing and enigmatic symbolic images. He went straight to it now and gazed with wonder at its shining surface. There was some evidence that all four golden shrines displayed in the Cairo museum, like the tomb itself, had originally been made for someone else and only hastily modified for the boy king. It was clear that all reference to the Akhenaten monotheism was missing. The rich metaphysics of the centuries before and after the Atenist revolution were in evidence.

When he had first seen them as a boy, Jack had interpreted the long lines of people linked each to a star by what appeared to be lines of force, as aliens who had landed on earth, but who still received their instructions from the command centre in the galaxy from which they had come. He imagined two bodies lying inert, enclosed in a coffin-like structure surrounded by a snake coiled three-fold around them, as space travellers kept in stasis during the long journey.

His fertile imagination had been fed for weeks by the science fiction stories he conjured around those tiny gold ciphers on Tutankhamun's second golden shrine. Now he wanted to know what exactly the ancient Egyptians had meant by their elaborate system of symbols, but frustratingly his rational mind was not up to the task.

To the ancient Egyptians the story line of these enigmatic ciphers must have been as clear as the stories of Moses and Christ are to Christians when depicted in stained glass windows in medieval cathedrals and abbeys.

'A pity we have lost the key,' Jack thought. 'What treasures of spiritual instruction must lie here.' It crossed his mind that it was a pity that they, who seemed to be 'remembering' something about those ancient times, could not remember everything. It was as though they were walking through a thick fog. An occasional dark object emerged which they interpreted as best they could, while so much more lay all around them – hidden.

He turned to the image that had fascinated him most as a boy and still fascinated him today – the one that depicted the mummified figure of the deceased contained within two circles consisting of snakes biting their own tails, with a third smaller circle contained within the body's sexual region, encompassing a bird with a ram's head and arms raised in prayer.

He now knew the serpent biting its own tail, the ourobos, often represented cyclic manifestation of birth and death, the cosmos itself following the same pattern. The ram headed bird with arms raised in adoration surely symbolised the power of the life force, as represented by the sexual organs, which is at once physical (the ram) and spiritual (the bird) – both aspects joined in adoration of Divinity.

Emma touched his arm and he started as though recalled from a long way away.

'What do you think?' she whispered. 'Do you understand it?'

He looked into her grey green eyes and saw there the mystery of life as those who had buried the young king all those centuries before had seen it. Nothing had changed in the fundamentals of life and death.

He felt the stirring of his own life force, his own sexual power, and wanted to take her in his arms there and then, making love in the place of death to enable the cycle to go on turning.

She must have seen it in his eyes, because she dropped his arm hastily, and moved back a step.

'Jack!' she breathed. 'Don't...'

Finn was behind her, and put his arm around her waist as she bumped into him.

Jack's expression turned from desire to anger. He glared at Finn and clenched his fists.

'I say,' said Bernard, beaming innocently, as he joined them.

'Have you ever seen such treasures? Do you recognize anything, Finn? They say some things in Tut's tomb belonged to Akhenaten.'

Jack turned and moved away quickly. He could feel Emma's eyes on his back. He left the room, and the building, and sat on a bench in the garden outside the museum, watching the men outside the fence washing their hands and kneeling toward Mecca for their five times daily prayers.

Confronted by their religious ritual he felt a gap, a hole, a loss, in his own life. Men and women had died for their beliefs since time began, and they were still dying in Northern Ireland, in Afghanistan, in India, in Israel... He felt nothing of their passion, their commitment... He still interpreted religious symbols and rituals as a child would a cartoon story. But in a child's story the good always won and the child was always on their side. During wars opposing sides prayed for help to the same god. And in an adult story evil often won, and the only reward for the good was the promise that in some distant and insubstantial future, justice would be done.

He had been cynical about religion for most of his life. But what if religious people were only wrong about the superficials of their faith, and there was something there that even they did not understand, something that was crucially important, without which life and death had no meaning? Was he missing out?

At this moment Finn and Emma came out of the main door of the museum together as though they were a couple. Bernard trailed behind. Jack frowned. Eliot had charged him with looking after Emma. What would he do if Finn and she indeed became a couple? Would he try to part them for Eliot's sake, or for his own?

When they joined him they discussed their reactions to the exhibits in the Museum. Emma had identified with the child on Akhenaten's knee and was more convinced than ever that she was a reincarnation of Setepenra.

'I feel so strongly Finn and I have been together before. If he was Akhenaten ... if he was my father...'

'Are your feelings towards Emma *fatherly*?' Jack asked Finn sarcastically.

Finn did not answer, but took out the flute he always carried with him, sat cross-legged on the sparse and dusty grass, and started to play.

Bernard, sweating in the heat, wiped his face and neck on a large white handkerchief and sat down on the bench next to Jack. Emma sat cross-legged on the ground opposite Finn, and rummaged in her string bag for a notebook and pencil. She began writing a poem while he played.

Passers-by stopped and stared. Jack reminded himself they were not in England where it was thought impolite to stare, and tried not to mind that they were the centre of attention when he would rather have had time to sort out his thoughts in private. Bernard too looked uncomfortable. But Finn and Emma seemed oblivious of all else. Jack envied them their self-containment.

Late that afternoon they went by taxi to the Giza Plateau.

Emma stared in disbelief at the city of Cairo pressing so close against the pyramids on one side. All the photographs she had seen had been carefully angled so that the ancient monuments looked as though they stood alone in the desert. Coach loads of tourists, like myriad coloured butterflies, fluttered around their base. Arab boys attached themselves to them as soon as they stepped out of the car, pestering them to buy postcards, 'genuine antiques', and misshapen little models of Egyptian artefacts. Others shouted invitations for them to ride on camels, horses, and donkeys... Emma bought one thing, feeling sorry for the ragged urchin who pressed it on her, but at once she knew she had made a mistake for she was given no peace by dozens of others who materialized out of nowhere and would not take 'no' for an answer. Jack rescued her at last, but only by losing his temper and shouting. Tears came to Emma's eyes. This was not as she had imagined her first encounter with the mighty and mysterious pyramids of Egypt.

She turned her attention to the Sphinx, and there again was bitterly disappointed. From where they stood it seemed so small and insignificant. It had none of the magnificent isolation she had imagined.

Jack had been to the plateau before and so was not surprised at anything he saw. But when he came before he had not paid much attention. Now he remembered the friend who had accompanied him had been speaking about a theory that the sphinx was much, much older than had previously been thought – by ten thousand years! The contention was that the ridges of weathering on its sides had been made by water and not wind. If this was so it must have been carved and standing centuries before the land became a desert. Jack knew that the one thing certain about the earth was that it was continually changing. He had been shown red sandstone cliffs on the way from Bath to Bristol that had been laid down when England was a hot red desert, millions of years before. It was not therefore surprising to him that the great deserts of North Africa had once been running with water supporting a green and fertile land.

Emma found a spot removed from the crowds to sit and meditate. Finn disappeared into what was left of the desert, riding a camel. Bernard, who had been reading his guidebook assiduously with only an occasional glance at the real structures, decided to enter the Great Pyramid, joining the last tour of the day.

Gradually the sun sank lower and that amazing flame colour that characterized sunsets in dusty lands began to suffuse the sky. Tour buses left, and Arab traders packed up their wares. Their taxi was soon alone in the parking lot, its driver alternately patiently smoking and dozing, clocking up his fare.

Bernard returned, puffing and sweating, with tales of how stuffy and narrow the stairwell had been and how the kings chamber was bare and bleak, except for the fifty tourists packed tightly into it!

Emma told them how Mary Brown had spent the night in the Kings Chamber on her first visit to Egypt. 'The group she was with bribed the guide and performed some sort of initiation ceremony there. She told me the sound effects in the chamber were spectacular, the five spaces above, that archaeologists claimed were to lessen the weight of the stone, acted as sound boxes and their chanting reverberated in the most extraordinary way. She said she felt she was in a space ship taking off for the stars!' laughed Emma, and then added, more seriously, 'I believe Napoleon also spent a night in the Great Pyramid, and he would never talk about what happened to him there. All he would say was that no one would believe him.'

Jack looked over his shoulder at the huge fireball disappearing over the horizon. Already the significance of the ciphers he had seen in the Museum on the shrines of Tutankhamun seemed less enigmatic. And as the sky darkened, losing its glow, and the stars appeared above those great pyramidal structures, he felt less and less alien to this ancient civilisation.

The sky was immense. The stars powerfully present. How could we, who lived in cities and rarely saw the stars, understand the metaphysics of a people who believed their lives were immediately and intimately bound up with them? They did not know what we now know about the physical properties of the universe ... the chemical composition of the matter that made up the nebulae, the galaxies, the suns, the planets. Imagine not knowing any of this and looking up into that darkness and seeing those vivid and mysterious lights! No wonder all their religion was influenced by what they saw in the sky. The sun, giving life and light in the day but disappearing at night. Many of the sacred texts were prayers and spells to bring about the rebirth of the sun at dawn. And many of the funerary texts emphasized union with the stars as being the fate of the pharaoh and the justified dead.

Jack wondered if knowing the physical properties of the universe these days spoiled the sky for us as a numinous and mystical experience. But here in the desert, he knew that it did not. He still experienced awe and wonderment at the unimaginable distances into which he was gazing. There were still major and profound questions unanswered. Why? And how and what had started off the whole thing – what had caused the "Big Bang" and why did it happen at that particular moment? Not only Genesis in the Bible mentions the Word, but also the great Creator gods of Egypt are credited with thinking and then speaking the cosmos into existence. At Karnak, Amun, 'hidden of aspect, mysterious of form', thought the universe into existence. At Memphis, Ptah thought and then spoke. Mary would say the Cosmos exists because Consciousness exists. Consciousness utters materiality. But what, Jack wondered, was consciousness, and what is the process of uttering, and how can it transform thought into matter? How could there be consciousness without a physical brain with all its brain cells acting and reacting? Yet at this moment he believed in a supernatural Consciousness that thought the Cosmos into Being, his own consciousness being only a small and insignificant flicker – a crystal set radio in comparison to a computerised satellite transmitter.

All four were silent, thinking their own thoughts, gazing upwards for a long time, awed by what they saw.

Nearly everyone else had left the plateau. Only a few young Egyptian couples were to be seen, sitting on the fallen blocks at the base of the Great Pyramid, talking quietly.

Finn pulled out his flute and began to play.

For once Jack did not resent the man, but almost loved him as the silver threads of his music, haunting and melodic, rose into the darkness and seemed to mingle with the stars.

Suddenly Jack felt they were not alone, and turned his head sharply. He saw no one but the four of them, but around them he felt the crowds gathering, the ancient dead, and the spirits of Amenti, yearning for their lives on earth. Not enough for them the cold stone tombs supplied with painted images of life, nor even the regions of dull perfection they now inhabited ... They wanted life in all its clamour and its complexity ... its pain, its dirt, its glory...

They arrived back late at the hotel in Cairo, but nevertheless decided to gather in the room shared unwillingly by Bernard and Finn. On Emma's suggestion Bernard was to try to channel Akhenaten before they set off for Amarna the next day.

At first it looked as though Bernard would fail. He said, after a few moments of strained silence, that he was too tired. Jack suggested they break up and retire to bed, and was already at the door, when Bernard's body gave a kind of jerk and his face distorted alarmingly. Jack paused with his hand on the door handle. Emma, who had half risen from the edge of the bed on which she had been perched, sank back again at once and stared with some alarm at the medium. His face did not resemble that of Akhenaten as it had before, but was a much more malevolent face, with eyes glaring and lips set in a hard line. There was the same rasping breath that had presaged the former transmission, but the voice that eventually came out of him was much deeper and more menacing. There was no welcoming pleasantries, but a stern demand that they not meddle with what they did not understand.

Jack let the door handle drop and moved back into the room. 'Who are you?' he asked, caught between scepticism and alarm.

He looked into the eyes that now bore no resemblance to Bernard's. The eyes stared directly back into his.

'What makes you think you will succeed where others have failed?' demanded the voice, now mocking.

'Because we come in good faith to bring help to a soul in need – and we have the forces of Light on our side!' cried Emma, recovering herself and leaping up to stand beside Jack. She took his hand in hers and he could feel that she was trembling. Finn rose too and stood beside her on the other side. The three, shoulder to shoulder, faced the malevolent force Bernard was channelling.

'What is your name?' they demanded with one voice.

The being gave a brief and sardonic laugh and Bernard began to choke. Red in the face at last after a fit of coughing, their travelling companion, as they knew him, emerged again. The stranger was gone.

Back in England, in bed asleep, Mary Brown dreamed that she was being sealed alive in a tomb deep underground – but she was not alone. In the blackness that surrounded her she could feel a presence. She backed against the wall, sobbing. She put up her arm to shield her face, as she felt an icy breath against her skin.

But suddenly she woke. Heart pounding, she stared around her pleasant and familiar room illuminated dimly by the streetlights outside her window.

She climbed out of bed, went into the kitchen, and made herself a cup of cocoa.

What was happening to the group in Egypt? Surely they had not left Cairo yet?

Before they left Cairo Bernard insisted they visit the Khan el Khalili. Friends at home had extolled the wonders of it, and he was hoping to get some good bargains for his family.

The great covered labyrinthine market seemed to stretch for miles. Emma noticed that men were staring at her as she walked with the group and, at first, was flattered. But soon it became oppressive, and when she became separated from the others and found herself alone in a shop, she was not at all pleased to see that three young men were crowding her into a corner. She looked up at them angrily, and said loudly: 'Excuse me!' and tried to push her way out. They did not give way, but pressed closer, grinning.

'Where your husband?' one of them asked in heavily accented English.

She shook her head fiercely.

'I have no husband – but my friends are...'

'No husband!' She caught the English word as they laughed and then broke into their own language.

One took her bare arm, another tried to kiss her on the mouth, and the third put his hand on her breast in her tight T-shirt. She struggled to get free, calling to the shopkeeper who was in full view leaning against the counter, smoking, and watching the scene with undisguised relish. They were in the back of the shop and not visible from the covered street beyond, where passers by would surely have helped her. She fought and kicked, but the more she did so the more the men seemed to be enjoying themselves.

But suddenly it was all over. An Egyptian man in a pearl grey Western suit, elegant and commanding, appeared and said something sharply to the men in their native language. They fell back at once.

'Come,' he said commandingly to Emma. 'You must get out of here. Come with me.'

Still clutching her string bag as though her life depended on it, and considerably shaken, she obediently came towards him. He took her arm and led her out of the shop and into the covered street.

'Where is your husband?' He asked in perfect English.

'I haven't got a husband!' she almost screamed. 'My friends...'

'Ah,' he said. 'Did you tell those men you had no husband?'

'Yes, of course. Why should I lie?'

'It would have been better had you done so,' he said gently. 'I have lived in England and I understand how differently you do things there. But to some of our men a woman who travels with men who are not her husband, father or brothers, is deemed at once to be a loose woman. You western girls should dress more modestly and respect our ways when you come to our country.'

'You mean wear a black tent!' Emma snapped angrily.

He smiled stiffly. 'Many women in Egypt do not wear traditional dress, but they do not travel so blatantly with men who are not related to them.'

At this moment she spotted Jack arguing over a silk tie at a stall not far ahead. She broke away from the man and ran towards him, flinging herself into his arms, weeping noisily.

'Why did you leave me alone!' she cried, beating him on the chest.

'I say, steady on!' Jack said in surprise. 'You're making a terrible scene here!'

'I don't care! I want the police! I could have been raped!'

Finn and Bernard had joined them now and her friends formed a comforting barrier around her against the staring, unfriendly eyes of the crowd who were gathering.

'Steady on!' Jack repeated, but he held her close. 'Calm down. Tell us exactly what happened.'

'That man there will tell you,' she sobbed, looking round for the man who had rescued her. But he was nowhere in sight. Nor were the men who had molested her. She could sense no sympathy from the crowds who were staring at her. No doubt they were thinking: 'A Western girl, flaunting herself ... They are all loose women ... they get what they deserve...'

'Oh, what's the point!' she burst out. 'Let's get out of here. I hate this place! This is not what we came for.'

The stallholder who had been about to close a deal with Jack for the tie protested, but Jack waved him away.

With his arm protectively around Emma, he started to move off, Finn and Bernard close behind.

With tear-streaked face Emma glared at the hostile faces around her.

'My husband!' she announced, stabbing Jack in the chest with her index finger. 'You see! My husband!' And then she pointed at Finn and Bernard. 'My brothers!' she shouted, turning her head as Jack hurried her away.

When they were well clear, Jack asked her what all that was about.

'You'll have to be my husband for the rest of the journey. I can't stand being treated like a whore just because I haven't got a husband.'

'Fair enough,' he grinned. 'Does that mean we can share a room?'

'No, it doesn't!' she snapped. 'You're as bad as they are.'

'Just kidding!' he laughed.

But she pulled away from him and strode ahead – but not so far ahead that she was out of range of his protection.

9

The Monastery of the Virgin

The next day they were late setting off because the unanimous decision was to hire a car rather than go south by train or bus to Akhenaten's city. While Jack arranged the car hire in the office, producing all the right documents, the others sat outside under an awning staring rather disconsolately at the gridlock of traffic in the Cairo streets.

'I hope Jack is a good driver!' Bernard said.

The others remained silent. Finn's flute lay mute in its box. Emma twisted the ring on her marriage finger round and round. It was not a wedding ring, but one of the many she normally wore, transferred to that particular finger in an attempt to persuade the locals she was a married woman.

When Jack eventually emerged from the office he led them to a sturdy four-wheel drive vehicle.

'He advises it for Amarna,' he told them. 'If we want to go off the beaten track at all, the going is rough.'

'I just hope we get out of Cairo soon,' muttered Emma. She sounded desperate.

'I rather wish we could spend longer here,' Bernard said ruefully. 'There's a lot we haven't seen. I felt we rather rushed the museum.'

'You can see it on the way back if you want to, after we have gone our separate ways. But now we should go straight to what we came for, as a group.'

'As Companions of the Benu!' Emma cried, her heart already lifting at the thought.

They stowed the luggage and set off.

A long while later, still in the outskirts of Cairo, their nerves frayed, they were snapping at each other as she tried to read the map and direct him.

'We're nowhere near where we want to be,' Jack snarled. 'Give the map to Bernard.'

But Emma was not about to add to men's belief that women could not read maps, and insisted on keeping it in her grasp. As always, the most important pieces of information were on the folds, and as she unfolded it the stiff paper flapped across Jack's vision. He swerved and swore.

Luckily at that moment she spotted a sign for the south printed in English. With lips set in a hard line, Jack drove south. No one spoke for a long time.

Emma blinked back the tears. She longed for magical, mystical experiences, but had felt closer to ancient Egypt in Mary's living room, surrounded by pictures and books, than she had since coming to this country. Was it a mistake to have come? Would everything be spoiled, as the first few days had been? Should they not perhaps have undertaken the whole mission on the astral plane – instead of the physical? The modern population of Egypt seemed to have very little to do with the ancient inhabitants. Since she had been here she had only seen one face that bore any resemblance to the faces in the paintings in the tombs and temples, and that, she mused, was the face of the man in the dove grey suit who had rescued her in Cairo.

In late afternoon they reached Minya and decided to stay there overnight. It was not far from Amarna, and was a pleasant enough little town. They had the choice of several hotels on the Corniche overlooking the Nile, and Jack suggested they approach the one named The Akhenaten, thinking that Emma, whom he was now trying to befriend again, would want that.

But surprisingly she said 'no' and directed them further, to one that was lying back surrounded by gardens, with scarlet bougainvillea spilling out from every balcony.

'Why not the Akhenaten, given the reason for our being here?' Jack asked.

'I don't know. Perhaps we shouldn't declare our loyalties too openly, given the warning we received,' Emma replied.

Jack laughed. 'You think we could fool that guy!'

'At any rate this looks more comfortable,' Bernard declared with satisfaction.

'It also looks more expensive,' Finn muttered.

Booking in was awkward. Minya was not a tourist town, but a sleepy provincial capital, and the clerk behind the desk, summoned by a bell and very tardy in coming forward, had very little English. Mindful that Emma did not want to be thought 'a loose woman', Jack booked a double room for them as a married couple. Emma insisted that it should be a room with two beds.

The rooms were large with working fans and a wonderful view over the balcony to the Nile and the distant mountains framed in bougainvillea flowers. It was a great improvement on the Cairo hotel.

There were two beds, but pushed together.

Jack, giving her a quizzical look, at once set about moving them apart.

Emma took a shower.

When they were clean and refreshed after the long drive, they found the others and decided to go for a walk before dinner.

After Cairo's noise and bustle this place was heaven. There were some beautiful Italianate mansions built in the last century for the rich cotton merchants, now crumbling and romantic behind overgrown gardens. Light and airy squares surrounded by palm trees supported small shops and street-side cafes, while a leisurely population wandered about, greeting each other and smiling on the strangers.

Jack suggested a drink at one of the cafes, but found that alcohol was not served. As though on cue an English-speaking guest from their hotel joined them, and suggested a drink that he translated as hibiscus tea.

Glasses of the crimson liquid were brought and they tasted it gingerly. But it was delicious and they settled down to a pleasant talk with the man, whose name, it seemed, was Mohammad Ali.

He smiled at their reaction, pre-empting the inevitable remarks, by saying he was not named for the American boxer.

When he heard they were going to Amarna he gave them good advice about times to allow for travel, ferry times, ticket prices for the site and so on, but stressed that there were other interesting sites around Minya they should see before they left. They did not tell him why they wanted to see Amarna, and he assumed they were just tourists generally looking around.

'There don't seem to be many tourists around here,' Bernard remarked.

'No. Since the shootings, tourists on the whole avoid what you people call Middle Egypt.'

'The shootings?'

'I don't want to alarm you, but Assyut and Mallawi, not far south of here, are dangerous areas for tourists these days. Assyut University is a breeding place for revolutionaries who want to bring Egypt under Sharia Law and make it a truly Islamic republic. Members of al-Jihad are welcome in those towns. You were sensible to choose Minya to stay. Here we steer clear of politics and live much more peaceful lives.'

Emma said a little prayer to her guardian angel. They had come to modern Egypt in haste and ill prepared. When they left Cairo they had intended to base themselves at Assyut, but 'chance', or their guardian angel, had directed them to Minya.

Mohammed Ali was insistent that they visit the Monastery of the Virgin on Gabel el-Teir, before they went to Amarna.

'To Christians it is very important,' he said. 'Joseph, Mary and Jesus stayed there when they came to Egypt. It is a place of great holiness to your people.'

Jack tried to protest, but Mohammed declared he would take them there himself the next morning. Bernard was keen to see anything of importance in the district, and Finn, who had grown up a Catholic, though had drifted into a sort of compromise between Catholicism and New-Ageism since, agreed he would like to see it. Jack tried to point out that their time was short.

'There is nothing to see at Amarna,' Mohammed insisted. 'You'll be finished there in a few hours. I will be leaving the day after tomorrow. Let me take you to this place before I go. Egypt is a holy land, not only for the ancient pharaohs and the Muslims, but for the Christians also. Your holy family spent years in Egypt when your Christ was a child and most impressionable. Much of your bible is influenced by Egyptian beliefs and events. And in the early years after his death on the cross, your faith in Jesus was kept alive in this country by hermits and monks in remote monasteries while the Romans persecuted the holders of your faith. When you in your country had not even heard of Jesus Christ, we in Egypt knew about him!'

It turned out Mohammed, though a Muslim himself, had a mother who was a Coptic Christian, and he was proud of both strands of his heritage, though he did not ordinarily admit to it among his Muslim friends and colleagues.

Finn clinched it by saying that he had heard the Copts used a language in their rituals that was known to be derived from ancient Egyptian.

'Many Egyptologists study the Copts believing that they are the last link we have with pre-Arabic Egypt,' he said. 'They have absorbed and transformed the ancient mythology. For instance, Isis and her son Horus, became Mary and Jesus. The Egyptian ankh became the Coptic cross. Who knows, they might well have preserved something from Atenism so near to Amarna.'

Jack was doubtful knowing that the early Christians were notorious for declaring the ancient religions demon inspired, and destroying every sign of them they found around. But perhaps Akhenaten with his attempt at monotheism might have been tolerated – if indeed anything had been known about him at that time.

Emma seemed keen to go too, so they agreed.

After a light meal they retired early to bed in various stages of nervous anticipation of what lay ahead of them. Jack's last thought before he went to sleep was that it would be no bad thing to delay the dreaded confrontation with Akhenaten's ghost.

Emma, in her separate bed, lay awake a long time wondering what Eliot would say about her sharing a room with Jack, and how he would have fitted in with their adventure. Her last thought was that he would not have done so.

The dreams of all of them that night were dark and confused, but not one of them remembered enough to tell the others in the morning.

Mary, in England, was feeling increasingly anxious about them, and prayed with passionate intensity that the Spirits of Light would protect them from any harm.

Mohammad Ali was waiting for them somewhat impatiently when at last they came down to breakfast.

'Where we are going,' he said, 'there will be no place to buy food or drink, so I have taken the liberty of providing a picnic lunch.' He patted a square, lidded basket at his side reminiscent of picnics in England during Edwardian times.

They crossed the new Minya Bridge to the east bank and about 20km further south came upon the cliffs of Gabel el-Teir, which Mohammed translated as 'Bird Mountain'. Perched on top of it were the remnants of the Monastery of the Virgin. They struggled over a bumpy track and then up a steep stairway in the heat to the church hewn out of solid rock at the summit. Normally, Mohammad said, they would have to get the key from the caretaker, but today it appeared to be wide open. He told them it had been founded in 328 AD by the Empress Helena over the cave in which the holy family had lived as refugees.

'It is famous for the miracles that have happened here. There is a picture of the Virgin that weeps holy oil.'

'Wasn't Helena the mother of Constantine who made Christianity the official religion of the Roman Empire in the fourth century?' Emma asked Jack. 'Wasn't it she who found the true cross in the Holy Land?'

Jack shrugged. He did not know.

It was dark inside after the brilliant sunlight, and for a while they stood in a tight cluster at the door.

'Here is where your Holy Family lived,' Mohammad Ali said in a low voice, leading them towards a cave. But then he stopped and held up his hand, cautioning them to keep quiet. It seemed he had heard a sound in the cave, and there certainly was a faint light emanating from it.

'Tourists!' thought Emma, disappointed. But having struggled up those steps she did not intend to go away without seeing the inner sanctum. She tiptoed forward and peered into the cave, the others pressing in behind her.

What they saw astonished them.

A small group was gathered, not western tourists, but locals. A family it seemed, with children and parents and grand parents. They were surrounding a tableau at the centre lit by one flickering candle. A young girl was kneeling on the rocky ground bound with huge iron chains. Above her was a hideous crone in black sprinkling something from a plastic bottle and muttering incantations.

Within seconds of their registering the scene, and before the inhabitants of the cave were even aware of their presence, Mohammad, in agitation, was pulling them back and whispering to them urgently that they must leave.

They left.

Once out in the sunlight again they all spoke at once, demanding to know what was going on.

'Shouldn't we go back and rescue that girl?' Jack asked, and the others clamoured that they should.

'No! No. We must not interrupt them.'

'But they are torturing her!' cried Emma.

'No. No indeed. They are helping her. That is an exorcism. She must be possessed by demons and they are freeing her.'

'She didn't look very free to me with all those chains!' Jack protested, believing he should go back, but hesitating to do so.

'It is the demons who are chained. The ceremony will drive them out and then the chains can be removed.'

The four westerners were silent. This primitive and macabre ceremony was performed in the holy of holies of a Christian church. Was what they intended to do – to rescue a ghost from a three thousand year old curse – so very different? Jack thought about the exorcisms he had heard about in England. There were no chains and no mumbo jumbo, no dark and furtive ceremonies, but a belief, nonetheless, that dark spirits *did* exist, and *could* take over the living. For the first time he felt truly afraid of what they were doing. Up to now it had seemed an adventure, almost a game. He realised that he had not seriously believed there was a real ghost, a real curse, and a real dark force they would have to confront. Belief comes in stages like the steps they had just climbed. At first you think you believe something – but don't really. The next stage is when you think you believe in something, and start to act upon it as though it is real. You play out the moves that are expected of you if what you believe is true. But your deepest consciousness is not engaged. But then suddenly something shakes you into really believing! And this stage is different from all that have gone before.

He looked at the others. Bernard was looking ill at ease. Finn's face he could not see, but Emma was plainly terrified. She too had met herself face to face in that dark place.

A blood-curdling shriek came from inside the cave, and Emma grabbed his arm.

He made a move forward, convinced they were murdering the girl, remembering all the horrific tales he had heard of how so called heretics and witches had been cruelly put to death.

But Mohammad again held him back.

'It is not the young girl shrieking,' he said, 'but the demons who are leaving her. We must not interfere. If we do, she will be destroyed along with them.'

'I don't believe it!' Emma sobbed. 'She was just a child!' And she rushed for the door.

Mohammad barred it. His expression was no longer amiable and polite, but stern and hard.

'I cannot permit!' he said.

'A guardian at the door!' Jack thought, remembering the long tradition of tomb guardians, one of which he had had in his home for so many years. Was Mohammad a friend of the Demons or the Beings of Light? That old crone had looked more evil than anyone he had ever seen.

He prepared to push Mohammad aside, by force if necessary, and could sense that Finn was coming to his side. Bernard, whimpering that it was none of their business, had retreated towards the steps.

What would have happened next had the situation inside the church not changed, they would never know.

Mohammad suddenly stood aside, and the three about to rush in were confronted by the family coming out. They were all laughing and happy, leading between them the young teenage girl who had been chained and was now free. She was very pale and seemed bewildered, but was apparently unharmed.

Behind them came an old woman, beaming – wrinkled and bearded, but not appearing in any way like the monster they had believed her to be when they had seen her at work in the cave.

That evening they sat on the bank of the Nile and watched the water flowing red in the dying light of the sun, like molten lava. It took a long time for all the sun's light to go, but eventually faint starlight appeared in the immeasurable darkness.

For a long time they said nothing. It was Jack who voiced their thoughts first.

'What if there is such a thing as possession by demons?' he asked musingly. 'What if Bernard is laying himself open to such possession every time he channels? What if that last menacing voice he channelled is still with us – watching us?'

'Don't say that!' Emma shivered.

'What if Finn is being over-shadowed by Akhenaten's ghost, and is not a reincarnation at all?'

'And what if when you sleep you are taken over by demons?' Finn countered.

'What if we're being led here to our deaths? Pawns in some ancient demonic game? Finn, you were told you would die at thirty-five. You *are* thirty-five. Are you not afraid?'

'Stop it!' cried Emma. 'Stop it at once!'

'Why? Do you not think all this is possible?' Jack persisted.

'Of course its possible!' she replied, her face flushed and her eyes bright. 'But what if it is true that Akhenaten was cursed, and we are the ones, his loyal companions and servants, who have sworn to release him? What if there are good spirits who are helping us? What if there are Guardians of the Light who are on our side and are protecting us at every step? What if what we do here in Egypt will defeat the demons and reinforce the strength of the angels?'

'I think...' said Finn quietly. 'If you believe in bad spirits you have to believe in good ones too.'

Jack threw a pebble into the dark water that flowed so silently past their feet.

'I renounce all dark demons,' he said as he heard the splash, 'and call upon the Beings of Light to help us, guide us and protect us!'

'Amen!' murmured Finn fervently.

'I, too!' cried Emma and threw her favourite silver ring into the ancient river as sacrifice.

Bernard remained silent. They all turned their heads to look at him, unable to see the expression on his face.

'Bernard?' Emma asked breathlessly.

'What?' he asked, jerking his head round as though he had been far away and had not heard a word they had been saying.

'What do you think? Do you make a vow to renounce demons of the dark and follow only the light?' Emma urged.

'Of course,' he said. 'Who wouldn't? But the problem is – how will we recognize which is which?'

There was silence between them once more. For the first time since they had met, Jack felt something other than impatience with

Bernard. He had asked a question that demanded their respect. Perhaps he had been underestimating him all this time.

In England, Mary Brown, eating brown toast with butter and honey, paused with a piece half way to her mouth. It was as though a cold wind had blown through the room though the curtains had not been the least disturbed.

What if they had allowed the gates between the worlds to open and had no control of what came through? Supposing imagination was more powerful than people credited and could manifest what they most feared.

Mary dropped the toast, picked up the phone and rang the hotel in Minya where Emma, who had phoned her on arrival, told her they were staying. She wanted to tell them to come home.

But the man on the desk insisted that they were not there and only agreed to take a message reluctantly. His English was not good and she could not be sure he had understood.

The group returned to their hotel that night in thoughtful mood. The desk clerk was nowhere in sight, and there were no messages left with their keys.

They retired to their rooms, Emma looking back over her shoulder to Finn as he unlocked his and Bernard's door.

Inside their own room Jack confronted her.

'Would you rather I exchanged rooms with Finn?' he asked outright, looking into her eyes challengingly.

She seemed taken aback by the question.

'Why do you ask that?'

'Never mind why I ask it. Would you?'

'Don't be silly,' she said impatiently, but he noted she did not look at him when she said it, and was already moving towards the bathroom.

He watched her shut the door, and then went onto the balcony. There he stayed for a long time watching the dark stain of deeper black made by the distant mountains against the sky.

When he came back into the room Emma was in bed, apparently asleep. He stood for a while gazing down at her, suffering an uncomfortable mix of emotions.

She lay motionless, awake, aware that he was watching her.

10

Akhenaten's City

In the morning they set off very early for Akhenaten's city. They missed another call from Mary, who, once again, left a message that was not delivered.

They drove south through the depressing town of Mallawi, and arrived in time for the first car ferry across to Amarna and the east bank. While they were waiting in the queue, Jack wondered if the others' hearts were beating as fast as his in anticipation of what they might find in the ruined city. But the loading was so slow and noisy and needed such concentration on his part, he almost forgot the significance of the place they were about to visit. Emma went to the front of the ferry and braved the stares of the locals to gaze out over the wide river, straining to catch the first glimpse of the fabled city. She had been warned that Amarna, having been flattened so soon after Akhenaten's death, and later quarried by the Greeks and Romans for their city of Hermopolis nearby, was not full of magnificent standing ruins like Luxor or Edfu or Abydos. But she expected *something*. There was very little. Modern cultivated fields and a grove of Palm trees lined the riverbank. Beyond there was a plain of almost featureless yellow dust stretching to the amphitheatre of cliffs that marked its boundaries.

As soon as they landed at el-Till they were surrounded by villagers and farm children trying to sell them things, mostly basket work, though some had the usual 'genuine' antiques found all over Egypt. Emma flapped ineffectually at them, saying over and over again 'no','no','no' – and then the sight of one little girl with running eyes on to which flies had stuck touched her heart, and she bought a misshapen rag doll stuffed with straw. Finn took her arm and hauled her to the ticket office where Jack was buying the tickets for the day. Emma's eyes were sad. Here they were, the Shemsu Benu, close companions of the Pharaoh, being made to pay to visit *their* city, the place where they had once been honoured and respected! She felt like screaming it out, wanting somehow to distinguish their group from the tourists in their cotton hats, pushing and puffing ahead of them.

Mohammad Ali had been right. There were not many tourists in this part of Middle Egypt – but enough to annoy Emma. She wished very much they could have the place to themselves.

'The last ferry back is at 6 pm,' Jack said, rejoining them.

'What's the matter with her?' he asked Finn, noticing how distraught and angry she looked.

'Don't you feel anything?' Emma snapped, glaring at him. 'Don't you ... oh! What's the use!' And she turned away impatiently.

He shrugged and walked back to the car.

'I hope we're not going to spend all the time in the car,' Finn said.

'Of course not. But it's a huge place. We'll drive a little and walk a little. I have a map, and Mohammad told me in which places to use the car.'

'Mohammad Ali told us there was nothing to see at Amarna,' Bernard said. 'I hope he wasn't right.'

According to the map a track running south from the ticket office was once Akhenaten's Royal Road, and they followed this to where the Great Temple of the Aten had once stood.

The site of Akhenaten's city had been well excavated, but it had not been easy, as villages and farms from time to time had sprawled over it.

There was very little left of the Great Temple to the Aten after Horemheb's devastation, and a Muslim cemetery had occupied the area. Nevertheless the four companions were determined to spend time there. Bernard insisted on reading aloud the guidebook description of how it had once looked, but the rest barely listened. Emma wandered off by herself, out of earshot.

She pictured herself as a young child, the youngest of the Pharaoh's six daughters, in the Great Temple, the House of Aten, a vast area of courts and altars open to the sun. It seemed to her she was standing at first with her father and the rest of the family in the House of Rejoicing, an ante-chamber from which the earliest glimmerings of the dawn were greeted. Then they moved on to the Gem-Aten where the serious dawn ceremonies took place as the world wakened to the full and glorious light of the sun. Beyond this, to the east, her father and mother presided over rituals that channelled through their own bodies the power and energy of the Aten to the population as a whole. She fancied she could smell the incense burning on hundreds of altars, and see the priests placing offerings before gigantic statues of the Pharaoh and his Great Royal Wife, pleading with them to intercede with the Aten for their well being and the well being of the Two Lands.

Phrases from the rituals passed through her mind like smoke.

'Given life forever, eternally, Aten, Living and Great, dwelling in the Temple of Aten in Akhetaten.'

'Aten, the Sole Creator, whose beauty bathes the earth with its beneficent rays.'

'Live the beautiful God who delights in Truth, Lord of all that His disk encounters.'

She heard the chanting of her father's hymn.

'Ah, beautiful is the rhythm of your setting and your rising.
How various is the world you have created,
each thing mysterious, sacred to sight.
O sole God
beside whom is no other!'

She hopped up and down on the steps of a plinth, happy, carefree, laughing, How unlike the gloomy solemnity of the old temples! No one told her to stop. The golden children of the Pharaoh were welcome wherever they went, whatever they did. Suddenly a shadow crossed the dusty plain at Amarna. Momentarily a cloud blotted out the sun.

Finn took Emma's arm. 'What's the matter?' he asked gently.

'It's all over!' she whispered. 'All the good times. I am frightened.'

He could see that she was not referring to the present time, nor was she speaking as Emma.

'What happened to you as Setepenra when everything was destroyed here?' he asked.

'I was hidden. I was taken away. And I never saw ... never saw my father or my mother again. No one said goodbye. No one told me what was happening. Oh, Finn – do you really think I am Setepenra and you are Akhenaten?' Suddenly she was clinging to him, seeking confirmation and comfort that all had not ended there and then – was not indeed ended yet.

'I certainly feel I've been here before,' he said. 'In fact I know I've been here before.'

But Bernard with his guidebook was getting nearer, pointing out where the archaeologists said there had been columns. Jack had left the temple site and was examining what was left of the Foreign Office – where a rich store of diplomatic correspondence had been found which illuminated the story of Akhenaten's brief life in the city. There was nothing much to see, but under the sand the foundations lay, and Jack had read some of the letters in translation. Nothing had changed. Diplomatic promises then were as evasive and as procrastinating as they are today. Akhenaten was accused of having let the great Egyptian Empire slip away from him because he did not send troops when they were requested, did not send payments due, failed to bribe or flatter the right people at the right time.

Next came the rectangles in the sand that were all that remained of the Royal Residences. Ben Wilson's journal had described the beautiful design of fruit and flowers, fish, birds and insects on the wall tiles of Nefertiti's quarters. But they were long gone. A farmer, irritated by the many visitors who walked through his fields to see it, had smashed it up. On Ben Wilson's second visit there was nothing left. Only fragments had been preserved in museums around the world.

The little group spent many hours in the hot sun tracing the last remains of these ancient buildings, trying to visualize them as they once had been. The great state palace over the road had once had a bridge linking it to the royal apartments. There the royal family had stood in the Window of Appearances, accepting the worship of the crowd, and dispensing gifts and rewards. They had seen pictures of these occasions, the younger princesses leaning eagerly over the sills, trying to identify people they knew in the crowd. The older ones trying to keep their dignity beside their parents.

And Jack had seen it all in his dream.

As the heat of the day started to increase approaching noon, Jack stood in the place marked 'the Sanctuary of the Aten' on the map, and gazed out over the ochre coloured sand plain to the eastern cliffs. Idly his mind started imagining how the city must have looked in its brief heyday, and then, as the air vibrated with the heat, it seemed the city itself lay before him, the mud brick buildings lining the straight streets, the pylons of the temples towering over them, flags hanging limp in the still air, the gardens of the Great Palace green and lush with trees and splashing water. People were going about their business, happy, well fed and well housed in the gleaming new town. Nothing was shabby or damaged as it was in the cities that had lasted for thousands of years. The lines of the buildings were straight cut, and the streets clean. What a dream it had been! Was there no way such dreams could be realised in the world? How many Utopias had failed to deliver their promises? 'The Golden Age' was always the nostalgic concept of people who lived in degradation and despair looking back to a time about which they knew little. What invisible tensions existed in this city? What boredoms, frustrations, rivalries and jealousies? Surely there were some. Surely the children laughing in the street went home to parents who worried about the future or felt guilty about the past? Perhaps not. Perhaps for its brief time it was perfection, and destruction came from without, and not from within.

The vision faded and Jack wandered back to join the others. Bernard was crimson in the face from the heat, and Emma sat drooping on the remains of a mud brick wall.

'Let's have our lunch by the river among the palm trees,' Jack suggested. 'We can't go much further in this heat.'

They sat in the shade, with the great river sliding past beside them, and took out the food they had brought. The water was lukewarm, but they drank it thirstily nevertheless.

When they had recovered somewhat they began to compare notes on their experiences so far.

Bernard was impatient with the slowness of their pace, and disappointed that there was so little of the old town left to see. He kept paging through his guidebook and looking longingly at pictures of the great structures at Luxor, Karnak, Abydos, Edfu and Denderah still standing.

'But those don't have connections with Akhenaten,' Emma pointed out.

'Karnak has,' Bernard insisted. 'Akhenaten grew up there and when he first became pharaoh he built a temple at Karnak east of the Great Temple of Amun. In fact that large statue of him we saw in Cairo Museum was from there.' The sound of the pages of his book turning resembled the sound of dry leaves in the wind.

'Here it is. Right at the beginning, when he changed his name to Akhenaten, before he'd even thought of founding his own city. "Colossal statues of him stood against pillars in a peristyle court," and reliefs showed Nefertiti worshipping the Aten. When the Priests of Amun came back to power they destroyed it, broke up the statues and buried them as deep as they could, "to a depth of seven metres",' he quoted.

'We are not concerned about his early life,' Emma said firmly, 'but the end. Later we can fill in the pieces, but now our task is to find him and set him free.'

'Can we do that without knowing more about him?'

Once again Jack looked at Bernard in surprised appreciation.

Emma chose to ignore the question and turned to Finn.

'What about you, Finn? What do you feel about the place?'

They all looked at Finn. He was sitting cross-legged as usual, gazing at the river glinting through the palm trunks. Jack glanced to the river, wondering what he was staring at so seriously. A blue grey heron was sitting on a rock watching for a fish as intently as Finn was watching him.

Was not the Benu bird sometimes depicted as a heron?

Jack looked at Emma. Had she noticed it?

But she was still gazing at Finn.

Jack was irritated with himself. It was a heron after all, an ordinary water bird, common in Egypt, going about its business of finding food for its family. Yet here he was, as bad as Emma, reading into it all kinds of symbolic significance for their journey. There was a faint splash as the heron dived, and this made Emma turn her attention to the river. She was in time to see the bird winging away with a shining silver fish struggling for life in its beak. She leapt up at once and ran to the waterside. 'Did you see that!' she cried excitedly. 'A heron! A Benu! It is a sign!'

Jack, who had thought the very same thing, was irritated at how silly it sounded when spoken out loud with such a blind conviction.

After lunch they explored the rest of the area once occupied by the principal buildings of the town. Finn was still keeping his own counsel, walking alone and not giving away any of his feelings. Emma was constantly remarking on things she 'remembered', rejoicing when they arrived at the remote southern palace of Meru-aten, claiming that she could smell the flowers, and see the lake on which she had spent so many happy hours boating with her sisters. Jack was increasingly disturbed by shadowy images that flitted across his vision and then were gone before he could properly identify them. It felt to him rather like the times in conversation when you cannot remember a word. You can feel the word just out of reach, teasing you. You know it is important, but it will just not surface in the conscious mind.

Bernard was still consulting his guidebook at every hump or lump, and did not seem particularly disturbed by the atmosphere of the place. Where the archaeologists had unearthed the studio of Thutmose the sculptor, and found all those beautiful stone heads of the royal family and local dignitaries, he spent most of the time bemoaning that they had all been removed and scattered around the world in various museums. He showed a photograph of one of the Amarnan princesses to Emma and asked why she was always depicted bald. Emma gazed at the exquisite sensitive face, and touched her own thick chestnut locks gratefully.

'It was the custom. Everyone who was anyone wore elaborate wigs for state occasions. We had our heads shaved to accommodate the wigs.'

'Perhaps the wigs acted like hats, preventing sunstroke. You never see a hat on an ancient Egyptian.'

'Trust Bernard to reduce romance to practicality,' Emma thought, and moved away.

Jack called to her.

'Do you want to see one of the boundary stelae?' he asked. 'There is time if we get a move on.'

She nodded at once, and the two of them strode ahead.

Akhenaten had set up stone stelae north, south, east and west, to mark the boundaries of his new and sacred city. Some were still in existence, having been carved against cliffs, set back in shelters. There the royal family were depicted, not yet with their full complement of daughters, offering to the Aten the sun disk with its rays each ending in a hand holding an ankh representing eternal life.

'As my father the Aten lives, I will make Akhetaten for the Aten my father in this place. I will not make him Akhetaten south of it, north of it, west of it or east of it. And Akhetaten extends from the southern stele as far as the northern stele, measured between stele and stele on the eastern mountain, likewise from the south-west stele to the north-west stele on the western mountain of Akhetaten. And the area within these four stelae is Akhetaten itself: it belongs to Aten my father; mountains, deserts, meadows, islands, high ground and low ground, land, water, villages, men, beasts and, all things which the Aten my father shall bring into existence eternally for ever. I will not neglect this oath which I have made to the Aten my father, eternally.'

They had agreed to take their exploration of Akhenaten's city slowly, 'acclimatizing' themselves to the atmosphere before they tackled the real purpose of their mission. They were disappointed that they were not allowed to stay overnight, but would have to leave on the ferry at 6pm and return again the next day. They planned to visit the town the first day, the northern tombs the second, the southern tombs, the third, leaving the great wadi with the royal tombs to the fourth day. Then, and only then, would they go into the desert and see if they could find the ghost of Akhenaten. Tired and dusty they drove back to Minya, each locked in his or her own thoughts, trying to digest the impressions of the day before they spoke of them to the others.

* * * *

That night Jack dreamed again.

He was standing watching a stela being carved, like the one he and Emma had seen that day. He must have been some kind of overseer or court official because he was criticising the workmanship and directing the stone carvers to make various changes. It must have been one of the earliest because the plain north of him was not yet filled with buildings under construction. There was a sense of urgency because the king himself was coming to view it shortly. Behind him, on the distant river, he could see the sails of the royal boat.

Suddenly, from above him, he felt he was being watched. Glancing up at the rugged cliff behind the workmen, he saw a lone figure standing. A sense of danger overcame him. He called out and indicated authoritatively that the figure should come down from where it stood. The man turned and walked away, disappearing behind rocks.

Jack scowled. Was he an assassin waiting for the king? Hastily he clambered up the low cliff. At the top he found no one.

As Jack woke, in half conscious state, he had an overpowering conviction that the man was Finn, and that the reason for his presence with them on this mission was not as they thought. But when he was fully awake, he dismissed the idea as ridiculous.

'I am jealous of him because Emma likes him,' he thought.

But he was disturbed and could not get back to sleep.

He went out onto the balcony and stayed there until the dawn light began to suffuse the eastern mountains with pink.

As strings of birds began to wing across the sky in search of arable fields, Emma joined him. Her hair was tousled, her cheeks flushed from sleep, a sheet draped around her beautiful body. He put out his arm and she nestled against him, both held entranced by the ancient ritual of sunrise the Egyptians had clothed in so many meaningful myths. They stood silently a long while, absorbing the beauty before them, a light breeze stirring the frame of bougainvillea flowers. There was complete peace between them.

Jack had been cold, but her body gave him warmth. He lowered his lips and kissed her hair. She looked up into his eyes.

And then they both remembered – and pulled apart.

If anyone had been watching they might have noticed that Jack and Emma were deliberately trying to avoid eye contact with each other at breakfast. On the journey back to Amarna Emma made a point of talking a lot to Finn and Bernard, and Jack avoided talking at all.

Before they took the route to the northern tombs, Emma wanted to wander the area of the town once more. This time they left the principal buildings they had concentrated on before, and explored the outlying districts where there was even less to see, apart from occasional shards of broken pottery and chips of stone.

Early on Emma found a sizeable piece of pottery painted duck-egg blue with the faint lines of part of the surface design still visible. She sat down at once in the sand and held it close to her forehead, concentrating all her attention on it.

'What is she doing?' Jack asked, puzzled, although nothing Emma did really surprised him.

'She is having a go at psychometry,' Finn replied, and then, when he saw that Jack was none the wiser, he added, 'trying to pick up vibrations and memories from the pot when it was in use.'

'It's unlikely to have been used by Akhenaten,' Jack said. 'These must have been the suburbs where the ordinary people lived.'

'This is where the pots were made for use in the temples and palaces. Who knows what she will pick up.'

Jack looked at her, an isolated figure in a vast expanse of dusty, ochre-coloured landscape, clutching her little piece of ancient pottery. But what he could not see was that Emma believed herself to be a long dead woman, carrying a water pot on her head along a crowded street, shouting out to friends, flirting with her eyes as she passed a slender young man leading a donkey laden with slabs of white stone, held firmly in place by a net of rope. He turned and looked at her when she had passed, and another man called out a lewd comment. He laughed and shook his head, but before he turned the corner into the next street he looked back. She had also turned and, in spite of the distance between them, their eyes met.

The vision ended. Emma stood up, satisfied, and put the shard in her pocket. She had experienced a moment in ancient Akhetaten, and had seen that it was not all religion and court intrigue, but a very human town, with very ordinary people not unlike today.

She glanced across at Jack as he stooped to pick up something. Could it be something the young man with the donkey in her vision had dropped? As improbable as it seemed, Emma was so convinced of the dynamic link between past and present, she would not have been surprised.

She called out, and Jack held up what he had found. When she came nearer she saw that it was a sliver of pure white stone.

'This could be some of the alabaster from the Hat-nub quarries,'

Jack said, 'used in the temples and the palaces. The stonemasons must have had work yards near here.'

Emma rejoiced secretly. The young man in her experiment with psychometry had been carrying stone for the stonemason's yards! What Jack had found *was* connected with what she had experienced. She would take this as yet another sign that they were in genuine communication with ancient Akhetaten.

They drove the few dusty kilometres towards the cliffs into which the northern tombs were cut. Jack was particularly interested in these, as he felt, if he had a past in this ancient drama, he was most likely one of the court officials close to Akhenaten. If Mary and Emma's theory of the Shemsu Benu was correct, these court officials were likely to be the ones who chose to join such a secret society after Akhenaten's death.

Since Ben Wilson had visited the temples and tombs, and written about them in his journal, much had faded or been lost. Bernard's guidebook suggested bringing torches with them – and this they had done. No electricity had been installed in these tombs, the only light coming into their dark depths was from sunlight reflected in by sheets of foil-covered boards and mirrors wielded by guards at the entrance.

The tomb of Ahmose, Akhenaten's fan bearer, was the first they saw but they found it somewhat disappointing. Not many of the wall paintings survived and those that did seemed out of character. One showed Akhenaten leading his troops into battle, a thing he rarely did, if ever. The group decided Ahmose could not have been one of the Shemsu Benu, because if warriors were what he admired he would certainly have been disappointed in Akhenaten who, according to the letters preserved in the archive, was notorious for avoiding military confrontation.

The tomb of Mery-Re the First, was more interesting. He was High Priest, the Greatest of the Seers of Aten, and some of the columns of painted flowers and reliefs of him and his wife were still extant. There was a depiction of Mery-Re receiving a golden collar, and Akhenaten riding in a chariot, with his face and the sign of the Aten scratched out. Was this done before Mery-Re was laid to rest in the tomb? Did this mean he had renounced Atenism during his lifetime? He must have been a man well on in years, and perhaps had been brought up in the old religion, for the tomb of his son was nearby.

Mery-Re the Second had been the Overseer of the Two Treasuries, a much more secular position. Near the entrance to his tomb there was an adoration scene and an inscription of Akhenaten's Hymn to the Aten, badly defaced. But on one of the inner walls there was a scene of Nefertiti straining a drink for her husband seated under a sunshade, and Mery-Re the Second receiving a golden collar like his father. Some of the cartouches had been scratched out and the names of Smenkhkare and Merytaten overlaid. So this tomb must have been finished after Akhenaten's death, but before the main purge of the Atenist cult started. Had Mery-Re himself lain in this tomb? The four sat in meditation, on Emma's suggestion, and tried to contact its ancient inhabitant.

For the first time since they had come to Akhetaten, Bernard let his guidebook slip to the floor, and went into trance.

'Thus speaks Mery-re, friend to the King. I will follow my Lord into the Everlasting and will speak his name though my tongue be cut out. He has been honourable and kind to me his servant, and deserves nothing of the hatred that burns around him. May my name be removed from the Tree of Records, if I let his name fade from my lips.'

The others looked at Bernard. He stopped speaking.

'Well,' Jack said, after a long silence. 'At least we know the name of one of the Shemsu Benu.'

'Call him back,' Emma urged. 'Ask him what our names were at the time of Akhenaten.'

Bernard shut his eyes and tried to concentrate. But nothing happened this time.

'I can't,' he said. 'I can't ever make them come if they don't want to. He has said what he wanted to say. We must be content with that.'

The next tomb was that of Pentu, a physician, and was almost totally destroyed. Real violence had smashed these walls and images. There was practically nothing to see. Bernard read out a passage from his guidebook that purported to be an inscription from this tomb.

'May you grant that I rest in my place of continuity, that I be enclosed in the cavern of eternity: that I may go forth and enter into my tomb without my Ba's being restrained from what it wishes; that I may stride to the place of my heart's determining, in the groves which I made on earth; that I might drink water at the edge of my pool every day without cease.'

'You know, all these inscriptions make one think that to be a ghost, still walking the earth after death, was the greatest desire of the deceased,' Jack said thoughtfully. 'Maybe we would not be doing Akhenaten any favours if we stopped him walking the earth.'

'A hermit choosing to live in a cell to further his spiritual development,' Emma said at once, 'is a very different case from a prisoner kept against his will in the same cell. Besides, the restraining curse might have been put on his *Akh*, his Spirit, and not on his *Ba* or *Ka* that want to be still linked to earth.'

Jack was silent. None of them knew what they were really doing in Egypt. None of them knew where their quest would take them. In this tomb, so badly smashed about, Jack had an overwhelming feeling of unease. It was a place of danger and despair, and Emma was now insisting that they meditate in a circle, holding hands, to increase the energy of the transmission she hoped Bernard would tune into from those ancient times. He could feel Bernard's hand in his growing hot. On the other side of him, Finn's hand was ice cold.

It was not long before a hollow voice began to come from Bernard's twisted mouth.

'Leave this place! Do you still mock me Priest of Darkness? Have you not done enough to destroy me and my children and my grandchildren, and all the generations that might have come after? Leave this place, the last sanctuary of my soul, hated and hateful.'

His voice rose to a scream and they dropped hands and scrambled for the exit, Jack on all fours. Only Finn stood for a moment longer and Jack, looking back, could not read the strange expression on his face.

Bernard was whimpering and shaking and demanding to be told what had happened. Emma was pulling his hand and jabbering that they should leave. Well down the corridor they were joined by Finn.

'What was all that about?' he asked casually, as though he had not been as terrified as the rest of them.

'What I want to know is,' Jack said, looking hard at Finn, 'who was he addressing?'

'I felt such hate directed towards us!' Emma said. 'Maybe he was one of Horemheb's cronies who hated Akhenaten, and does not want us to free him.'

'Or maybe he was close to Akhenaten and recognized, in one of us, an enemy of Akhenaten.'

'Don't be silly!' Emma cried. 'We are all here to help Akhenaten!'

'I must have some air, 'Bernard declared. 'I can't face any more tombs.'

No one demurred. They tumbled gratefully out into the sunlight and sat for a while on a pile of rocks trying to collect their thoughts. Finn took out his flute and started to play.

Jack, studying him, remembered his dream, and found it difficult to dismiss the growing unease he felt towards him.

* * * *

After lunch they returned to the tombs, but decided not to meditate or invoke the spirits.

Huya's tomb was the most impressive. He had been a high official in the administration of Akhenaten's father and there was a well preserved version of the Hymn to the Aten, and a banqueting scene delightfully depicting several of the princesses and Akhenaten's mother, the dowager queen Tiye, the much beloved commoner wife of the great king Amenhotep III. There was a procession to the Hall of Tribute, where diplomats from Syria and Kush waited for an audience with Akhenaten and Nefertiti.

Huya was Steward to Queen Tiye and Superintendent of the Royal Harem, and there were elaborate scenes of him receiving honours from the Window of Appearances. Ben Wilson's journal spoke of the mummy of Huya actually being found in a burial shaft within the tomb. But the four found they had no great interest in him, and soon left.

About 500 metres south along the cliffs there was the isolated tomb of the High Priest Panhesi, but this had been used as a chapel by early Copts and the Christian vibrations were so strong in the place that the little group found it difficult to receive any sense of Panhesi himself.

'But a High Priest of the Aten!' Emma said. 'Surely he would have been one of the Shemsu Benu.'

It was frustrating being unable to get a sense of him, and Jack joined Emma in pressing Bernard to try once more to contact the spirit of the tomb.

At first he refused, but Emma was not one to give up easily, and eventually he agreed.

They sat as before, holding hands, with eyes shut, trying to breathe easily and float loose from the moorings of their ordinary bodies. It took much longer than before, and they were about to give up when Bernard uttered that now familiar rasping breath and began to speak in a voice not his own.

'Bless the Lord, Oh my soul. Oh Lord my God, thou art very great; thou art clothed with honour and majesty. Thou coverest thyself with light as with a garment; and stretchest out the heavens like a curtain. Thou layest thy beams on the waters, and makest the clouds thy chariot. Thou walkest upon the wings of the wind and maketh thy angels spirits, and thy ministers a flaming fire. Thou has laid the foundations of the earth, that it should not be removed forever....'

They could not tell if it was a Christian Copt speaking, or the Great

Seer Panhesi himself. Bernard's voice faded and they sat silently for a long time.

'I've heard that before,' Emma whispered. 'Somewhere in the Bible. A Psalm, I think.'

'It may have been from the Hymn to the Aten,' Jack suggested.

'It is as though the two religions have grown together like the roots of two trees, and we are sitting in the shade, not knowing which is which.'

'Does it matter if we can't distinguish them, as long as we are filled with respect for what lies behind them?'

When they left Panhesi's tomb, they carried with them a strong sense of mystery and awe, but as soon as they climbed into their hire car and started the engine, all sense of it disappeared.

11

The Southern Tombs

At home in England Mary tried several times to contact the group by telephone, and on the fourth attempt, when she asked for Miss Emma Forsyth directly, she was told that there was no person of that name staying at the hotel. Responding to her obvious agitation at this piece of information, the desk clerk called for the assistance of someone nearby who could speak a little more English.

Mary insisted that she had been told her friend was staying at that hotel and was travelling with a group of three other English people. The voice at the other end, interrupted by constant crackling, admitted there was a group of four English at the hotel. There was a pause as he consulted the clerk in his own language, and then came back to Mary to say that there was a Mr and Mrs Wilson, a Mr O'Connor and a Mr Meech.

After taking a deep breath, Mary then asked to speak to Mrs Wilson. But the line had gone dead.

Mary put her own phone down and considered the matter. It was very likely Emma had taken on this persona as self-protection in a country where women, however liberated, did not travel unnoticed with a party of men. On the other hand she had noted the electricity that passed between Emma and Jack on more than one occasion, and would not have been surprised if...

But before she could formulate the thought her own phone rang loudly right beside her, and made her jump.

'Hullo,' she said.

A man's voice speaking with an American accent asked if she was Mary Brown. When she answered that she was, he gave his name as Eliot.

'You don't know me,' he said, 'but I am a friend of Emma Forsyth.'

'Oh yes,' she said, remembering at once who he was and gasping at the timing of the call. 'But I thought you were in South America.'

He laughed. 'I was,' he said cheerfully. 'But I came back early. I was wondering if you have Emma's address in Egypt. I thought I might join her.'

There was a long pause while Mary tried to collect her racing thoughts.

'Mrs Brown?' Eliot prompted.

'I'm sorry... I'm ... I'm just looking for...' She rustled papers loudly on the little table, wondering if she should tell him what she had just heard. He must certainly be told before he went rushing out there.

'I'm sorry to put you to so much trouble,' he said politely. 'If you haven't got it to hand, perhaps you could ring me back when you've found it.'

'Perhaps... perhaps...' She stammered desperately. 'Perhaps you could come and see me and ... and help me look for it.' It would be better to discuss the matter face to face than blurt it out on the phone. Besides, she might be able to get hold of Emma before that.

His voice was still polite, but somewhat puzzled when he replied.

'Of course, Mrs Brown, but ... Do you in fact have the address?'

'Yes, yes. Of course. But my things are in such a muddle and I'm a very old lady you know ... my eyes are not as good as they should be.'

'All right. I'll come. Will it be all right if I come right away? I could be with you in ten to fifteen minutes.'

'Yes. Yes. That will be fine. So sorry ... so sorry...' and she put the phone down as though it was burning hot.

What extraordinary bad luck! Why could he not have stayed in South America as he had planned? And what was the point of his going to Egypt when, according to Emma, he had no interest in the country or in any of the issues they were now investigating?

She feared it was Emma who was drawing him, Emma who, no doubt, was now sharing a room with Jack as Mrs Wilson.

She tried phoning Minya again, but there was no reply. She was still trying when Eliot rang the doorbell.

She let him in and at once insisted they should have a cup of tea.

'I've found the address,' she said, more cheerfully than she felt. 'But I've been trying to phone them for days and have not been able to get hold of them. The desk clerk not only doesn't speak English, but also is totally inefficient. I can't believe they haven't received any of my messages.'

'Never mind,' said Eliot. 'I wanted to surprise her anyway.'

'You don't mean to say you'll go all that way without contacting her? They might have moved on by the time you arrive.'

'You'll probably know the route they intend taking. I'm sure I'll find them. They're quite a distinctive group!' And Eliot laughed heartily, visualizing Finn with his lean and sepulchral look, and

Bernard, who he hadn't met, but heard described as a 'fat business man'.

'I still think it would be wise to make sure Emma knows you are coming. They are not on a scheduled, well-organized tourist trip you know. From day to day their plans could change if the mood takes them, or something unexpected crops up.'

'Oh, it will be all right,' he said confidently. 'I should never have let her go on such a crazy expedition. I only did so because I knew my family would not approve of her, and she would be uncomfortable with me at such a family gathering. But when I was away from her I knew I didn't care what they thought of her. I'm going to Egypt tomorrow to sweep her off her feet and marry her – and to hell with what my family thinks!'

Mary's face was a study, but Eliot was not looking at her.

'Tomorrow?' she murmured weakly.

'I've wasted far too much time. Now that I've discovered I can't live without her I want to tie the knot as soon as possible.'

'Marriage is a long and serious commitment,' Mary said. 'And from what I've heard, you and Emma have very few interests in common.'

'Haven't you heard the expression "opposites attract"?' he asked smugly. 'I have to admit her bizarre ideas sometimes irritate me, but she'll grow out of them. We are good for each other. We're good in...'

'Bed.' Mary filled in the missing word as Eliot hesitated to say it, suddenly remembering he was speaking to an elderly lady.

'Mrs Brown,' he said earnestly, looking her straight in the eye at last. 'I have to go. I have to stop Emma going on with this lunatic expedition and exposing herself to all kinds of danger. I have to make her see the sense of leading a normal life. Who knows, by now she might have had enough and be longing to come home.'

Mary pressed her lips together, and looked at him hard.

'She is living in that hotel registered as Mrs Wilson,' she said, suddenly choosing to be blunt.

At first he didn't grasp the significance, and then, when he did, he looked at her in astonishment.

There was a long pause.

'I'll thank you to give me the address now, Mrs Brown,' he said icily.

She had been clutching a piece of paper in her hand all this time.

Now, without a word, she handed it to him.

He glanced at it, put it in his wallet slowly and deliberately, and then stood up.

'Thank you for the tea,' he said, ever polite. 'And for the information. I'm sorry I troubled you.'

'I think we ought to talk about this,' Mary said urgently. 'There may be a perfectly innocent explanation...'

He raised his eyebrow sceptically.

'You don't know. It might be for her protection in some way. Islamic countries have a very different attitude...'

'I thank you for the tea and for the information, Mrs Brown,' Eliot repeated, 'but I don't want to discuss it with you. It is a matter entirely between Emma and me.'

'And Jack,' Mary wanted to add. She liked Jack and had taken a dislike to Eliot. So, she would 'grow out of' all her deepest, most passionately held beliefs living with him, would she?

But he was gone, the door shut between them.

What happened now was a matter of fate.

However she did try to reach the hotel in Minya several times more.

On the way back to Minya after visiting the northern tombs at Amarna, Emma's little group discovered they were low on petrol and stopped to refuel in Mallawi.

While Jack was attending to that, Finn wandered off and returned with a newspaper and a worried expression on his face.

'What's the matter?'

'Look at this.' He held out the front page. The writing was unreadable by them, but the picture was unmistakably of a tourist bus and a great many bodies lying around, obviously dead or wounded. Some, still alive, were crouching against the bus, weeping.

'Oh, my God!' Bernard gasped. Emma paled, putting her hand over her mouth to stop herself crying out.

'It looks bad,' Finn said.

'Where? Where did it happen?'

'I don't know. One of the tourist spots. Not Cairo, I think.'

'Jack!' called Emma urgently, remembering what Mohammed Ali had said about Mallawi. She was now anxious to get out of there to safe and pleasant Minya.

But Jack was arguing with one of the men from the petrol station, and, as they watched, a small and menacing group was gathering around him.

'Jack, pay the man whatever he asks and more, and lets get out of here!' Emma shouted.

Bernard and Finn joined her in urging Jack to come back to the car quickly.

He glanced at them in annoyance. He was being seriously

overcharged and he did not see why he should let them get away with it. He seemed not to have noticed the odds stacked against him as more and more men gathered around him.

With an impatient exclamation Finn leapt out, grabbed Jack's arm and more or less pulled him back into the car. Startled and protesting, Jack would have fought him off had he not glimpsed fleetingly the faces of Emma and Bernard, distorted with fear.

'Have you paid?' Emma shrieked.

'No. I won't pay those prices...'

With a hysterical gesture she pulled what money she had out of her faded tapestry purse and flung it out of the window.

'Drive!' Finn commanded.

'For God's sake, drive!' Bernard yelped.

'Why...? What...?'

But even Jack could now see that something was seriously wrong. Some of the men were leaning down and peering into the car, their faces angry. Emma and Bernard had closed the windows and locked the doors, but they were banging on the glass and on the bonnet of the car.

'Drive!' screamed Emma. And this time Jack started up and screeched away.

Looking back they saw a man just emerging from the door of the office, holding up what looked like a gun. Whether it was a gun or not, and whether he would have fired it at them or not, they did not know. They were already well away, the car enveloped in a cloud of dust.

'Good grief! I thought the Egyptians enjoyed bargaining!' Jack said, half laughing when they were sure they were clear.

'It was not about the price of petrol, mate,' Finn told him, and held up the picture of the massacred tourists. Jack sobered up immediately.

'Christ! Was that today? Where?'

'It's today's paper. But we can't read where it happened.'

'We must go home,' Bernard gibbered. 'We must go tonight!'

'Hang on!' Jack said. 'We need to find out more about it first.'

'What more do we need to know? They're murdering tourists! We are tourists!'

'But we knew such attacks happened before we came. They're trying to cripple Egypt's economy so that the government will fall and they can take over. We're not in a tourist area. They target the big money making areas. And now more than ever there will be security forces around. We'll probably be safer tomorrow than we were today.'

116

'We didn't appear to be very safe at that petrol station,' Emma said. She shuddered.

'You should have paid them what they asked, mate,' Finn said, with a slightly amused twist to his mouth.

'I would have, if I'd known what you were screaming about!'

'Its no laughing matter,' Bernard snapped irritably. 'We are likely to be in serious danger and I, for one, believe we should go back to England.'

'Oh no! We can't go now!' Tears filled Emma's eyes. 'We've come so far!'

'We'll talk about it when we get back to the hotel,' Jack said sensibly. 'Let's not go off half cock.'

The image reminded them of the gun they had seen, and there was silence in the car as Jack broke all speed limits to Minya.

Mary, watching the television news in England, was horrified to see pictures of the tourist massacre in Egypt. Graphic images of bleeding Americans, and interviews with hysterical survivors trying to face the cameras and describe how they felt having just been dragged out of a bus and shot, occupied the screen for some minutes. Five had been killed, twelve wounded and the rest were in a state of shock. There were the usual heads of state condemning terrorism, but all Mary could think of was that her premonition of danger had been justified. It is true she had not thought of terrorists, but more of nebulous dark forces. But dark forces need people through whom to work. Surely there was no readier a channel than those with huge grievances and an unshakeable conviction that they were in the right and God was on their side?

When she had turned off the television and was thinking about all she had just seen and heard, she saw the parallels with the situation in the ancient world Emma and her companions were investigating. Was that not also the result of religious conflict – both sides convinced they knew the will of the gods, and both sides with power to gain or lose?

When Jack and Emma and the rest arrived back at the hotel in Minya that night, they were exhausted. Without even checking for messages they went straight upstairs.

After showering and changing their dusty clothes, they had arranged to meet for a discussion in Jack and Emma's room. None of them felt like dinner, so during the evening they finished off the bread, fruit and nuts left over from their picnic lunch.

Bernard was calmer, but still sure they should abandon the project and return to England. If they were not all prepared to go, he said, he would go alone. Finn, used to terrorism in Northern Ireland, had already adjusted to the news, and argued that they could just as easily be killed in a car crash as by Islamic Jihad.

'More easily, in fact,' he added.

'I narrowly escaped an IRA bomb in London a few years ago,' Jack confessed. 'Finn's right. Danger is everywhere. One can't avoid it.'

'But surely it is better to watch an angry tiger from outside the cage, than to get in there with him?' Bernard argued. 'There are acceptable and unavoidable dangers, and there are unacceptable and avoidable ones.'

'I think we should all stay. I feel there is a real possibility that we are on the right track,' Emma said. 'What happened in those two tombs, Mery-Re's and Pentu's, was really something! Spirits were actually speaking to us. And if you leave Bernard, how will we be able to communicate with them?'

Even Jack, who had been so reluctant to come in the first place, was eager to stay. He felt to go home with nothing resolved would doom him to a lifetime of disturbing dreams and weird occurrences. He wanted the matter settled once and for all.

In the end they persuaded Bernard to stay. Perhaps his pleasure at being made to feel he was indispensable sidetracked his fear. Before this he had felt he was an outsider in the group, barely tolerated by Jack, and ignored by Finn. Only Emma had shown him any consideration and kindness, but even that was only in a sort of scatty, absent-minded way.

The next day they planned to explore the southern tombs at Amarna. As they were about to leave the dining room after breakfast a new guest arrived, and Emma was astonished to recognize him as the man in the light dove grey suit who had come to her rescue in the Cairo souk.

Their eyes met as they passed close by, he coming in, she leaving. He showed no sign of surprise at seeing her, though there was no doubt he recognized her. She walked past without greeting him. But once out in the reception hall she grabbed Jack's arm and babbled, 'that was the man, you remember? The man in Cairo!'

'What man?' he asked, genuinely puzzled.

'You know, the one who saved me from being raped!' Emma insisted.

'Oh, I didn't get a look at him. Are you sure.'

'Isn't it extraordinary that he should turn up here?'

'Not really. This is his country.'

'But *here*! Where *we* are! I must go back. I never thanked him.'

'Don't make a fool of yourself, Emma. Even if he is the one, he won't remember you.'

'He recognized me. I swear he did!'

'He's probably groaning even now to think how unkind Fate is to make his path cross with yours again!' He was holding her arm, laughing at her, and pulling her towards the outer door.

She struggled free and turned to go back.

'I have to say something to him. He might not be here when we return.' And she rushed to the dining room, hair, beads and string bags flying, coming to a halt beside his table.

'Excuse me,' she said to the back of his head.

He turned and looked up at her and then rose to his feet. He had a handsome face, with dark and penetrating eyes. 'Like Horus!' she thought. But those far seeing eyes were showing a trace of tolerant amusement now. 'Jack is right,' she thought. 'I am making a fool of myself.' But nevertheless she was determined to say what she had come to say.

'You probably don't remember me,' she burst out, 'but you saved me from a very unpleasant situation in Cairo, and I didn't have the opportunity to thank you.'

There! She had said it.

'I do remember you,' he said quietly. 'I trust you have had no more problems.'

'Oh, no! I mean, yes, but not the same ones...'

'Is there anything I can do to help?'

'No. No. I'm sorry. I didn't mean to interrupt your breakfast. I just saw you... and... and I was so sorry I hadn't been able to thank you properly last time...'

He bowed.

'Would you care to join me for breakfast?'

'Oh no!' She found herself blushing with embarrassment. 'My friends are waiting. I just wanted to...'

Completely flustered, she fled. He stood, gazing after her until she was through the door, and then sat down and resumed his breakfast. The other guests, who had been watching the scene with close attention, relaxed and resumed their own conversations.

At el-Till, where they bought the tickets for the day, they were not at all comforted to see that the representatives of the Security Forces provided for their safety were two youths, still subject to acne, armed with the most fearsome weapons they had ever seen.

The ticket officer tried to persuade them not to go so far afield, claiming that the southern tombs were at least fourteen kilometres away, and the route over some rough ground. But when they assured him they had every intention of going, and pointed out their perfectly adequate vehicle, he insisted they take one of the boy soldiers with them. They tried to refuse, but it was clear he would not let them go without 'protection'. He reminded them about the terrorists attack the day before, and made it clear he deeply regretted it.

'These people don't speak for Egypt,' he said. 'Egypt wants to be friendly with all peoples.'

'We know,' Jack said sympathetically. 'Egypt is a great country. I am sure we will have no trouble at the southern tombs. All who visit here have to come past you, and I'm sure you would be able to spot terrorists at once.'

The man shook his head gloomily. 'They look like ordinary people,' he said. 'It is impossible to tell. My government wants you to have protection and has provided this armed soldier for you.'

Jack looked at the boy. He was the sort who was not above playing 'bang-bang you're dead' with his mates. But now he had real lethal weapons to play with. Jack was more nervous of the protection than of the dangers from which he was supposed to be protected.

But there was no getting around it. They had to take the boy. How could they explain that the only dangers they might be likely to encounter in the tombs were impervious to guns and armaments, and certainly to untried and callow youths.

It was a nuisance to have him with them, but at least he did not speak English, so would not be able to understand their conversations. Quite how he would react to the meditations and the spirit voices they hoped to hear would only be shown later.

There were several tombs of court officials scattered among the low hills to the south east of the city. According to Bernard's guidebook, and Ben Wilson's journal, the most interesting by far had to be the tomb of Ay. He was the old man who had succeeded the boy Tutankhamun briefly before General Horemheb had finally, and openly, taken over the country. Ay had been an important man at the court of three pharaohs. He was Vizier to Amenhotep III, Akhenaten and Tutankhamun. There was some evidence that he was the father of Nefertiti. He and his wife were sometimes described as 'Divine Father and Mother', which suggested they were parents of royalty.

The tomb itself had been dug and designed during the golden days of the sacred city, and contained some of the best-preserved and most interesting images of Akhetaten. But Ay himself was never buried there, for when Tutankhamun succeeded and the court moved, and later he himself became king, he had another tomb prepared for him in the Valley of the Kings at Thebes. At the time this tomb at Amarna was dug, no one had any idea that he would be pharaoh one day. There were scenes of his receiving honours from the hands of Akhenaten and Nefertiti at the Window of Appearances. There were pictures of his other daughter, Nefertiti's sister, Mutnodjmet, and her two famous dwarfs, before she married Horemheb. And on one wall there was an almost complete text of Akhenaten's Hymn to the Aten, with Ay and his wife making obeisance.

Emma's little group walked among the columns and spent a long time looking at all there was to see. They gained a real impression of the living city from the images of dancers and harp players, servants cooking and sweeping, scribes writing, guards guarding ... and one woman having her hair styled. They could almost hear the sounds of the busy street life, the shouts of vendors, the lascivious remarks of soldiers aimed at girls gathered at street corners...

'Shall we meditate?' Jack asked. 'Ay must have known Akhenaten from birth to death.'

'I don't feel he is here,' Emma said musingly. 'Besides, if he became pharaoh after Tutankhamun when the whole country had returned to the old religion, he would be unlikely to be a member of the Shemsu Benu.'

They moved on, passing their boy protector who was smoking and chatting to the caretaker of the tombs. He followed them at once to the tomb of Mahu, Akhenaten's Chief of Police, and insisted on coming inside with them.

Consequently they gained nothing, and passed on, disappointed, to the tomb of Tutu, the Foreign Minister.

This time the soldier preferred to sit outside and doze in the shade of a thorn bush.

Emma recommended meditation, and they were soon sitting in a circle, holding hands, and bracing themselves for whatever might occur.

Tutu was a long time coming, but when he did he complained bitterly that none of it had been his fault and he did not deserve what had happened to him. Bernard's voice came out thin and whining, and his face began to resemble that of a small, mean man.

'What did they do to you? Emma asked. 'What was it that you did not deserve?'

Bernard gave a long, rasping sigh.

'I was accused,' he said, *'of letting the Empire slip away. It was*

not my fault. The King would not act. I advised him well... but he would not listen... They threw me in prison... they tortured me...'

'Did they assassinate the King?' Jack asked, leaning forward, for all the world as though he was talking to a real person standing before him in the room.

The man laughed, a dry, crackling, hopeless sound. '*Yes. Yes. They punished him too – but he deserved it. He ruined the country. Not I. Not I!*'

'Who? Who assassinated him?' Jack asked, holding his breath for the answer.

But Bernard started screaming and shielding his face with his arms as though to avoid blows.

Emma and Finn leapt up and Emma started beating the air, demanding that the spirit vacate Bernard's body immediately, while Finn put his arm around Bernard's shoulders and shouted commands loudly into his ear. Jack did nothing but mutter 'Oh my God! O my God!'

Their boy protector, alerted by the shouting, had rushed in and was waving his gun at random into the chamber.

At last Bernard managed to break free and, pale and shaken, was embraced by both Emma and Finn.

Jack tried to reassure the guard, and at the same time shoo him away. He would never forget the boy's expression of total disbelief that anyone could behave as they were behaving. No doubt it was being confirmed for him that all Westerners were mad and ought to be eliminated.

When they were outside they saw him describing what he had seen to the caretaker. There was much waving of arms and mock screaming. The caretaker looked at them with deep suspicion and told them in broken English that as they did not know how to behave with proper respect in the tombs of his ancestors, they would have to leave at once.

For a moment they stood before him like naughty school children caught in an unforgivable act behind the cycle sheds, and then Jack, at least, rallied. They had not yet seen the tomb of Ramose, Steward to Amenhotep III, and who thus must have known Akhenaten since childhood. Jack was particularly anxious to communicate with him, as his name had featured in one of his dreams.

He brought out his wallet, and after a somewhat embarrassing and acrimonious wrangle, persuaded the caretaker to let them see one more tomb, and with more judicious bribery convinced the soldier to stay outside when they entered.

The others watched in admiration as Jack deftly negotiated the deal, and complied at once when he indicated imperiously that they should follow him.

At the entrance to the tomb of Ramose, Bernard refused to go in, and after some hesitation and consultation, they unanimously agreed that he had put himself in enough danger for one day, and they would let him give this one a miss.

'We won't meditate,' Emma assured the others. 'We'll just look.'

Jack was disappointed – torn between his unease at what they had been doing, and a desire to obtain first hand information from the spirits of Akhetaten. 'A shame,' he thought, 'we've made this decision just when we may have had a chance to contact a man I am positive *was* a member of the Shemsu Benu.'

Inside the tomb chamber they explored silently for a while, and then each sat down on the floor as far away as they could from each other. There would be no linking of energy this time. Jack rested his back against the cold wall and tried to recall the details of the dream in which he had been at a meeting of the Shemsu Benu with Setepenra the youngest daughter of Akhenaten, then a mature, beautiful woman. Ramose had been present, he was sure. An old man, but very much alive.

He glanced across at Emma. She believed she was a reincarnation of Setepenra. If she was – who was he? Who was Finn? Was it as neat and easy as that – actors donning different costumes to play different roles?

The place was very quiet. Very, very quiet.

Jack shut his eyes. If he could sleep now perhaps the dream would come again. Involuntarily he was turning Akhenaten's seal ring round and round on his finger.

Perhaps this was a better way of doing it, he thought. Invoking no one. Channelling no one. But allowing oneself to drift into an atmosphere pregnant with possibilities. But how could one distinguish between imagination and true information when images started to form?

At last he felt himself floating between realities. He seemed to be following an old man into a cleft in the mountains. He could feel the heat of the rock on one side of him reflecting from the sun's rays. He could see a hawk high above them, poised apparently motionless, in a sky of cobalt blue. The old man was wiry and agile. He himself was out of breath trying to keep pace with him.

When he was almost dropping with exhaustion they came out into the open and found the desert stretching before them to the horizon. The old man pointed and Jack's eyes followed. It was no longer a featureless plain as it had been in the dreams of the tomb guardian.

There were rocks and hillocks among the sand.

'Ramose,' he said, 'is that...?'

But Ramose was gone. The desert and the mountains were gone. The Horus hawk was gone. He was in a tomb with his back to the wall and Emma sitting across from him, rocking backwards and forwards with her head in her hands. Finn had left.

'Emma,' he spoke her name softly. And then, as he came across the chamber to her and took her in his arms, he whispered: 'Setepenra'. She clung to him and he held her close. Was she the one whom he loved more than life itself, the daughter of his King, or was she the woman he was growing to love more than any other – Emma, the infuriating, the fascinating, the beautiful?

A shadow darkened the doorway.

Finn was silhouetted there.

'I think we ought to leave. The soldier is getting restless and muttering what sounds like threats. I don't think Bernard can keep him occupied much longer.'

He made no comment, seeing them there, locked together.

Emma lifted her head from Jack's shoulder.

'We must go,' she whispered, and there was a deep sadness in her voice... the sadness of many lifetimes.

12

Locked out

When the group burst into the hotel lobby that evening, tired and dusty as usual, with plenty to talk and think about, they noticed the desk clerk, usually so disinterested and noncommittal, animated almost to the point of excitement.

Jack, seeing how his eyes lit up with anticipation when he saw them, asked if there were any messages.

This time he got more than a grumpy 'no'.

There were several messages, all from England, from a Mrs Brown, 'and...' he was beginning to say, when Jack interrupted him to call out to the others that there were at last messages from Mary. They crowded round at once, grabbing the slips of paper from the desk clerk's hand and reading them eagerly. All were written in a spidery, almost illegible hand and badly mis-spelt. There was nothing there but a request that they phone her and, on the last one, the one word 'Elat' spelled out in big letters.

'Elat?' Jack said, puzzled. 'Isn't Elat in Israel – not Egypt?'

'I think he means Eliot,' a voice drawled behind them. They swung round to see Eliot, dressed elegantly in lightweight trousers and jacket, looking as casual and handsome as ever, showing no signs that he had been dashing across the world from Chile, to England, to Egypt, driven by a sudden and overwhelming passion.

'Eliot!' shrieked Emma, and rushed towards him. Then she stopped. There was something in his eyes, a wariness, a suspicion. She remembered the charade she and Jack were playing. Other guests who knew them as man and wife were passing through the lobby. She was almost sure she caught a glimpse of the man in the grey suit.

Jack stepped forward.

'Eliot, old man,' he said. 'What brings you here? I thought you were on the other side of the world.'

'The other side of the world is not so far these days,' Eliot said. 'I missed Emma,' he added, looking at her closely.

She flushed scarlet, and lowered her eyes.

Eliot? Here? He did not fit into this part of her life. It was as though a character from a romantic novel had crossed over into a powerful fantasy novel, and totally confused the story line for the reader. Why could he not have stayed in his separate compartment?

Bernard was unaware of the nature of the emotional bombshell the stranger had dropped, and excused himself. He had had yet another exhausting day and was longing for a shower and a rest.

Eliot ignored Finn, though they had met before. His attention, like a cat watching a mouse, was focussed on Emma and Jack. Finn shrugged and followed Bernard up the stairs.

With bright, expectant eyes the desk clerk looked from Eliot to Emma and back again. He knew something was definitely going on, though he did not know what. He had had his suspicions from the start that Jack and Emma were not married. And here now was this other man who had made very pointed and exhaustive enquiries about them, including their sleeping arrangements, when he arrived. He must be the real husband. The clerk was hoping for bloodshed. Nothing much ever seemed to happen in this quiet town, but now it just might, and in his very own hotel!

Jack suggested Emma and Eliot should go out to dinner alone and, while she went to the room to change, the two men sauntered out into the garden and there, smoking, Jack explained the situation. It was already dark, and the streetlights did not penetrate so far into the garden. The two friends could not see the expressions in each other's eyes. Perhaps it was as well, for, though Jack's explanation was delivered in a calm, orderly fashion, his heart was crying out for the loss of the woman he now desired. Eliot himself apparently accepted his friend's words without reservation, but in his eyes there was an acknowledgement that he was poised over a precipice, and nothing could ever be taken for granted again.

Emma did not return to Jack's room that night.

He lay awake watching the stars wheel slowly across the sky through the window, and when at last first light came creeping over the mountains, she returned, tiptoeing like a thief across the carpet.

He pretended to be asleep, but heard every sound she made in the bathroom, and then as she flung back the bed clothes and flopped wearily into bed.

They were both woken by Finn banging on the door. The sun was high already, and Bernard and he were impatient to get going.

Breakfast was over when Jack and Emma came down, but neither were hungry. Bernard, Finn and Eliot were waiting at the car.

Jack looked at Eliot in surprise.

'Don't tell me you're coming to brave the ghosts with us?' he laughed.

'I wouldn't miss it for the world!'

'A pity,' Jack thought. This was to be an important day. They were finally going to visit the Royal tomb. Eliot, with his supercilious attitude to Emma's beliefs (and now, he had to admit, to his own) might spoil everything.

He glanced at Emma, but her face was turned away.

Bernard climbed into the front seat beside Jack, and Emma sat in the back between Finn and Eliot. They drove the now familiar route to Amarna.

The Royal Tomb is not generally open to the public, but permission can be obtained if one follows the right procedure. Jack sent Eliot to negotiate, just in case their disgrace of the day before in the southern tombs had been reported back at el-Till. Having arrived late, there were more tourists at the site than usual and luckily the boy soldiers were fully occupied elsewhere.

They slipped away fairly easily and drove across the plain to the great valley that led to Akhenaten's tomb. Walking the final distance they found Eliot's presence a definite annoyance. He chatted about his sister's wedding in Chile when they would all have liked to be silent. Jack and Finn moved swiftly ahead, while Bernard lagged behind, leaving Emma to take the brunt of the distraction.

As far as Eliot was concerned, the evening with Emma had gone well. He told her that Jack had explained the circumstance of the shared room satisfactorily. During a good dinner at a hotel that served alcohol, he listened patiently to her wild tales of what had been happening in Egypt, and only once interrupted to assure her that what she had described could not possibly have happened. When she was mellow with wine he told her he intended to marry her and, because he had not anticipated any disagreement, he interpreted her shocked silence as a positive response.

They had ended up in bed together, Emma too confused and uncertain to protest – but during the lovemaking she had found her attention wandering.

She told him firmly that she was not going back to England until they had done what they had come to do, and she was not making any decisions about her future until she was back in England. There was nothing for it, Eliot decided, but to humour her and stay with her the couple more days he estimated it would take for them to discover how ridiculous this so called 'mission' was. He agreed, for appearances sake, that she should continue to pass as 'Mrs Wilson'.

As they walked the Royal processional route to the tomb, Emma's thoughts were in turmoil. She had been happy with Eliot in England, and was still not sure she did not want to be with him forever. But she wished he had not come. She wished him anywhere but in this special place with her. She tried to shut out the sound of his voice but could not.

At last, exasperated, she stopped and, red in the face, demanded that he be quiet.

'You don't understand,' she said. 'We have to be quiet to get the atmosphere of such a place.'

'Sorry,' he said at once. 'Not another word!' And he made a gesture with his hand to show his lips were sealed. His eyes sparkled with amusement at her earnestness.

They set off again, and he did not speak. But after a while she stopped again.

'I cannot do this,' she burst out.

'What?'

'I cannot walk with you.'

'But I'm not doing anything.'

'You are!' she almost screamed. 'You are emanating criticism, judgement, disbelief!'

'I'm not, I assure you. I'm just walking here beside you. If I am emanating anything it is heat. The only thing I am feeling is hot!'

'There!' she cried accusingly. 'The only thing you are feeling is hot? You might as well not be here. This is a terrible mistake. You should never have come.'

'Emma...'

'No. I won't go another step with you. Either you go back to the car and wait for us, or...'

'Or what?'

'It is over between us!' He was about to argue, when Bernard puffed up to join them. 'I say – its a long way. Are we nearly there?'

'No!' she snapped.

'Its too hot for such an expedition. Would you not agree?' Eliot spoke directly to Bernard, hoping for an ally. 'Why don't we all go back to the car?'

Bernard looked as though he might give in.

'No!' Emma said desperately. 'Bernard and I are going on. We've come so far we can't turn back now. But you – you, Eliot, are not part of this chosen group of Companions of the Benu. You can go back. In fact you must go back!'

Eliot thought about it. He did not want to lose Emma, and he certainly did not want to see a smelly old tomb. He would wait in the car.

Bernard looked after his retreating form longingly, but Emma was already pulling on his arm, encouraging him to move forward.

Without Eliot's immediate presence Emma was no better off. Her mind was seething with resentment, and she found herself going over and over what she wanted to say to him, leaving no room for experiencing the magic of the great Royal route. She barely noticed the rocky cliffs, the straggling thorn bushes, some with their roots grotesquely exposed like dangerous snakes, and the tough little herbs struggling for existence in the inhospitable environment, but scenting the air nonetheless. She did not notice the Horus hawk hovering over the wadi, high in the sky, as though watching to see what the Companions would do. No water had rushed down this dry riverbed for centuries, and recently something of a road had been built for tourists, though lately very few tourists had come.

Today they had the place to themselves. It would have been ideal for 'tuning in' Emma thought bitterly, if only Eliot had not insisted on coming with them. She tried to remember the relationship they had had in England. It must have been good or she would not have stayed. Yet now she could scarcely recall what they said or did together. She knew he had never shared her beliefs, but somehow that had not mattered. She realised her 'beliefs' then had all been part of an elaborate game she played with herself, a speculation she enjoyed. But now the game had become serious. Either what she believed was true, or it was not. If it was not, she might as well go back to Eliot and live a life of comfort and pleasure. But if it was, there would be no going back. She would be committed to a complete change of life. Partly this prospect frightened her, but partly it excited and stimulated her. To live, interacting, not only with the people that you saw around you, but with an invisible world as well. She remembered Mary's image of the sky at night. The most ancient experiences of the world would be hers as surely as what happened to her today. How much richer the texture of life would be. Even the most devastating personal disappointment or suffering would be seen from the perspective of a wider dramatic context, and thus, meaningful, would be less painful.

Akhenaten's tomb was down a smaller, side wadi. Finn and Jack were seated on rocks when Emma, closely followed by Bernard, arrived.

'How considerate,' Emma thought. 'They've waited for us.'

But she soon noticed the gate was locked and there was no sign of the caretaker.

'Where's Eliot?' Jack asked at once.

'I sent him back to wait in the car,' Emma said. 'He was spoiling everything.'

'He arranged this. There is supposed to be a caretaker here with a key.'

'Oh no!' Emma flung herself down on the ground, hot, tired and now bitterly disappointed and angry. It was almost as though Eliot was deliberately trying to sabotage their mission.

'Perhaps he has the key himself,' Bernard suggested.

'They'd never let tourists loose in this place without a guard. No, he has screwed it up in some way!' And Jack uttered a few expressive expletives. 'One of us will have to go back and find out what has happened.'

But it was already past noon and they would have very little time left by the time they had gone back to el-Till and returned again.

For a while they sat against the rock wall, trying to get what little shade there was, and fumed.

Finn seemed to be the only one not agitated by the situation. He took out his flute and started to play. At first the sound irritated them, but then it began to soothe. Even the insects creaking and chirruping from the cracks in the rocks, and under the dry bushes, seemed to pause to listen. A bright eyed bird, a wagtail, came amazingly close and stood watching them warily, but curiously.

They sat still, held in the web of music, in this remote and potent place. Even Emma forgot Eliot.

Finn's melody was from an Irish mourning song, and Emma found such sorrow welling up in her heart she could hardly contain it. She was mourning for her father, whose tomb this was, and for her sister, Maketaten, who had died young in the Golden City, and been buried here while the family were still in power. Tears began to gather in her eyes, and she remembered her own baby sister in England, who had died before her first birthday, and her grandfather ... Mortality seemed so inexorable and cruel. If there was nothing after death, there was nothing worth having before!

And then she felt a hand on her shoulder, comforting her. She thought it was Jack and felt love for him welling up. He understood. Unlike Eliot, he did not mock her.

But Jack was sitting opposite her, and she realised that he could not possibly have his hand on her shoulder. Finn? But Finn was too far away and both his hands were occupied with the flute. Bernard? She did not want it to be Bernard, but found that he too was not within reach of her. Startled, she looked round to see who it was. Surely Eliot had not dared return after the ultimatum she had given him?

There was no one there and the sensation of a hand on her shoulder had gone.

Her heart lifted. 'Someone is here!' she thought. 'Someone we can't see.'

She wanted to alert the others, but was afraid the delicate thread that held the being in contact with her would be severed. She whispered, so softly it was hardly distinguishable from breathing.

'Who are you?'

She felt a dreadful loneliness and pain in her own heart, but she knew this time it was from his.

'*I am no one,*' he sighed.

'That cannot be,' she whispered. 'What is your name?'

'*I have no name. I was buried for the King, and my name was taken from me.*'

'Buried for the King? What do you mean?'

'*I was the slave chosen to carry the King's name in death, so that neither of us would live.*'

Emma's heart was beating so fast she was afraid the noise of it would drown out his voice, so small, so faint, that it was hardly sound at all.

'You mean – the King was not buried in this tomb? You were.'

'*Ay ... ay...*'

'Can I do something to help you? Perhaps if I find the King and...'

'*He has no name. I have no name. We can never be called into life again.*'

'But he has a name. We are seeking him. We use his name every day.'

She felt the thread weakening between them – the silence returning.

'And you?' she cried. 'What is the name you had as a child? You must remember. Surely you must remember what your mother called you?'

But he was gone.

Finn had put down his flute.

'Go on playing!' she urged him, wild eyed. 'Don't stop. Don't stop. The thing you were playing before. Play it again.'

Finn looked surprised but started to play the same tune again. Jack and Bernard were looking at her with intense interest, realising something was happening to her which they could not see.

But though Finn played the tune again and again, the nameless slave did not return, and Emma, shaking with disappointment, told them what she had experienced.

'Perhaps if we link and meditate as we did before, we could call him back,' Jack suggested. 'Perhaps Bernard could channel him.'

She did not want Bernard mouthing his words. She wanted to return to that wonderful feeling of union with him, that private and secret communication – but she finally had to admit that to link and meditate and let Bernard try to channel was all that was left to them.

But Bernard stayed mute. Nothing came though. And Emma had to accept that the being was gone.

'We'll have to come back tomorrow to get into the tomb,' Jack said. 'Perhaps he'll speak again then.'

Bernard, upset that another member of the party was starting to channel, started back towards the car without them. What if Emma could do what he had been doing for them? Would he then be redundant? Part of him wanted to be shot of the whole thing and return to the comforts of England, but his curiosity and his pride were roused. He wanted to play an important role in the unfolding drama.

Jack and Emma walked side by side, and were aware of no one else.

'If he mentions Eliot, I'll scream,' she thought.

'What if,' he said, seriously, tentatively, staring at his feet treading the sandy floor of the road. 'What if the ancient Egyptians were not so crazy when they believed that the pharaohs went to the stars after death. If, as we now know, there are billions of stars like our sun in millions of galaxies, and even the most cautious scientists agree that there must be planets circling some of those suns, and some of those planets might have intelligent life...'

'What if,' cried Emma, totally in tune with his thought. 'What if reincarnation is a reality, and our spirits after death, released from the physical body, are not limited to this planet but can live again on other worlds in other galaxies?'

'And when we doubt that aliens can come from other galaxies because of the distance, they are already here, not landing in space ships, but being reincarnated as ourselves!'

They both stopped walking, tremendously excited by the thought. Memories of ancient Egyptian texts Mary had shown them came to mind.

'...grasp the King by his hand and take the King to the Sky...'

'I make the sunshine to flourish on the sides of the ladder which is made to mount up to the Unwearying stars...'

'You shall ascend to the sky, you shall traverse the firmament, you shall associate with stars...'

132

'O Imperishable stars, hide me among you...'

'You shall separate head from head when approaching the Milky Way...'

'For I am he who crosses the sky ... limitless eternity is given to me, for I am he who inherited eternity, to whom everlasting is given...'

'The doors of the sky are opened for me...'

'How could so many people have missed the true implications of these words? How could so many people have believed we are limited to this world, even in an afterlife?'

'The ancient Egyptian obsession with astronomy in their tombs has a very practical application. The images are guiding the spirit to its next physical home.'

'And the ducts and vents that have been found in the Great Pyramid pointing at Sirius and Orion's belt are not just symbolic pathways, but actual pathways to the pharaoh's next destination!'

Jack and Emma looked at each other and suddenly, laughing, hugged each other.

'Someone once said to me that reincarnation could not be true because the population of the world was growing so rapidly it couldn't consist of just recycled people! Clever ancient Egyptians to know the truth of it, all those centuries ago.'

'They knew the world we live in is not only extended into the invisible realms Mary talks about, but is linked in literal and physical reality to all those millions of other worlds out there.' He waved his arm at the vast and apparently empty sky above them. For a moment he seemed to glimpse the galaxies, the stars, the planets, the nebulae, the quarks, the pulsars, the white dwarves and black holes and all the rest about which astronomers knew so little, but talked about so glibly. His little life opened up into a magnificent progress of unimaginable variety and interest across the great tracts of Space and Time. He was living a multi-dimensional life in a multi-dimensional universe.

'We must free Akhenaten to continue his journey – and that nameless slave too!' Emma cried. 'What a cruel thing to do – to limit a being to only one planet!'

Finn was approaching and they could feel themselves being pulled apart by forces beyond themselves. Soon they would rejoin Eliot, and the great certainty they had shared would weaken and dissipate.

When Mary and Emma spoke on the phone at last, Mary told Emma how uneasy she now felt about the whole expedition, and had been trying to recall them.

'The fact that you could not get hold of us must mean something. Perhaps we're not meant to abandon the project?'

'Or perhaps someone wants you to go on, in order to harm you?'

'Oh dear,' Emma said. 'Is nothing ever clear cut and simple?'

Mary laughed. 'Only on television and in the tabloids,' she said. 'Never in real life!'

The phone line crackled alarmingly.

'Have you seen Eliot?'

'Yes. He wants me to go back to England and marry him.'

'And will you?'

'I don't know. I certainly don't want to go now. What do you think? Have you a good reason for asking us to come back? We've been making contact with other members of the Shemsu Benu ... and I've been remembering all sorts of things. I can't believe we're supposed to just walk away now.'

Mary was silent. Fear was not always a reason to retreat. Was she being nervous unnecessarily?

'I don't know what to say. Think hard about it. Discuss it with the others. Make a communal decision. But whatever you decide, remember to be careful, and never take a step without asking for protection from the Spirits of Light.'

'Of course.'

The line finally gave out and Emma put the phone down. She stood for a few moments staring at it, and then went to join the others. She did not tell them what Mary had said. She gave them no chance to make a communal decision. She was determined to go on and find her father, Akhenaten, and release him from this planet.

The next day the group set off for the Royal tomb again. This time Jack was to make sure the caretaker would be there with the key.

Eliot had been persuaded not to come, and was left still asleep when they drove off. Emma and Jack felt a twinge of guilt at their relief, but soon forgot it in the adventures of the day.

They were told they would have to wait a while for the caretaker to arrive at the tomb, so they decided to visit Nefertiti's northern palace which they had missed before... It was set where the plain narrowed and the cliffs almost came down to the water's edge. Emma was ecstatic, claiming to remember the garden, the pool, the cool northern breezes blowing through the spacious rooms. Remnants of mosaic floor were left, but most of the beautiful painted floor of marsh scenes that had once been there with wildfowl, fish and flowers, was now in the Cairo museum. They had marvelled at it only a few days before, but now the memory of it evoked the palace as it had once been – elegant, colourful, and luxurious. Bernard's guidebook described toilets and bathrooms, and oil lamps that made night almost as light as day. Emma 'remembered' playing in the garden at night with lamps hanging from the trees; the moon, stars, and lamps all reflected in the still lotus pool while her mother's guests, seated beside scented bushes, discussed things she did not understand. Sometimes gusts of grown-up laughter would float across the pool to where the children played, and they themselves would laugh, not wanting to be left out. She had always been happy there – even when, occasionally, she heard her mother and her father arguing.

Jack stood aside and watched her. Her very movements were that of a child. She was running, pretending to smell flowers that were no longer there, pointing out things only she could see. Her face was beautiful, lit with joy. He longed to take her in his arms.

13

The Royal Tomb

By the time the group arrived at the Royal Tomb the caretaker was there, chatting to two men – not tourists, but Egyptians. They stared at the new arrivals in none too friendly a manner. The caretaker stood up at once and moved towards the rusty iron gate with a large bunch of keys jangling in his hand.

Emma looked back uneasily at the two left squatting beside the guard's stool. She felt she had seen them before, but could not remember where.

At last the tomb was open and they climbed down the steps into the long sloping corridor cut deep into the rock. They had been warned that most of what had been there in ancient times had been smashed by enemies of the King, or removed by tomb robbers later. Archaeologists were still sifting through the dust and measuring things, but very little of interest was left for the ordinary tourist to see. Ben Wilson's journal waxed almost lyrical about the wall images in one of the side tombs off the main corridor, and Emma went straight there. This was where Maketaten, Akhenaten's second daughter, had been interred when her father was still alive, and the scenes of mourning on the walls were still powerfully moving.

The three men, after a brief look around, moved on, leaving Emma alone in the chamber, sensing that she would want a moment of privacy with her lost 'sister'.

Jack was curious to see how Finn, in particular, reacted to the main burial chamber even though it was probable the King himself had never been interred there. If Emma's 'ghost' was to be believed, a slave had lain in the magnificent royal coffin. While it was being built the King must have expected to lie there among magical pictures of his dream city, not suspecting the events that turned his fortunes around and caused him to be cast out into the desert.

It was always difficult to fathom what Finn was thinking or feeling. His lean, dark face was not expressive, and unlike every other Irishman Jack had encountered, he was not prone to blarney.

'Perhaps he learned to keep his own counsel when he had those experiences as a child that made him believe he was Akhenaten,' Jack thought. 'He knew he would be ridiculed, so he became secretive. And now it is a habit.'

The burial chamber, entered by a further set of steps at the end of the corridor, was as bare as they expected. Their torchlight in this dim place revealed the usual well cut into the floor. There were a few scanty remains of reliefs left on the plastered walls... One side of the pillared hall had been extended, and, according to Bernard's guidebook, this was where the royal sarcophagus had lain, contained, it was believed, in a series of golden shrines like those in Tutankhamun's tomb.

Jack watched Finn closely. Did he feel anything? Was he a reincarnation of Akhenaten as he said he was? Or was he someone, as Pentu had indicated, antagonistic towards Akhenaten? Was he the shadowy assassin Jack had 'seen' above the boundary stele? Or was he just another person deluded into believing he was someone important from the past, in order to make up for his inadequacy in the present?

Jack began to feel agitated. Whatever the truth of it, they had all been drawn here by strange and compelling events in their present lives. He felt he had endured a long preparation for a difficult test, and here he was, on the brink of it, and he did not know what it would be. He remembered those dreams he had had at school and university, dreams of entering an examination hall, sitting down, laying his pens neatly in front of him, looking confidently at the outer covering of the examination paper, and then, when the examiner gave the signal to start, opening it and reading the questions inscribed therein, not one of which he could understand, let alone answer.

Just at that moment he thought he heard a muffled scream from somewhere back along the corridor.

Emma!

He turned and ran up the coffin ramp between the steps. Bernard and Finn, who had heard nothing, looked after him in surprise, but did not follow.

He was filled with dread. Whether what he had heard was Emma screaming or not, he was acutely aware of danger. Something was threatening them.

There was no sign of her in the main corridor, so he turned into the side chamber where he had left her.

Bursting into Maketaten's burial chamber he saw Emma struggling on the floor with one of the men who had been waiting outside. The other was leaning back against the wall watching.

Shouting, Jack rushed in and grabbed the shoulders of the man on top of Emma.

He managed to lever him up sufficiently for her to roll out from under him. But the other was attacking from behind.

Jack, now being pounded from both sides, nevertheless put up a good fight. Emma rushed to the door and yelled for Bernard and Finn before she turned back to help him.

This time the others heard her and came running.

Halfway back along the corridor they could hear the sounds of fighting, the shouting and thudding, and Emma's shrieks as she beat on the struggling bodies of the strangers as best she could.

As Finn reached the entrance to the side chamber, he was in time to see one man pulling out an ugly looking knife and plunging it towards Jack, who was being held down by the other man. Emma flung herself bodily forward against the side of the man holding the knife, and managed to push him off balance, so that he missed Jack's heart and struck his arm instead.

Finn plunged in at once, but Bernard ran for the exit shouting for the caretaker. There was no sign of him, and Bernard, distraught, ran back towards the fight. He had never fought anyone in his life and he was terrified at the thought. But he knew he had to do something.

What he did was not very heroic, but actually helped a great deal. He shone the beam of his powerful torch full into the eyes of the man who looked as though he was getting the better of Jack, while Finn and Emma together felled the other one.

His attacker momentary blinded, Jack took the chance he needed to turn the tables, and before long both of the attackers were beaten to the ground.

'Let's go! Let's get out of here!' Emma cried. 'Before they recover.'

Jack's arm was bleeding profusely, and Finn had a gash on the side of his neck.

'We must get help. Come. Come quickly!'

They did not need a second telling. Shaken and confused they stumbled out into the sunlight and back along the path to the car. Emma, looking back over her shoulder more than once, established that they were not being followed.

'What happened to the caretaker?' Jack muttered.

'I tried to find him,' Bernard whimpered. 'They probably paid him to get lost.'

But then they saw him, sauntering back along the main wadi towards them, as though he did not have a care in the world.

When he was within earshot they all shouted at him at once. He looked genuinely shocked when he at last grasped what had happened. He insisted on coming back with them to alert the police, no doubt, Jack thought, because he wanted to put his story to the police before he was maligned by the foreigners.

'Who are those men? You seemed friendly enough with them when we arrived.'

'I never see them before. They came to see the tomb. I speak friendly to anyone who comes to see my tomb.'

'They were locals, not tourists.'

'Not local here. From Mallawi, they said.'

'That's where I've seen them before!' Emma cried. 'At the petrol station. Remember?'

The others did not, but were prepared to take her word for it.

'Why would people who live in Mallawi want to see your tomb?' Finn continued the interrogation. He was holding a handkerchief against his neck.

Jack was staggering. Emma's arm was around his waist, trying to support him. Her scarf was wrapped tightly around his upper arm to stop the flow of blood.

At last they reached the car. There had been no sign of the two villains following. It would be too much to hope that they would just lie there until the police picked them up, but none of the group, nor the official caretaker, could face attempting to detain them themselves.

Bernard drove like a lunatic over the bumpy terrain back to el-Till.

There their story was told to a gathering crowd.

While the local policeman and several sturdy men set off in an aged jeep for the tomb where the outrage had occurred, a local villager hurried them to his home. First aid was given immediately and soothing hot drinks were passed around. The family was horrified at what had befallen 'the English', and the villager's wife and daughters made a fuss of Emma. The man of the house did not want to listen to this part of the story, but was all attention when the knife was mentioned, and the fact that the men had come from Mallawi.

'There are bad people in Mallawi,' he said. 'The assassin of President Sadat lived there, and many still do not want us to be friendly with your country. Many young men are in prison. Mallawi and Assyut are not good towns for tourists.'

'We were told that, and that is why we decided to stay at Minya, though it is further from Amarna.'

'Much better. Minya much better.'

'We heard about the shooting of the people on the tourist bus...'

The man shook his head gravely. 'A bad business. They drive the

139

tourists away and we will all starve. They do not think, the tourists are our food.'

'They will not drive us away. We are staying,' Emma said firmly, warmed and comforted by the care and sympathy of the villagers, and already coming to terms somewhat with the violence to which she had been subjected.

'I say,' demurred Bernard, who had decided he could not wait to get out of Egypt after all. 'We need to talk about this.'

'We will talk,' Jack assured him soothingly, but to the anxious villagers he said, 'Don't worry. Tourists will not stop coming.'

At this point Bernard reminded him that it was almost time for the last ferry.

The villager at once suggested they spend the night in his home.

'You must wait until the police get back,' he said.

'We have made a statement,' Bernard said. 'We must get our friends to hospital. In Minya we will go to the police station and give more statements if necessary.'

Reluctantly the villagers let them go. They were seen off at the ferry by what seemed to be the whole village, for once not trying to sell them anything, but pressing gifts of food and drink on them for the journey, and tearful apologies for what had occurred to visitors in their country.

Bernard was not a good driver, but Jack and Finn were too weak to drive, and Emma had only recently learned and was not confident enough in this alien country where the local drivers seemed to have no sense of danger. She had heard that a visit to Mecca qualifies one to be a driver. No lessons needed. The euphoria she had experienced in the comforting presence of the friendly villages was wearing off, and she was beginning to shake uncontrollably. Bernard was not the only one desperate to get home.

But if Minya was home, they were destined not to get there as soon as they hoped.

On the outskirts of Mallawi the car broke down.

'I don't believe it!' muttered Jack. The night was not far off, and this was the town against which they had been warned. Bernard became almost hysterical.

'What can we do? What can we do?'

Jack ordered him to look under the bonnet, but Bernard was no mechanic and did not know what he was looking for. With great difficulty Jack struggled out of the car and peered into the engine. His eyes were blurry and he could see little. Finn was lying on the back seat looking as though he was about to faint. Emma was distraught. It could not be worse! The two wounded men were

140

looking as though they could not hold out until Minya hospital even if the car had not broken down. Bernard was incapable of making a decision.

She must. She must make the decision. She must be the strong one.

There was not much traffic on the road, but occasionally cars passed. She told Jack to get back into the car, leaving the hood up so it was clear that they had broken down, and ordered Bernard to stop a passing car.

'What if it's a terrorist?' he wailed.

'Not all Egyptians are terrorists. In fact very few are. It's our only chance. Mallawi must have a hospital. We must get these two there or they might die.'

'I can't...'

'You can!' she shouted at him. 'Do you want to stay here and be murdered or not? At least at the hospital we'll be safe.'

This decided him, and he put out his hand tentatively as the next car approached. It drove past – not even slowing down. A second passed ... Throwing all caution to the winds Bernard stood out in the road and with sudden determination flagged down the next vehicle – an open truck full of chickens. The driver stopped. He spoke no English, but he could see they were in trouble. He peered into their engine and shook his head as though he knew exactly what was wrong and that he would not be able to fix it. He was about to return to his truck when Emma leapt out of the car and, shouting and gesticulating, tried to make him understand they needed a lift. She repeated the word 'hospital' over and over again. He did not understand until Bernard, waving his precious guidebook, started shouting 'mustashfa' at the top of his voice. The driver of the truck nodded at last and indicated that they should climb into his truck.

It was not easy. Jack and Finn squeezed in beside the driver, and Emma and Bernard, the able bodied, climbed in among the chickens. Agitated and squawking at their unexpected companions, the chickens let the two know they were not welcome. Bernard, who had a tendency to asthma, began to wheeze as chicken feather dust flew around him in a foggy haze at every bump and pothole over which the unsprung vehicle lurched.

Emma was past bursting into tears. It was a nightmare.

At the hospital they had more problems with language. They were kept in an over-crowded reception area for ages, trying to explain that they needed immediate attention. Jack gave Emma their insurance documents to show, but this did not seem to be enough. Something else was expected. Emma produced some money, but this seemed only to cause offence. She was at her wit's end, when one of the other casualties waiting patiently for treatment showed some knowledge of English, and told them they had to pay a deposit of several hundred Egyptian pounds before they would be admitted.

'Insurance companies do not pay for a long time,' he explained.

Emma looked at the other patients and could not believe that between them they could raise even half that amount. Their interpreter, seeing her expression explained softly that it was only because they were foreigners. There were other arrangements for locals.

Emma slapped the money down on the reception desk, pooled from all their wallets, and glared challengingly at the clerk. This was a mistake. Her aggression brought her nothing but more delays, as the clerk deliberately took his time writing out every unnecessary detail. He also put their passports out of reach and would not give them back.

Their interpreter shrugged when Emma looked in alarm at him.

'You will get them back at the end,' he said.

'But only two of us need treatment. Why does he keep all four?'

The interpreter shook his head. This was evidently beyond even his understanding.

They were told to sit down and wait. The atmosphere in the room was surly and hostile. No doubt there was little love for foreigners here, and the highhanded way they had pushed ahead and demanded treatment for themselves before those who had been waiting for hours did nothing to lessen the prejudice.

'I'm going to phone Eliot,' Emma announced desperately. But that entailed going back to the desk and negotiating with the unfriendly receptionist again. She asked the English speaker if he would help once more, and after some hesitation, he did so. He spoke rapidly to the man at the desk. The initial response did not look hopeful, but after more persuasion she was allowed to use the phone – but at a price. After this they had no cash left and she could not imagine how they would be able to rescue their car and get back to Minya. What if there were more charges at the hospital? The receptionist had already refused to accept their Visa cards and travellers cheques.

The English speaker helped her get through to their hotel at Minya and she waited in agony while the desk clerk there went off to find Eliot.

At last she heard his voice and the relief of it made her burst into tears. Eliot had already been worrying about them as they had not returned at the time they had said they would, and when he heard her sobbing at the other end of the line his fears were confirmed. Somehow she managed to convey that they were in hospital at Mallawi and needed help before the phone went dead. The English speaker had gone back to his seat and the receptionist was not about to let her make another call without paying. She retreated to where her group were seated and flung herself against Jack, sobbing uncontrollably. Every single person in the room stared at them. With his good arm he held her against him, his face grey with pain.

It seemed a long time before a doctor saw to them, disinfected the wounds, administered a few stitches and told them they were very lucky as the wounds were not deep.

'Allah has been good to you!'

'Yes. Very good!' thought Jack bitterly.

'But,' the doctor continued, 'it would be best you go to Assyut hospital in case there is infection.' Meanwhile Emma and Bernard had been left in the reception area, sitting in gloomy silence close together.

Suddenly there was a flurry at the entrance and Eliot strode in imperiously.

Both Emma and Bernard cried out in relief, and she rushed into his arms.

'What's going on here?' he demanded. 'Are you all right? What's happened?'

'Jack and Finn have been stabbed, and Emma was raped!' Bernard burst out.

'Our car broke down and we've no money!' Emma added hysterically.

'Raped?' Eliot almost shouted.

'Bernard exaggerates!' She said hastily, trying to calm him down. 'I'm all right. Jack saved me. He and Finn...'

'Where are they?'

'The doctor is seeing them at last. Oh Eliot we've used up all our money and they won't take visa cards and they've taken our passports...'

'Have you been to the police?'

'We reported it at Amarna. But we've had no time to go to a proper police station. We were trying to get back to Minya when our car broke down ... a chicken lorry brought us here...'

'And I have asthma!' Bernard added, determined his suffering should not be left out of the catalogue of misfortunes.

'Who has your passports?' Clearly Eliot had taken charge, and would stand no nonsense.

When Emma indicated their passports were with the receptionist, Eliot strode towards the desk.

And then, to Emma and Bernard's astonishment, he demanded them back in perfect Arabic. Emma had known that Eliot's father had been a diplomat and the family had lived abroad for most of Eliot's childhood, but she had no idea he could speak Arabic. Their angels had not deserted them after all!

Although he was arrogant and aggressive, the receptionist must have been impressed by his command of the language for he handed over Bernard's and Emma's passports, but insisted on keeping the others until their treatment was completed.

Just at that moment, the doctor came back into the room, followed by a very sorry looking Jack and Finn.

'Transfer these patients to Assyut hospital,' he instructed.

Eliot turned his attention to the doctor at once and spoke volubly in Arabic. The doctor replied in Arabic. The others tried to understand what was being said by following their body language and eye expressions, but could not.

The upshot of it was that Eliot was going to drive them back to Minya in the taxi he had waiting outside, and they would not go to Assyut, but to a hospital in Minya. They had to sign a waiver that they would not sue if they got an infection, as they were refusing to obey the doctor's instructions.

Only then were the passports and the relevant insurance documents returned to them.

On the long uncomfortable drive back to Minya, Eliot berated them for their irresponsibility in going about unprotected it a notorious terrorist area.

'It wasn't terrorists that attacked us, but ordinary randy criminals!' Emma protested. 'The local villagers at el-Till could not have been more kind and supportive.'

'Nevertheless, political and religious intolerance and unrest in this part of the country leads people to treat foreigners as fair game for any kind of humiliation.'

And then, as though they had not had enough horrors for the day, Eliot described in detail the massacre of tourists a few days before and the horrific scenes at Hatshepsut's temple at Deir el Bahri in November 1997.

'These people have no concept of other people's right to live or have their own opinion. If you don't do what they want you to do, they swot you like flies. I believe the six men who slaughtered those fifty-nine tourists at Deir el Bahri were laughing and joking when they left. And they had not only shot innocent people, but also taken delight in hacking them to death. Can you imagine the mentality of a man who hacks small children to death! They pretend it is for a religious reason! But that's just a cover for the blood lust of insanity. The same thing happened during the Middle Ages when so-called Christians tortured and burned anyone who did not toe the line.'

'I wonder if it was the same in Akhenaten's time?' Jack pondered. Emma believed that everything that happened had a meaningful connection with everything else. If she was right it would not be inconceivable that 'the Universe' (as she called her God) was pointing out to them how nothing had changed since Akhenaten's time. Religious dogmatism and intolerance was still a force for evil in the world, offering an excuse for murder and sadism to unstable and underdeveloped psyches.

Did Akhenaten himself smash images and destroy temples? Did he order the killing of those who worshiped in them? He hoped the Sun King had not achieved *his* revolution by bloody and violent means. But what did they know of him? What did they *really* know of him?

When they reached Minya, Jack and Finn refused to go to the hospital. They were desperate to get to bed, and argued that they would have another long wait in a reception area, a filling in of forms, and a paying of deposits...

'We've got antibiotics and painkillers to take. We've been stitched and patched and disinfected. What more would they do tonight?'

They promised to go to the hospital in the morning, but now insisted on going to bed.

Emma too was at the end of her tether. She felt like a rag doll with half its stuffing removed. Eliot almost carried her into the hotel, so heavily was she leaning on him. She had been brave and decisive and got them home, and now she could do no more.

The desk clerk noted that she had changed 'husbands', and handed Eliot his key with a knowing look.

The group limped upstairs and fell into bed.

Eliot covered Emma with a sheet and then, because she was shivering in spite of the warm night, he added the only light blanket provided, and his own jacket. He sat down on the side of the bed and stroked her hair until, at last, she fell asleep, her cheeks pale and tear stained.

Then he left her and went downstairs. He was sorely in need of a drink. He knew that the hotel did not serve alcohol even to foreigners, but he knew one that did. He had spent a long time there in the middle of the day, drinking and wondering what to do about Emma.

He was about to cross the reception lobby to the main outside door when a man in a pale grey suit, who had been speaking to the desk clerk, came across and addressed him in impeccable English.

'Mr Ravenscroft, I believe you are with the party that has just had a spot of trouble at Amarna?' he said.

Eliot looked at him in disbelief.

'A spot of trouble?' he repeated sarcastically.

'I apologise. I chose my words carelessly. "A great deal of trouble" at Tell el-Amarna,' he revised.

'Yes,' said Eliot guardedly. What now? The press?

'I wonder if we could talk? In private,' he added as Eliot seemed doubtful.

'I really don't feel like talking right now,' he said. 'Perhaps tomorrow.'

'Perhaps I should introduce myself. I am Ahmed Hassan – of the Tourist Police,' he added, after a slight pause.

Eliot's interest was at once engaged. This was someone with whom he wanted to talk.

In fact he had been considering that after the much needed whiskey he might contact the police.

They sat on the veranda of the hotel, gazing out into the shadowy garden, the Nile lying dark and secretive beyond, as it had lain for many thousands of years while civilisations rose and fell.

'Have you heard if they have caught the men at Amarna?' was Eliot's first question.

'I'm afraid not. There was no one in the tomb when the local police arrived.'

'But surely they must have looked around. I believe they were quite badly hurt. They couldn't have gone far.'

'There was a thorough search, but no one was found. My colleague there was surprised the party did not wait to make a proper report.'

'As I understand it they gave their names and addresses and passport numbers – but two of my friends were severely wounded and needed to get to a hospital. Mrs Wilson needed attention too. She was very shaken by what happened.'

'I hear from the hospital at Mallawi that the wounds were not deep, but they were advised to go to the much better equipped hospital at Assyut, in case there was infection. I believe Mrs Wilson did not ask for examination or treatment at Mallawi.'

So he had been in touch with the hospital at Mallawi already. It was comforting to know someone was on the case – but why the remarks about Emma? Were they going to deny she had been attacked because she did not complain enough?

'She was anxious about her friends, and the hospital kept them waiting for a long time. In fact,' said Eliot, 'my friends were most disappointed by their treatment there and will no doubt be lodging a complaint.'

Hassan shrugged.

'If Mrs Wilson had been examined by a doctor we, the police, would have more to go on.'

'You mean you won't just take her word for it?'

Hassan smiled at Eliot as though the two of them were men of the world, and understood that young girls sometimes exaggerated.

Eliot was angry. 'Two Englishmen have been seriously assaulted in trying to save an Englishwoman from abuse – and you doubt...'

'I do not doubt, Mr Ravenscroft. But the courts might, given the fact that she made no complaint at the hospital, and that the irregularities of her relationships with men have been noted at this hotel.'

Eliot looked at him in astonishment. He could see how the whole thing could be twisted. Was this Hassan on their side or not?

'We will do everything in our power to catch the two men, Mr Ravenscroft. You can be sure of that. We do not condone our visitors being harassed.'

'Raped and attacked,' Eliot amended.

'Of course,' Hassan agreed smoothly.

'My friends believe they saw the two men previously at a petrol station in Mallawi, and that these men were part of a group threatening them.'

'I would be grateful if your friends would come to the police station first thing in the morning and give us a statement and a description.'

'They will be there. They were too exhausted tonight even to report to the hospital.'

'We have two good hospitals in Minya. They would be well advised to see a doctor at one of them first thing tomorrow.'

'Before or after reporting to the police?'

Hassan looked at Eliot, and a slight shadow crossed his face. He could sense the hostility in the question.

'Perhaps you had better have your whiskey, Mr Ravenscroft, and we will continue our talk when you are less stressed.'

Eliot nodded, and Ahmed Hassan stood up to leave.

Just as he was about to step down on to the path that led to the Corniche road, he turned and looked at Eliot.

'Where did your friends leave their hired car, by the way?'

'Somewhere on the outskirts of Mallawi. Still on the main highway. If I give you the registration number now could you...'

'I know the registration number, and I have already made enquiries. But I am afraid there is no car of that description abandoned on the highway, or on any of the roads leading towards the hospital.'

'Perhaps your people missed it.'

'Locals do not have such cars,' Hassan said. 'If it was still on the road we would have found it.'

'Perhaps you should check at that garage where they saw the two men.'

'I should like to Mr Ravenscroft, but I have not been given its address.'

Eliot sighed. He knew it would be sensible to get onto the problem right away, but that would entail waking his friends. The hire car must have been insured against theft. At any rate, they would not need it any more, as he was going to make sure they returned to England just as soon as they had reported to the hospital and the police station.

Maybe before, he thought. Why wait around for slow wheels to turn here? If they did not press charges they could be home in twenty-four hours.

To Hassan he said: 'In the morning.'

Hassan nodded.

'In the morning. Allah is good,' he said.

That night in England Mary Brown had a very disturbing dream. She tossed and turned as the little group were pursued down dark and narrow tunnels by demonic figures, some in the shape of ancient Egyptian gods. She recognized Anubis of the Necropolis, Set, the storm god, and Amun himself as a ram with an enormous phallus. Other figures less clearly defined, wielding knives, sprang up ahead of them screaming imprecations, ripping at their clothes. The dream ended as a great flock of carrion birds came swooping down on them in the confined space...

Shuddering, she sat up.

All was not well. She could feel it.

What had happened? Something terrible.

She held her friends in her heart with passionate intensity as she prayed for them to be helped, guided and protected.

14

Finn's Encounter

Emma, on waking, found herself in bed with Eliot, still in the dusty bloodstained T-shirt of the day before. She crept out and had a shower before he woke, and made her way back to Jack's room for clean clothes.

There she found Jack already awake, taking his anti-biotic capsules with tonic water. He was not as pale as he had been the night before, and seemed, on the whole, to be on the mend. As the doctor had said: God had been good to him, and the cut was not deep. He knew, if Emma had not intervened, he might be dead, or at least lying much more seriously injured in Assyut hospital.

The two confronted each other awkwardly.

'You look like hell,' he said.

'So do you,' she replied. They both laughed nervously.

'I need my clothes,' she said.

'Right,' he said.

But neither moved.

Their eyes locked – speaking volumes.

At last Jack lowered his gaze and moved aside for her to get to the wardrobe. He sat back on the edge of the bed while she went into the shower room to change. She emerged in an ankle length blue cotton frock, her hair still damp from the shower, but already drying and curling up in the warm Egyptian air. He took a deep breath.

She pottered about the room, moving things, tidying things up. He watched her every move. She avoided meeting his eyes again.

'What are we going to do?' He spoke at last.

Whether she understood what he was really asking, or not, he could not tell.

Her answer could have been to a different question.

'Eliot wants us to give up and go back to England. But I don't want to. What about you?'

'You mean abandon the project and go back with nothing accomplished?'

'Yes.'

'I don't want to.'

Her face lit up. 'Even if the others decide to go – *we* could stay?'

At this moment the door burst open and Eliot stormed in.

'So there you are!' he snapped. 'I was worried.'

'Where else would I be?' Emma countered. 'But in my husband's room!' Eliot did not appreciate the joke.

'This has gone far enough. Everyone in the hotel is talking. Even the desk clerk has noticed...'

Emma looked shocked.

Jack swore. 'You have to be kidding!' he added.

'No. I was speaking to a policeman last night and that is exactly what he said.'

'We had it all sewn up till you came,' Jack complained bitterly. 'No one questioned that she was not Mrs Wilson until she started flitting between rooms at night.'

'I asked you to look after her,' Eliot said, equally bitterly. 'Not to go to bed with her.'

'He didn't! We didn't!' Emma cried. 'He hasn't touched me! You can see the beds are quite separate. I insisted on that.'

'Oh, yes,' Eliot sneered. 'I might believe you, but who else would?'

'Its nobody else's business!'

'Until you start lodging a complaint with the police about rape!'

'Well, if that's how they are going to react, I'll not press charges. I don't need the humiliation of injustice on top of that horrible experience. You should be thanking Jack for getting there before it went too far. He nearly lost his life defending me.'

'I might still if this goes septic,' Jack muttered.

'All right. All right. I *am* grateful. I think none of us should press charges, but just get out of this damn country as soon as we can, this very morning! The whole escapade has been ridiculous and you're lucky to have got away as lightly as you have.'

'Oh, yes. God is good,' Jack said sarcastically.

'Think about it!' Eliot snapped. 'Think about what happened to those tourists at Deir el Bahri.'

'We're not leaving,' Emma said firmly. 'Not until we have lifted the curse on Akhenaten.'

'There *is* no curse!' Eliot shouted in exasperation. 'There *is* no ghost of Akhenaten!'

But now he had gone too far and it seemed as though a barrier had come down, and from that moment on, as far as she was concerned, it was over between them.

'That is what we are trying to establish,' Jack said diplomatically. 'Whether there is, or not.'

'You're as mad as she is,' said Eliot irritably. 'We're leaving! I'll make all the arrangements,' And he strode angrily out of the room.

Emma looked at Jack, shocked.

'Do you doubt that he exists? That the curse exists?'

Jack took a moment or two before he replied.

'Emma, we can't know for sure. How can we know for sure?'

'But so much has happened! Mary's experiences. Your dreams. My memories of Setepenra. And all the channelling Bernard has done! We have nearly been killed in Akhenaten's tomb by the dark forces trying to prevent us going any further!'

He seemed uneasy.

'That probably had nothing to do with it...'

'How can you say that? In *Akhenaten's* tomb! It *must* have been connected.'

'But...'

From pleading, she became angry.

'You are as bad as Eliot! I'm going to stay, and I'm going to find him and lift the curse by myself if necessary!'

'Don't be crazy. You can't possibly stay here by yourself. Look what has already happened to you with all of us around you!'

'I don't care. I'm staying.'

He sighed. 'Okay. I'll stay with you.'

'Don't bother, if you don't believe!'

'I didn't say I didn't believe. Its just that one cannot be certain.'

'Its the same thing.'

'No. It is not. Certainty makes for closed minds; uncertainty leaves the mind open for the possibility of change if new information is received.'

'Oh, you always have all the answers!'

He laughed. 'That's just what I'm saying I don't have.'

She sulked for a while, and then decided to let it go.

'You will stay with me?'

'Of course.'

When they came down to breakfast Jack found a letter addressed to him at the reception desk. He was just about to open it when Finn appeared in a high state of agitation.

'He lost his flute at the tomb,' Bernard, following on behind, explained. 'He's thinking of going back for it. I've been telling him it would be long gone. He'd be better to tell the police.'

'I'll tell the police. But if they don't produce it I'll go back for it. I might have dropped it in the main chamber before I ran. The police would only have looked in the place where Emma was attacked.'

'Oh, Finn, I'm so sorry,' Emma said.

'Where's Eliot?' asked Jack.

'He has gone to arrange our trip home,' Bernard said with satisfaction.

'We're not going home,' Emma announced.

Bernard looked startled. 'Eliot said it was all agreed.'

'Jack and I aren't going,' she said firmly. 'We told him. How about you, Finn?'

'I'm not going without my flute,' Finn said.

'I'm going,' Bernard said vehemently. 'I've had enough. Next time we might be killed. I can't believe you want to stay after all that has happened!'

Eliot came striding back into the dining room looking pleased with himself.

'There's a flight we can take at 6pm,' he said. 'That'll give us just enough time to get back to Cairo.'

'Eliot, I told you I will not go home yet.'

'Come Emma, don't be silly. You know you can't stay by yourself, and the others want to go.'

'Jack and Finn don't,' Emma said triumphantly, looking at Jack to confirm what she said. But Jack was not listening. He was reading the document in his hand with growing excitement.

'I say,' he cried. 'We've got the permit for the Eastern Desert!'

He had claimed to be a writer working on a book about his great-grandfather, the famous archaeologist Ben Wilson, and needing to retrace Ben Wilson's steps from his journal. He knew permits were difficult to get and he had half expected his application would fail. But here it was, just at the very moment they needed it.

Emma was delighted. 'You see! We are meant to go on. We *can't* go back now!'

Eliot's face was black as thunder, Bernard's alarmed and frightened. Finn did not seem to have taken it in. He was still worrying about his flute.

Eliot decided to play his trump card.

'Even Mary Brown says she regrets that she sent you, and was trying to make you come back when I saw her.'

'She did not *send* us,' Emma declared hotly. 'We chose to come.'

'But you wouldn't have come if she had not encouraged you.'

'Who knows if we would? Jack was having dreams. Finn was having convictions. Bernard was channelling. We were meant to come, and we came.'

'And what made *you* come, Emma? You were having no dreams, convictions, channelling!'

'How do you know? We never talked about anything important to me!'

The others were beginning to look uncomfortable as this seemed to be turning into a domestic row between two lovers or, as Jack hoped, ex-lovers.

Finn stood up. 'I'm going to find out about my flute.'

'And how are you going to do that without knowing a word of the language,' Eliot rounded on him. 'You people think you can swan around the world without any preparation, language or knowledge of local conditions. You are like infants playing on a motorway.'

'We've managed so far!' Emma snapped.

'Right. I had forgotten how well you'd been managing!' Eliot said sarcastically.

She turned scarlet and if he had been nearer, instead of across the table from her, she would have hit him.

'Let's stop this row right now,' Jack said. 'We've got the permit for the desert. We need to make plans. Not least among them to retrieve our car. '

'Oh, that!' Eliot said scornfully. 'It's been stolen.'

They looked shocked.

'How do you know?'

'An official from the Tourist Police was here last night. They'd been looking for it.'

Bernard stood up. This was the last straw. 'I'm going to pack,' he announced.

No one argued. No one even seemed to notice as he left the room and, muttering to himself, went upstairs. He would be on that 6pm flight whether the others were or not.

The others went to the police station and there, to Emma's surprise, was her friend in the dove grey suit, evidently a high-ranking plain-clothes member of the Tourist Police. He took them into an inner office at once and made them comfortable. Finn asked about his flute, and a message was sent immediately to check with the el-Till security.

Eliot asked if their car had been found. It had not, and there was a great deal of paperwork to fill in regarding the hire and the theft. While Jack was working on this the message came back for Finn that his flute had not been found. His face darkened with disappointment, and Emma took his arm sympathetically.

'Never mind, Finn,' she whispered. 'I'm sure we'll all help you to get another.'

He turned pain-filled eyes towards her, but it was as though he did not see her. Then, shaking himself loose from her caring hand, he turned and walked out of the room.

Ahmed Hassan was now wanting to concentrate on the details of the attack, and the mysterious men spotted at the petrol station in Mallawi, but Eliot, before either Jack or Emma could say a word, declared that they had decided not to press charges or pursue the matter further.

Hassan looked up from the papers on his desk, and raised an eyebrow.

'Is this true?' he asked Emma.

She looked uncertainly at Jack.

Jack was annoyed Eliot had answered for them, but had decided independently not to press charges, because he thought doing so would delay their journey to the Eastern Desert.

But there was some explaining to do. Although Hassan did not argue, he asked some very searching questions. So searching indeed that Jack and Emma nearly revealed the real reason for their trip. But in the end it was the explanation Jack had given on his application form that was given and, apparently, accepted.

'It is not a complete lie,' Jack thought. 'We *are* retracing Ben Wilson's steps, and I may write a book, or at least an article, about it. If we survive!' A small unwelcome voice added its warning.

Eliot remained silent through the interrogation, no doubt wishing not to appear involved in such totally idiotic plans as the real ones. At least the writing of a book was a respectable one.

But when everything was settled, he tried once again to persuade them to abandon the project and go home.

Jack was immovable on this.

Ahmed Hassan watched with hawkish eyes and a slight smile as the two friends argued, getting more and more heated. Emma, seeing that soon they might lose control and say things best left unsaid, began to fuss about Jack going to the hospital. Hassan rose, and ushered them out of the office.

'Mrs Wilson is offering good advice,' he said, smiling at her. 'You will not be able to go anywhere if the wound is not healing properly.'

Once outside they noticed that Finn was no longer with them, so they returned to the hotel. There Eliot established from the desk clerk that Finn had ordered a taxi, and set off for Amarna.

'He's going in search of his flute,' Emma cried. 'He shouldn't go alone. We must follow him.'

'No,' Jack said. 'He's capable of looking after himself. If we want to set off for the desert tomorrow, we've a lot to do today.'

Bernard emerged, already packed and dressed for England, sweating in his Harris tweed jacket.

When Emma grasped that there would be no changing his mind, she made him promise he would go straight to Mary, and tell her every detail of what had occurred, and ask for her prayers for what was still to come.

Bernard expected Eliot to be going back with him, but Eliot, glowering and tight-lipped, declared that if Emma was going to be such an idiot the least he could do was to stay and try to protect her.

'I don't need your protection!' she snapped.

'I entrusted your safety to Jack and look what a botched job he made of it!'

'Can't you see – I don't *want* you to come!' she cried.

'That is irrelevant. I am coming. You don't know what you want at the moment, and you are at your most confused and vulnerable. God knows what crazy situation you'll get yourself into.'

'Come back with me, Emma,' Bernard pleaded. 'Let Jack and Finn sort it all out. I'm sure Mary would be glad if you came back.'

Even Jack let her down. 'Perhaps they're right, Emma. You do seem to get into more scrapes than the rest of us. Finn and I are quite capable of finishing the mission.'

'No. No. No!' she shouted. 'I *will* go. I *have* to go. Don't you see how involved I am? I have to see it through.'

'All right. All right,' Jack said. 'Don't lose it, Emma. Of course you can come if it means that much to you.'

'If Emma goes into the desert, I go,' Eliot said. His voice was hard as iron. There was no arguing with it.

Emma looked at him in despair. She had won the right to stay, but would it be worth it if Eliot was there too?

'You must realise, Eliot, that when this is over I will not be coming back to you. It is over between us.'

Jack could feel the tension between the two as the silence lengthened.

Eliot broke it at last. 'We shall see. But whatever – I would not be able to sleep if I were not there seeing that you are all right. If nothing else, my knowledge of Arabic will be of help. You don't expect anyone you're likely to meet in the desert will be able to speak English, do you?'

'But you will disrupt everything we do with mockery.'

'I promise I won't. I will be there purely as guardian and translator. You can do whatever idiotic thing you choose...'

155

'You see!'

'Sorry. Whatever you choose,' he corrected himself. 'I will not interfere.'

Emma knew that it was no good continuing to argue. He would accompany them.

Bernard left with many an anxious and regretful backward glance. If Eliot was with them perhaps they would be safer, but his bags and his psyche was already turned towards England. They would face the last stage of the mission without him. He knew he was letting them down... but...

The visit to the hospital confirmed that Jack's wound was clean and on the mend.

He spent the rest of the day with Eliot trying to organize the hiring of a jeep and a tent. He had to admit Eliot's command of Arabic was invaluable. It was eventually from a farmer, and not an official car hire company, that they took possession of a battered vehicle that had seen service in the Six Days War, but whose engine was still in good condition. They paid a hefty deposit, and set off back to the hotel in some excitement. The two friends had avoided the subjects of Emma and Akhenaten the whole time they were together, and had concentrated entirely on the practicalities of the matter in hand.

Emma, meanwhile, had been buying provisions.

It was well past noon when Finn eventually arrived at the Royal Tomb at Amarna. He had had difficulty in arranging for the caretaker to open just for him, but a judicious bribe using the last of his rapidly dwindling funds did the trick. He was soon walking down the corridor towards the furthest chamber.

He stopped first at Maketaten's burial chamber, though he had no great hopes that the flute would be there. It must have been thoroughly searched for clues of their attackers.

Finding nothing, he walked on.

There in the columned hall of the actual chamber he searched desperately, trying to recall his every movement, and how and where he could have dropped his precious flute. It had been with him all his life, and was intimately bound up with every significant emotion and event. It was part of himself, and no other flute bought in a shop could ever take its place. He had inherited it from his grandfather who had died when Finn was an infant, and who, he always believed, would have understood him better than anyone else.

Gradually, hope of finding it faded. There was no sign of it.

He sat down on the dusty floor, cross-legged, with his face in his hands in despair.

It seemed to him his identity had deserted him. Who was he without his flute? The playing of it was the one thing that made other people sit up and take notice of him. When he was sad it comforted him. When he was happy it celebrated with him. Women who had ignored him flocked around him when they heard him play. The threads of music his breath drew from it were woven inextricably into his being. He could not imagine life without it.

For the first time he had to face despair in silence. Nothing stirred. No sound from the living world penetrated so deep underground. He would have been glad of a rat scuttering, or a beetle gnawing wood...

The weight of his dark mood eventually silenced even his own thoughts, and he sat, empty of everything, unaware of the time passing.

But then the whispering began.

He tried to catch the words, but it was wordless whispering without variation in tone.

He strained every fibre to understand. He was used to catching meaning in wordless music, and now used this skill to interpret the paradox of the soundless sounds he was experiencing.

It seemed to him he was hearing accusations, condemnations, pleadings...

'Who is there?' he breathed.

'*You should know,*' he seemed to hear. '*You put me here.*'

He lifted his head from his hands and peered around him. The torch he had brought with him and left lying on the floor at his side only partially illuminated the chamber. Beyond its beam the rest was in shadow. He could see no one, but he knew someone was there.

'I don't understand.'

'*Do you come back to mock me – or to release me?*'

'I don't know what you mean. Release you? Are you Akhenaten?'

Finn had found the journey to Egypt very disturbing. He had not been able to talk about his feelings with the others. Their insistence that Akhenaten remained in ghostly form wandering the desert instead of being reincarnated in him had undermined the foundation on which he had built his personality. And now his flute had deserted him!

As he spoke these words he felt a surge of suffering. Was it his own? Or that of his invisible companion? Or both?

'I have not come to mock you,' he said. 'Tell me what I must do.'

For a while the pain was too much, and the wordless words swirled around in the darkness making no sense.

Then: '*You were the one who buried me here. You, a traitor to your King. You took my name and left me without a means to leave this dark place. You who know my name, give it back to me.*'

Finn staggered and leant against the cold wall, his hands covering his face. He was not Akhenaten as he had always believed, but one of those who had conspired to destroy him!

Naked without his flute to hide behind, he knew the disembodied voice was speaking the truth. The being must be the nameless slave Emma had encountered. But that *he* was the one who had condemned both slave and king to everlasting exile was a devastating thought. How could he have been so mistaken? He thought back over all those years he had dressed up as Akhenaten – all those books he had read about him, all those times he had declaimed Akhenaten's Hymn to the Sun Disk in the cold rains of the Burren in Galway. Was it guilt, rather than love, that had driven him to identify with the king? And was he being drawn back now to set right what he had done?

He fell to his knees.

'Forgive me,' he pleaded. 'I did not know what I was doing. But now I understand. Tell me what I must do to set you free.'

'*Give me back my name and the funeral rites you denied me.*'

Thoughts were hammering in Finn's head now. Bits and pieces of memory from those ancient Egyptian days...

It seemed to him he saw the slave being put to death on his own instructions... He saw the embalmers dragging out his entrails and putting them in royal canopic jars. He saw himself walking in the royal funeral procession, and felt his own unholy glee thinking how he, and his fellow conspirators, had fooled so many people...

He had no vision of what happened to Akhenaten. Perhaps others had carried out that part of the plot.

He heard the slave's voice crying in the tomb. '*What is my name? Give me a burial with my rightful name.*'

He tried to think. He strained and struggled. He would give anything now to undo what he had done. But the name eluded him.

He, who had felt desperate loneliness at the loss of his flute, knew now what it must feel like to be adrift in the universe without an identity. He sorrowed that he had put other beings through this torture.

The slave he had chosen was one of his own personal servants. He saw him standing with a tall water jar on his shoulder, silhouetted against the sunlight of the doorway.

'Come, Ba-ben, serve my guests.' He had said the name because it was a familiar name, without hesitation.

'Ba-ben!' he shouted now in the icy tomb. 'That was your name.'

'*Ba-ben! That was my name!*' came back the words, rejoicing.

It seemed to Finn that he remembered the ancient rituals and performed them now, using the name he had remembered. He intoned the spells to preserve the man's soul throughout the journey into the afterlife, to guide his steps through the dangers and tests he would have to endure before he reached Amenti.

When he was finished Finn lay on the floor, spent, exhausted, but more or less at peace.

15

The Book of Thoth

It was late that evening when Finn returned to the hotel. They were all worried about him and Eliot had just suggested they alert the Tourist Police when Finn limped up the path to the hotel.

'Finn!' cried Emma, rushing at him. She was about to hug him when she noticed how ill he looked.

'Oh my God! Finn?' Jack said and took his arm, leading him to a chair. He fell into it as though he could not have taken another step.

'We must get a doctor!' Eliot said, while Emma at once produced some homeopathic pills she claimed were good for shock.

'How do you feel, old man? Do you need a doctor?' Jack asked.

Finn shook his head wearily, but Emma turned to Eliot, and Eliot, without a word, went to consult the desk clerk. When he returned he said authoritatively that he would take Finn to the casualty department of the hospital.

Finn shook his head again.

'I can't afford...' he murmured.

'Nonsense,' said Jack and Emma together, each taking an arm and helping him towards the door.

Eliot drove the jeep round to the front, and they helped him in.

'It's his neck,' said Emma. 'He should never have gone off like that.'

'Perhaps now you'll listen to me,' said Eliot, 'that Finn and Jack at least are not fit to travel into the desert. Imagine if this sort of thing had happened when you were in a remote area.'

The doctor pronounced Finn unfit to travel the next day. His wound had opened up again and was bleeding. He had been on the road trying to hitch a lift for many hours. They decided to keep him in overnight for observation.

Gloomily Jack and Emma returned to the hotel. Eliot drove with a somewhat smug expression on his face.

Bernard had left and was probably already landing at Heathrow. Finn was ill. Eliot was fighting their every suggestion. Jack and Emma felt the whole project was coming to a frustrating and unsatisfactory end, without resolution. They were silent the whole way back to the hotel, and when they arrived there Emma announced that she was going to sleep in Finn and Bernard's vacant room. Neither Jack nor Eliot argued. It seemed, under the circumstance, the best solution to the emotional mine field of the night.

'Feel like a proper drink?' Eliot asked Jack when Emma had left them.

'Why not.'

The two young men walked back along the corniche to the hotel that served alcohol to foreigners, and settled down in the lounge, each with a double whiskey.

It was a long time before either spoke, and then it was only to order another drink.

During the second whiskey Eliot said to Jack: 'What do you really think of all this crap? You surely can't believe it?'

Jack did not answer immediately, but sipped his drink and stared into the distance.

'I mean, it *has* to be crap, hasn't it?' Eliot persisted.

'I don't know. I really don't know,' Jack said at last.

'I know Emma's gorgeous, and one goes along with her...'

'It's not just Emma,' Jack said.

'What then?'

'Its just that so many things came together in my life – dreams, strange feelings, coincidences that seemed too perfect to be coincidences, meeting Mary Brown...'

'Mary Brown is an old woman with an overactive imagination. Surely you're not going to be influenced by her!'

'I might have rejected what she said if it had not rung true against my own experience. I was having encounters and strange convictions. And then there was Bernard. You should have heard him, Eliot, in the tombs speaking with the voices of the dead...'

'Any actor can do that...'

'I don't think he was acting. The whole atmosphere of the place...'

'You don't *think*. Listen to yourself Jack! You used to be a rational man.'

'I still am,' Jack insisted, annoyed at Eliot's accusation. 'It may be that *you* are the one not thinking. Listen to *yourself*. You have shut the door on any explanation for things other than the one you have had drummed into you since birth.'

'Do you deny that what I have said is true about Mary and Bernard?'

'I accept that what you have said may be true, but a jury has to be sure beyond all reasonable doubt. I have doubt. I cannot convict them. And I have doubt because I know what I have experienced, and I know *I* am not faking.'

'What have you experienced? Dreams!' Eliot snorted. 'How can you quote dreams as a source of truth? I dreamed last night I was standing on the top of the Empire State Building and Emma was flying past in a helicopter waving at me. How could this have any basis but my concern that I am losing her?'

'It could mean that your inner, deeper self has recognized at last that she is on another level of development from you. You are rooted to the physical ground, even though you have climbed a thousand steps. But she is still above you, flying, in the Spirit realms. It could mean that man-made buildings, representing all that formal education has taught you of the material world, can get you no higher than the top of the Empire State Building. You have to take off, leave the ground, leap into the Unknown, to find your true love – Truth.'

'Such a leap could kill you.'

'True. But it might also reveal the meaning of everything.'

'I despair of you, Jack. You're as mad as she is!'

'It may be so. But at least I'm trying to see beyond my own nose – trying to interpret my dreams intelligently.'

'What "intelligent" explanation do you give for the dream you had about that tomb guardian of yours leading you into the desert? And don't tell me he was leading you to Akhenaten's ghost, because I won't accept *that*!'

'At first I thought that must be the only explanation. But now I'm not so sure. This journey to Egypt – this search for Akhenaten's ghost – has made me aware of things I've never noticed before. It has opened the door you keep so nervously barred. I admit all that is pouring through might not in the long run be acceptable, but I am slowly learning to distinguish things – not from books or from other people's opinions – but from my own experience. I am beginning to think Akhenaten was a hero because he questioned the status quo established over thousands of years, but a failure because he did not find the right answers.'

'And I suppose you think you are going to find the right answers?' Eliot sneered.

Jack was silent.

'I can't believe you are as arrogant as that,' Eliot added.

'I'm not. Its just that I *want* to find the right answers, and I've come to believe that if I follow that dream apparition into the desert I *might...*'

Eliot shrugged, as much as to say, 'I give up!'

He ordered another drink for them both, and when the conversations started up again it was on a different tack.

'Do you think Emma meant it when she said we were finished?' he asked.

Jack shifted in his chair uncomfortably. He had hoped the conversation would not get around to this.

It was his turn to shrug.

'Who knows?' he said.

'*You* might,' Eliot said, looking at him hard. 'It seems to me you and she have become closer than you were at home.'

'It is inevitable. We're sharing a pretty potent experience here.'

'I don't mean the ghost thing,' Eliot said impatiently. 'I've noticed the way you look at each other... and the room...'

'We've both told you – that was a charade for the locals. We didn't share a bed.'

'I know that is what you told me, but...'

'There is nothing more to tell.'

Eliot did not seem convinced, but said no more for the moment. An awkward silence fell. It was Jack who broke it.

'It seems to me, old man, you don't really appreciate Emma.'

Eliot raised his eyes swiftly.

'I mean – her beliefs are a very important part of her. Take those away and she may fall apart.'

'So now we get to the real reason you are pretending to believe all this bullshit!' Eliot said bitterly.

'No. We are not. I am exploring my own beliefs – not hers. But, because I now know what it means to explore beyond the material world, I can appreciate her doing so.'

'Do you love her?' Eliot leaned forward, his eyes boring into Jack's.

Jack hesitated for a moment, and then said simply:

'I do.'

Eliot sat back suddenly in his chair, as though knocked off balance. His face was ashen white.

'I thought I'd find you here,' another voice spoke above their heads. Both looked up to see Ahmed Hassan smiling down at them.

'May I join you?'

Neither man answered. Hassan saw that he was not welcome, but drew up a chair and sat down anyway.

'I've been thinking,' he said cheerfully, ignoring the tension in the air. 'You cannot go into the Eastern Desert without a guide. What better guide could you have than myself? I know the desert well. I was brought up by the Bedouin and only came to the cities as a teenager. Besides,' he added, 'I will have the power of the police behind me if there is any trouble.'

163

* * * *

That night Emma found herself in a house she often visited in her dreams. As far as she knew she had never seen it in waking life, but it had been with her since childhood, hauntingly familiar. A large house, of many rooms. No matter how many she walked through, there were always more beyond the next door. Sometimes she encountered people in the rooms, but this time she wandered through alone. On the hall table lay an address book and she found herself opening it. The names and addresses were strange to her. As though she knew she was dreaming, she made a note in her mind to try to find out who those people were when she was awake. She then went into the first room. It was cluttered with toys and children's books lying open on the floor as though a child had grown tired of playing and gone on to other things. She opened the door on the other side of the room and passed through, finding more books, some shut, some open. Continuing through, in each room she found books and, opening them at random, read a paragraph or two before passing on to the next one. As she progressed through the house she left a trail of open books behind her, only partially read. She seemed to be searching frantically for something in them – some information – some answer. But the answer she sought eluded her.

Eventually she came to a room in which there was something she had never seen in the house before – a ladder leading up to a trap door in the ceiling. The whole room was filled with books, flung every which way about the place, most lying open, some yellowing as though they had been open a long time. She had become impatient with the books and fixed her attention and her hopes on the unexpected ladder.

She climbed – heaved on the trap door – and at last it gave way with a groan. She managed to swing it open with a tremendous effort. With heart beating fast in anticipation of what she would find in this unknown and unexplored attic, she took another step up the ladder. Peering in – half in, half out – she was astonished at what she saw.

The rest of the house had been very much the sort of house she was familiar with in England – the rooms carpeted, with furniture, fireplace and lights that switched on and off. But this – this room was like nothing she had ever seen. It blazed with light emanating from no visible source. Columns of green malachite stone supported the ceiling of crystal through which the whole universe could be seen – a billion galaxies whirling and swirling, stars dying and being born, comets trailing clouds of shimmering ice...

Emma gasped, and, trembling, climbed another few steps so that

164

she could see more. At the centre of the room stood a figure. Was it Djehuti, the ancient Egyptian god who recorded past, present and future in his fabled book? He was looking directly at her and holding out to her a tightly rolled scroll of papyrus. She climbed the last few steps of the ladder and found herself standing on a floor of deepest purple amethyst. She knew suddenly that all she had been seeking in those other books left abandoned on the floors of the house below was in that scroll – and more. She had to have it!

With it she would change the world and make it a better place ... with it she would find Akhenaten and release him to eternal life ... With it she would show Eliot how stupid and blind he had been, and make him appreciate her!

She reached out her hand ... Her eyes were burning from the light that blazed into them ... She could hardly bear it, but she was determined not to close her eyes in case she lost sight of the scroll which she now desired with painful intensity.

She sensed he was beginning to withdraw it, and called out desperately.

But he was gone. The malachite columns and floor of amethyst were gone. The heavens 'fretted with golden fire' were gone.

She was standing in the dusty attic of an ordinary house, and she could hear the death-watch beetle slowly, but inexorably, destroying the timbers...

When she woke, Emma lay a long time thinking about the dream.

She remembered that the Egyptian god Djehuti, called Thoth by the Greeks, was supposed to have possessed a book in which all the knowledge and wisdom of Existence was recorded, a book so precious that men throughout the centuries had risked everything in search of it. There was a story that Khaemwasat, First Prophet of Ptah, High Priest of Ra, Chief of Seers, and honoured son of the Pharaoh Rameses II, had broken through some fearsome spells to obtain it from the tomb of a Sorcerer prince, but it had done him no good. For no sooner was it in his possession than he misused it and, eventually, when he had destroyed everyone he loved, he returned it to the tomb from which he had taken it, declaring that he understood now that we learned more from seeking it than possessing it.

16

The Flute

It was several days before they could start their journey to the Eastern Desert. Finn did not seem to want to get better. The doctor told Jack that the wound had been restitched and showed no sign of infection and he was free to leave hospital. But Finn turned his face to the wall and refused to get up or even speak to them. Emma concluded that it was the loss of his flute that was the problem.

'There is something about that particular flute,' she said. 'We have to get it back for him.'

'How do you propose to do that?' Eliot asked impatiently.

'I don't know,' she answered. 'But we have to!'

Jack was by now desperate to get going, and suggested they leave Finn behind.

'The local police will find it if it can be found,' he said.

Emma went to see Ahmed Hassan personally. He assured her that they would do everything they could do to recover it.

'A description will go out to all offices, as far afield as is necessary. Has he marked it in some way? Does it have any distinctive features?'

'I don't think so.'

Hassan's pen paused over the paper on his desk.

'All I know is that we must find it. Since its loss my friend seems to have given up on life...'

'Are you sure it is the loss of his flute?'

'Of course.'

'It seems to me it is not the loss of the flute, but something else that is troubling him.'

Emma looked surprised. She was about to deny it, but something in the steady gaze of Hassan gave her pause.

There was silence between them for a long minute.

'What are you *really* doing in Egypt?' he asked at last, and he was no longer smiling.

Emma caught her breath.

Should she tell him? She wanted to, but something made her

cautious. Their mission would seem absurd to outsiders. And to the police? They had lied to get the permit for the Eastern Desert. Would this not make the authorities distrustful of anything they might say and refuse to let them go?

He watched her face, noting every fleeting change as she battled with her conscience.

'We've told you,' she said at last, avoiding his eyes. 'Jack's doing research on his great-grandfather...'

'Yes. You have told me,' he said quietly.

'I – I must go. The others will be waiting. You promise to do your best to find my friend's flute? We don't mind about the car, but the flute is irreplaceable.'

'Of course,' he said politely, and stood up.

She walked towards the door feeling acutely uncomfortable. She would ask the others if she could tell Hassan the whole story. She felt he might understand, and surely they would *have* to tell him if he was accompanying them to the desert.

Bernard visited Mary just as soon as he could on his arrival back in England. She questioned him closely about all that had happened and tried to correlate her own disturbing dreams with events that had occurred to them.

She was clearly frustrated not to be taking a more active part in their adventures.

'Perhaps now that you are here,' she said, 'we can help them in some way. My telepathic link has been weak and erratic, but with your skill at channelling we may be able to make a stronger connection.'

She did not know how telepathy worked, but she believed it could be some kind of impulse or wave transmitted by our brains, broadcast and travelling through the air until a sensitive receiver picked it up.

Bernard agreed at once, glad to have the chance to reconnect with what was happening in Egypt.

He and Mary settled down in her jewel-box room, full of gleaming colour and light from the stained glass at every window, and tried to 'go into the silence'.

It took a long time for the mood to be right, and they had almost decided to give up when Bernard's face began to change and words that appeared to be other than his own began to come through.

'*Watch to your left and your right,*' he intoned, '*before and behind. Trust no one. Those that appear to be one thing, may be another.*'

And then he stopped.

'Go on,' Mary urged. 'Who should they not trust?'

But Bernard was shaking his head. The spirit, if spirit it was, had passed.

Under questioning he admitted only to a feeling of unease.

Mary held his hands and, together, they tried to project this warning telepathically to the group still in Egypt.

Whether they succeeded or not, they could not tell.

'If only psychic messages were clearer,' Mary thought. 'Partial knowledge is sometimes more dangerous than no knowledge at all. If their message reached the group in Egypt – would it not cause dissension and suspicion among them? Would it not disrupt the single minded drive of the mission and make them jump at shadows instead of being wary about the real problems that they had to face?

Emma decided to conduct her own enquiry into the whereabouts of Finn's flute. She announced that she was going back to the village of el-Till to question the villagers. Eliot insisted on going with her, while Jack was persuaded to stay behind to rest. He intended to spend a quiet day reading Ben Wilson's journal, much of which was still virgin territory to him.

He, Mary and Emma had concentrated on the parts that described Akhetaten and the finding of Akhenaten's seal ring in the eastern desert. But because of the difficulty in deciphering the spidery writing, there were great chunks of the journal as yet left unread.

Jack discovered that day that Ben Wilson had been one of the archaeologists present at the ill fated dress rehearsal of the play in 1909 that Mary had told them about, and his great-grandfather confirmed that there had been 'something eerie' about the way storms had suddenly interrupted the drama. He was sceptical that the curse really existed and that Corinna and Hortense fell ill because of what they had dreamed, but Jack noticed how many paragraphs he devoted to trying to insist that everything that happened must have been 'coincidence.'

'Old Ben is as eager as I am to find alternative explanations for strange events,' Jack thought, smiling.

Ben's journal then continued about other matters and Jack stopped reading. He sat for a long time pondering the possibility that the storms that put a stop to the play were supernaturally induced. If they were – what forces were they themselves going to encounter when they raised the matter of Akhenaten's release? He shivered, but was even more determined to go ahead. He had tried bungee jumping, white water rafting, and parachuting ... Surely this would be no worse than these experiences?

* * * *

Eliot and Emma drove a long way in silence. Jack's declaration that he loved Emma was still ringing in Eliot's ears, and he realised this might be the last time he and Emma would be alone together in Egypt. The time was now or never to try to win her back. Did she feel the same way about Jack? He would rather not ask her outright. Once put into words things could take on a life of their own.

He asked her instead when the ferries ran, and she answered him briefly, and was then silent again. She gave every indication that she resented his presence.

While they waited for the ferry he apologised for his opposition to the whole expedition and promised her he would keep an open mind from now on. He described an incident in his youth he had never mentioned before. It seemed he had lain awake one night worried about a close friend who was away on holiday. He was unable to get it out of his mind that his friend was in danger. Later he heard that his friend had drowned during a midnight swim at the exact time he had been thinking about him.

Emma looked at him with sudden interest. This was the first time he had ever admitted to anything even bordering on a psychic experience.

'Why didn't you tell me this before?' she asked.

'I don't know. I was very young. I suppose I forgot about it.'

'Forgot! How could you forget something like that?'

'I probably thought it was just coincidence. I'd often thought about friends and nothing had happened to them.'

'But the exact time he died!'

Eliot could see that the chill between them had gone, and her eyes were shining into his.

'I know. I've thought about it sometimes when you've been telling me about your experiences,' he lied. Until this moment he had not thought about it since it happened. He was not even sure of the exact timing – but he was not prepared to admit that to Emma now.

As the ferry arrived, Emma slipped her arm through his.

'I'm glad you came with me,' she said. 'Your knowledge of the language will be invaluable.'

They questioned the ticket seller at el-Till first, then the security guards. All complained that they had already told everything they knew to the tourist police. Finally, they located the family who had been so kind to them on the day of the attack, but they also could not help.

Emma and Eliot walked around the village, wondering what to do

169

next. They soon acquired a retinue of dusty children from the mudbrick houses, some wanting baksheesh, others pencils for schoolwork, and some to have their photographs taken. They were offered rides on donkeys and several 'priceless antiques' taken secretly from the tombs at dead of night! Eliot humoured them by handling the crude copies of genuine artefacts as though he believed they had value, while Emma obliged by taking photographs of the children. One boy hung back from the others, saying nothing, but watching their progress with an intense stare. Emma sensed that he may know something about the flute, and whispered her hunch to Eliot. As soon as the boy saw that they were whispering and looking at him, he ran off and disappeared among the maze of mudbrick houses.

At once Eliot asked the other children who he was and where he lived. They volunteered noisily to lead them to his home. Eliot tried to stop them, realising a mob descending on the young fugitive would certainly make him run away again. But he could not dampen their enthusiasm for the chase. It seemed the boy was pretty much a loner and not very popular in the village.

Emma was sorry she had drawn attention to him, seeing the delight with which the children engaged in the hunt.

He was not at home, but the way his mother answered their enquiries confirmed for Emma that they were on the right track. The children must have thought so too, for they streamed out over a neighbouring hill in full cry. They seemed to know where they were going, and would not stop no matter how much Emma and Eliot called after them to come back.

They stopped following and waited at the edge of the village. Looking back, Emma could see the boy's mother still standing at her door gazing after them anxiously.

'I wish I hadn't said anything,' Emma said. Was a chance of getting Finn's flute back worth the possibility of a boy's life being ruined?

'Go after them, Eliot,' she said. 'See that they don't hurt him.'

Eliot set off slowly and rather unwillingly. It was a hot day, and the rocky hill was steep.

Before he had gone far they could hear the others returning, shouting triumphantly. They were pulling the boy roughly between them, and one of them was holding up the flute.

Emma's emotions were mixed. She was delighted of course for Finn, but sorry for the boy. It must have been such a wonderful find for him. Who knows, he might have one day become a famous flautist himself because of what he found that day!

She ran to meet them and spoke rapidly to Eliot. He looked surprised and a bit disapproving, but he did her bidding. He took the flute in his own hand and commanded the others to release the boy. The culprit stood with head down, a trickle of blood at the side of his mouth where he had been hit. The children were chanting with cruel glee, yet Emma suspected there was not one of them who would not have done the same thing given the opportunity.

She dictated what she wanted to say, and Eliot, after hesitation, translated her words into the local language.

He thanked the children for the return of the flute, and thanked the boy for keeping it safely. He then dispensed baksheesh to all of them, including the guilty boy. So astonished were they at the turn of events the children's mood changed at once to one of eager rejoicing and a counting of coins. They made sure the boy who had kept the flute was given no more than the rest of them.

The boy himself could not believe the value of coin that was thrust into his hand, and looked up at Emma with such heartfelt gratitude, and such a deep and yearning look on his beautiful, gentle face that her heart melted at once.

She ordered them all to sit down and commanded the boy who had found the flute to play it for them.

Hesitantly, wonderingly, trembling slightly, he took the instrument once more in his hands and, after checking that indeed he had been asked to play it, he blew, and the air was filled with a most exquisite plaintive melody unlike any Emma had ever heard before.

The other children listened in silence, entranced. The music was fumbling and imperfect, but it was clear the urchin had a very considerable natural talent. Tears came to Emma's eyes and she hugged him when she took the flute back into her care.

She then walked back to the boy's mother, holding his hand, and asked Eliot to explain that her son should have music lessons and she would send an instrument for him, possibly a recorder, when she got back to Minya.

When they arrived at the ticket office and the guards, Eliot explained that the boy had found the flute and returned it to them in good condition.

'You're crazy, Emma,' Eliot said when they were on their way back to the ferry. 'Where do you think that boy will find music lessons?'

'I don't know – but certainly not in jail.'

She looked back at the knot of people gathered at the ticket office gazing after them. It was difficult to tell if the boy would be safe amongst them or not.

On the way back to Minya, Eliot make it clear that he thought Emma had made a mistake in rewarding the thief.

'He had not, in the strict sense, stolen the flute,' she countered. 'He had found it, and he might well have handed it in eventually. He tried it out as might anyone, and his dreary life was suddenly lit with magic. Thank goodness he did! Because otherwise he might never have known he had that amazing talent!'

'Telling his mother to get him music lessons!' Eliot jeered.

'Music is universal. Egypt must be as full of it as everywhere else. I didn't mean send him to the Royal Academy of Music in London – though he might very well end up there!'

Eliot drove in silence for a while. Why did he love this girl? She was impractical, zany, gullible, and eccentric. Her values were totally different from his own – yet he would hate to live without her.

When he spoke again he tried to make his voice sound casual.

'You have spent a lot of time with Jack,' he said. 'How have you been getting along?' He gazed straight ahead at the road, automatically avoiding the line of donkeys laden with reeds swaying across into his lane.

Emma did not reply at once. This he took as a bad sign. She was usually so spontaneous.

'Well...' she said at last, cautiously. He sensed the unsaid.

'He can be difficult sometimes,' he continued, trying to draw her out.

'Oh, yes, I've noticed!' she replied.

'You haven't fallen in love with him have you?' he asked suddenly, directly, glancing sideways at her.

She caught her breath. How to reply?

'I don't know,' she said, after a long pause. And that was perhaps the truth. He pressed his lips together in a hard line, and said no more.

When they swung into the hotel driveway, still no more words had been spoken between them. Emma climbed out, and watched him pull away to park the jeep.

Jack was standing on the steps of the veranda watching out for them.

They set off for the south the next day.

Finn recovered quickly from his malaise when his flute was returned to him, though he was still even more withdrawn than usual. Emma began to wonder if Hassan had been right about there being something else that was worrying him, but when she asked, and he replied rather irritably that of course there was not, she let the matter drop.

Hassan was not coming with them for the first part of the journey, but arranged to meet them at Qena in a few days time, from where they would start their trek into the desert.

Jack had decided they should have a few days in Luxor to see the place where Lindon Smith and Weigall had tried to lift the curse on Akhenaten in 1909. The others were happy to go along, as much to see the famous monuments in that area as to test out the antagonism of the Priests of Amun in their home territory. Jack had read aloud the pages from Ben Wilson's journal regarding the play and the sudden storms and illnesses. Eliot could not resist using the word 'coincidence', though he was trying very hard to appear to be open minded concerning Emma's beliefs.

When they reached Luxor, Eliot insisted on booking in at the Sheraton, offering to pay for Finn and Emma, even though Emma was intent on having a room to herself. Jack was none too pleased to be sharing with Finn, whom he found even more dour than he had been at the beginning of the journey, but, since his announcement that he was in love with Emma, the atmosphere between Eliot and himself had become very strained. It would have been much worse to share with Eliot.

That evening they met on the terrace for drinks and dinner, and an argument soon developed between them as to whether Hassan should be told about the real purpose of their expedition. Emma wanted to tell him. Finn was silent on the matter. Eliot was determined that he should not be told.

'How crazy will he think we are?' he said.

'How can we not tell him?' Jack asked.

'If we have to tell him anything, we must make out it is all in Ben Wilson's journal and we are only checking the information given there.'

'But Ben doesn't mention meeting the ghost, only that he found the ring in the desert.'

'Hassan won't read the journal. I'm surprised anyone can! He need not know that you have made up the whole thing.'

And then he met Emma's eyes, and stopped short.

'I mean...' he added lamely.

'I know what you mean,' Emma said coldly.

'It may be as well to do as Eliot says,' Jack intervened. 'I can't believe a policeman would be any more enlightened than Eliot.'

'I say!'

'Besides – its best we stick to the story I put on the form to obtain the permit. Since those shootings the police are very twitchy about unauthorised travel arrangements.'

Eventually they all agreed on the story they would tell Hassan.

'I wonder what he will think when we find the ghost,' Emma mused.

'If we find the ghost!' said Eliot.

Emma decided not to rise to this. She was exhausted after the long drive, as were they all. They retired to bed early with no further conversation.

17

Luxor

When Emma woke in the morning she went straight out onto the balcony and gazed over the calm silver-blue surface of the Nile. In the distance she saw the mountains that had held the tombs of the pharaohs so secretly in their clefts and chasms, until first the robbers, and then the archaeologists, had come to desecrate them. She held her breath. Such beauty! Such an awesome feeling of time having ceased to run forward. Nefertiti and Akhenaten must have gazed at the same scene. Setepenra must have played in her grandmother's garden over there, beneath the pink mountains where Amenhotep and Tiye had one of their favourite residences. Akhenaten himself would have grown up there. According to the guidebook Bernard had left with them, there was nothing to see of the old palace now. The only monuments dating to that time were the two colossal statues of Akhenaten's father now left isolated on the flood plain at the edge of the cultivated fields. They had once stood at the entrance to his magnificent mortuary temple, which was already ruined by the time the Greeks came to Egypt. Evidently, more than two thousand years ago, when the Greeks ruled Egypt, one of the colossi emitted a strange sound at sunrise. Travellers came from far and wide to consult it, believing it to be the Oracle of Memnon, until the Roman, Septimus Severus, well meaning but misguided, repaired the cracks in the statue and left it mute. How she wished she could hear its voice now in the cool dawn air!

Her heart was full of confusion. She longed for Jack, yet she was not free of Eliot yet. Something in him still held her. Something that made no sense.

They were beginning the most dangerous part of their mission. This was Amun territory. This was where Akhenaten had dispossessed the priesthood and ordered the shattering of the sacred statues of Amun. It was, no doubt, priests from here who had plotted that deadly curse she and her companions were now trying to reverse – priests so powerful they had sent thunder and lightning, hail and wind, to drive Lindon Smith and his friends scattering from the

175

Valley of the Queens into the hospitals of Cairo. They needed all their wits for this place.

What would they find here? Would they ever reach the Eastern Desert and find Akhenaten? Or would they... But her dark thoughts were interrupted by Finn calling out that they were going down to breakfast in order to get an early start. She picked up her string bag and her straw hat and followed him.

Having crossed over the Nile to the west bank, they paused on the long straight road to the mountains to greet the statues of Akhenaten's father. Beside his knees were small statues of his wife. Could this be Tiye, Akhenaten's mother, or one of his many other wives taken from the royal families of vassal or enemy countries to ensure the peace? Emma felt it must be Tiye because she was his Great Royal Wife, his favourite. He married her, though she was not of royal blood, and ordered giant stone scarabs and stelae erected to her all over the country, declaiming his love for her. It was said she was the power behind the throne, and after his death continued to exert influence on her son, Akhenaten.

Emma wondered what Nefertiti felt about her mother-in-law. They were both strong women. Tiye was not as beautiful as Nefertiti, but her face was full of character, and her body had been found with wisps of reddish hair still adhering to the skull. Did she resent her daughter-in-law's influence on her son?

'I see Amenhotep's wife is still portrayed as much smaller than her husband, waiting patiently at his knee,' Jack said, 'whereas Nefertiti was nearly always portrayed as the same size as her husband, taking her place as an equal beside him.'

Eliot had wandered off and was gazing over the green fields of corn towards Luxor as though not in the least interested in the statues or anything they represented.

Finn had climbed the statue as far as he could and settled down to play his flute.

Emma felt as though the sound of his music was the ancient pharaoh speaking again – his words floating out across the landscape, giving them courage to rescue his son.

Jack moved close to her and they held hands as they listened.

They had been alone at first, but another party was approaching, taking photographs of Finn as he played.

Eliot called out impatiently that they should leave.

Emma and Jack dropped hands and moved apart. The moment was gone.

Because they had set off from the hotel early they reached Hatshepsut's temple at Deir el Bahri before most of the tourists arrived and had it almost to themselves for a while. Numerous heavily armed police lolled about the place watching them closely. This had been the scene of the horrific massacre of tourists in November 1997.

Jack shivered, imagining how it must have been that terrible day. And then it seemed to him he was witnessing an earlier and similar violence. Akhenaten's men must have come here, rather like the men of Henry VIII in England, smashing and destroying everything of the old order in a zealous frenzy in the name of 'religion'.

Amun had been raised to supreme power at the time of Hatshepsut. He was her special god. There were carvings on the walls of this very temple declaring that Hatshepsut herself was fathered by the God Amun.

He made his form in majesty like that of her husband, Aa-kheper-ka-Ra. He found her sleeping in the beauty of her chamber. She wakened at the fragrance of the god and he took her in his arms and had his desire of her. Then he caused her to see him in his form as a god and she rejoiced at the sight of his beauty. His love passed into her limbs and she was flooded with his divine fragrance. All his scents were of frankincense and myrrh. Then did the king's wife and king's mother Aah-mes, speak in the presence of this great god, Amun, Lord of Waset:

'How great is thy presence, O Lord! Thou hast united me to thee with thy favours – thy dew is in all my limbs.' Then did the majesty of this god do all that he desired of her, and at the end he uttered these words:

'Khenemet-Amun-Hatshepsut shall be the name of this my daughter, whom I have placed in thy body. She shall exercise excellent kingship in this whole land. My soul is hers, my treasures and my crown, that she may rule the Two Lands, she may lead all the living to know that I am I.'

A century later, Akhenaten, rejecting Amun and believing his own favourite god to be supreme, had ordered the desecration of the place. Images and inscriptions had been hacked out, sacred statues toppled. Had the priests who had tried to defend the place been killed?

The feeling of violence still lingered. The Christians had come here too in the early centuries after Christ and, believing the ancient gods to be demons, they smashed more than a few images themselves.

It was difficult now to tell which wave of religious iconoclasts had done what damage.

'Strange,' Jack thought. 'All these centuries have passed and people are still intolerant of other people's religious ideas and are prepared to kill for them.'

Yet in spite of it all, Hatshepsut's beautiful temple rose grandly against the desert cliffs. It was extraordinarily modern looking with its clean, plain lines, the terraces of columns echoing the rock formations of the mountains behind it.

Eliot was striding up the first ramp with an expression of eager anticipation.

In the Metropolitan Museum in New York, at the age of thirteen, he had first encountered the beautiful Hatshepsut. Subsequently, whenever he visited New York he returned to her statue, drawn to it as though to a living woman. At one time he had found a single red rose lying on the plinth at her feet, and smiled to think that someone else was also under her spell.

Now he was in her temple. Now he was standing where she had stood!

He gazed over to the distant river and for a moment he fancied he saw the gleam of gold from the tip of the obelisk at Karnak that she had erected to Amun.

'Probably sunlight shining on the windshield of a car,' he corrected himself hastily. Whatever he did he must not become as crazy as Emma and the others.

Finn had found an out-of-the-way nook to sit and meditate and play his flute.

Jack and Emma found themselves together.

She looked at him.

'This is where it all started,' she whispered, hardly daring to speak aloud, so convinced she was that ancient spirits still inhabited the structure.

'If Hatshepsut hadn't given her priests so much power they might not have been corrupt enough to offend Akhenaten, nor strong enough to challenge him.'

Jack nodded. He too felt wary of the atmosphere.

'Shall we go into the sanctuary of Amun and pray for Akhenaten's forgiveness and release?' she breathed close to his ear.

He hesitated. He was not sure he wanted to confront Amun in his holy of holies but, on the other hand, where better to plead for Akhenaten?

He nodded and she took his hand. Together they climbed the ramp to the second terrace. Eliot had disappeared into a side chapel. The top terrace where the ruins of Amun's most sacred sanctuary were being restored was closed to tourists. Archaeologists were clearly working there, and the barriers and notices were unequivocal. No unauthorised visitors were allowed.

Frustrated and yet secretly relieved, they wandered on the second terrace admiring the beautiful carved reliefs of Hatshepsut's expedition to the land of Punt to bring back frankincense trees in honour of her god. There they also found the reliefs depicting her divine origins. Neither could read the inscriptions, but the beauty of the images carried them back to her lifetime. They felt her presence.

'Perhaps we should ask her to intercede for us,' Emma suggested.

'Why should she? She would have been very angry with Akhenaten herself if she had still been present as a *Ka* when he attacked her temple.'

'I feel she would understand loneliness and exile. She too suffered annihilation at the hands of an enemy. When Thutmosis III finally took the throne she had usurped from him, he destroyed her statues and removed her name from history. She too might be wandering as a ghost.'

Jack looked over his shoulder. He did not want Eliot spoiling the mood. Finn's music, faint and distant, enhanced it. He could hear a tour bus arriving at the gate. They would not have long to conduct a private ceremony.

He took both her hands in his and they stood facing each other, with eyes shut.

It was Emma who voiced the invocation and the plea.

'Daughter of Amun,' she whispered, 'we come in humility to ask a favour of you. We ask you to intercede with your father Amun for the forgiveness of Akhenaten Wa-en-ra, who has been doomed to everlasting exile by his priests. We cannot believe your Father himself, Great in Majesty, Rich in Names, would wish punishment to last forever. Wa-en-ra has suffered, as you have suffered, wandering nameless between the worlds, for too long. Surely the gods can be merciful as well as mighty...'

It seemed to her that her voice was very loud, though it was in fact no more than a whisper.

She took another deep breath, preparing to speak again, but Eliot came striding towards them.

'What are you doing?' he shouted angrily – so angrily indeed that both looked at him in astonishment. For the moment they could have sworn he was taller and fiercer than the man they knew. It was almost as though the air was seething around him like a dark and ominous storm cloud. He was blotting out the sun.

But at that moment tourists arrived, chattering. Jack and Emma drew apart, and Eliot became his usual suave and handsome self.

'What were you doing?' he repeated, now in a mildly curious voice.

'Nothing,' Emma answered at once, with a quick look at Jack.

Eliot shrugged.

'If you two can't keep your hands off each other,' he said, 'you might try a more private place to do it!'

After Amun's temple at Deir el Bahri the group skirted the mountains against which it was built and arrived in the valley behind it, the Valley of the Kings. There, after running the gauntlet of the vociferous souvenir sellers with stalls on either side of the road, they came to the tomb of Tutankhamun.

The boy king was probably the son of Akhenaten by a minor wife and was married to his half-sister Ankhesenamun, daughter of Akhenaten by his Great Royal Wife, Nefertiti. By a strange quirk of fate, this teenager, whose reign had lasted no more than a few years, and who was buried in haste in a tomb too small for him, has become the best-known pharaoh of Egypt. Perhaps the insignificance of the tomb had fooled the ancient tomb robbers into thinking it would not be worth stripping. But they were wrong, and Emma and her group had seen in the Museum of Cairo how wrong they were.

It was likely he had died from a blow to the head at the age of seventeen or eighteen. But whether this was assassination or accident the experts were uncertain. An educated guess would suggest that Tutankhamun had been killed on General Horemheb's orders to speed up the process of returning the country to stability under the old gods. It was certainly true that within a few years of the boy's death, Horemheb himself, a powerful commoner, declared himself pharaoh and ruled the Two Lands with a rod of iron for many years, himself choosing his successor, a general from his own army, Rameses.

Musing on this, Jack remembered that in Ben Wilson's journal it had been a statue of one of the Rameside kings, who had come 'alive' in the dreams of Corinna Lindon Smith and Hortense Weigall after the ill fated rehearsal of the play invoking Akhenaten, and it was this 'living' statue that had beaten them with flails. He made a mental note to visit the Ramesseum on the way back to Luxor, to confront the very statue that had featured in those extraordinary dreams.

But meanwhile they had arrived in the small chamber open to the public. Others were there before them, and more were coming down the steps. The guard was hurrying them all along. There was no time in that crowded cell to meditate on the figure lying encased in gold in his open sarcophagus, bullet-proof-glass shielding him from vandals and trophy hunters.

Behind him on the opposite wall was a painting depicting the 'opening the mouth' ceremony, when the lips of the deceased are touched with an adze of meteoric iron to give him speech in the Otherworld, and influence in this. Ay, the old courtier who briefly succeeded Tutankhamun before Horemheb became pharaoh, was performing the ceremony dressed in ceremonial robes.

Emma was responding as though she knew these people personally, and had practically to be dragged out as the guard became increasingly angry with her for standing in the best position beside the sarcophagus, excluding all others.

Eliot and Finn had barely glanced in and were already waiting in the sun, side by side on a stone wall overlooking the steps, when Jack and Emma emerged.

'I can't believe all that stuff I've seen in books could have fitted into that small space,' Eliot said. 'Why didn't they give him a decent burial for god's sake!'

Jack laughed. 'It was probably for 'the god's sake' they didn't!' he said.

Emma was shivering, and not amused. All three men stopped laughing and looked at her. Jack, the nearest, put his arm around her.

'Come,' he said.

He too felt chilled to the marrow in spite of the body heat of all those people crowded together. He was now warming up rapidly as the sun blazed down. The glare on the pale dust was almost blinding.

'Enough of tombs!' Eliot said. 'Its macabre, grotesque, to get so worked up over something that happened so long ago!'

'I thought we were going to see Horemheb's tomb?' Finn complained.

'We must at least see Horemheb's,' Jack insisted.

Eliot shrugged.

'Whatever turns you on!' he jeered.

Emma glared at him, frowning, her anger for the moment driving out the disturbing shadows she had found in Tutankhamun's tomb.

Jack could see that she had been deeply affected by the place. He would have to wait to be alone with her to find out what she had experienced. But there was little chance at the moment. Eliot had established himself at her side as they walked the dusty road to the tomb of Horemheb.

Jack's companion was Finn, walking silently, staring at his feet.

'What do you think of Tut's tomb?' Jack asked.

Finn shrugged as though disinterested. 'Too crowded,' he said.

'If you were Akhenaten, Tutankhamun was probably your son. Did you feel anything looking at his coffin?'

'Not a thing.'

But there was something in Finn's expression – something in his voice. Jack suspected he had some feelings but was not prepared to talk about them.

'I felt an overwhelming sense of waste.' Jack decided to talk on, hoping his confessions would encourage Finn to speak. 'Such a young lad. I'm sure he was murdered.'

'We don't know the full story. He might have been about to upset the apple cart again. After all, he'd grown up under Akhenaten.'

'You're saying his murder was justified?'

'No. Of course not. But we don't know the whole story. We don't know the truth about any of it.'

'That's what we've come to find out,' Jack said soberly.

Finn looked up at last, into his eyes.

'You mean you have an open mind as to whether Akhenaten deserved what happened to him or not?'

'No man has the right to stop another from progressing as far as is possible in this world or the next.'

Finn grinned. 'You sound like Mary.'

'I have a great respect for Mary. She may not know the whole truth, but she's made a pretty good stab at it. Until proven otherwise I've decided to go along with her beliefs.'

'I agree that no one should be subjected to such a curse. But we have to take into account the provocation.'

'Provocation is in the eye of the beholder.'

Finn was silent.

'How do you propose to discover the truth?' he said after a while. 'All my life it seemed true to me that I am a reincarnation of Akhenaten. And yet that may not be true at all. How can we *know*? If we can't even know the truth about ourselves and the people close to us, how can we know the truth about what happened three thousand years ago?'

'I don't know,' Jack said. 'Perhaps there are different kinds of truth. There is the Court of Law kind, the scientific laboratory kind, the kind that is written down at the time and becomes accepted as historical fact no matter how false it might be ... But even these are subject to the psychological agendas of the judge, the witness, the juries, the scientists, the observers, the recorders ... We don't see the same war our fathers did when we watch documentaries...'

They walked side by side, without speaking, for a while.

Ahead of them, Eliot was holding Emma's arm and she was laughing up at him.

'What kind of truth do you think we are pursuing here?' Finn persisted.

Jack shrugged. 'Mary talks about Mythic Truth, Imaginal Truth. This Truth has no basis in fact but illuminates the mind in such a way that for the first time we understand the meaning of life.'

The great cliffs that held so many secrets towered above them. The tourists and souvenir sellers were dwarfed beneath them, the cliffs themselves dwarfed against the sky, immeasurably high. A profound Silence that was not silence hung over Jack and Finn. Meretseger, the goddess of the great pyramid shaped peak that watched over the Valley of the Dead, 'She Who Loves Silence', seemed to speak to them.

'*What are three thousand years to me?*' she whispered. '*What are they to you?*'

Suddenly the silence was shattered by a gunshot that echoed among the cliffs. There were screams behind them and when they turned, half the tourists had scattered like leaves before the wind, while others lay flat in the dust.

Only the souvenir sellers were upright, laughing. Jack and Finn stood, frozen to the spot.

A tomb guide striding along the path towards them, having already passed Emma and Eliot, called out cheerfully. 'Don't worry,' he said, 'it is only a Japanese film crew making a movie.'

When they reached the entrance to Horemheb's tomb Emma drew back and said she would not enter.

She said Horemheb was the general who had taken power after Akhenaten's death and had supervised the return of the country to the old religion of Amun and the other gods. She was sure he had been behind the plot to assassinate Akhenaten and may have even masterminded, or at least encouraged, the curse. From his point of view, even if he were not a religious man, he would know the people believed a dead king could still exert influence from the Otherworld if he was not prevented in some way.

'He believed that once cursed, Akhenaten's influence would cease with his death,' Emma said. 'The irony is that it is that very curse, and the efforts Horemheb made to remove all trace of his name from history, that has led to his having a greater influence than almost any other pharaoh. Three thousand years from his death Akhenaten is more powerful than Horemheb!' she declared triumphantly.

'If he was working with the priests of Amun to destroy Akhenaten, it is very important we face him now,' Jack said. 'We might learn something that will help us when we find Akhenaten.'

'What are you afraid of?' Eliot said. 'If there were such things as ghosts they would long since have been chased out of here by all the millions of tourists that came gawking about the place!'

Emma ignored him and looked fearfully at Jack.

"Do you think I should?' her voice was pleading for him to say 'no' – but he nodded and said 'yes'.

Finn walked ahead, ignoring the argument, locked in his own thoughts as usual.

Emma hesitated a few moments longer, the two men on either side of her watching her face, waiting for her to make up her mind.

Suddenly she took a deep breath and marched ahead, following Finn into the long cold corridor cut deep into the mountain. On either side of her marched the gods of ancient Egypt... with Horemheb between them: Horemheb offering to Anubis the god of the necropolis; Isis and Osiris blessing him... no doubt rewarding him for having re-established their worship in the Two Lands. Emma averted her eyes angrily from the rich colours and beautiful images. How dare he! How blind these gods must be if they thought he was someone to be trusted!

Deep inside the tomb she found Finn in a small chamber gazing at a wall painting of Osiris in white on a background of green. This was probably the room in which the Osiris shaped bed of earth was placed and planted with seed to grow after the tomb was sealed. This was the room that promised new life, resurrection.

Tears were streaming down Finn's cheeks. Startled, Emma forgot her own feelings, and put her arm around him to comfort him.

'What is it?' she whispered.

'It is the promise,' he whispered back, his voice catching on a sob. 'It is the promise of redemption...'

Emma did not know that Finn was thinking of himself, so her reaction was anger. Why should Horemheb be redeemed, when he denied it to others? Why should he live again, when her father could not?

Eliot moved in behind them.

'What's going on?' he asked loudly.

Emma rounded on him and her face was dark with anger.

'Why don't you go away?' she almost shrieked. 'All this means nothing to you! You'd have been just the sort of person whom Horemheb would have used to do his beastly work.' She broke away from Finn and began beating at Eliot. Jack, coming in just at that moment, caught her wrists and held her back.

'I say,' he said, 'steady on!'

'Let me go!' she shouted.

'No,' he said. 'Emma, calm down. Eliot isn't your enemy, Horemheb is. You should be confronting *him*, not Eliot.'

'Where is he then?' she demanded. 'Show me where he is!'

'The sarcophagus is in a chamber further down. We haven't reached the bottom of the tomb yet.'

He took her arm and led her out. Eliot stood back, a sort of sneering smile on his face.

When they reached the last chamber it was bare of everything except the tremendously heavy stone sarcophagus. All the rich grave goods that must have been buried with such a powerful and long-lived king had been stolen long before the archaeologists reached the tomb. Ben Wilson had been there at its opening, but had not stayed beyond the first few days of digging out. He described the corridors choked with piles of chippings and dried mud from several flash floods.

At the corners of the sarcophagus goddesses were carved protecting the pharaoh with their wings.

Emma glared at it, firmly held under the restraining arm of Jack.

On the wall behind the sarcophagus there was a line drawing of the judgement scene in the Hall of Osiris. The tomb was evidently not finished before Horemheb died and no colour had been applied to the icon.

Emma turned her attention to it and derived some comfort from the fact that it was not finished.

'Perhaps,' she said, 'he was never properly judged before the throne of Osiris, so perhaps he too has not been able to progress through the other worlds.' The scales where his heart should have been weighed against the feather of Maat, the goddess of Cosmic Order and Truth, looked empty. He was not justified! He had not passed on!

Her black mood lifted.

She turned her face up to Jack's and kissed him passionately.

There beside the open sarcophagus of Horemheb, the daughter of Akhenaten celebrated life and love...

Eliot was standing at the door ... watching them.

It was not until mid-afternoon that they reached the Valley of the tombs of the Queens and began to look for the place where the ill-fated play had been rehearsed by Weigall and Lindon Smith and their wives in 1909. Ben Wilson's journal was not precise, but it was not long before they found what must have been the natural amphitheatre Lindon Smith described in his account of the incident.

Most tourists were clustered round the tombs that were open to the public, so they were little disturbed when they reached the spot.

Eliot had been sullen and morose ever since he had witnessed the kiss in Horemheb's tomb, and refused to show any interest in the place. He sat on a rock a little to one side and waited impatiently for them to finish their ridiculous business. The others tried to ignore him, but there was no doubt his resentful presence affected the atmosphere of the place and the mood of each one of them.

For the first time Jack actually asked Finn to play his flute, hoping it would improve the vibrations, but for the first time Finn did not feel inclined to do so.

After a while among the hot rocks of the desolate valley with nothing apparently happening, Jack suggested they leave.

'What if we declaimed Akhenaten's Hymn to the sun as they did,' Emma suggested. 'It was when Corrina Lindon Smith as Queen was reciting those words that the storm broke.'

Jack was hot and tired and irritated with Eliot, and with Finn for not playing when he was asked, and was beginning to think longingly of the hotel bath and several cool drinks, but he gave in to the extent that he agreed she could, as long as she did not expect him to join in.

Both Finn and he found places to sit – probably where the audience of eminent archaeologists had sat all those years before, and Emma climbed a little knoll and started to chant the ancient hymn to the Aten.

The words echoed against the cliff walls, her voice booming out far more strongly than they would have expected. Jack could feel the 'Silence' growing around him, enclosing him, distancing him from the sound. It seemed to be coming from the mountains around them, not from the slight figure of the girl with stick arms raised to the sun, with sweating armpits and long cotton skirt thick with dust around the hem.

'You are in my heart, and there is none other that knows you except your son, Neferkheperure, Sole-one-of-Ra, whom you make to comprehend your design and might...'

She had just reached this point in the hymn when suddenly there was a sharp crack and, from the cliff behind her, a large piece of rock broke off and came thundering down. For a moment the sun illuminated the cloud of dust that enclosed her and she seemed transformed into a supernatural being. The boulder missed her, and her voice did not waver though all three men leapt up and rushed fearfully towards her.

She came to the end of the hymn and looked at their faces below her in triumph.

'How about that!' she cried exultantly. 'He tried, but he didn't stop me!'

'Don't tell me you think that was the force of Amun that dislodged that rock?' Eliot jeered.

'What else?'

'The racket you were making caused vibrations that dislodged a boulder already poised to fall.'

'Don't you think it's pretty strange that both times that hymn has been spoken aloud in this valley something dramatic has happened?' Jack asked, himself undecided as to the supernatural origin of the event, but inclining to accept it as such.

'No, I don't. We know flash storms and floods occur in this area, the debris washed into tombs tells us as much. It could have been pure coincidence that other time. And this – well – you heard the echoes. I've never heard Emma shout so loud. If this was the Alps she would have started an avalanche!'

'Thanks!' Emma said bitterly. He always spoiled things. It could not have been a natural happening. It had to be Amun or the spirits that attended him. She had felt like a warrior shouting out a battle cry – and a warrior had answered her challenge. When the rock had missed her and fallen harmlessly into the gully behind her she had felt a second surge of confidence, to confirm the one she had had in Horemheb's tomb. She believed they could indeed defeat the dark forces that had destroyed her father and were threatening them.

Jack insisted that there was one last visit they had to make before they returned to the hotel. Hortense Weigall and Corrinna Lindon Smith, who had played Akhenaten and his mother in the play, had an identical dream on the night after the aborted rehearsal. They both saw a statue in the Ramesseum come alive and beat them with flails. They both succumbed to serious illnesses after this dream.

Jack wanted to see that particular statue in the Ramesseum. After his own strange experiences with the image of the tomb guardian at his home, and the haunting dreams and disturbing thoughts he had, he was curious to see if he could sense 'life' in that statue. The ancient Egyptians believed statues could house the spirits of the dead (and the gods) and take an active part in the affairs of this world. Most statues in Egypt were now broken and ineffectual, yet some still retained their ancient magic.

It was almost sunset when they arrived at the Ramesseum en route for the river crossing that would take them back to Luxor for the night. The sun was still visible as a burning copper disk, the sky staining red around it. Soon the colour would tinge everything – every last breath of the sky – every rock of the mountain and drop of water in the river. The burning afterglow of an Egyptian sunset is something that will never be forgotten by anyone who has ever seen it.

Birds were winging home in long strings from the cultivated fields as they entered the temple precincts. This was a Rameside temple, built after Akhenaten's lifetime, and erected in honour of Amun. Jack had seen one of the two giant heads of Rameses II that had once been here, in the British Museum in London. The other was lying where it had fallen.

As soon as he saw it, Eliot started quoting one of Shelley's poems, 'Ozymandias', written about it.

> '*I met a traveller from an antique land*
> *Who said: Two vast and trunkless legs of stone*
> *stand in the desert... Near them on the sand,*
> *Half sunk, a shattered visage lies, whose frown*
> *And wrinkled lip, and sneer of cold command*
> *Tell that its sculptor well those passions read*
> *Which yet survive, stamped on these lifeless things.*
> *The hand, which mocked them, and the heart, that fed.*
> *On the pedestal these words appear,*
> '*My name is Ozymandias, King of Kings:*
> *Look upon my works ye Mighty, and despair!*'
> *Nothing beside remains. Round the decay*
> *Of that colossal wreck, boundless and bare*
> *The lone and level sands stretch far away.*

'You see,' he said at the end, 'Amun approves. He hasn't thrown any rocks or thunderbolts!'

'You don't understand a thing!' said Emma bitterly, walking away from him.

The mortuary temple of Rameses II, one of the longest lived pharaohs of ancient Egypt, was still in a good state of preservation considering it had been built too near the flood plain of the Nile. But there were no complete standing statues that Jack could find that would answer the description in Lindon Smith's book.

When they were discussing it, Finn suggested that in their dreams the women had seen the temple as it was in its heyday, and that it was one of the giant statues of Rameses II himself that had arisen from its throne and beaten them. Emma, Finn and Jack surrounded the head on the ground, while Eliot, annoyed at Emma's remark, went on his own to look at the wall reliefs of the various battles of which Rameses II was so proud.

But no matter how hard they stared at the fallen head and no matter how hard they concentrated, nothing happened. Emma even tried declaiming Akhenaten's hymn again, but this time her voice sounded ordinary, and the only untoward sound was a brief snort of mocking laughter from Eliot as he came back and found out what they were doing.

It was getting dark, and Eliot reminded them they had to take a ferry over the river and they had not checked how late they operated. The first stars were beginning to come out as they floated across the Nile. The afterglow had gone, and with it their strength and enthusiasm.

That night in England Mary dreamed that she was being pursued through a rocky chasm by a giant stone statue, lashing out with his flail.

She woke before she knew whether he would touch her with it or not.

The next day they visited Karnak.

They walked down the long avenue of ram headed sphinxes, animals sacred to Amun, and stood at the entrance to the great Temple of Amun embellished by so many generations of pharaohs. Hatshepsut had erected mighty obelisks here. On the one she had inscribed the following:

> *She made a monument for her father Amun – two obelisks of enduring granite from the south, their upper parts, being of electrum of the best of all lands, seen on the two sides of the river. Their rays flood the two lands when the sun-disk rises between them at its appearance on the horizon of heaven. I have done this with a loving heart for my father Amun after I entered unto his secret image. I slept not and I turned not from what he ordered until it was complete. I have paid attention to the city of the Lord of the Universe – for this city is the horizon of heaven upon earth, the place of ascent and the sacred Eye Of the Lord.*
> *I was sitting in the palace and remembered the One who*

created me: my heart directed me to make for him two
obelisks of electrum, that their pyramids might mingle with
the sky from the pillared hall between the great pylons of my
earthly father, Aa-kheper-ka-Ra. Each would be of one block
of enduring granite without joint or flaw. My majesty began
work on them in Year 15; second month of winter, day 1,
making swift time in cutting them from the mountain.

I acted in this way with love and respect as a king does for
his god. Let no man say it is boasting when I say that I have
used the finest quality of gilded electrum measured by the
sack like grain. Let them rather say: 'How like her it is, she
who is truthful to her father.' The god Amun, Lord of the
Thrones of the Two Lands, knows it in me that I am his
daughter in very truth, who glorifies him.

On the other she had inscribed:

I am the beloved of His Majesty, Amun-Ra, who placed the
kingship of Khemet, the deserts and all foreign lands under
my sandals. My southern border is at the region of Punt... My
eastern border at the marshes of Asia... My western border at
the edge of the horizon... From all these places I have brought
gifts for my Lord: incense from Punt, turquoise from Sinai,
tribute from Libya...

The Thutmosid kings who succeeded her, Akhenaten's father,
Amenhotep III, Horemheb and the Rameside kings, all had a hand in
the mighty pylons that gave entrance to sacred space after sacred
space. Chapels were added during almost every reign for two
thousand years. There were even additions by Alexander and the
Macedonian Ptolomies.

Jack took Emma's hand as they passed through the towering
gateway into Amun's most important precinct. When it was roofed it
must have been a dark and impressive place, and even now with the
sun blazing down into it, it was still awe-inspiring. Poor Akhetaten
had nothing on this scale, nothing that was still standing to cause the
visitor to gasp and want to fall to his or her knees. They walked
forward. As in the great Gothic Cathedrals of Europe the eyes were
drawn upwards. Everything soared above them, dwarfed them, and
humbled them. Eliot strode ahead as though he owned the place. He
was impressed with this in a way he had not been with the dusty
plains of Amarna. Finn too wandered off, staring and curious.

Only Emma and Jack stood still in a courtyard and hesitated to go forward. Jack would not have been able to describe exactly how he felt, but it was something to do with scale. 'Alice in Wonderland' crossed his mind. She must have felt like this when she was suddenly reduced in size and the most ordinary objects, normally so small and insignificant, became giant size and threatening.

He pulled Emma towards him and held her. He could feel that she too was overwhelmed.

'I want to get out of here,' she whispered fearfully. 'I don't feel well.'

'Let's go!' he said at once, and drew her after him back towards the entrance. But at that moment a mob of tourists came pouring into the place, and whether it was in dodging them, or whether it was because he was suddenly disorientated for other reasons, the gap in the wall they went through was not the same gap through which they had come.

They found themselves in an open space outside the main temple, but still contained within the precinct walls. Laid out in row after row were carved blocks of stone like pieces of a jig-saw waiting to be assembled, apparently put there by archaeologists working on the site. They had the area almost to themselves except for the official guide and guardian in his dark brown galabiah and white skullcap. He had been dozing in the shade, but as soon as he sensed their presence he got up and walked towards them.

'Oh, no!' muttered Emma.

Jack asked him the way out. But the man was delighted to have a couple of customers at last and was determined to show them around. He would not be diverted and led them from row to row pointing out this and that about the blocks. The two followed him in something of a daze, until Jack spotted a shed and asked if they might see into that.

'No. Not allowed,' the guide said at once.

Just at that moment another man appeared back at the entrance, shouting something to their guide. He shouted back, and then started hurrying towards the man who was now beckoning urgently.

Jack looked at Emma, and with one accord they moved towards the shed.

It was locked. The windows were small and high but standing on an old box they found they were able to peer in. With Jack holding her to steady her on the none too steady box, Emma saw more blocks of the type they had already seen, but these were better preserved and the carvings were recognisable. Emma gasped.

'What? What do you see?' Jack asked, frustrated that he was still on the ground.

'I see the rays of the Aten. I see Akhenaten and Nefertiti and...

and the princesses!' She almost screamed with excitement over the last words.

'These must be blocks from the Temple to the Aten, erected here by Akhenaten before he moved to Amarna – the one Horemheb later destroyed.'

Emma climbed down and let him climb up. She held him as he had held her, but tighter, leaning her head against the small of his back, her heart beating with the joy of the discovery.

'It is a sign!' she said. 'We were meant to see this.'

Jack could not argue. They had stumbled into this area with no foreknowledge of what they would find here, and the guide had been called away just at the right moment. He was coming back now, weaving his way through the rows of stone blocks, shouting and waving his finger at them as though they were naughty school children caught stealing apples.

Jack climbed down at once and they stood patiently while the guide berated them. As the words washed over him Jack was thinking that he very much regretted not taking photographs through the window. He must have fingered his camera at that thought, because the guide suddenly turned his attention to it and demanded that he hand it in to the authorities.

Jack protested that he had taken no pictures and refused to part with the camera. Another guide appeared from nowhere while they were arguing and joined in the fracas. Emma asked why the contents of the shed should be kept secret.

'Its just old blocks of stone like these out here,' she said scornfully.

The guides were beginning to run out of steam. In truth they did not know the answer. They had only been told the shed was off limits to tourists. They began to calm down, and when some coins had passed hands they seemed ready to let the matter drop and suggested the two might find more of interest through an open doorway to the east.

Jack and Emma followed the suggestion and found themselves near the sacred lake at the south side of the main temple.

They sat beside the water and discussed what had happened.

'I think it is yet one more confirmation that we are doing the right thing,' said Emma. 'We are being given glimpses into Akhenaten's life that were supposed to have been long since lost and destroyed.'

'It is rather like that children's game when something is hidden and the finder is told when he is getting warmer or colder in relation to the hiding place.'

Emma laughed. The dark shadows were no longer troubling her.

'I wonder how Finn and Eliot are getting on?'

As though on cue they saw Finn sauntering further round the lake. He was looking at the giant stone scarab Amenhotep III had had erected and carved in praise of his wife, Akhenaten's mother, when he married her against all protocol. As they watched, Finn started to walk purposefully round and round it.

Emma called out to him, but it was only when Jack added his voice to hers that Finn looked round and noticed them.

'What were you doing?' Emma asked as he joined them.

'I was told if you circled it three times you could wish.'

'What did you wish?' Emma cried in delight.

Finn grinned. 'That would be telling! Why don't you go and make your own wish?'

Before the last word had left his mouth Emma was off running towards the scarab. Just in case three times was not enough, she circled it six times, and then once more, a seventh, for luck.

'Seven is the most magic number of all,' she told herself.

Jack and Finn, watching her, laughed.

'It'll probably not work at all now,' Finn said. 'I was told three times.'

'Emma always has to take everything one step further than the rest of us,' Jack said. 'She has probably unleashed a devastating force by all that activity. Hey, Emma!' he called. 'That's enough.'

She came dancing back to them, her face alight.

'We should be all right now. That old Amun can't touch us now!'

'Ssh – don't *say* that!' Jack warned, half joking, half serious. 'Not in his own temple by his very own sacred lake!'

'I don't care,' she said. 'I feel we have been given a mandate by a higher power.'

She leapt up onto a block of stone that was beside them and raised her arms towards heaven.

'Do your worst!' she yelled. 'Bring on a storm this very minute to show your power – or forever hold your peace!'

Both men had stopped laughing and were watching her uneasily.

They waited. No thunder. No lightning. No squalls of hail stones as big as tennis balls.

All that happened was that seven geese that had been swimming at the far end of the lake took to the air and, beating their wings and squawking noisily, flew over them, headed off to the south.

'You see!' cried Emma jumping down from her rock. 'No thunder! No lightning!'

'Only laughter,' Jack muttered under his breath, for that is what the noise the geese made had sounded like to him. He knew that the goose was the sacred bird of Amun.

But Emma did not catch what he said, and went cheerfully to find Eliot in the temple, no longer afraid.

That night Eliot came to Emma's room.

She woke to a knocking at her door. Still half dazed, she stumbled across the floor, opened the door and stood blinking in the light from the corridor. Eliot was casually leaning against the door jam, smiling. He moved in at once, firmly shutting and locking the door behind him. Emma rubbed the sleep from her eyes and pushed the tangled hair from her face. The loose T-shirt she was wearing as a nightdress did not reach her thighs.

'What's the matter?'

'I need to talk to you,' he said.

'What's the time?' She looked vaguely round the room as though expecting to see a clock. Eliot had put on the light and, taking her arm, was leading her back to the bed.

She was awake enough at last to protest, and pull back.

'Don't worry. We're only going to talk,' he said soothingly.

Whether she believed him or not she was still sleepy enough to protest no more, and thankfully climbed back into bed.

He sat on the edge, looking down at her.

'What do you want to talk about?' She was beginning to feel uneasy. The sexual attraction between them had held them together for a long time, and she could feel it now, against her wishes, against her will. Her mind told her to send him away at once, but her body wanted him to stay. He brushed a few strands of hair from her cheek and she experienced that old familiar stirring in the rest of her body.

'Damn!' she thought.

They made a pretence of talking.

Eliot claimed to have experienced an exhilaration in the Temple of Amun that he could not explain, and wondered if this meant he was becoming less sceptical about her beliefs. She thought it might be. And then, softened by his unusual humility on the subject, she did not push his hand away when it touched her shoulder.

Before long his robe was on the floor and he was in her bed.

In the small hours she fell asleep, curled in his arms as she had been for so many nights in England.

She was still asleep when, just before dawn, he crept out of her room.

Finn, turning into the corridor from his own room on his way to watch the sunrise on the banks of the Nile, saw him.

* * * *

When Emma awoke and found him gone. She lay a long time regretting what she had done, and thinking about Jack. The light was blazing through the curtains and she stood up and went to the balcony. It was early and most of the hotel guests were still fast asleep. She saw servants pouring water onto the paved paths in the garden, while others swept it afterwards into the flowerbeds. 'What a good idea,' she thought, 'no waste.' At the same time she was appreciating the beauty of the scene beyond the garden, and was wrestling with the problem of Eliot and Jack and the tousled bedclothes behind her.

A lone figure was seated right at the river's edge, gazing out over the water. Finn.

She turned back into the room and pulled on her clothes as quick as she could, ran a comb through her hair, and splashed water on her face. Then she ran. Ran down the deserted corridors, into the empty lift, across the deserted reception area and out into the garden.

Finn was still there when she arrived breathless, at his side.

He looked surprised, but not displeased. There was something in his eyes she could not fathom, but then she was used to that with Finn.

'Did you see the sunrise?' she asked.

He nodded.

'And you?' he asked.

She shook her head. It was clear she wanted to talk about something. Her manner was agitated and nervous. But he stayed silent, waiting until she was ready.

At last it came.

'Do you think...' she burst out. 'Do you think it is possible to love two people at the same time?'

Finn stared at the water flowing past them.

'I don't see why not,' he replied.

'You don't think it is unnatural?'

'Monogamy is a convenience, not a natural state,' he said.

Emma's expression was still troubled.

'Do you think it is possible to love two people *equally*, but in different ways, for different reasons?'

'Love is not an object like a cake that after cutting it in half you have two smaller pieces. Each true love is unique and whole in itself, and is not lessened by any other love you might have. Parents know this. It's more like a hologram than a cake.'

Emma was silent. She had picked a twig from a pomegranate bush and was pulling it apart abstractedly.

Finn looked sideways at her.

'You are thinking of Eliot and Jack?'

She flushed, 'How did you know?'

He laughed. 'I'm not blind.'

In a way she was relieved that she no longer needed to talk obliquely.

'I wish I didn't have to choose between them. I love them both.'

Finn grinned. 'I thought they both irritated the hell out of you!'

She smiled ruefully.

'That too!'

They sat side by side quietly for some time, each with their own thoughts, while a barge loaded with blocks of stone passed them just as it might have done a thousand, two thousand, three thousand years before. Birds on their way to the fields flew overhead in neat formation.

After a while several other guests began coming out into the fresh early morning air of the garden.

Emma heard a voice calling her name. They both turned round and saw Jack approaching. She must have looked guilty because he asked: 'What are you two plotting? You look as thick as thieves.'

'We were just thinking,' Emma replied, a touch of irritation in her voice.

Jack laughed. 'Where is Eliot? We ought to have breakfast and be on our way.'

Finn stood up. 'I'll rustle him up,' he said, grinning at Emma. Emma flushed.

'Finn is a good friend,' she said. 'He understands things.'

'What things?'

'Oh, just things,' she said. And he had to be content with that.

18

The Eastern Desert

They would have liked to stay longer in Luxor, but their permit was not open ended and they had arranged to meet Ahmed Hassan at the police station in Qena at a precise time on Saturday.

As it happened they were an hour late and they found him drinking tea and gossiping with the Chief of Police. Both men were relaxed, leaning back in their chairs while junior officers beavered away at desks, and answered telephones.

Hassan smiled at once when he saw them and rose to greet them. Dapper as ever, he had abandoned his dove grey suit for neat, crisp new khakis. His colleague glanced at their permit and passed it back to them with a grin. In very broken English he indicated he thought they were mad, and his friend Hassan was equally mad to be going with them.

'What is there to see?' he asked. 'Nothing!'

'There is always *something*,' Emma declared with spirit.

Hassan met her eyes and smiled, but Eliot was already hurrying them to leave. He was impatient to get the whole thing over as quickly as possible. Apart from his natural antipathy to what they were doing, he was the only one of them with a regular job, which required him to be back in England the following Monday.

Hassan enquired closely about the provisions they had made for the expedition, and insisted on checking what they had in the jeep. He was instantly critical and suggested they spend more time in the town stocking up with more water and petrol and rations for emergencies.

'We won't be in the desert for more than a couple of days at most,' Jack protested, but Hassan said the desert was unpredictable and they must always prepare for the worst. Eliot groaned inwardly. There was even a moment when he contemplated leaving them in Hassan's capable care, but the sight of Jack and Emma drawn back from the others, out of earshot, close together and talking most earnestly, decided him to stay.

When Emma rejoined them she was wearing Akhenaten's seal ring.

Throughout most of their time in Egypt Jack had kept the ring hidden. Only in Akhetaten had he brought it out to see if it would guide them in any way. Now he decided it was time to use its ancient magic – and who better to wear it than Akhenaten's daughter?

Hassan too noticed the ring, and asked to see it more closely.

Jack explained at once it was a legacy from Ben Wilson and that he had come by it honestly.

'He had permission to take it out of Egypt,' Jack lied.

Hassan did not look convinced, but he chose not to pursue the matter further at that time.

'No doubt you have the appropriate papers,' he remarked casually, and then turned back to checking the provisions.

Jack, Finn and Emma looked at each other, but said nothing.

The road from Qena on the Nile to the Red Sea is not a bad one. They set off with spirits high, exhilarated by the prospect that, for good or ill, they were at last starting on the last phase of their mission. The road was so good they wondered if they really needed a jeep for the journey. But they soon had to turn north on to a much less travelled road, following in some places the track at the bottom of a wadi.

Emma had not known what to expect, but she had thought it might be like the Sahara, mile after mile of undulating sand dunes. There was certainly some of that, but mostly it was rough and rocky. The road twisted and turned among the mountains, hair-pin bends with craggy drops below them were common, and Emma's knuckles were white as she gripped the back of the front seat as they bounced along. This desolate region had yielded precious metals and gems in ancient times. The Romans had extensively quarried good building material here. Mons Claudianus, for instance, had supplied the granite for the Pantheon and Trajan's Forum in Rome. Further north, near Jebel Abu Dukhaan, they quarried the magnificent purple porphyry that was such a feature of Roman architecture at the height of the empire.

The heat was oppressive. Most of the water and their perishable provisions were stored in cold boxes. Jack remembered that in the journal Ben Wilson had described how they had carried water in canvas bags hanging from the backs of the camels, evaporation acting as the only cooling system.

They soon became aware why it was obligatory to have a guide on this journey. The Eastern Desert had been heavily mined during a war with Israel, and the only way one could tell a minefield was by the rusting barbed wire that surrounded it. In some cases sand had buried the wire, and only Hassan's military map indicated where the deadly traps lay.

'Another religious war!' Jack thought. Would humans ever learn – ever change?

They camped that night in the mountains, and found it extraordinarily cold. Emma stayed in the jeep, but the others lay in the tent, pitched against the shelter of overhanging rocks.

Jack kept thinking about Mary's enthusiasm for the universe and her description of the time distortion as the light of distant galaxies travelled towards us. He was not a church going Christian, but he sort of believed in Christ. Was he the saviour of all the distant galaxies as well, or just our world? Were there other Christs for the inhabitants of those other worlds? Questions would not let him sleep. He thought of the ancient Egyptians – the pharaohs who believed they journeyed to the stars if the right rituals were said over them at their funerals. Did they choose the star to which they wanted to go after death while they were still alive? It would seem so if it was true that a duct in the King's Chamber in the Great Pyramid at Giza was aimed directly at a particular star in the belt of Orion, and another, from the 'Queen's chamber', at Sirius. But if the light had left a million years before, the star itself might not still exist by the time the deceased reached it.

As he stared and pondered, the great arc of the heavens above, studded with a billion lights, seemed to turn inside out in some way, so that all that complex splendour was within his own consciousness, and not as points of light, but as mighty interactive systems. He experienced the universe – and not just as an observer!

A phrase he had read came to mind. Was it spoken by a Hermeticist?

'As above, so below?'

At that moment he was aware in startling clarity of the similarity of the universe within him and the universe without. The cells in his brain, with the intricate dance of molecules, atoms, nuclei, the electrical and chemical charges that fired their relationships and brought about the miracle and mystery of consciousness and thought, mirrored the greater but similar dance of stars and planets, galaxies and nebulae. In that moment he could believe that what caused consciousness in the individual brain was the same as caused consciousness in the universe. Was that Greater Consciousness the Super-consciousness that Mary talked about? The God that so many sought? He no longer felt that he was an individual unit observing the universe 'out there', but was an integral part of it and if he was snuffed out at death, as some people believed, a vital connection would be cut in the interactive process and the whole would malfunction like a person with dementia. But if he was not snuffed out, but transformed in some way, so that he was still part of the Whole, then the Whole would function as normal.

Mary jerked awake at 3am hearing the sounds of shouting outside her window. With heart beating she struggled out of bed and peeped through a gap in the curtains. There, in her garden, was a crowd of angry people shouting and shaking sticks at her house.

The harsh orange light from the street lamp illuminated every grotesque feature.

Drawing in breath sharply, she realised these were not local people... or if they were, they were clad in macabre costumes with hideous masks upon their heads.

She looked again. They were not people at all, but ancient Egyptian gods, and the sticks they were shaking at her were the staffs they carried in all the reliefs and tomb paintings she had seen of them.

Behind the screaming mob, she could sense other sinister figures standing silently in the shadows of the bushes and trees. She strained to see who they were, but could not. She felt they were somehow willing, and orchestrating, the scene.

Then she sensed someone standing behind her in her room, and turned in alarm. It was Akhenaten, as she had seen him in the desert near Abydos, his skin rubbed all over with gold dust, calmly gazing past her at the melee in the garden with his golden eyes, sadness on his golden face.

'You see what happens when priests manipulate the gods like puppets for their own gain?' he said.

'You mean...'

But he was gone. She turned again to the drama in the garden and could now see more clearly the figures lurking in the shadows. They were indeed the priests of the various sects in Egypt. As she looked at them directly, in recognition, they faded like mist at dawn, and their creations with them...

Rich and magnificent the golden disk rose and bathed all in light....

Her garden lay shadowless ... flawless ... beautiful...

She knew now that she was asleep.

After some hard driving the next day Jack and Emma and their group reached the area Ben Wilson had been exploring when he found Akhenaten's ring.

'Why would he have come here?' Hassan asked, puzzled. They had left the road system at noon, which, although rough and sparse, had afforded them some comfort. For the past two hours they had been following a compass into the desert along Bedouin tracks. Hassan and Eliot had kept up a chorus of protests, but Jack and Emma were determined not to turn back before they had a chance to bring their mission to some sort of a conclusion.

'He was trying to find an ancient route used by the miners to transport silver and amethyst back to the Nile,' Jack said. 'This area of the desert is full of mines worked in ancient times.'

They had stopped driving and were sheltering in the shade of the jeep. They were hot and exhausted, and Eliot was not the only one wishing he had not come.

There was an ominous silence about the landscape. No birds. No insects. Just rock and sand baking in the devastating heat of the sun.

Where exactly in this vast area were they to look? Not for the first time Jack felt truly daunted and wondered if they were indeed insane even to attempt such a task. What were they expecting to find? A ghost? But surely a ghost could wander the earth and turn up any place? He had often wondered why 'grey ladies' appeared always on a particular flight of stairs in an old house as though they were a replay on a video machine. If that was all the ghost of Akhenaten was, they were wasting their time.

He glanced across at Emma. She was rubbing cream into her arms. Her face was too red, her nose raw. They had been taking the normal precautions against sunburn and sunstroke, but they had never before encountered a sun so relentlessly fierce.

'When this is over,' he thought, 'Emma and I...' But the reverie was not completed.

Hassan was standing up and looking anxiously over the bonnet of the jeep back towards the track they had created in the sand. There was a faint, strange, moaning sound in the distance.

'What is it?' Eliot asked.

Hassan held up his hand for silence. They waited, straining to hear.

Suddenly he seemed very agitated and ordered them to gather everything they had scattered around outside the jeep, put it back inside, and climb in themselves as fast as they could.

'What? Why?' they all chorused.

'Sand storm!' he shouted.

They could hear it now, approaching with incredible speed, whining and screaming, the sky blackening behind it.

Without any more argument they stumbled about, the sand already stirring around them, gathering up water bottles and packs of food, and everything they could lay their hands on. As the storm struck, Hassan, the last one in, pulled the door shut behind him.

The sand battered against their flimsy windows, mended in several places with insulating tape. Small rocks must have been caught up by the wind because they could hear them banging against the metal sides of the vehicle.

'Oh, God!' muttered Jack.

'The curse of Amun,' whispered Emma, terrified, clinging to him.

Hassan in the confined space was still issuing orders. He had seized his jacket and was trying to cover the window with it.

'Where's the tape? Cover all the windows in case they give way. Quickly! Quickly!'

They struggled to obey him, finding whatever clothes they could and fastening them to the windows. When they had done this they were in darkness, and the howling of the wind, tearing at their shelter in a powerful frenzy, seemed even more terrifying. They cowered together, each with their separate and private fears.

'To die like this ... without completion...' Finn was remembering the ouija board that had told him he would die at thirty-five. It suddenly seemed as though Death was leaning over him. He could feel its chill already on his spine.

Eliot was thinking: 'How long will the air last in here with five of us breathing it?'

'The windows will never hold. Oh my God!' Jack prayed with no clear idea to whom he was praying. The Super-Consciousness he had glimpsed with such tantalising briefness the night before seemed now such a disappointingly impersonal force.

'May Allah's will be done. But why did I let these crazy English people persuade me to come this far?' Hassan muttered to himself.

Emma folded her hands and shut her eyes. 'Oh please, Great God over all other Gods, protect us from the curse of Amun and all malevolent forces. Forgive us whoever we are and whoever we have been. Christ said "forgive them for they know not what they do!" Please ... please ... we are stumbling about in a dark world, taking all sorts of wrong turnings ... Forgive us!'

She turned her face into Jack's neck and sobbed.

'Its all right,' he murmured, holding her close. 'It'll be all right.' But he had no hope that it would be.

How long they were trapped in that small space while the dark forces of the storm tore at the fabric of their vehicle, they could not tell, but at last the noise subsided and they ventured to pull the covers down from the windows and look out. Sand had found its way into the jeep through tiny cracks and Emma's face was streaked where the tears had run down through it.

Thankfully they opened the windows and forced the doors against the sand that had piled up around them, and took great gulps of fresh air. The sky was blood red.

And then they stumbled out and looked around.

The landscape had completely changed. Sand had covered many of the rocks that had been visible before, and exposed others that had not. But strangest of all strange sights were the skeletons of military tanks and guns now lying before them.

They looked to Hassan for an explanation.

'They must have been left behind after the war,' he said. 'They were buried under the sand.'

'Just under the surface,' Jack thought. 'The ghosts of religious wars.' How many other wars lay covered, biding their time to resurface?

'We can't go on,' Eliot declared. 'We nearly died in that storm, and who knows what unexploded bombs lie around these parts. We have to go back.'

'If we can find our way back,' Finn muttered gloomily, staring at the changed landscape around them. The fear of immediate death having been lifted he was still not convinced he would be allowed to live beyond his thirty-sixth birthday.

They shook the sand out of clothes and boxes, and cleared up their vehicle and themselves. The sun had set and the red glow was already fading from the sky.

At that moment Hassan called out. 'We'd better get ready for the night before all the light goes. No one is to wander from the camp. Eliot is right. There may be unexploded bombs. We will return to Qena the first thing in the morning.'

In the morning they did not notice at first that Emma was missing. They thought she had just gone behind a rock as she usually did to relieve herself. But it soon became clear she had left the camp and no matter how they searched and called, she was nowhere to be found.

Hassan muttered several Arabic swear words and looked really worried.

'You had better tell me right now,' he said angrily to Jack. 'What is the real purpose of your visit to this part of Egypt?' He caught the look that passed swiftly between the three men. It was Eliot who spoke first, in Hassan's own language.

Jack was annoyed, not knowing what he was saying.

Hassan turned on him when Eliot had stopped speaking.

'A ghost hunt!' he exclaimed. 'Are you mad? Risking all our lives for such a thing!'

'It is not just a ghost hunt,' Jack protested. 'I don't know what Eliot has told you, but he has never understood what we have been trying to do.'

'An ancient curse! Please! Give me some credit for intelligence.'

'What did you think we were looking for?' Finn asked suddenly.

Hassan looked at him – the silent one – the mysterious one – and then he turned back to Jack.

'I thought,' he answered with irritation, 'and I still think, you are looking for treasure your great-grandfather found, the ring being part of it. I came along with you to make sure you didn't smuggle it out of Egypt as he did the ring.'

Jack was astonished. Of course! That would make perfect sense to a policeman.

But Emma was missing and this was not the time to pursue the matter. If she believed they were abandoning the mission she might well be trying to complete it by herself.

'We can sort all this out later,' he said. 'We must look for Emma.'

They gazed anxiously over the desert ahead.

The early light picked out everything with great clarity, including the stark rusting metal of the broken tanks and the long barrels of the missile launchers. Luckily in this sandy terrain footprints were not easily hidden. They could see the direction in which she had left the camp. To have disappeared so completely she must have left many hours before. Not one had noticed her going, though none of them had felt they were soundly asleep. A torch was missing, and a water bottle and some dried bread and dates. She had not taken much.

Hassan supervised the packing of provisions and the medical box, and protection against the sun. He insisted on leaving the jeep behind, as it would be more likely than themselves to set off unexploded bombs.

'She couldn't have got that far on foot,' he said.

They hoped he was right and set off in some agitation.

It was in the heat of midday that Jack first caught sight of her. He and Eliot, ahead of the others, had reached the top of a ridge and were gazing out over a flat plain, mostly sand with occasional wind-weathered rocks rising black above it. If she had not moved they might not have seen her.

'There she is!' cried Jack at once, pointing to a small dark object moving across the sand in the distance. He turned to Eliot to see if he would confirm the sighting and was startled to catch his expression. Eliot's face was fearsomely angry, taut lines distorting his mouth, his eyes, seemingly blazing with hate.

'What on earth?' Jack muttered, hardly crediting what he saw.

But Emma was his priority and he put aside the question that needed asking. He turned, scrambling down the steep and rocky slope towards the plain. The sand made it difficult to run, but he ran. The sun blazed down like a blowtorch at his back, and sweat poured from him, running into his eyes and obscuring his vision. Impatiently he wiped it away with the back of his hand, blinking against the glare. The air seemed to be liquid, bubbling in a cauldron. He felt as though his heart was bursting, but he ran on.

It was not so easy to see her now that he was on her own level, but instinct and desperation kept him moving in the right direction.

Suddenly he noticed what looked like a brown column reaching to the sky. He stumbled to a halt, the better to identify it. Another appeared. Straining his eyes into the heat haze he identified two thin twisters, two desert whirlwinds tearing the sand off the earth and sucking it into the sky.

'Emma!' He started to run again, calling her name, over and over again.

He could see her running between the two columns, clutching something to her breast, dodging as the two veered towards her. It looked for all the world as though the two were pursuing her, trying to squeeze her between them.

Running and calling, Jack was frantic. In that moment of extreme anxiety he saw them as alive, two fearsome supernatural enemies trying to destroy her and what she carried.

He made one last desperate effort and flung himself forward, taking her into his arms. They were together when one of the whirlwinds reached them, and even with their combined weight it lifted them off their feet and flung them against the rocks. Jack heard the screaming of the wind in his ears as a voice full of hate. When it passed the other struck and buffeted them further across the desert. His skin was burning from the bombardment of millions of grains of sand. He tried to cover Emma as best he could with his own body, but the wind was trying to tear them apart. They clung with a surprising tenacity to each other, believing that if they let go they would die.

At last, with a final violent shake, the wind dropped them and, shrieking in apparent frustration, moved off across the plain to follow its companion.

Sobbing, Emma clung to Jack. Blood was running from a cut on her forehead. He himself was bruised and bleeding, the skin of his left arm grated raw by the sand. But they were alive.

After a few moments of relief at their escape, Emma began to look around them as though seeking something she had lost.

'The bones!' she cried. 'Where are the bones?'

'What bones?' he asked, drawing back from her.

'The bones of Akhenaten! I found them! But now they're gone.'

He remembered how he had seen her clutching something before the wind struck.

If she had indeed had the bones of Akhenaten in her arms, perhaps he had not been wrong after all to think the whirlwinds were not natural phenomena, but somehow consciously trying to destroy them. Even as the thought crossed his mind, he dismissed it angrily. 'I'm becoming as crazy as she is,' he told himself. But he could not get the image of Eliot's extraordinarily violent rage out of his mind.

Emma had left his side and, limping badly, was desperately searching the sand in a wide arc around them, muttering to herself.

Jack was bending down helping her search when he noticed that the light had dimmed. He glanced up, hoping that a merciful cloud would give them some respite from the scorching heat. But what he saw horrified him. His mouth fell open as he stared upwards, scarcely crediting what he saw. There seemed to be a vast circle of billowing black clouds, like a wheel, slowly turning in the sky, the centre still blue above them, but an unnatural electric blue. Every second the circle was closing in. Around the edges the light was livid, vile, piercing and destructive.

As the huge clouds, like a vast whirlpool sucking everything into its depths, churned around them, he grabbed hold of Emma again. She too was gazing upwards in alarm.

The last blue disappeared. Lightning pierced the blackness, striking the ground all around them as though Set, the mighty storm god of ancient Egypt, was personally trying to destroy them. The two twisters that had seemed so frightening a short while before must have been no more than outriders, heralds, of this storm.

There was nowhere to run. Nowhere to hide.

Jack felt in that moment that he would die and, like Akhenaten, have no great journey to the Otherworld, no vision of what the Reality of Existence was. His heart was beating like a drum in the vast cacophony of thunderous sound that cracked and roared and rumbled around them.

He looked back in a frantic attempt to see what was happening to the others, and there he saw, looming out of the swirling fury of the storm, the faces of the hostile gods, the gods Akhenaten had offended.

206

And on the hill where he had last seen Eliot, was a huge, dark figure, many metres high, with arms raised, orchestrating the storm – the centre of an immortal hatred, an everlasting demand for vengeance.

Jack held Emma close. If they were to die, they would die together. He closed his eyes.

But when his lids came down and the fearsome visions were shut out, another vision took over. He had had this vision before. It was of the magnificence of the universe.

But now a further understanding came to him.

However vast and impressive the universe appeared – it was still only matter. What was greater was spirit and, that mystery of all Mysteries, Consciousness, which in its higher form can remake the universe as a child remakes a house of cards.

He opened his eyes and stared defiantly into the eyes of the gods that leaned over him from the swirling clouds. Their eyes were darker than the blackness that surrounded him, but his consciousness penetrated their shadows, and he knew they were limited beings, only fragments of the Everlasting – not of Eternity. They, like him, and Emma, were subject to Time in their earthly form. But there was another reality their shadows did not touch. The state of being that was utterly other than anything any of them could imagine. A state of being that had nothing to do with time or matter.

If Akhenaten had grasped this, the Priests of Amun would have had no power over him. Perhaps even his vision was not enough to free him from the shackles of time. Perhaps even he had not completely understood the complete otherness of Eternity. And they, the Shemsu Benu, had likewise perpetuated his imprisonment century after century by believing in the curse, believing he was trapped.

Jack screamed out in a voice that seemed to fill the vast desert and the black, swirling clouds above it:

'You have no power in Eternity. Only on this earth, and only if we let you!'

At this moment he believed Akhenaten was in Eternity and had always been in Eternity. Only his shadowy Ka was held prisoner – and now even it would be released to go on its way...

For a moment the malevolent figures seemed to grow stronger, larger, more threatening. But he held his ground.

And then the figures began fading fast, the clouds drawing apart, the blessed light of the sun returning.

As he turned his head to the west he saw it shining through a break in the clouds in long separate rays that fanned out across the earth – the cipher Akhenaten had chosen to represent his god, the Aten.

Jack and Emma were alive.

* * * *

When Finn and Hassan caught up with them, there was no sign of Eliot.

Emma was lying on the ground looking drawn and faint.

'Give her water,' Hassan said at once, and Finn held his water bottle to her lips. She drank thirstily, but when she turned her face to look at them, they noticed her eyes were shining feverishly.

'I've found him!' she said. 'He is here.'

Finn looked enquiringly at Jack.

Jack shrugged his shoulders.

Emma was on her hands and knees now searching the sand again frantically.

'She seems to have found some bones she believes are those of Akhenaten,' Jack explained, 'but she dropped them when we were caught up in a whirlwind.'

'There must be lots of bones in this desert,' Hassan said, 'animal as well as human.'

'I think we should help her find them,' Jack said quietly. 'Whether they are his or not, she won't leave until she has them.'

The men joined the search.

It was Finn who found the first one, and Emma who found the rest. She cradled them in her arms as though they were those of a lost infant. Jack and Hassan watched her in some alarm. The bones were indeed those of a human, and old, cleaned and whitened by years of wind and sun, but whether they were those of a man who lived more than three thousand years ago, or that of a Roman, or a Bedouin, or even those of a soldier from the most recent religious war, they could not tell. But no one tried to take them from her. Still holding them she allowed herself to be led back towards where they had left the jeep.

They found Eliot on the ridge where Jack had last seen him. He was sitting on the ground with his head on his knees, as though exhausted. He glanced up as they approached, and his expression was strained and weary, as though he, and not Jack, had run through the heat of the desert. He listened silently when Finn told him Emma had found the bones of Akhenaten, a bitter twist to his mouth the only change to his expression.

Jack stared at him, puzzled and uneasy. He had known him a long time, but now he seemed like a stranger. Emma must have sensed something too, for she walked past him without a greeting.

* * * *

When they were safely back at the jeep, Finn urged Emma to tell him how she had found the bones.

'Leave it for now, Finn,' Jack cautioned. 'She is in no fit state to answer questions.'

'We must know more!' Finn seemed agitated. In fact, he was more agitated than Jack had ever seen him. 'We may have a chance of giving him a proper burial at last if they really are his bones.'

'Not now, Finn. Let it be.' Even Hassan could see that Emma was not herself.

'I need to know,' Finn persisted.

Jack was about to intervene again when Emma started to speak. She sounded almost as though she were drunk or drugged.

'I saw him. I saw him standing in the desert. I walked towards him and he didn't move. He pointed at my hand – the hand with his ring. I thought he was asking for it and I was prepared to take it off and give it to him, but when I was as near to him as I am to you now, he disappeared.' She gave a sigh. 'And then I saw the bones in the sand exactly where he had been standing.'

They listened in silence.

Jack wondered what Hassan was thinking. If he believed there was a chance of their being genuinely the bones of Akhenaten he would have to take them to the authorities to be examined and put in a museum. Jack hoped for Emma and Finn's sake the sceptical expression on the policeman's face would mean they could take them off and bury them as Finn had suggested.

Jack wanted the bones to be those of Akhenaten. They all needed closure on a physical, ordinary level. Already his magnificent understanding in the black vortex seemed unreal. How could he possibly convey it to the others? Besides, he did not know if Emma would be able to accept that the bones were not what she believed them to be. He had been alarmed at the look in her eyes when she had been seeking them after the whirlwind.

As for Eliot! He turned his attention to his old friend. He remembered that Eliot had been trying to stop them and take them back to England from the very first. If they were all reincarnated protagonists in an ancient drama, and if Emma had been Setepenra, as she believed, Eliot might well have been Horemheb or one of the Priests of Amun.

There was a full moon that night. The milky light created an eerie, unearthly landscape. Pools of silver sand lay between islands of the deepest, blackest shadow. It was a landscape in which one could believe anything could happen.

* * * *

In England Mary, restless and unsleeping, went out into her garden to watch the huge silver sphere of the full moon rolling across the sky above her. She was thinking about the expedition. Emma had phoned from Qena to say they were going into the Eastern Desert.

They must be there now, seeing that same moon.

She felt calm, as though something good had happened.

The group slept one more night in the desert, too exhausted to drive on by the time they reached the jeep. The bones were placed carefully in the strong cardboard box in which many of their provisions had been packed, wrapped tenderly in a spare blouse of Emma's. She curled up on the back seat, her eyes shining with the sense of achievement. She was feeling an amazing sense of relief, and had no doubt at all that she had found what remained of the body of Akhenaten, and they would be able to free his soul at last. Neither she nor Jack mentioned anything about their extraordinary adventure. It was as though they knew they couldn't describe it, so there was no point in trying.

Eliot was restless. His head ached and he had an uneasy feeling that something had happened to him he could not quite remember. Only Hassan spoke to him on the long walk back. The rest were cold and distant. He could get nowhere near Emma, and he had to endure the sight of Jack walking close to her, often helping her when she stumbled. That last night in the Sheraton at Luxor seemed a long time ago. What had happened? Why was she so antagonistic? He did not believe for a moment the bones were those of Akhenaten, and he suspected that neither did Hassan, but they could see how important it was to the others, so both men were playing along with it. Hassan had said he would take the bones back to Cairo for examination, and Eliot could not be sure whether he meant to do so or not. Probably he was intending to throw them away as soon as the others' backs were turned. But whatever happened, this ridiculous expedition, or 'mission' as they called it, was thankfully over.

Before dawn Eliot wriggled out of his sleeping bag and climbed the small knoll that loomed darkly behind their camp.

Sitting down with his back to a rock, he shivered and drew his jacket closer around him. The moon had set and the darkness of the desert was oppressive. Above him the sky was where the action was – a billion pinpoints of light reminded him of a vast city. He let his mind wander to the cities he had known – anything to take his mind off the empty, alien desert. In a city there were people, movement, noise, life, a thousand things to keep one occupied and distracted. He was never at a loss in a city. Here, with everything stripped away, he felt lonely, vulnerable. Unwelcome thoughts were beginning to crawl into his mind. The cities that had seemed so full of life and interest before began to seem less so. He began to notice the back streets, the dirt, the disease, and the children being abused – the suburbs where the householder was clutching his worthless possessions so closely a thief had to kill him to get them away from him... Then other images crept in ... the Ku Klux Klan in the Southern States of the USA echoed in England with a petrol bomb through a letter box because a neighbour had a different coloured skin ... the Spanish Inquisition ... slave ships and gas chambers ... 'ethnic cleansing'... generations of suffering because some people believed that they were superior to others and thus had the right to wield power over them.

And then suddenly, at the centre of the malaise, he saw himself.

The desert lying at his feet suddenly seemed familiar. He had been here before. Uneasily he began to remember that other time... He and his fellow priests circling the body of a man – speaking the fearful words that stripped him of everything he possessed including, they believed, his right to eternal life...

Eternal Life? The American Eliot had not thought he believed in it, and until this moment, in this desolate and haunted place, he had not thought he needed to believe in it. But what if one *was* accountable for one's actions, and not only in this life? What if there was a series of realms through which one had to progress, watched and tested all the time? What if he had lived before and committed unspeakable deeds for which he would have to pay? What if – and the thought would not go away – what if *he* was the one who had cursed Akhenaten and was himself locked, like him, in the savagery of that curse forever. Mary had said a curse binds him who is cursed and him who curses. He suddenly remembered what had happened when he was alone on that ridge watching Jack run towards Emma. He had felt ungovernable rage. What his hate had created all those centuries before was about to be destroyed! His anger had taken on fearsome form. He felt it was he who had stirred the desert up to form the twisters, and then, when that failed, he who had commanded the dark and whirling vortex.

When the rage had passed he had felt empty, desolate and spent. He had hardly been aware of the others passing him.

He thought back on his life. It had not been a bad one. He had always had plenty of money. He had gone to good schools and a good university. He had a good job. He had Emma. But – and here for the first time he realised something about himself – he had not been 'awake'. He had not been 'engaged' in it as though it were real. The days and nights had passed and not once had he noticed the meaning of them. He would die and someone would ask him about his life and he would not know how to reply. 'Life?' he would say. 'What life? I didn't notice it. It just passed.'

Was this the working out of the curse? Akhenaten could not live again and progress meaningfully through the rich and varied realms of Being, but neither could he. He could have been born again and again, but the lives he lived were empty, wasted. Even his love for Emma was not true love.

He had no feeling of 'being' with her in mind, soul and spirit.

He stood up suddenly, shocked and agitated.

Somewhere in the distance a jackal howled, a lonely and a desperate sound.

In the morning when the others arose and set about finishing what food was left, and then packing up to leave, Eliot was silent and subdued. Jack glanced at him once or twice, wondering about him. But nothing was said.

They drove back to Qena, each busy with their own thoughts. Emma seemed to have recovered, and, though still elated at her find, was no longer feverish and half demented.

At Qena, Hassan was to be returned to the Police Station where they had picked him up. They had made no further arrangements. While he went in to see if there were any messages for him, the others waited outside.

Eliot was bent on flying back to England as soon as possible and suggested they returned to Luxor and took a flight from there.

Finn pointed out that they should return the jeep to the farmer who had rented it to them at Minya.

Eliot said the farmer would not lose out for they had paid generously for it, and he would send him some more money in compensation. 'Its an old wreck anyway, practically on its last legs.'

But Finn seemed determined that it should be returned, and declared he would drive it back himself.

Jack was almost as keen as Eliot to return to England, but Emma was insisting on accompanying Finn, so he said he would go with them.

Eliot was about to burst out with one of his hostile quips, but bit his lip, and said nothing.

A few moments later he declared that, as far as he was concerned, the expedition was over, and he would return to Luxor and take a flight from there back to England whatever the others decided to do.

No one argued.

Jack helped him disentangle his luggage from the others.

'What's the matter, old man? Are you feeling okay?'

Eliot looked at him and Jack was surprised at his expression.

'I've some serious thinking to do,' he said soberly.

They stared into each other's eyes for a long time and Jack knew his friend had taken a great leap forward towards better perception and awareness.

Eliot glanced over towards Emma who was now sitting on the steps of the police station in earnest conversation with Finn.

'Look after her,' he said, pretending a lightness he did not feel. 'She may well be better off with you.'

At that moment Ahmed Hassan came rushing out of the door and spoke to Finn and Emma in some agitation. Jack could not hear what was said, but in the end he hurried back into the station with only a quick wave towards Eliot and himself.

Finn and Emma at once came towards Jack and Eliot.

'What's happening? What did he say?' Jack asked.

'It seems there's some big thing he has to deal with urgently, so he's leaving us now.'

'What about the bones?'

'He didn't mention them, so I think we're free to take them back to Amarna for proper burial,' Finn said.

'Perhaps he doesn't really think they are Akhenaten's.'

'He seemed very distracted. Something really nasty must have happened.'

'Well,' said Eliot, 'you're on your own if you insist on doing this. I'm leaving.'

'That'll be no bad thing,' said Emma sharply.

'Won't you reconsider?' Jack spoke quickly. 'You've come this far. Why not be in at the end?'

'It *is* ended,' Eliot said with conviction.

'Not quite,' Finn said, with equal conviction.

'For me it is,' Eliot said, and there was almost a touch of out-of-character humility about the tone of his voice.

Emma looked at him in surprise. 'No!' she thought. 'He is not doing this to me again. Every time I try to get free of him, he pretends to be sensitive to my beliefs, and as soon as I decide to stay he goes back to his old ways.'

'Well, its best that you go now then,' she said heartlessly. 'We won't drive you to Luxor because its in the opposite direction, and who knows, Hassan might change his mind and demand the bones back. We must get going fast.'

'I say...' Jack protested.

'Its all right,' Eliot said. 'I'll be okay. You can drop me in the town centre. There'll be plenty of transport there.'

So that is what they did. Emma did not even look back to wave.

The drive north was an anxious one. They were determined to stay overnight in Minya again, though this time they decided to try another hotel.

Jack was convinced Hassan would never have let them go with the bones if he had thought for a moment they were those of Akhenaten, while Emma believed that the forces of Akhenaten were now working with them to give them every assistance. Finn was looking over his shoulder at every car he heard following them, terrified they would be stopped before they could perform the ceremony and complete the process of his redemption.

They did not reach Minya until late and signed in at the hotel that served alcohol to foreigners. They had no trouble obtaining rooms, one double for Mr and Mrs Wilson, and one single for Finn. Emma stood quietly by when the booking was made and did not complain when they found their room had only a double bed. Jack tried not to think of Eliot as he stood back for her to enter. More things were coming to a head than their mission to free Akhenaten. How would it be? He had wanted this for so long and now that he almost had it, he was nervous and unsure of himself.

When they eventually climbed into bed, he turned his back on her.

He lay for a long time, unrelaxed, thinking about all that had happened – the change in his own perceptions and beliefs since he had come to Egypt, and the change he had seen in Eliot when they had said goodbye. Whether he himself had been some specific character in that long ago drama he did not know, and no longer really cared. He was alive now and what he had done was what he needed to do to free himself, as much as Akhenaten, from the invisible threads that apparently held him to the past. Emma might have been Setepenra, or she might not. He wondered how she would react when Akhenaten was finally buried in his tomb. He could feel her warmth against his back, but he did not turn. It was not the right time yet. What would he do if she could not leave the ancient past alone, even after the final ceremony? He did not think he could live with a woman who was not fully engaged in the present, no matter how she attracted him.

What would Mary think of how things had turned out? It was extraordinary that they had found the bones. Had Emma really seen the ghost of Akhenaten beckoning her? Or had she seen yet another whirlwind, so common in the desert? It may have been coincidence that the whirlwind had disturbed the sand enough to uncover bones that had lain hidden for centuries just as Emma approached.

It was not until the small hours that he fell asleep, unaware that Emma herself was now experiencing a dream which she believed was illuminating, at last, their ancient relationships.

Setepenra walked in a garden late in the evening. The main flush of the sunset had passed. One star was hanging in the sky like a lamp. The last few birds were settling into the trees. The lilies drooped on the pool. Ra's strength was leaving the world and everything was closing down, losing energy, going to sleep.

As she stared at the star her heart ached. Was this the star where her father even now should be? Was this the star he had been denied?

She had only recently learned her family's tragic story, and she was not sure she knew it all yet.

She had spent her early years in Akhetaten, the City of the Sun, carefree and joyful, the privileged youngest daughter of the King, with friends and sisters to play with, and servants to minister to every whim, surrounded by flowers and pools and shady trees.

And then, without warning, she was taken from her bed at night, her mouth stuffed with cotton to stifle her cries of alarm, swathed in a heavy cloak. Her captor ran a long way with her, his arms uncomfortably tight around her, others beside him, hurrying him on. She could hear the thud of their feet on the dusty road, the change in sound as they ran over wooden planks. She felt a sickening motion, and knew that they must be on a boat. She heard sharp orders given as the sails were unfurled, and then the creaking of boards, and the swish of water against the sides.

At last she was released and stared, blinking, up into the face of a young man. She could barely make out his features in the darkness, though a billion stars and a crescent moon gave faint light. She hit out at once, scoring his cheek with her nails, screaming imprecations.

It was only later that she learned that he had saved her life.

Later still she was reunited with two of her sisters. The three youngest daughters of Akhenaten and Nefertiti had been smuggled out of the city for their own safety when the Atenists fell from power. They stayed with a family, secretly loyal to their father, on a remote country estate. They grew up far from the power struggles of the court, never sure why their lives had changed so dramatically, but eventually accepting the pleasures and privileges of their new home.

Only Setepenra, the youngest, wept for her father every night before she went to sleep.

Sometimes the exiled princesses overheard things being discussed by the grown ups. It seemed Ankhesenpaaten, one of their sisters left behind in Akhetaten, had become great royal wife to their half brother Tutankhaten, who was now, it seemed, pharaoh, and had changed his name to Tutankhamun.

It was at this moment Setepenra finally accepted that her parents must be dead.

The young man who had so roughly bundled her out of her bed that horrifying night, Rekhmire, still bearing the faint scars of her nails on his cheek, had become her closest friend, and it was to him she turned in her despair.

'Tasherit and Neferne don't seem to care,' she sobbed. 'They say we'll be going back soon now. Ankhesenpaaten will send for us, but how can I bear it without father and mother? What happened to them Rekhmire? Why has everything changed?'

Rekhmire, whose name meant 'wise-like-Ra', sighed. He was young, but he had already noticed that the one certainty in life is change. He knew his father did not want the little girls troubled with too much political detail. He told her only that some bad men had been angry because her father had taken away their riches and their privileges and they had had him murdered.

It was not until much later, when she herself was grown up, and married to a man she did not love, that she learned of the curse on her father.

It was then she joined the Shemsu Benu, and Rekhmire and she became secret lovers.

When Jack woke at dawn he found Emma curled around him, awake.

This time he did not hold back.

Before they set off for Amarna Emma insisted on doing some shopping. He was surprised that she was not as impatient as Finn clearly was to get going, but when she returned with her arms full of flowers he saw what she had in mind. She filled the back of the dusty, dilapidated jeep with glorious blooms.

'For Akhenaten?' Finn asked. She nodded.

They drove to Amarna in a state of tense excitement. At the back of their minds was the fear that they might be stopped, plus an anxiety that they would not be able to perform a ceremony effective enough to send his soul on its way. They knew quite a lot about the traditional methods of burial in ancient Egypt – the casting of spells from the Book of the Great Awakening (or The Book of the Dead as some called it!) – the placing of food and drink for the deceased's journey into the Otherworld – the placing of familiar possessions around the coffin so the traveller would not feel lost or homesick – the placing of an Osiris shaped tray planted with seed to indicate new life germinating... but all these things had probably been dropped by Akhenaten. He believed he would go straight to union with the Aten, the blazing disk of the sun, without passing the seven gates, fourteen mounds, twenty one doors to face the forty two assessors in the Hall of Osiris where his heart would be weighed against the feather of Maat, the representative of Truth and Cosmic Order.

Their ceremony would of necessity have to be an invention of their own, bearing in mind as much as they knew of Akhenaten's beliefs. What they lacked in knowledge they would have to make up for with the passion and sincerity of their hearts. They were no longer living at the time of Akhenaten. Through many lifetimes they had become who they now were, and as they were now they had to perform a ceremony that would free a soul.

After establishing at el-Till that the Royal Tomb had been opened already for some earlier visitors, they set off. The drive across the plain of Amarna, keeping in sight the gap in the range of hills where Akhenaten's god rose in glory to shine upon his city and his tomb, and the walk through the wadi towards the remote royal tomb, seemed much longer than usual.

But all went well, and they arrived at the tomb just as the other visitors were leaving. The guard was different from the one before, so mercifully did not recognise them as 'those trouble-makers'. He was an old man, the father of the regular guard, standing in for him today as a favour, more interested in the breakfast he was chewing than the fact that the tourists were carrying so many flowers into the tomb.

Once inside, Finn unpacked his rucksack where he had hidden the bones, and laid them carefully on the floor where the sarcophagus would have been. They would not have made a complete skeleton, but the skull at least was there. Tenderly he arranged it with the others.

Jack stood back, feeling almost an intruder.

Emma took Akhenaten's ring off her finger, and with no more than a quick enquiring look at Jack, laid it beside the skeletal hand.

Then she arranged the flowers around him. When that was done she took a leather pouch out of one of her string bags. She opened it and Jack peered curiously over her shoulder. Inside were candles and a collection of exquisitely formed quartz crystals. With great care she placed them at intervals around the body and throughout the burial chamber. Finn lit the candles.

'Now we can begin,' she whispered, and beckoned Jack to come forward.

But before they started, Finn spoke the name of the slave who had been buried without his name all those millennia ago, and then he and Emma took it in turns to intone prayers and supplications to counteract any residue of spells and curses that might still be active, pleading for help, guidance and protection for themselves and for the souls about to embark on the greatest journey in existence.

As he watched the makeshift ritual and heard Emma call upon Akhenaten's god to take the pharaoh and the slave together into union with him at last, Jack wondered again about the dark vortex they had experienced in the desert. He remembered Elijah in the Bible had been taken up to heaven in a whirlwind. He remembered Jehovah speaking to Job out of a whirlwind.

'Who is that that darkeneth counsel without knowledge?'
'Where was thou when I laid the foundations of the earth?
Declare, if thou hast understanding...'

Where indeed?

Jehovah, Aten, Amun, Allah – a different name from every culture on earth did not mean there were as many gods ... A different image drawn from the environment of every country ... the sun that blazed down so relentlessly in Egypt ... the whirlwinds that stirred up dust in ancient Canaan ... even the hot springs that were a feature of his home town in England, giving rise to the image of a goddess associated with them... None of these meant that the mighty first cause, that which Was, Is and Always Shall Be, is not single and unique.

Jack knew now with extraordinary conviction that there was some inexplicable, unimaginable Consciousness beyond all the naming and the imaging. He knew that we see this Consciousness shaped by who we are and how far along the path of enlightenment we have travelled.

What the truth about Akhenaten was they might never know. But whatever it was, the search for it had changed the course of his own life forever, and possibly the lives of the others as well.

He saw Finn leaning forward and touching the mouth of the skull with his flute as an ancient priest might have done with meteoric iron to 'open the mouth' of the deceased. Jack felt a sudden change in the atmosphere of the tomb. He lifted his head and looked around in astonishment. Wherever Emma had placed the crystals it seemed a fine, laser-like beam of light had sprung into being. Within seconds the whole chamber was criss-crossed with threads of light radiating out from the body, enclosing it in a kind of protective temple structure. He gasped. There was a very strong feeling of an invisible Presence beside them.

Finn had now put the flute to his own lips and beautiful and haunting music was coming from it. Tears were streaming down Emma's cheeks. Jack too was blinking back the tears.

Finn was ecstatic. He knew he had, at last, been forgiven.

19

Back to England

At Cairo airport late that night, just as they were getting their boarding passes, Emma heard her name spoken and swung round. It was Ahmed Hassan in his dove grey suit.

He seemed friendly enough, but behind him were two policemen.

'A formality, you understand,' he said with his usual suave politeness. 'I'm afraid we have to check your luggage.'

They were led into a side room and thoroughly searched by the two policemen while Hassan made polite small talk.

'We buried Akhenaten in his rightful tomb,' Emma said. 'We are taking nothing back to England.'

'I know. We found the burial,' he said quietly. 'Even the ring.'

'Then why are you searching us?'

'My dear friend, I am only carrying out a little search to placate my colleagues. You must understand my position. If I let anything out of Egypt that should not go, just because I have grown fond of you...'

'What will become of the bones?' Jack asked.

'I'm afraid they can't be left where they are.'

'Why not?' Emma cried. 'You could put glass over them like you have over Tutankhamun.'

'If they are proved to be those of Akhenaten, they will certainly be treated with respect.'

'Will you let us know the result?' Jack asked.

'Of course.'

They could hear their flight being called, and Hassan walked them to the plane.

'Goodbye,' he said at the foot of the steps. 'I will not forget you.'

Jack met his eyes and for a long moment gazed into them. Startled, he realised they reminded him of the eyes of a man he had encountered twice before. Once in the dream of the meeting of the Shemsu Benu and, secondly, in his vision in the tomb of Ramose at Amarna.

He opened his mouth to say something, but the flight attendant hurried him on to the plane.

At the top of the steps he looked back, but Hassan was already walking away.

Jack was hardly aware of being shown to his seat or of putting Emma's string bags up into the overhead lockers.

Almost before they were settled Jack turned to Emma to tell her about his suspicion, but she was already speaking about Hassan.

'You know I think he was also one of the Shemsu Benu,' she was saying. 'Did you notice how he protected us, all the time? I don't think we would have got through it without him. He saved me from those men in Cairo. He was in charge of the investigation after what happened in the Royal tomb. He came into the desert with us and saw that we avoided the minefields and the unexploded bombs.'

'He made sure we had enough food and water, and warned us of the sand storm in time for us to take shelter!'

'Who do you think he was?'

'He could have been Ramose who had been the steward of both Akhenaten and his father. I had a vision of a man in the tomb of Ramose at Amarna. He led me out as though he was trying to guide me to something in the desert.'

'I wish we had told him what we were trying to do right from the beginning,' Emma said. 'I *knew* he would understand!'

'I don't know. Everything seems to unfold at its own pace. If we'd spoken up too soon who knows what would have happened.'

'He even knew before we did that it was something more than the loss of his flute that was bothering Finn. Why, oh why, didn't we suspect him before?' Emma cried.

Jack was silent, remembering how many times he had fought to avoid recognition and acknowledgement of the unexpected and unfamiliar. This was no exception.

When they arrived back in England nothing specific was said, but Emma went home with Jack. As they threw down their luggage on the floor of the living room, she reached up her arms and gave a long, luxurious stretch as though she were a cat glad to be back at her own fireside.

The very next day they went to see Mary. She had invited Bernard and Eliot, but only Bernard had come. He was overjoyed to see them and almost overwhelmed them with his eager delight.

Mary smiled politely in the background, wishing she had seen them alone for at least the first time. She was longing to hear every detail, but Bernard would not stop talking. He gave a long explanation of how he had felt he ought to come back to England when he did, how he owed it to his ailing, elderly mother not to put himself in any unnecessary danger, how he had regretted it as soon as he left Egyptian soil, how he had missed their camaraderie as much as the dramatic experiences they were having...And then came the questions.

At last Mary intervened.

'Bernard,' she said firmly. 'Give them time to answer, for heaven's sake!'

At once he started apologising and only stopped that when they began to talk over him.

Jack had a question of his own. 'Have you seen Eliot since he came back?'

'No,' Mary replied. 'I didn't know until Emma's phone call that he had left before you. As soon as I heard, I phoned him, but I only got his answering machine.'

'I hope he is all right,' Jack said anxiously.

'Of course he's all right,' Emma said scornfully. 'Why wouldn't he be?'

'I don't know. I think he was pretty shaken by the revelation that he may have been one of Amun's gang.' Jack had spoken about his suspicion on the plane.

'He didn't care at all,' Emma said. 'He was every bit as arrogant as he always is!' She would not forgive herself for having lived so long with the enemy, or him for having deceived her.

'Are you going to be as unforgiving as he?' Mary asked mildly.

Emma flushed slightly.

'No, of course not, but...'

'The important thing,' Mary continued calmly, 'is that you have all learned from the experience...'

'I have,' said Finn suddenly.

They all looked at him. On the way back he had told Emma and Jack why he had been so anxious to bury Akhenaten properly this time.

'I have learned that I must not batten on to a figure in history and try to live out his life instead of my own.'

Mary nodded. 'We only get hints from the past, and if we build on them too elaborately we are in danger of going horribly wrong.'

'Rather like archaeologists who construct a temple from a few bricks – when they were actually the remains of a latrine,' Jack said. They laughed. They had all been following hints and clues. Who could tell whether they had found the truth or not?

'Now, begin at the beginning,' Mary said. 'Tell me everything that happened.'

As they spun the tale, she found it interesting how often they interrupted each other to correct a detail or two. Jack was always seeing ambiguities, Emma certainties, Finn, things that went unnoticed by either of the other two.

As Mary listened she was weaving into their story her own experiences of dreams and visions and insights. The adventure had occurred on many levels. At some moments she had felt they were playing a game of three-dimensional chess in several parallel universes at the same time. The drama had been played out on one level among the dust and flies of modern Egypt, with the ever present physical dangers of rapists, thieves and terrorists representing 'Evil', while 'Good' had been represented by the kindness and help of villagers and tourist police. But the drama had started in ancient Egypt and old scores had needed settling. Beyond this, on yet another level, each of their individual souls was engaged in its own journey towards enlightenment and redemption. Whether Akhenaten's ghost had been laid, or indeed had ever existed was, in this sense, irrelevant.

Mary looked at Emma thoughtfully as the story unfolded. What had she learned? She could see how profoundly changed Jack and Finn were. But Emma...?

She thought about herself. What had she learned? She had always known that nothing was as simple as it seemed, but recent events had driven home to her that imagination is the most powerful and underestimated activity of the human brain, being the bridge that carries the human soul from the individual human consciousness to union with the higher consciousness. We cannot know what is beyond us but by the activity of the imagination. Many fear the bridge and keep the gate to it locked and barred. But she and this little group had opened the gate of imagination and followed the rush of visions into the alien landscape beyond, without any thought of the consequences. They had been in very real danger.

They were lucky they had all returned safely. Some with spiritual treasures of great value. But if risks were not taken and the gate of imagination was kept tightly shut, she thought, one would never know the capability of the human soul.

Her train of thought was interrupted by Jack.

'Is it truly over now?' he asked.

Mary sighed.

'Who knows?'

'I know one way we can find out,' Bernard said importantly.

'How?'

'Let me channel Akhenaten and ask him direct!'

'I don't know...' Mary said uncertainly.

'It's worth a try,' Jack said.

'I need to know. I need to speak to him,' Emma pleaded.

Mary shrugged and settled back in her chair. The others gazed expectantly at Bernard. He composed himself. Eyes shut tight he waited for the familiar feeling. He expected his limbs to become heavy, his tongue like lead... He waited. They waited.

Nothing happened.

At last Bernard opened his eyes, disappointed.

'He's gone!' Emma did not know whether to rejoice or cry.

Jack felt only relief. With any luck he would now be free of those disturbing dreams.

Finn was relieved too. What he had done was undone.

Only Bernard felt bereft. What kind of life would it be for him if he could no longer channel? How would people regard him without his voices?

Jack tracked Eliot down after a few days and met him at the Crystal Palace pub for lunch. Emma was not with them. He had thought it best not to tell her. He found Eliot already in denial. He pretended not to know what Jack was talking about when he asked him what he had discovered about himself in Egypt.

'I still think the whole trip was nonsense,' Eliot declared. 'And as for those old bones! I'm astonished Hassan has taken them so seriously.'

Jack decided to let the matter drop.

He cleared his throat.

'Emma and I are living together now,' he said, waiting somewhat anxiously for Eliot's reaction.

Eliot shrugged. He seemed resigned rather than angry.

'I gave it my best shot,' he said ruefully, 'and it didn't work out. I hope you have better luck.'

There was an awkward silence, and then Jack asked how he had found work on his return. Eliot seemed even gloomier.

'I don't know. It seems pretty pointless – making rich people richer. I think I'm bored with it. I need a change.'

Jack wondered if this was a result of the change he had sensed in Eliot that last day in Egypt.

'Where will you go? What will you do?'

'I don't know,' Eliot was frowning. 'Something new. Something different.'

'I was thinking of writing a book about our experiences in Egypt,' Jack said.

Eliot gave a short, mirthless laugh.

'That should be a bestseller!' he mocked.

'I'm not aiming at the bestseller market. I just want to sort it all out in my own mind. So much happened in such a confusing way. I need to come to terms with it – to find out what it all means – to make sense of it.'

Eliot stared into his beer sombrely.

'If you ask me it meant nothing at all.'

'Emma would say "nothing" does not exist. And Mary would say – even the spaces between the stars are filled with "something".'

'You've been brainwashed, I see!'

'No. I've opened my eyes – and I don't want to shut them again.'

Eliot looked up at him and, for a moment, Jack thought he understood what he meant.

But nothing was said, and after a long, painful silence, Eliot changed the subject.

'I've resigned already. I'll be leaving soon.'

'I thought you hadn't made up your mind what you wanted to do.'

'I haven't. But if I don't get started now, I never will.'

'Do you want to say goodbye to Emma before you go?'

Eliot shook his head. 'Best not,' he said.

Jack nodded.

Somehow there did not seem anything more to say, and they parted company as casually as though it were old times and they expected to see each other every day.

Finn celebrated his thirty-sixth birthday with them before he returned to Ireland.

'Weren't you supposed to die at thirty-five?' Jack asked, remembering the prophecy of the ouija board.

Finn grinned. 'There were a couple of times I thought I would,' he said, remembering the knife fight in Akhenaten's tomb, the long hitch-hike back to Minya when the wound had opened, and the sandstorm in the desert. 'But it seems I did not. Unless...' and here he paused thoughtfully, '...unless I misinterpreted the message. In a way "the old me" *did* die in Egypt. Illusions died, and a new me was born.'

'It just shows one should not take predictions too literally,' Jack grinned.

Finn shook himself. 'It feels good to be thirty-six. I tried not to believe the prophecy but there were moments when I was really afraid. I even wondered if the plane would crash on the way back now that I had done what I was meant to do, and no longer had a reason for living.'

Emma looked shocked. '*Never* say that!' she cried. 'There are *always* reasons for living. Lots of them! Even when they are hidden and you haven't noticed them.'

Finn laughed, 'Don't worry. I know that now.'

As the months went by, the experiences of Egypt settled into place, and what passed for normal life in England resumed. Jack suffered no more bad dreams, and busied himself writing a book about his journey of discovery.

One cold winter's day during Christmas week Jack and Emma were sitting on the floor by a crackling log fire, opening Christmas cards.

'Here's one from Eliot,' Emma said. Apart from the printed message wishing them a Merry Christmas, there was writing so small and squashed she could scarcely decipher it.

'Where is he?'

'He's back in America,' she said. 'I can't make it out. He is describing a dream he had. He is crossing a long, high suspension bridge over a chasm and two men approach, one from each side, and attack him. He fights and lays them both out. He gets to the other side and tries to get the police to help, but the police are ex-directory and he can't get hold of them. Meanwhile, one man he hit is lying where he left him, looking as though bones are broken and he is near to death. He asks,' Emma added, puzzled, 'that you interpret this for him.'

'Why me? You would be better at it,' Jack said.

He specifically says "Jack",' she replied.

Jack thought for a moment and then suggested: 'He is crossing from one reality to the other. It is not without danger. Doubts attack. He overcomes them, but feels he has damaged and almost killed something that should have been kept alive. He tries to rescue it, but can't reach those who could help him.'

'Who would they be?'

'I don't know. You, maybe. You were always "laying down the law" to him on spiritual matters. The police? But now he can't draw on you for help because you are "ex-directory", unavailable.'

She shrugged, but her attention was already on the next envelope.

'This one is from Egypt,' she said. 'It doesn't look like a card.'

'It must be from Ahmed Hassan,' Jack said, reaching out his hand. But she held it back, staring at it thoughtfully.

And then, suddenly, she threw it into the fire, unopened.

'No!' Jack cried, leaping forward, trying to pluck it out. But the flames were already consuming it.

'Why did you do that?' he demanded. 'It was probably the result of the tests on the bones.'

'We don't need it,' she said. 'We know Akhenaten's ghost is laid.'

'But we cannot be sure!' he shouted. 'That letter might have given us the proof.'

For all he now understood about the different types of reality and truth, and even that so-called scientific truth is continually subject to change under the pressure of new research, he still longed for the kind of certainty he believed in as a child.

For the first time in months he felt the irritation he used to feel towards Emma welling up again. It was all he could do not to shake her.

But she, unconcerned, had returned to opening Christmas cards. The firelight glinted on her hair, and on her silky skin.

Notes

Chapter 5: The Shemsu Benu
The fullest description of the play that went so disastrously wrong in Egypt in 1909 can be found in *Tombs, Temples and Ancient Art* by Joseph Lindon Smith, edited by his wife, Corrina Smith, pub. University of Oklahoma Press, USA 1956, p.105-15.

Chapter 6: Akhenaten Speaks
"Hymn to the Aten" from *Ancient Egyptian Religious Beliefs and Practices* by Rosalie David published by Routledge, Kegan, Paul, London.

Chapter 7: The Journal
"He is not the Sun..." from *The Egyptian Book of the Dead* by Charles H. S. Davis.

Chapter 10: Akhenaten's City
For information about Amarna I have particularly consulted the invaluable guide book *Egypt: The Rough Guide* by Dan Richardson and Karen O'Brien, pub. by Rough Guides and Penguin, 1993; and the magnificent catalogue of the exhibition of the Amarna dynasty, *Pharaohs of the Sun*, pub. by Museum of Fine Arts, Boston, USA 1999.

Phrases from the rituals have been taken from the book by George Hart: *A Dictionary of Gods and Goddesses*, p.44, pub. RKP, London, 1986.

"How various is the world ..." from the Hymn to Aten on p.100 of *Pharaohs of the Sun*, pub. Museum of Fine Arts, Boston 1999.

Quotations for the boundary stele at Akhetaten from *The City of Akhenaten and Nefertiti* by Julia Samson, and from J D S Pendlebury, *Tel el Amarna*, pub. Lovat Dickinson & Thomson, 1935.

"May you grant..." p.171 of *Pharaohs of the Sun*. Inscription from tomb of Pentu at Amarna.

"Bless the Lord, Oh my soul..." Psalm 104, v.1-5 from *The Bible*.

Chapter 12: Locked Out
Most of the quotations about the stars are from *The Ancient Egypt*

Book of the Dead by R O Faulkner, pub. British Museum Publications, 1985

'You shall ascend to the sky...' Spell 16

'I make the sunshine to flourish...' Spell 98

'O imperishable stars...' Spell 44

'You shall separate...' Spell 58

'For I am he...' Spell 62

'The doors of the sky...' Spell 68

Chapter 17: Luxor

'He made his form in majesty...' – Translation from J H Breasted, *Ancient Records of Egypt Vol.2*, pub. Russell & Russell, New York 1962. A translation of the wall inscriptions in the Temple of Hatshapsut at Deir el Bahri.

'I met a traveller...' – The sonnet *Ozymandias* by Percy Bysshe Shelley.

'She made a monument...' – Translation of inscriptions on the obelisks of Hatshepsut at Karnak from Breasted, *Ancient Records of Egypt Vol. 2*, and *The Obelisks of Egypt* by Labib Habachi, pub. Dent, London, 1978.

For more information about Mushroom Publishing
and Bladud Books, please visit
www.mushroompublishing.com

You can learn more about Moyra Caldecott and her
work, and sample some of her writings at
www.moyracaldecott.co.uk

Lightning Source UK Ltd.
Milton Keynes UK
02 October 2009

144412UK00001B/17/A